# THE
# SWAN LAKE
# MURDERS
## A Mary Wandwalker
## Mystery

I0565728

## By
## Susan Rowland

CHIRON PUBLICATIONS • ASHEVILLE, NORTH CAROLINA

www.ChironPublications.com

Interior and cover design by Danijela Mijailovic
Front cover image by artist Brigitte Werner, reproduced with permission
Printed primarily in the United States of America.

ISBN 978-1-68503-570-9 paperback
ISBN 978-1-68503-571-6 hardcover
ISBN 978-1-68503-572-3 electronic
ISBN 978-1-68503-573-0 limited edition paperback
ISBN 978-1-68503-574-7 limited edition hardcover


Library of Congress Cataloging-in-Publication Data Pending

FOR JOEL WEISHAUS, BELOVED,
AND FOR ALL THOSE SUFFERING
IN THE CLIMATE EMERGENCY,
ESPECIALLY IN THE
ASHEVILLE NC FLOODING OF 2024
AND THE LA FIRES OF 2025

## The Mary Wandwalker
## Mystery Series by Susan Rowland:

# ACKNOWLEDGEMENTS AND HISTORICAL NOTES

More people than I can mention here deserve heartfelt thanks for helping me with this book. In particular I thank the kindness and tolerance of my family without whom *The Swan Lake Murders* would have flown into the ether, rather than materializing into a book. Thank you, Cathy and John Rowland and others. Thank you also the wonderful team at Chiron!

However I must offer special mention to friend and brilliant artist Dr. Mary Antonia Wood whose gift of Shakespeare's curses found its way into the witches lair of Holywell. Students and colleagues at Pacifica Graduate Institute have inspired and informed the way I try to imagine the importance of witches and indigenous Celts to the climate crisis of the twenty-first century.

My long suffering friends in the US and the UK have supported, encouraged and provided me with essentials such as coffee, tea, cake and refuge. In particular, this book owes a lot to Christine Saunders, Leslie Gardner, Caroline Barker, Margaret Erskine, Kathryn Le Grice, Ailsa Montagu, Evan Davis, Guillaume Batz and Mr. Whippy.

More in this story is true than might appear. The witches of today do try to ameliorate the climate emergency much as mentioned here. The debate in magic between a dark side of predatory power versus attempts to better the world by loving co-operation with the nonhuman, these currents are perennial and pertain to more than the world of witchcraft.

The historical Dr. John Dee is a big influence on my fictional Billy Dee. He was an important astrologer, mathematician and magus in the court of Elizabeth 1<sup>st</sup>. He did practice spiritualism with the aid of dubious medium Edward Kelley. Of course *The Swan Lake Murders'* plotting of Kelley's descendants comes from my imagination.

This is not a 'ballet' novel in the conventional sense. Rather it completes my quartet of Mary Wandwalker novels on the ancient four elements – this one being 'air and spirit.' *Swan Lake,* the ballet nevertheless roots the story in the Celtic hinterland of the dreamworld, which connects to ancient cultures everywhere in the motif of people becoming birds and the reverse.

In particular, the relationship of the vulnerable feminine and the majestic swan, of the traumatized and wild nature, is at the heart of this tale. It is entirely fitting that it begins with a doomed attempt to stage *Swan Lake* in the pre-Christian greenery of Greenwich park, beneath the Royal Observatory. It concludes with a triumphant revision of the ballet that just might be truer to its Celtic origin story.

# DRAMATIS PERSONAE

*From The Depth Enquiry Agency*

Mary Wandwalker (early sixties): leader and formerly Chief Archivist National Government Archives

Caroline Jones (early forties): detective and Mary's daughter-in-law (husband deceased)

Anna Vronsky (early twenties): detective, a theoretically rehabilitated criminal and Caroline's lover

*From the Government*

Robin Prince aka Robbin' Robin (58): formerly chancellor of the Exchequer, now Minister for Northern Ireland

Mr. Jeffreys (don't ask): Senior Civil Servant with links to the Security Services, former boss and frequent sparring partner of Mary Wandwalker

Billy Dee (mid-forties): mysterious origins, dubious reputation. A choreographer, sorcerer and spiritualist, he is an unofficial adviser to the PM and was instrumental in his defeating Robbin' Robin in the election for party leader

*From the Prince family*

Helen Morgan (50): ex-wife of Robbin' Robin and not impressed. Employs Billy Dee as choreographer in her new Greenwich Ballet School

Irina Prince aka Irina the ballerina: fifteen years old, she is daughter to Robbin' Robin and Helen Morgan, and a ballet student at her mother's school

*From The Holywell Retreat Centre*

*Witch-Therapists*

Dorothy Chamberlayne (48): harassed manager

Naomi Wildfire (71): Earth magic

John Tring (50): nonbinary in a relationship with Linda, studying weather magic

Linda Chow (47): in a relationship with John, also studying weather magic

Janet Swinford (76): herbal healer with mental health issues

Cherry Arbuthnot (41): cook and food magic

Meredith Kelley (31): new to Holywell, and a former nurse

*Clients (formerly trafficked young women)*

Sarah: from the Congo, in the process of choosing a new surname
Other young women who wish their names to be withheld. They are known as 'gels' in the story

*Guest*

Agnes: name unknown, believed to be late seventies, receiving hospice care

*From the Police*

Detective Inspector Kirpal Singh plus unnamed officers and forensic crime scene personnel

# CONTENTS

# CHAPTER 1
# LONDON FOG

*Thursday 21 September, morning.*

At the exit to Parliament Tube, Mary Wandwalker blinked and paused, eyes wide at the lack of light. Where were her familiar London streets? Fog had swallowed the city. She ran her fingers through her stylish grey bob, yes, damp already. Condensation from her mac dripped onto the hem of her burgundy suit.

"Watch your step, Caroline," she said to the woman beside her. "The fog makes everything slippery."

Immediately Caroline Jones stumbled. Mary reached out to steady her. Twenty years younger and eighteen pounds heavier, Caroline's thrift store coat and dress suited her faded once-copper curls, Mary thought. After all, no one could miss her warmth despite (Caroline said 'because') of her bouts of her clinical depression.

"There's something in the air," she announced. "Besides this damn fog, I smell trouble. Whatever happens, we've got to keep our first meeting with the minister."

Caroline took Mary's arm. "So we don't lose each other," she said.

We cannot be late, Mary Wandwalker fumed silently. Thanks to the weather, we might miss the boat, river taxi, whatever. She strode across the road wary of the glowing eyes of hooting traffic. Caroline trotted to keep up.

We could be in the marshes of two thousand years ago, thought Mary, then shook her head. Her vision adjusted.

1

Cobblestones and a few commuters materialized. Mary tapped Caroline's arm and turned into a side street at a brisk pace. She was a woman on a mission. *She* had researched the angry minister they were to meet. *He* had no idea of what he faced with Mary Wandwalker and her Depth Enquiry Agency.

*****

Minutes later Mary and Caroline found the entrance to the riverside dock. They prepared to confront their possible client. The minister had declared that he could not take his embarrassing problem to the police. Just what was his mysterious feud? Mary and Caroline knew the name of the minister's nemesis, a Romanian called Billy Dee. A ballet choreographer, he was in London for an experimental production of *Swan Lake* in Greenwich Park.

"Aha," Mary had remarked. "A fairy tale with the tragic ending intact. The lovers remain stuck as swans, don't they?"

"That's right," Caroline had said. "Anna would say fairy tales are real."

"Well, she should know," Mary had returned. Anna seems like a fairy tale character to me, she had thought but did not say to Caroline, who was also Anna's lover.

Mary dwelled on this exchange as they struggled through the fog to Parliament Pier. Fairy tales contain magic, thought Mary. How fitting since my research on social media suggests Dee also practices what he calls sorcery.

As the two women reached the dock, Mary almost fainted with relief at seeing the minister's boat. Before she could speak she coughed. Caroline banged on her back, then cleared her own throat. Mary stuck out her tongue and tasted the London smog. No, there was something coiling above the Thames: an electrical storm? Caroline nodded, green eyes wide.

"You're getting it too?" Mary said. "Whatever's in this fog, it's stronger now."

Caroline nodded. "Bad spirits," she said, sagely. "Exactly why we're here, after all." It was rare for her to be the confident one, particularly when meeting a new client.

"I heard that," said a petulant voice behind them.

They swiveled to find a wall of men in dark suits. Glued to their phones, none of them had spoken. No, the plummy voice came from behind. The wall parted to reveal a man carrying too much weight for his dark blue coat. He needed a haircut as well as a comb, Mary thought.

"Miss Wandwalker, you're late. Follow me please onto the boat."

"Has he any idea we're doing this for his fifteen year old daughter?" whispered Caroline.

"Not a clue," returned Mary. "Everything is all about him."

The minister and his seemingly identical aides descended steps to the launch that bobbed below them on the tide. Mary let Caroline follow. That sense of something not right held her back. Yet she had agreed to talk to the minister.

He looked around for her, the flame-haired politician known as Robbin' Robin. Mary Wandwalker's raised chin did not go unnoticed.

"Bad spirits," snapped Robbin' Robin from the cabin doorway. "The subject of our meeting, Miss Wandwalker, Mrs. Jones. Jeffreys guaranteed you'd be here ten minutes ago. I hate a lack of punctuality."

And yet you waited, thought Mary to herself. Interesting.

Beyond the minister, Mary glimpsed the grey head of Mr. Jeffreys, her former boss and senior Civil Servant.

"Minister, we need to leave," said Mr. Jeffreys, peering out to address Mary. Polite attention appeared on his impassive face. Mary could feel his impatience.

With a pout familiar from news bulletins, the minister waved Mr. Jeffreys aside then disappeared with his entourage, followed by Caroline, glancing back at Mary.

"Miss Wandwalker, time to board," said Mr. Jeffreys, now filling the doorway. "Mrs. Jones will save you a seat." He glanced at his old-fashioned watch.

The engine throbbed.

Mary stepped onto the gangplank, then paused. "Doesn't the fog make the river dangerous?" she called to Mr. Jeffreys, feeling foolish. She pointed beyond the boat. "Aren't those waves getting bigger? Or, is it the current? You know I'm not keen on boats."

"The captain says the fog's clearing," replied Mr. Jeffreys.

Mary took another step. "A likely story."

"Miss Wandwalker, too much is at stake. Get on the goddam boat."

Mary sighed. I have a bad feeling about this, she said to herself.

The boat pulled into the choppy water. Behind them, the Houses of Parliament leaned over the river like the haunted mansion in a morbid ghost story, Mary thought. Caroline beckoned her from the rows of seats. Waves slapped, and the boat rocked.

The fog did appear to be thinning. Perhaps this meeting might yield clarity, hoped Mary. If not, she would never forgive Mr. Jeffreys. For yesterday he'd imparted a secret, a secret so shocking that if released, it would terrify the nation.

## CHAPTER 2
# THE DAY BEFORE: ALL ROADS LEAD TO YOUR DOOR, MISS WANDWALKER

*Wednesday 20 September, morning.*

"Chance of paid work would be a fine thing," grumbled Mary the previous morning about to compose yet another advertisement for the Depth Enquiry Agency (we go deep where the police cannot). With Anna on an unpaid assignment, and Caroline fretting for Anna, Mary was left to worry about the mortgage. She barely registered the shocking news from the radio. After the fog, a hurricane would strike southern England. *Yes, a hurricane*, said awed meteorologists, for the first time since the Great Storm of 1986.

What with the fog dampening sound, Mary did not hear the chauffeur-driven vehicle as it crunched to a stop at their modest house in Surrey. The doorbell no longer chimed as it used to. Today it sounded a howling gale. Mary jumped up, then groaned. Drat Anna, with her tricks from the Internet, and her strange humor. Surely it would be some delivery. In the kitchen, Caroline brushed crumbs from her sweatshirt. Screaming wind again. Caroline answered the door. She recognized the large man tapping his foot.

"Mary, your old boss," she yelled, then retreated so that Mary could take her place. Only Mary merely put her head out of the dining room that doubled as an office.

"Oh, it's you," she said.

The unexpected arrival left her irritable. Mr. Jeffreys knew her too well. She did not want him to guess the financial woes of the Depth Enquiry Agency, not when he had fired her for being digitally incompetent.

"What now?" she said as the man removed an old fashioned trilby and shook it to dislodge water drops.

"First, I'd like to come in out of this fog," said Mr. Jeffreys, stepping over the threshold. "My driver will be back for me in an hour."

Mary sniffed, then pointed him to the sofa in the front room. "Too long," she groused. "For whatever you want in this crazy weather. I remember that hurricane of 1986. Climate crisis means more wild skies," she muttered.

"I expect you want coffee," said Caroline, brightly. "Sit down, both of you, and I'll make it." Mary frowned at her.

Mr. Jeffreys settled his bulk into the sofa, then held out a scarlet carrier bag. "Actually, I brought coffee," he said with the ghost of a grin.

Seizing the bag, Mary extracted a foil brick. "Good God, Mr. Jeffreys. Gold Mountain Special Reserve." She narrowed her fine grey eyes at him. "You must be desperate. Is there some really horrible job you're offering the Depth Enquiry Agency?"

"The desperation belongs to the Prime Minister," returned Mr. Jeffreys. "Thank you Mrs. Jones. While you brew the coffee, Miss Wandwalker and I need to talk about a sorcerer."

Caroline gasped. "Sorcerer? Prime Minister? I'm staying for this," she flung at the visitor.

"Your expertise is most welcome," said Mr. Jeffreys gravely.

Mary retreated to the kitchen to inhale coffee tones from figs to fresh blueberries. As she poured water into the filter, Mr. Jeffreys's words sank in. He didn't say *sorcerer*, did he? Unless? No, too much of a coincidence. *And yet.* Mary abandoned the coffee maker to Caroline and returned to Mr. Jeffreys. It gave her a chance to judge the body language of her old sparring partner.

Minutes later Caroline brought in a tray with two coffees and a mug of tea for herself. "No chocolate biscuits," she said, looking away from Mary. "I ate them all when Anna left."

"Ah, where is Miss Vronsky? I hoped to consult all three of you."

"Anna's undercover," said Mary, peering at the yellow tinge of the coffee before taking her first sip. *Buttery, spicy, fruitcake on the tongue.* She'd cancelled her regular blend as an economy measure.

"Vronsky's out there alone? You terrify me," said Mr. Jeffreys, picking a piece of lint off his tailored suit. The charcoal wool had the merest hint of blue, Mary noted. Caroline bridled at the implied accusation of Anna.

"Spill the beans," said Mary hastily. Coffee beans were on her mind.

Mr. Jeffreys looked carefully at Mary. He smiled. "The coffee is a gift," he said.

Mary got down to business. "Thank you. I believe you mentioned the Prime Minister?" She would not make it easy for him.

Mr. Jeffreys sighed. "When the fates of the powerful are at stake all roads lead to Miss Wandwalker."

"Not anymore," said Mary. "You fired me."

"I'm here because of your *confidential* service at the National Archives, Miss Wandwalker," continued Mr. Jeffreys. "I know what you can do. You've tracked down lost secrets, found documents hidden for centuries, forestalled *scandals*."

Mary caught his emphasis as she was meant to.

"Scandals?" Mary prompted.

"Of course we can be trusted to keep our mouths shut," burst out Caroline. "Anna too."

Mr. Jeffreys and Mary exchanged a glance.

"Did I hear you mention a sorcerer?" said Mary as more coffee brushed cobwebs from her mind. "Is this where I say I don't believe in coincidences? We have a sorcerer. You won't

7

know this, but we are doing deep background on a man called Dee. It's for our friends at Holywell."

"Same sorcerer. Different problem. Better pay," said Mr. Jeffreys, succinctly.

Mary set her coffee down and met Mr. Jeffreys' frown. "From the start, please."

"It began with a call from our old college," he said. "St Julian's wanted information on Billy Dee on behalf of your witch friends at Holywell. He describes himself as a sorcerer and spiritualist as well as his day job choreographing ballet."

"Therapists," said Mary, automatically. "The witches at Holywell are also accredited psychotherapists."

"Witch-therapists," said Caroline, firmly. "Why ask you, Mr. Jeffreys?"

"I'm on St Julian's College's Governing Board," Mr. Jeffreys replied.

"And St Julian's oversees Holywell," Mary reminded Caroline.

"Yes, but Holywell is worried about Dee visiting them because he's a sorcerer. They think his magic is not like theirs, so it could be dangerous."

Mr. Jeffreys blinked at Caroline. Mary sighed.

Caroline ploughed on. "Up to now Dee has been in touch with Holywell by email and Zoom. But now he insists on visiting in person. Why would a top Civil Servant know about magic stuff?"

Mr. Jeffreys cleared his throat.

"It seems they, that is your witches, watch the TV news. Recall the new PM's photo op inside Parliament. Dee stood among top Civil Servants, the only person without an official position." Mr. Jeffreys scowled. "Social media speculated on how a choreographer with a sorcery practice could be connected to the new PM. Since your witch friends are aware of my role at St Julian's and my... er government contacts..."

"Come off it, Mr. J." broke in Caroline. She's cross about his Anna jibe, Mary thought. "Everyone knows you're tight with the security services. Plus you run the Archives. It stores the government's dirty linen since the year dot."

Mr. Jeffreys nodded appreciatively. "I confirmed to St Julian's that Holywell would be wise to refuse Billy Dee. His reputation in ballet companies abroad is…" He searched for a suitable epithet. "Unsavory. After that phone call I did not" –he turned back to Mary– "expect to hear from a cabinet minister about Mr. Dee." He paused.

"No," said Caroline. "No way are we going to help this despicable, incompetent government."

Mary waved her down. The coffee had improved her mood. She motioned Mr. Jeffreys to continue.

"Thank you, Miss Wandwalker. The call came from the PM's defeated rival. He'd been demoted from Chancellor of the Exchequer to Minister for Northern Ireland."

"*Robbin' Robin*," gasped Mary. "You expect us to help Mr. Brexit? He who forced through the 'Leave the European Union' law and made us all poorer?"

"That man." Caroline looked nauseous. "Real name is Robin Prince; he pretended he would be a Robin Hood Chancellor, taking from the rich to give to the poor."

"Instead he raised taxes on those least able to pay. Calling himself Robin Hood was a stunt to get elected," said Mary. Recollection heated her until she felt steam on her forehead. "The press dubbed him *Robbin'* Robin, and it stuck." She glared at Mr. Jeffreys. "So the ex-chancellor doesn't like losing the election to be prime minster. Tough cheddar. We don't care."

"We want nothing to do with him," said Caroline, folding her arms.

"Are you both finished?" said Mr. Jeffreys mildly. He turned to Caroline. "Ask Miss Wandwalker how she and I met. That will convince you I'm no fan of Robbin' Robin, with his racist and homophobic remarks to titillate the right wing. That, and opportunist populism, fueled his rise to power."

"Oh," said Caroline, looking a bit lost. "Mary never talks about how you two met."

Mr. Jeffreys cleared his throat. "Back in the Dark Ages, Mrs. Jones, I was St. Julian's first Black British student. Our Mary Wandwalker washed the blood off my face after an excruciating encounter with the all-white Rugby Club."

"Oh," said Caroline again, flopping back onto the sofa.

Mr. Jeffreys and I never discussed that night, thought Mary. Even though she could still hear the ugly shouts from the drunken players, could recall lamplight gleaming on the blood dripping from the young Jeffreys' nose. He'd been twenty, she eighteen. After graduation, when she had found herself alone and pregnant, Jeffreys, already a high flyer in the Civil Service, had given her a job.

When did Mr. Jeffreys get old? thought Mary. We're almost exact contemporaries. Well, we're both grey, aren't we.

"Robbin' Robin called me," repeated Mr. Jeffreys in harsh tones, "or rather one of his flunkies summoned me on his behalf. Naturally I refused."

"Naturally," agreed Mary.

"Then the Prime Minister's office got in touch."

"Oh dear," said Mary.

"Indeed," said Mr. Jeffreys. "That meeting I had to take. The country is in crisis, Miss Wandwalker, and only you can stave off a worse disaster. Let me put it simply. You take on Robbin' Robin as a client and he will hold his tongue about a scandal that would terrify the country at a delicate moment." He glanced at Mary, his watch, then jumped to his feet.

"Good God, woman, we have a hurricane and a fragile government. Now Robbin' Robin threatens us with the occult."

Mr. Jeffreys sat back down, removed a handkerchief and wiped his face. "Sorry ladies," he said. "You won't believe how hard it was to the get the Prime Minister *and* his political enemy, Robbin' Robin, to this point. No, let me explain." He held up his hand to Caroline who had begun to expostulate. Mary gave her a slight nod and she subsided.

"Listen to what the Prime Minister told me. In thirty-six hours a hurricane will hit England. It is likely to cause widespread flooding. While our emergency services are as prepared as they can be, ordinary people will be very frightened. During the days or weeks before normality can be restored, Robbin' Robin will accuse the new PM of using black magic to steal the election. He'll say he got Billy Dee to change votes by occult, and frankly terrifying, means."

"Nonsense," said Mary. "No one will take such rubbish seriously."

"The problem is…" Mr. Jeffreys sank back into the soft chair. "It's true."

"I don't believe it." Mary neither believed, nor approved of, magic, any magic.

"I do," said Caroline. "Remember, Mary, what I said earlier? When we woke up this morning to fog? I said it was a dark cloud from the PM election, didn't I, Mary?"

"I hoped you didn't mean *magic*," said Mary. "Mr. Jeffreys, what's happened to you? So the PM has a friend claiming to be a sorcerer. How much damage can Robbin' Robin do with that?"

"Enough. Because for once he can stick to the facts of what *really* went on," said Mr. Jeffreys heavily. "As I mentioned, Billy Dee's so-called sorcery includes spiritualism. He did séances in Parliament during the election, recorded them. These convinced wavering Members of Parliament to change their votes. Dead politicians persuaded live ones to vote against Robbin' Robin."

Mary laughed. Then she saw Mr. Jeffreys' face.

"The PM hated telling me this," said Mr. Jeffreys. He looked grim. "Dee came to him with the plan, an offer to destroy Robbin' Robin's chances. Why, no one knows."

Mr. Jeffreys looked sadly at his empty cup. When neither woman took the hint he resumed.

"So now the PM is desperate to have Robbin' Robin silenced. Sending him to Northern Ireland is not enough in these social media times. Can I find someone to persuade Robbin' Robin that if he holds off she'll get the goods on Dee? The minister could then do a private deal with the PM. And perhaps the PM would agree to step down in Robbin' Robin's favor after a year or two. Much better for Robbin' Robin than another election he could easily lose. What the PM needs, what the country needs," his mouth twitched, "*is an enquiry agency like yours with the strength, determination and imagination to keep him quiet. Can I count on you, Miss Wandwalker?*"

Mary sat very still. Fog on the windows spread, formed drips. She watched them grow big enough to run down the glass. She had a question. "With everyone focused on the weather, does it really matter if Robbin' Robin makes a scandal?"

"Black magic, conjuring the dead in Parliament? You think it won't frighten the horses?"

"We might get a General Election." Caroline clapped her hands. "Get a decent government instead."

"Not if half the country is flooded for weeks," retorted Mr. Jeffreys. "Rather there would be a mass panic with the best result being Robbin' Robin becoming prime minister now rather than later."

Mary looked up. "But you said…"

"A lot can happen in a year, Miss Wandwalker. Many of those Robbin' Robin stabbed in the back tell me they can neutralize him with more time. You can get that time for us, Mary. You and your…" Mr. Jeffreys' eyes strayed to Caroline in her frumpy clothes chewing on her finger. "Er, remarkable associates."

Mary could not refuse.

"Let me get this straight. We're to convince Robbin' Robin to keep quiet by telling him we'll get incontrovertible evidence of Billy Dee sabotaging the election. Failing that, we find other dirt that he can use to blackmail the PM. We can't appeal to his decency at a time of crisis because he has none."

"Blackmail, such an ugly word," murmured Mr. Jeffreys.

Caroline spoke quietly. "Billy Dee could really have allowed the dead to speak."

Mary and Mr. Jeffreys ignored her. They faced each other with matching frowns.

"I'm a Civil Servant," said Mr. Jeffreys at last. "Forbidden to meddle in politics. However, a scandal now, one that would terrify a frightened population with talk of the dead? No, that cannot be allowed."

Mr. Jeffreys stood up. "The fog's getting worse, and I'm needed in London. Tomorrow the minister has booked a boat taxi to Greenwich. He's popping into a ballet rehearsal. Something about his daughter and *Swan Lake*." He picked up his hat. "I fear his real reason is to confront Billy Dee, who is the *Swan Lake* choreographer. So I need you there, Miss Wandwalker. Be at Parliament Pier by 8.50 am. Convince the minister en route. After Greenwich he gets a helicopter to his new post in Northern Ireland." He gave Mary a wry smile as she stood up. "This is your chance to save your country from a storm in government. We can't do anything about the one in the skies."

Caroline jumped up. "No, no, not Robbin' Robin, I can't!" Caroline spoke as much to Mary as Mr. Jeffreys. His gaze focused on Mary. Her features gave nothing away.

Harsh chords shattered the tension. These turned into "God Save the Queen" by the Sex Pistols. Caroline ran from the room.

"Anna," muttered Mary. "She changes ring tones to get my goat."

Mr. Jeffreys took a few steps, then turned back.

"Miss Wandwalker, I know I can trust you. Persuade Mrs. Jones, or leave her at home. Besides you are already looking into Billy Dee for your Holywell friends. Ah." Mr. Jeffreys relaxed. "They can't be paying you much. We'll double your usual fee."

Mary drew herself up. "Triple it and we'll take the meeting with Robbin' Robin. I'll find a way to keep him quiet."

Mr. Jeffreys grinned. "Pleasure doing business with you, Miss Wandwalker. I'll see you on the boat."

"Um, about that boat…" called Mary. But Mr. Jeffreys was gone.

"Drat that man," said Mary to Caroline later. "I've half a mind to cancel, but he has a point about the hurricane and not making it worse for people."

Caroline looked gloomy. "I take back what I said before. We've got to talk to Robbin' Robin after what Anna just told me. She's doing great undercover in Greenwich, by the way. Billy Dee let her into his senior ballet class."

"You don't look very happy about it."

"Because Dee is creepy around sixteen- and seventeen-year-old dancers. Even with Irina, the daughter of the school's owner, Helen Morgan. She's Robbin' Robin's ex-wife. The girl is only fifteen and obsessed with Dee. Anna thinks he put a spell on her."

"Robbin' Robin's the girl's father?" said Mary, slowly. "From what Mr. Jeffreys said, Dee has some animus against the minister…"

"Don't we all," muttered Caroline.

Mary stared out at the fog. "You're right, Caroline. We *were* checking out Billy Dee for Holywell. Why does he want to visit the witches in person? That puzzle gets darker with the potential harm to children. Tell Anna to meet in us in Greenwich tomorrow when we get off the boat with the minister. It looks like we've got one more day before the hurricane makes landfall. At least the fog will be gone in the morning."

The next morning the fog was denser than ever. Mary and Caroline got into the car provided by Mr. Jeffreys. Too dangerous to drive into Central London, the chauffeur explained. He'd drop them at the nearest Tube Station.

By the time they reached the pier and boarded the boat, a stiff breeze whipped the waves into a frenzy. Mary's tongue tasted bitter. I have a bad feeling about this trip, Mary repeated.

Carrying the new Minister for Northern Ireland, his aides, a senior Civil Servant, and two members of the Depth Enquiry Agency, the battered river taxi pulled into the heaving river Thames. The captain set a course for Greenwich, the direction of the open sea.

## CHAPTER 3
# TEMPEST

*Thursday morning.*

Minutes later the fog cleared with a speed that turned heads to the windows. Waves slopped onto the deck. The boat rocked prow to stern, then side to side. Caroline gripped Mary's hand. Mary ignored the sudden pain, for she'd noticed the trees outside the National Theatre. Their branches shook as if trying to dislodge beetles crawling up their bony arms.

"The big storm's come early," said Mary, feeling her cheekbones tighten.

"Impossible," said Mr. Jeffreys from a row behind. "Hurricane's not due for twelve hours."

Later Mary would insist that the launch plunged forty-five degrees as they were sucked down by the current around Blackfriars Bridge. It felt like minutes, not seconds, before the prow heaved back towards the charcoal-colored clouds. Resuming the horizontal did not return the boat to the crew's control. Immediately the vessel spun clockwise towards the underside of the bridge. Cracked bricks and green slime rushed towards the boat, under the transparent roof the passengers clutched anything they could grasp: seat backs, roof supports, each other.

Outside the wind screamed. With a screech that Mary hoped did not come from the engine, the nose of the vessel found the open arch and the boat plunged into wild air. A bright light exploded, shaking the bridge behind.

"Lightning," yelled an amplified voice that made Caroline jump and Mary fall back. "It's a storm, not a bomb. Nothing to worry about. Stand by for the Captain."

Drumming came from all sides as water hammered the boat from river and from sky. So fierce was the downpour that Mary could not distinguish between waves and rain.

Hissing and crackling gave way to a strained voice from the loudspeaker.

"This is an important message to passengers. Remain where you are. There are life jackets under each seat. Put them on. The crew is monitoring the weather. Everything is under control."

"No, it isn't," muttered Mary as she tugged at a package of orange plastic. "That's what they say when everything is *out* of control." As she helped Caroline with the straps of her life jacket, despite orders not to move, two aides fought their way to Robbin' Robin.

Ignoring Mary and Caroline, they dragged the stunned minister back to the other aides at the back of the boat. Two aides scrabbled to hold out protective gear for the Minister. Only when Robbin's Robin's red hair vanished beneath the wall of suits did they secure their own life belts.

Mary let her gaze linger before a gasp from Caroline made her swivel back to the river ahead. A wall of water rushed towards them. In obeying the Captain, Mary and Caroline had stayed in seats near the prow. Their part of the boat would be swamped first. Mary braced herself, dimly aware that Mr. Jeffreys had joined them.

"Hang on," he shouted. "To anything you can."

Waves came from all directions and tipped the boat. The wall of water crashed down on top of the transparent roof. At the same moment as lightning streaked across the sky, Mary gazed in horror at the pattern of cracks in the boat's roof. Transparent no more, it resembled a giant leaf. Mary clutched Mr. Jeffreys' arm.

"It won't break," he said in her ear. "Bulletproof glass installed last year."

"You said the weather was nothing to worry about," yelled Mary over the continuing thunder.

He ignored her dig.

"Protocol," he shouted, nodding in the direction of the Minister, submerged beneath black suits. "Idiots. They might overbalance the boat."

Mary's hand tightened on his arm. Caroline moaned. Mr. Jeffreys grinned.

"Fortunately, I am worth several of those skinny ferrets," he called above the roaring rain. "See."

He pointed to a figure of indeterminate sex who swung from side to side in the door of the engine room. Clad in a yellow sou'wester, the person was a hood with waving arms. Seeing their upturned faces, one hand went onto the rail while the other did an exaggerated thumbs up.

"*Stay where you are, passengers,*" blasted the speakers. "Weight distribution is life and death with storms. Running around will cause us to capsize."

Mary gulped. "Why aren't we heading for shore?" she mouthed at Mr. Jeffreys.

"Currents and tide," he replied. "Can't mess with the Thames. They say when the wind gets bad, the river is another creature entirely."

"The Thames is a familiar spirit, a horse used to human riders. Usually. Now, that horse is wild, untamable." By some miracle Caroline's rapt tone was audible to Mary and Mr. Jeffreys.

"A horse, Mrs. Jones?"

Mary sighed. "Caroline is studying magic and the old gods," she explained. "She's remembering the Celtic goddess, Eponia," she said. "Also the river Thames, some say."

"Mrs. Jones still consorts with those witches, I see."

"As I reminded you yesterday, those witches are trained counsellors helping formerly trafficked women," Mary snapped. "Stop trying to distract us. By the way, the witches called me last night. They are really worried about Billy Dee. He's obsessed with Holywell, they said."

"Dee has an agenda we know nothing about," Mr. Jeffreys said slowly. "Most odd. Shooting down Robbin' Robin's career and harassing Holywell cannot be connected. Or can they, Miss Wandwalker?" A blast of thunder burst overhead. It drowned Mary's attempt to reply.

She tried again. "All we know so far is that Dee will show up at Holywell if we can't stop him. He refused to say why he must be there in person."

"If he's as creepy as Anna says, he'll freak out the girls," added Caroline. "Oww." She stumbled as the boat shook from side to side. Mary grabbed her shoulder.

Mary shut her eyes as the next wave hit the prow, opening them to find Mr. Jeffreys scrutiny at its most piercing. She saw words forming...

"Don't worry," she raised her voice over the churning river. "We've not forgotten about keeping the lid on Robbin' Robin. But Holywell wants Dee vetted – by us. Given their vulnerable young women, they are not keen on an alleged sorcerer and choreo...*oh, oh no.*"

Without warning, lightning snapped the sky into three. There followed a sound like splitting stone. It will tear apart the river itself, thought Mary in despair. The boat dived down and so slowly rose up, its occupants gasping for breath.

"Sorry Mary," bellowed Mr. Jeffreys. "You were right about something in the air. I've never seen a storm come on so fast. *Hold on.*"

The three of them grabbed the seats again, as the boat rose up like a bear on hind legs. It rocked from side to side, then appeared to dive into oncoming waves, each with an open mouth that foamed.

"Climate catastrophe," Mary gasped. "I heard those predictions of hurricanes and storms. Never before in London."

"Or the storm could be black magic." Caroline's squeak startled Mary and Mr. Jeffreys. Both exchanged a look. "Caroline…" began Mary.

"No, no, stop," shouted Caroline into the oncoming rain.

The three of them cried out. Again the boat pointed at the riverbed. There was a flash, followed by an explosion overhead as the storm whipped the vessel and its prow rose skywards, before flopping down again. Mary muttered under her breath, "Until we get to shore it's a gallop up and down over ridges of water."

"If the boat does not flip over," said Mr. Jeffreys.

Mary put her hands over her ears, then thought better of it, and replaced a hand on the rail attached to her seat. There was another burst of light followed by what sounded like boulders rolling overhead.

Caroline had lost her earlier pink color. I must be that pale too, thought Mary. Caroline's green eyes now reflected the dark grey waves. Thank God I never get seasick, was all Mary could manage. Then she felt bad. I don't want to drown with Caroline thinking me unsympathetic, she thought grimly.

"What did you mean about magic?" she called to Caroline. Mary never wanted to hear about spells, but she knew it comforted Caroline.

Caroline opened and shut her mouth, then seemed to make up her mind.

"I saw a man on Westminster bridge," she yelled through chattering teeth. "He had a rope and untied the last knot, looking straight at us. You never undo the last knot of three. Weather magic," she added, with a glance at the skeptical Mr. Jeffreys. He put his head in his hands.

"A terrible thing," continued Caroline, yelling at Mary. "At Holywell they are doing reverse spells – trying to drain the energy from that hurricane in the Atlantic."

"That's madness, Caroline," screamed Mary over the howling outside the boat.

"Fifteen minutes to Greenwich," came the amplified voice again. Then came static and a burst of annoyance from the speaker. "No, no, minister, we can't 'pull over.' This is not a car. The Thames is no road. There are rocks and debris in the shallows. We could be wreck..." The public address system snapped off rather late.

"The captain revealed too much. Robbin' Robin must have got to him on one of those satellite phones. The rest of us have no service in this..." Mr. Jeffreys scowled in the direction of the minister. This time Mary glimpsed some red hair as the suits pulled him down and the boat dived yet again.

Mr. Jeffreys is more disturbed than he appears, thought Mary. He never shows emotions. He's the perfect Civil Servant.

Caroline pointed down the boat to the aides with their yellow lifejackets over black suits. "Bees frightened of the rain," she whispered.

Mary smiled. The boat tilted up, and the clouds parted for a second to reveal a square structure ahead of them.

"Tower Bridge," said Mr. Jeffreys unnecessarily. "Shouldn't be too bad, this one, there's more clearance."

Mary nodded to him. Caroline clung to her while she gripped onto the seat back. The younger woman shivered. "Anna," she moaned into Mary's too-thin coat. Despite the river bus being enclosed, water surged around their ankles; when the boat rocked it splashed onto clothes. Mary had the sensation of damp soaking through. A "shower proof" coat is not enough for twenty-first century weather, noted Mary. Caroline went on...

"Anna will be waiting. Wish I'd gone undercover with her."

The boat tilted from side to side then, slowly, began to spin.

*Whirlpool,* screamed a voice from the back of the boat.

"Certainly not." This time the disembodied voice sounded rattled. "We are navigating the effect of wind, high tide, and foundations of the Bridge. Keep calm. We will soon dock at Greenwich."

The captain must have forgotten the switch again, because another voice, female, spoke out. "Sir, there's a waterspout reported at Woolwich. Other side of the Thames Barrier. They are lowering it to prevent flooding..." There was an audible click.

"Safe?" croaked Caroline. "Anna will be so scared for us," she wailed.

"Snap out of it, Caroline. Anna knows no fear. Tell me about weather magic?"

Caroline managed a tiny smile. Mary tried to be so proper, so rational. Yet when pushed, no one was more creative. She wove webs between institutions, could divine their most cherished secrets, yet she was no bureaucrat. Caroline had been with Mary when she drove through a wildfire, when she defied kidnappers. Together they'd fought for the truth about the death of Caroline's beloved husband, who had also been Mary's lost son. A bullying government minister meant nothing to Mary Wandwalker.

With that thought, the boat shuddered. Caroline shot a glance at newly constructed condos on either side of the approach to Greenwich; their glass skins trembled in the storm. Caroline shut her eyes briefly. She trusted Mary with her life.

There came a muffled scream from further down the boat, which now faced backwards. Mary pressed her arm around Caroline's shoulders as the vessel turned. At least the up and down motion had moderated, slightly. Mary would be that precise, Caroline thought wryly.

As the wind lessened, the rain increased, pasting the veined glass above them. Caroline cleared her throat.

"You don't want to know about those spells," she said sadly. "You only tolerate my learning magic to help with my depression."

"Not true." Mary's voice was hoarse. "Your... your temperament is an asset to the Agency. You understand about people, why they do terrible things." Mary could tell without looking that Mr. Jeffreys had raised his eyebrows. Ignoring him, Mary kept one hand on the seat for balance and took Caroline's hand in her left.

\*\*\*\*\*

Nobody drowned. Within arm's length of the shore, the wind and rain dropped as quickly as they had risen. Robbin' Robin stomped off at Greenwich Dock, yelling, "Someone will pay for this." He, of course, had a limousine waiting, large enough to swallow his aides. Another black vehicle opened its stubby wings for Mr. Jeffreys. The latter directed a rueful grin at Mary as he slipped into the seat by the driver.

Both cars vanished between dripping trees before Mary and Caroline drew a breath. Together, they staggered past the ticket office and onto the path that led away from the Thames.

"There's Anna. She waited, thank the gods." Caroline dashed towards a dark-haired young woman in a grey robe. Energy radiated from the woman, even as her expression remained enigmatic.

To let them have their reunion, Mary leaned against the nearest tree. Her back felt comforted by familiar bumps of peeling bark. Slowly, her muscles relaxed. No, the park, like the boat, did not sway beneath her sore feet. This was normality. Forcing herself to breathe deeply, she told herself to put the adventure on the river behind her. She had work to do.

Given what they faced with Robbin' Robin and Billy Dee, her next task would be to get Caroline and Anna to focus. To keep faith with Mr. Jeffreys and Holywell, and perhaps the Robbin' Robin's young daughter, they must find the truth. Billy Dee bizarrely connected politics, a therapy center, and *Swan Lake*. Mary could feel something twisted about him.

Pulse returning to normal, Mary let her eyes wander over the classical complex known as the Old Royal Naval College, now home to the University of Greenwich and a music school. Young people with backpacks bent over phones while they scrambled between colonnaded buildings. Mary's legs felt leaden. Two more minutes before she had to get Caroline's and Anna's attention.

Light increased through thinning clouds until Mary had to shade her eyes. Constructed on the site of a Tudor palace, the former Naval College framed four quadrangles. Lawns and fountains added elegance to the wilder river and park. Mary glimpsed the domed roof of the Maritime Museum behind the Naval College. If she craned her neck, she might spot their destination at the top of the hill: the Greenwich Observatory.

With an eye on Caroline and Anna, Mary pondered, could a ballet happen here? Stone flags made for a firm surface, but what about damp leaves? Mary had a vision of a line of swans toppling. What if it rained?

She remembered crossing Greenwich Park in freezing winter dawns. One December she was stunned by a huge gold moon. Violins wept from lit windows in King William Court. Then she recalled a childhood trip to the Observatory with her teacher parents. The home of time itself, her father had quoted. He had held her hand while they walked the iron meridian line. He had lifted little Mary so she could look through the public telescope. Mary had gasped and clapped as the tiny streets jumped close. While she had trembled with excitement, her mother had unpacked egg sandwiches and a bottle of lemonade.

Adult Mary shut her eyes. She could still feel the roof of her mouth smarting from the tart sweet drink. So long ago. Her parents had died of influenza the autumn Mary departed for Oxford.

After college Mary joined Mr. Jeffreys at the National Archive beneath St Paul's Cathedral. Mourning the death of her fiancé, and trying to forget the baby she'd given up, Mary bought an apartment near her childhood home in Greenwich. Her grandparents had labored all their lives as servants. Their parents were farm laborers. These thoughts at the memory of the Observatory. For centuries this building brought the planets closer. A Wandwalker might have scrubbed the floors or made the fires.

Caroline's perspective on the World Heritage site was rather different.

"The Greenwich site is a place of magic and ancient power," Caroline said to her barely-listening friend. "There's a ley line through the park, and across the Thames, energy currents in the earth linking sacred places."

"I know about ley lines," returned Mary, not looking up from Mr. Jeffreys' latest email. "Your witch friends say there is one connecting Holywell and Oxford. Nonsense, of course."

Raised voices brought Mary back to the present. A family tumbled off a bus. Two boys tussled over a football. Their harassed mother with a pushchair avoided Mary's eyes. Even Caroline and Anna stopped kissing. While Caroline gave the mother a look of sympathy, Anna made a rude gesture at the departing boys. Mary beckoned. Time to get going.

When Anna got close, Mary noticed Caroline frowning at the young woman's clothes.

"Anna, those rags are... a bit strange," Mary said. Grey cloth wrapped around her torso did not make Anna into a Cinderella, reflected Mary. Rather Anna looked inhuman. Perhaps it was the jagged cuts that made up her short skirt. The young woman's black eyes gleamed.

"Hullo Mary. This is my *Swan Lake* costume. Don't you know I'm a sorcerer now?"

"She means the character in the ballet." Caroline spoke too fast. "Anna's standing in for Billy Dee as the evil sorcerer in *Swan Lake*. I don't like it. He's trouble." She frowned at Mary. "Can you see a whole ballet *here?*"

Mary followed Caroline's arm across the grassy slope. She imagined girls in white tutus, in a *Swan Lake* that included oak trees, the river, and those white columns. A shiver ran through her whole body.

"Ballet here at Greenwich," she croaked. "You know it could be, make sweet airs visible..."

"Magical," mocked Anna. Caroline sighed.

No, no, Mary thought. She tried to hang onto her vision. The doomed lovers echo the twice daily pas de deux between river and sea.

Then Mary mentally slapped her forehead. She heard the mocking voice of Anna, *get real.*

"Yes, all right," she conceded. "Undertrained teenagers and *Swan Lake* is a stretch."

"Not to mention it's a totally new ballet school," added Caroline.

"The Principal is out of her depth," said Anna with brutal certainty.

"Ah," said Mary. "So *Swan Lake* at Greenwich is a stroke of genius only if it's not a terrible mess. Enough, let's get to the rehearsals. Did you tell Anna what we... I... promised Mr. Jeffreys?" Caroline nodded yes.

As Mary led the way, an anguished cry caused her to look back. Caroline called to Mary: "Stop. We can't go on. Look at Anna's belt."

Mary sighed and joined them. "It's not very artistic," she began. Anna stamped her foot, making sharp noises from metal at her waist.

Caroline swallowed. "No, Mary, it's not costume jewelry, nor Billy Dee's bad taste. Anna's wearing charms, ones with real power."

Mary ground her teeth. "Well, you would know."

This time Anna and Caroline exchanged glances.

"You misunderstand me, Mary," began Caroline with dignity. "Magic is not all the same. These symbols are forbidden at Holywell. Look." She pointed with an apologetic glance at Anna's blank stare. "See, warped crosses, and pentangles with knives, teeth and horns." She gulped. "I feel sick. Darling Anna, that belt could hurt you. Please take it off."

Mary shot a warning look at Caroline. Anna had already taken a warrior's stance: feet apart, hands on hips.

"Let the stupid belt be afraid of *me*," she said.

"Well," began Mary. "You've got to admit that Caroline does know magic from her apprenticeship at Holywell."

*Don't upset Caroline*, she meant. She's vulnerable. Caroline appeared nervously determined. She reached out to stroke one of Anna's arms.

"Darling, listen to me. You've met Billy Dee. You know he's not a simple ballet choreographer. Him doing séances for the new PM means he likes power, likes getting it the wrong way. These are dark, dark symbols."

Anna made an impatient snort. Caroline raised her arms and fixed her green eyes on her lover.

"Let me examine the belt." Caroline knelt briefly, then rose. "As I thought, horns not moons. Boar tusks, violent dark energy."

"You don't know," snarled Anna. "Not for sure. This combination isn't on the web. I searched."

Anna swung between Caroline and Mary. Her knuckles whitened on the belt. So she's not taking it off, thought Mary. Should we be worried? Is this Anna's bullheaded determination not to be diverted from trouble?

Tossing her flowing dark hair, Anna started up the hill.

"Have you…?" called Mary after her. "Wait. Don't go so fast, Anna. We've not all had ballet training."

With exaggerated forbearance, Anna paused until they caught up.

"No," said Anna.

Mary could not tell what she was refusing. Anna kicked the signpost which sprouted arrows pointing to the Naval College, Museum and Observatory. "No, and no and no."

"Stop kicking," said Mary. "You'll hurt your toes. Did you find any link to connect Dee and Holywell online?"

Anna merely scowled.

"I think that's a no," murmured Caroline.

Mary saw a new tightness around Caroline's mouth.

"Stop looking at my belt, Caroline," Anna ordered. "The belt is raw power," Anna growled. "Dee said so."

For once, Caroline ignored her. "*The forbidden books*," she said so quietly Mary had to check what she heard.

Anna snorted again. Mary felt a surge of impatience.

"You mean forbidden as in…?"

"Dark, occult, cruel. I found a torn-out page with several of those symbols in a book of herbal remedies. Dorothy, the Holywell Manager, got angry. You know she's not someone who yells." Caroline paused. "But she looked daggers before she took the page and the herb book away. Said they needed to be destroyed. Like that belt should be."

Mary wasn't sure how to respond to Caroline's fear. Was this the moment to challenge Anna? A spark in Anna's black eyes suggested not.

Mary cleared her throat. "I respect Caroline's… erm, esoteric knowledge," she began.

"Later we consult Holywell," she continued. "Now we get to the Observatory and whatever mess they are making of *Swan Lake.*"

Shaking her head to clear it, Mary signaled to Caroline and Anna to follow her up the steep slope.

CHAPTER 4
# THE BLACK SWAN AND HER PARENTS

*Thursday late morning.*

With the Observatory closed for the minister's visit and ballet rehearsals, Mary anticipated negotiations at the entrance. That Mr. Jeffreys had not arranged official passes made her purse her lips. Anna grinned. Before Mary could march into the ticket office, the young woman disappeared around the side of the building. When Mary followed she saw Anna had folded herself through an open window. A brown hand pulled Caroline after her. With a sigh Mary allowed Caroline to help her into a dim gallery.

"Clocks," said, Caroline, puzzled. "Clocks everywhere." Large brass and enamel clocks, some with pendulums like giant genitalia, some mounted on the walls, so many that it was hard to maneuver between them. Their dusty faces watched the intruders. Caroline shivered.

"Welcome to Greenwich Mean Time," explained Anna. "Where the guides talk about it. A lot. I got the tour of the entire World Heritage Site with the ballet students. The Observatory is clocks and telescopes. Now it includes a ballet about swans. Billy Dee is on another planet about doing *Swan Lake* here. '*Where time begins, the spirits gather*,' he said to Morgan. She repeated it at the warmup yesterday."

"Morgan?" queried Mary.

"Helen Morgan, formerly Helen Prince, when she was married to our minister. It's her ballet school, you know."

Mary nodded. "I'd forgotten."

"Getting Billy Dee to choreograph *Swan Lake* is a double win for her," continued Anna. "Famous choreographer and enemy of her ex, Robbin' Robin."

"Dangerous," said Mary. "Poking the bear."

She wanted to stamp her feet like Anna and argue with mystery man, Billy Dee. Where time is *measured,* not originates, she wanted to say. Oh, for solid ground – okay, a wooden floor – in this weird enquiry. We are about to enter a ballet about girls magicked into birds, not to mention we're in a world in which powerful men, *MPs no less,* got ensnared by a magician. Anna seemed at home with this craziness, while Caroline's furrowed brow furrowed. Where is this going? Mary thought.

She took a deep breath. "You know why we're here. Let's find the minister before he swings a punch at Billy Dee."

After checking with aides wandering the first floor, the three women climbed the stairs to a room almost entirely made of glass. Robbin' Robin stood alone, staring from one of the eight windows in the famous Octagon Room – floor to ceiling windows on eight sides. Mary blinked. You could almost see the telescopes gleaming in moonlight, hear men in funny accents muttering and scratching in their notebooks.

This morning offered too much light, she thought, eyes dazzled. As Robbin' Robin faced the three of them, Mary was unable to make out the minister's shadowed expression. She was electrified by the echo of footsteps on stone stairs. Too late, Mary realized.

The women moved to allow a short, lithe man in his forties to enter. In an instant, scorching heat flared between the two men, thought Mary. Her heart sank as she recognized Billy Dee from the internet sources Anna had provided.

With a snarl, the minister took a step forward.

"You… you," he stuttered.

The man in black dance attire put up his hand like a policeman stopping traffic. Robbin' Robin's mouth contorted. No words came out. Nice trick, thought Mary. Dee plays games.

Midnight hair sleeked back, Dee's red lips on too white skin fascinated Mary because… Ah, he's smeared a white cream on face and neck, she realized. Dee looks weirder in real life than in that news broadcast. Does he never go outside? What was that about vampires and sunlight?

Dee made an ironic bow in the women's direction, before taking a step towards Robbin' Robin. He's taut as a blunt instrument, thought Mary. How come he hates the minister so much?

Robbin' Robin hissed. Dee stopped.

"As you see Miss Wandwalker, Mr. Dee is really a toad." Robbin' Robin spoke hoarsely.

Dee's eyes flickered. His mouth contracted. Then he straightened, and stood aside for the arrival of a teenage girl in a black tutu that subtly echoed his own garb. Her expression betrayed nothing. Her youth is locked away, thought Mary. Even so, the girl caused gasps when her red ballerina bun caught a shaft of sunlight. Then she moved into shadow, drawing eyes to her stiff skirt that stuck out almost at right angles. Uncanny, thought Mary.

Dee broke the silence. "Ladies and…" he stopped, staring at Robbin' Robin until the insult struck home. He spread his arms, "I present… the black swan. The sorcerer's daughter," added Dee, with a sly glance at Robbin' Robin, who was turning purple. "Leave now, minister, because she and I are about to rehearse."

Black feathers glued to Irina's skirt reminded Mary of an unfledged baby crow. Was it the youth of the girl that hinted at trouble? No, her skin, Mary realized. She's too sallow for that hair. Also, the girl's dark eyes never left Billy Dee.

"Too young," whispered Caroline. "Depressed, I should know."

"Don't worry, Caroline." Mary whispered back. "We'll talk to her. Find out what's going on." She raised her brows at Anna, who nodded.

"Irina darling, what are you doing here?" Robbin' Robin sounded petulant. He did not forget to glare at Billy Dee. The choreographer did not take his eyes from Irina.

Ah, red hair, realized Mary. Irina gets it from her father. Hers is lighter than Robbin' Robin's, probably because of his sweat.

The minister shuffled a few steps towards his daughter. She shrank back. His hurt surprise struck Mary. What a contrast to politicians parading their adoring family for photographers.

Dee cocked his head at a series of clicks. A woman in high heels entered, expensively dressed with too-bright blond hair. Nodding first to Billy Dee, she glared at the minister.

"Leave Irina alone, Robbin' Robin. You don't care. No cameras here."

Her harsh tones cut the room. So this is Helen Morgan, realized Mary, mother of Irina, divorced wife of Robbin' Robin, and the woman behind the Greenwich *Swan Lake* production. Her contemptuous pronunciation of nickname conveyed so much.

*Robbin' Robin, what a brand.*

Anna took charge. She propelled Caroline and Mary to the side of the Octagon Room. Keeping us out of the sightline, Mary thought. Or is it the firing line? With Dee leaning against clocks set into a wall, only the divorced couple's speechless daughter remained between them.

"Go chase another headline, Robin. Everyone calls you *Robbin'* Robin because it's what you do: steal."

The Minister flinched. He knows she's only getting started, thought Mary.

"You steal love. You give nothing back. Time for you to leave our Irina alone." Morgan paused. Mary swore she licked her lips when she said this. "Billy is here for a *private* rehearsal. Irina is the perfect black swan."

She stopped. Mary locked eyes with Caroline. Was there a tiny crack in the facade when Morgan proclaimed a private rehearsal? Caroline bit her lip. Mary felt her coat for her glasses, then remembered she'd left them at home. Robbin' Robin's mouth moved, yet no sound emerged. Morgan became louder.

"The media have deserted you to applaud *my* corps de ballet, my swans, at the Naval College. The BBC have booked nine whole minutes for the ten o'clock news."

Robbin' Robin gaped.

Ah, she's won the publicity war, realized Mary.

Helen Morgan could not stop. "After *Swan Lake,* would-be dancers will beg me for an audition."

"Bully for you," Robbin' Robin said rudely. "You *are* a bully, ex-wife dear. You'll do anything to make more money than I have."

"After what you left me in the divorce…" began Helen, then seemed to remember the three women watching. She clamped her lips so tightly Mary worried she'd bruise them.

At last, Dee gave Irina a hand signal. She took up first position. Despite her mother moving to clutch Dee's elbow, the girl took no notice of either parent.

A cry of outrage made Mary's ears ring. Boy, does he hate being ignored, she thought. Like a spirit struggling for air, Robbin' Robin pushed past the three women to stumble out. He slammed the door. Caroline jumped.

Robbin' Robin is remarkably unsophisticated, Mary decided, even for a politician.

Breathing more easily, Dee and Morgan swept the room with their eyes and made a silent acknowledgement of Anna. As the replacement for Dee in the ballet, she was permitted to watch. To Caroline and Mary – they paid no heed. That interested Mary.

"No, watch Irina," muttered Caroline in Mary's ear. Mary could feel the tension radiating from her.

"Quiet over there," Morgan snapped.

Mary and Caroline stood up straighter, arms by their sides. Like grade schoolers, thought Mary, crossly. Who does this woman think she is?

"Stand still, Irina, so I can check the costume." Morgan poked at the skirt. "Keep your hands away," Morgan told her daughter. "The feathers will come unstuck if you fiddle with them."

Irina shot her arms down. Sallow-skinned and petite for her age, thought Mary. And not happy with either parent, from the anger radiating from her jaw. Irina's bottom lip pouted.

Truculence, decided Mary.

As Morgan paced around her daughter, Mary was struck by her stiff way of moving, a contrast to the flow of an experienced dancer. Helen Morgan had studied ballet into her late teens, Mary recalled from *Daily Telegraph* profile of the Minister and his wife. Never a professional dancer, then, this tight woman. Could Morgan really pull off *Swan Lake* at a World Heritage site?

Under Morgan's suit, an unfortunate color of wilted lettuce, Mary had the impression of a greyhound insufficiently exercised. The way she banged her high heels on the polished floor radiated buttoned-down energy. In one of Anna's phone reports, she'd remarked that Helen's shoulder length hair had been styled to soften her sharp chin and nose. Even Mary could see that the woman's makeup was too thick, her lips too scarlet. *What is she hiding?*

Caroline must have been following Mary's observations because she whispered again.

"The woman's dangerous. She's after power."

"Power is addictive," said Anna, quietly.

"If you have no love," returned Caroline. She slipped her hand into Anna's and smiled at Mary.

There was a sweetish, oily smell in the room. Probably polish for the old floor, Mary guessed. Morgan removed her high heels and pointed accusingly at Mary's court shoes. Shrugging, Mary slipped them off, followed by Caroline unbuckling her sandals. Anna's exquisite pumps remained on her feet.

No more time to talk. Morgan clapped her hands.

"Irina, get into position for the black swan pas de deux. We'll do a run through with Billy in the Prince's part."

Mute Irina found the center of the room and pointed her right leg. Her face registered nothing. Her immersion in the world of the ballet had drowned her.

Extracting a phone from a golden bag, Morgan nodded to Billy Dee who put a hand on Irina's shoulder. Ominous chords filled the room. Mary's hands turned into fists.

On the note of a high clear horn, Billy Dee bowed to Morgan then locked his gaze on Irina. Removing his hand to three inches from her, Dee's black male body began to circle her black female one. In response, Irina rose on her pointes. A graceful pirouette by Dee ended in him brushing close to Irina's lips. Mary heard a growl from Anna.

Then Caroline shouted.

"STOP. Mr. Dee, what about Holywell?"

Dee and Irina broke apart. Morgan snapped off the music.

"Get out, whoever you are. How dare you interrupt." She stamped her feet, then winced without her high heels.

Mary stepped forward. "Ms. Morgan, we are not leaving until we have an important conversation with Mr. Dee. He insists on going to Holywell Retreat Center despite their policy. We need to know why."

"Miss Vronsky is dealing with Holywell for my school," Morgan stormed. "Talk to Mr. Dee later. I'm here to get *Swan Lake* ready."

She's scared, realized Mary. Morgan's taken on too much with barely trained teenagers. *Swan Lake* at a World Heritage site means critics. *Morgan's looking at a public relations disaster.*

Before Mary could intervene, Caroline put her hands on her hips. "Not later. We talk to Mr. Dee now. Right now."

Mary felt like cheering. Never mind recurrent depression, the tempest on the Thames, and Anna's occult belt, Caroline was making a stand.

Mary adopted her most uncompromising expression. "Mr. Dee? Why do you want to go to Holywell?"

A muscle at the corner of Dee's mouth twitched. He stared through Mary's body and out the glass window behind her. She could feel it.

"Ms. Morgan," Mary began. "Irina looks tired. Perhaps she could do with a break?"

Very slowly, Billy Dee stretched out his right arm again to Irina, like a snake uncoiling. Irina began to shake. Even her mother noticed and frowned.

"Irina," shouted Anna. She's trying to smash her way into the girl's mind, thought Mary. Mary wanted to gasp for air. Something had to be wrong with Irina. She'd not said a word.

"Irina, are you wearing a wig?" Mary called.

Tension shattered slowly like statues toppling. Mary heard a scream. They moved so fast. Hand in hand, a swirl of black, eyes dark as tunnels, Dee and Irina scooted from the room. All that remained was the tapping of ballet shoes down the stairs. Afterwards the silence deafened.

At last, Morgan moved as if she was in pain. "Irina... No," she yelled. "Irina, come back here at once. You'll lose your part if you don't rehearse today."

Mary and Caroline stood open-jawed. Morgan stumbled over to the window that overlooked the courtyard. Mary, Caroline, and Anna peered through the next one.

"Nooooooo," Morgan wailed, fierce enough to blow a hole in the glass. "No, no. Oh, that's all I need." She rested her forehead on the window.

Finally, Morgan turned back to where Caroline was biting her lip.

"Look what you've done."

"Look what *you've* done," responded a furious voice from the door. Flanked by two aides, Robbin' Robin's forehead dripped with sweat. Drops splashed onto his pale cheeks. No longer was he the brick red inspired by Billy Dee. Not angry, frightened, understood Mary.

"I told you. I *warned* you, Helen. After costing me the prime minister job, that witch Dee's stolen our daughter, our

Irina." He grabbed his ex-wife's arm. "They're off to some godforsaken hole called Holywell, he told my aides. The thief's taken *my* limousine. I saw them setting off down Greenwich hill. How dare he take my car. I'm a government minister. It's *mine*."

Robbin' Robin let go of his ex-wife to lean against a wood panel. Morgan appeared blind to his bleakness. Her body slumped.

"You're fuming about your bloody car when our daughter's gone God knows where?"

"Where has that sorcerer gone with my limo – and our daughter?"

"I don't know. You said Holywell. He never said anything about taking her away. Un-bloody-believable! Problems with Irina are your fault." Morgan's chest heaved. "As a father you're bag of hot air. Always your career and never our family. That never-ending seduction of female aides…"

"If you hadn't neglected me, *me* – and our daughter for your vanity project, this ridiculous ballet school…" The minister looked around. He seemed to notice the three observers for the first time. Turning back to his main quarry, he produced a stronger blow. "Face it, Helen. Your *Swan Lake* is a farce."

"Farce? How dare you. What about you, thinking *you* could be PM… Ha… How Billy and I laughed."

Robbin' Robin roared towards his ex-wife. Anna leapt at him, seized both arms and forced them behind his back. Caroline came to help while Mary planted herself between the couple.

"Stop this at once," she demanded. "What about Irina, Minister? Has she gone with that man?" Mary switched her weight to address Irina's mother. "You cannot possibly believe she is safe with Billy Dee."

Morgan slumped again. Slowly she turned to each member of the Depth Enquiry Agency with unfocused eyes. Last was Anna, who had dropped her hold on Robbin' Robin after a nod from Mary.

"Anna Vronsky, you told me Holywell was a charity, a therapy center for trafficked girls." Morgan spoke in a small voice. "Billy only wants to help me. He's doing research for *Swan Lake*."

"How can we be sure he's taking her there," wailed Robbin's Robin. "Stop looking at me like that, Miss Wandwalker. I won't hurt Helen. I *never* hit my women."

His puffed out his chest and beamed. Mary was revolted. Anna mimed being sick behind his back. Morgan caught Caroline's look of disgust. She turned pink.

How is this helping Irina? thought Mary.

"Wait a minute," called Caroline. "Stop yelling. This is tricky." She did something complicated with her phone and moved to the window for extra light. Gentle music wafted from Caroline's device. A spirit of harmony, thought Mary, thank goodness. Caroline took her call.

"Dorothy, you got my text? Have you heard…? ETA three hours, maybe four. Isn't that…? Oh, I see, the strikes, the traffic. Even in a ministerial car? Fine, we'll be there."

Shoving her phone in her jacket pocket, Caroline directed her news to Mary. "Irina and Billy Dee will reach Holywell late this afternoon. Dorothy spoke to them. Irina sounded fine, she says. I think we can trust it because…"

"Because Dee is determined to get to Holywell," finished Mary. "His insisting worries the witch… er, therapists. They've got vulnerable clients." Mary moved so she could address both of Irina's parents at once.

"Holywell is a charity Retreat Center whose endowment is managed by St. Julian's College, Oxford." She frowned first at the Minister and then at the girl's mother. "Irina will be safe there. We, that is Caroline, Anna, and I, have worked with them before. The witch-therapists are our friends. You may trust Holywell's reputation for excellent, if unconventional, therapy."

"Did you say witches?" Robbin' Robin spat out. "Fakers like Dee?" He'd gone red again.

"Not like Dee," Mary muttered. She shot Caroline a speaking look and silently moved her lips, *later.* Caroline nodded. Getting Irina back was the priority. Defense of Holywell's combination of psychotherapy and spellcraft could come later.

"Holywell has *no one* like Billy Dee, Minister," Mary emphasized. "Of all the places they could go, Holywell is probably the safest place in Britian for a troubled girl like Irina."

"My daughter's not troubled," bristled Helen. "She's a star in the making."

Caroline clapped her hands. "Of course. *You're in love with him*, with Dee." A stunned silence greeted Caroline's insight. Morgan opened and closed her mouth.

Robbin' Robin choked. He stared blankly at Caroline.

"You… You," he stuttered. He began to wave his arms like a tree in a big wind. Then he collapsed, landing on all fours. A howl arose. Mary and Caroline rushed to help him to his feet.

"Are you all right?" hissed Mary. Ignoring both helpers, Robbin' Robin's howl became darker, more primal. His ex-wife backed away, darting glances at the door.

"Minister, behave yourself." Mary's admonishment had more effect that she expected. I must sound like his nanny, she reflected.

Robbin' Robin shook himself like a wet dog. When it came his voice was subdued.

"No need to run away, Helen. I see the fat woman is right. I saw how you looked at him – Billy Dee. He's your lover. Compared to my harmless affairs that man's a monster."

"I AM NOT FAT," yelled Caroline. Something glittered in her eyes. Anna hissed, and Mary remembered that she carried a concealed knife.

"Don't be silly, Anna. The man's too ridiculous."

Robbin' Robin jumped as if stung by a bee.

Good God, thought Mary, Irina's been bewitched by the man sleeping with her mother.

# CHAPTER 5
# FLYING

*Thursday afternoon.*

Gusts of wind made the helicopter swing right and left. Mary didn't like it. The roads might be jammed, but she wished she, Caroline, and Anna had not agreed to accompany Robbin' Robin and Helen Morgan on the flight to Oxfordshire. Drained by the tempests of the morning, Mary leaned her head against the seat in front.

It had all happened too fast. Whatever was going on in the minister's family created strange currents. She shut her eyes to review her own impressions of the runaways. If Dee went where he said, Robbin' Robin was in for the culture shock of his life.

The minutes before the flight had been dominated by the exes at war. Regrouped outside the Observatory, a waiting helicopter could be glimpsed in the open space at the top of Greenwich Park. Leading the way, Helen Morgan and Robbin' Robin kept up their furious silence for at most two minutes, calculated Mary. Then they resumed the blame game over Irina's escape with Dee.

"How could you, Helen? How could you let that man near our daughter?"

"Billy promised we'd be a family," Morgan retorted. "Me, him and Irina." Then she shouted. "*You* were never there for her."

The minister went white, then brick red, and the yelling started.

The minister's aides were waiting with the helicopter pilot. They lifted their heads from their phones, but could not snare Robbin' Robin's attention. Mary paced up and down. Anna slipped over to the helicopter and counted its seats. Caroline sat on a wall chewing her nails.

At this rate, we'll be stuck in Greenwich, Mary fumed. Dee and Irina might as well be migrating swans.

Finally Robbin' Robin shouted over his ex-wife.

"Fuck you, Helen. Fuck the PM. I'm taking the ministerial chopper to get my hands on Dee." He seemed to notice his audience. "I mean retrieve my daughter," he said with an attempt at dignity.

Morgan gave him a dirty look. The minster did not notice, as his aides had surrounded him, protesting. They're clamoring blackbirds, and he's a greedy pigeon, thought Mary.

The aide in the smartest suit had the loudest voice. He announced that the helicopter had been booked to take the minister to Northern Ireland. Only the Cabinet Office or the PM could override the pilot's orders. The minister's incoherent reply sent his aides into a tapping frenzy. Fingers like hungry beaks, thought Mary.

Her attention fell to Morgan. She, stony-faced, began two conversations, one into her phone, the other with the helicopter pilot, an Asian man in a military uniform.

Anna whispered that Morgan had the Cabinet Secretary on speed dial. Irina's mother's body language implied volcanic energy. She switched posture to bark instructions to the pilot. First he shook his head, then shrugged his shoulders.

Meanwhile Anna perched next to Caroline and busied herself with her iPad. She claimed she could hop over firewalls that protected the communications of government officials. I won't ask, Mary thought.

"All invisible, done by spirits," Caroline said.

"What are you talking about?" Mary's head throbbed.

"Online and out here," said Caroline, serenely. "It's not what you see that counts. The minister is shouting, the helicopter blades are whirring. Yet the real events are on pulses of electricity: invisible energies. Magical spirits are the same principle."

Mary blinked. "I'm more concerned what Anna might be doing online," she said under her breath.

"Never doubt her," said Caroline, stoutly.

Anna stood up from the wall. The blackened charms were no longer around her waist, but rather hung from her shoulder. Her belt jangled as she returned the iPad to its sleeve. She thrust belt and device into a cloth bag she pulled from a pocket in her ragged costume.

Mary was distracted by an exclamation from Morgan, who threw her phone in her gold purse. The pilot saluted, and nodded. Swinging into the cockpit, he began what appeared to be pre-flight checks. Mary wondered what Morgan had said to get her way.

Marching over to Robbin' Robin, Morgan cut through the twitter of aides. Like a tempestuous spirit from the morning's storm, she lunged for her ex-husband, seized an earlobe in finger and thumb, and spoke rapidly. His face changed. After a longing glance at his aides, he signaled them to back off. Swiveling to face the three detective women, he beckoned to Mary.

"Get in the helicopter. We're going to that place, Holywell. Hurry up Wandwalker, Fat Lady and Miss Vronsky." He pouted. "Those Holywell witch... er, therapists want you three with us."

They got in. It was a tight squeeze for five passengers. Headphones came as standard so they could talk above the engine's roar, at least in theory. Irina's parents sat directly behind the pilot and leaned away from each other. Mary, Caroline, and Anna crammed themselves in seats that would barely fit two. Robbin' Robin continued to grouse.

"My wife, okay, my ex, got to the PM when he would not take my calls. The chopper will put us down in the field next to that damn Retreat Center. Dee told them he would come later with Irina."

"We know," said Mary. "We told you. Please pay attention, Minister."

Caroline found her voice. "Fat?" she spluttered. "How... how?" How can you not see your own over-indulged stomach, Mary guessed she wanted to say. She touched Caroline's arm. Caroline muttered, "If I were as fat as you, you'd have to leave me behind."

Anna glared at the back of Robbin' Robin's head. Fortunately, the entire party had to scramble to fasten seatbelts as the helicopter rose alarmingly fast. That had been before wild-spirited winds began to toss it from side to side. Nothing, however, could tear Robbin' Robin from his own troubles.

"Why can't the police intercept Dee and Irina? Take that man-witch into custody. My limo has GPS?" Robbin' Robin grumbled at his ex-wife, yet also aimed his question over his shoulder at Mary.

"The police won't find them," returned Morgan, not moving her head. "Billy can disable the GPS."

She would not look at Robbin' Robin. Her words sounded forced. After a pause, Mary could feel heat radiate from the back of the Minister's neck. Yes, he was brick red again. Before he could explode, Morgan cleared her throat. "The police say the limo has been disconnected from the grid. They're trying to locate it. Us being at Holywell is the best chance of getting Irina back."

With a grinding noise the helicopter wobbled in the darkening sky.

Mary shut her eyes. Please, not the forecast hurricane. There were hours to go before it was supposed to make landfall. To divert her stomach, she pondered Morgan's ability to re-route a government transport. After all, given the strikes and imminent storm, all vehicles that could soar above roads and floods must be at a premium.

"Ms. Morgan," she shouted above the engine, "I guess the PM is worried about Billy Dee too." Morgan stiffened, her head resolutely forward. Mary continued, "With Mr. Dee so connected to his election success, it's not a good look for the sorcerer to disappear with a fifteen-year-old girl."

"Child," muttered Caroline.

Morgan would not acknowledge Mary. By contrast, her ex-husband could not pass up mention of Billy Dee.

"I'll see to it that your affair with Dee gets out." Robbin' Robin shot a poisonous look in Morgan's direction. A fist slammed into his shoulder. "Owww, that hurt."

The ex-wife rubbed her knuckles as if surprised they stung.

"Keep your dogs under control," she snapped, indicating the Agency women with a brief turn of her head. She leaned on the window to her right. Thin glass, Mary thought. All that separates her, any of us, from early afternoon breezes over the ploughed fields of England.

Wanting to doze, Mary could not relax because her left side was jammed against Caroline. Anna, nonchalant and elegant, somehow maintained her own space on the other side of her lover. Caroline began to wriggle her right shoulder. She almost poked Mary in the eye getting her arm free. Finally, she waggled her fingers towards Morgan glued to the window. Mary saw the tears drop from her cheeks to jaw to shoulder pad.

After a moment, Morgan sat up, scrubbed her face with her sleeve, and resumed her position slumped on the glass. Mary frowned at her own handbag only reachable by one toe. No, offering Morgan a tissue would embarrass her.

The remainder of the helicopter ride passed in the ping of messages to the minister. Several elicited swearing from Robbin' Robin. Once Morgan demanded news of Irina. There was none. Only her parents and the Wandwalker Agency were invited to rendezvous with the missing girl. No aides would be permitted on the premises due to the vulnerable residents. Even the police agreed to keep away until Irina could be confirmed safe.

Mary's headache increased to a drumbeat in her skull. Caroline spotted her frown. She knew that one. With a foot she shifted her own purse to where Mary could reach it. Hooking it up by her ankle, Mary stretched to where she could rummage for aspirin and the bottle of water that Caroline kept for her own medication. The pill fizzed on Mary's parched tongue. Bending to replace the purse, Mary noticed that Anna had not moved a muscle during the wriggling beside her. The young woman's fixed stare added to her headache.

*Anna's flying*, a voice said inside Mary. Well, yeah, in this helicopter, tossed back common-sense Mary. *No, Anna's flying on emotions. She couldn't stop Billy Dee from taking Irina. Anna's locked herself in.* True, said reasonable Mary to the spirit dwelling inside her. It's true and its terrifying. She swallowed, and then felt heat of Caroline in her left ear.

"It'll be okay," whispered Caroline. "I'll look after her."

Turning to see that Caroline indeed spoke of Anna gave Mary a crick to add to the headache. She shut her eyes and tried a visualization trick she'd used in the Archive for eyestrain headaches. Five minutes later she was disturbed again.

"Oxford, Oxford Mary, can you see it?" Caroline dug in an elbow. Mary winced. The helicopter began to circle. Groggily, Mary turned her head to the window and saw far below a forest of spires. Sprinkled between stone spikes were tiny houses with spirals of smoke. Dark woods filled the valley in every direction. Surely Oxford was bigger than that?

She blinked several times. The smoke vanished to be replaced by a brownish film hovering about the ring road and the motorways. Yes, there were the famous spires and towers, the broad streets, one actually called The Broad. There was the bulge where the car plant used to be, the new build apartments, glass, steel, and air. Where had the woods gone to? Cool air brushed the back of Mary's neck.

"This is the pilot speaking: ten minutes to landing. There may be turbulence as we descend. Be calm."

We are calm, thought Mary crossly. What's he on about?

Without warning the helicopter swerved left, then right, then up and down.

"Not again," shrieked Caroline. "Not like this morning on the Thames."

Fortunately, the intercom crackled into life. Mary couldn't follow the words, but their import was adequately covered by a steep descent through blustery gales.

"No problem," came an even louder voice. "A bit of blowing about. We'll land in a jiffy."

"Stop, stop," yelled Robbin' Robin.

Morgan tightened her seatbelt, and the women sitting with her did the same.

Seven minutes later the helicopter landed in a field. The pilot said to remain seated until the blades stopped rotating.

*Mary was back on the boat. No, the boat was in the air, spinning in a cloud. Caroline clutched her arm. Mr. Jeffreys pulled Mary to his shoulder. Mary smelt his after shave, Old Spice, her father used it too. Or he did before he died in the months before she left for Oxford; her mother followed him barely two weeks afterwards. Caroline began speaking but with no sound. Someone forgot to switch on the mic.*

"Wake up, Mary. We're getting out," Caroline hissed in her ear. It tickled.

Oh, yes, helicopter, Mary recalled. A huge insect swallowed us in Greenwich and regurgitated five passengers and one pilot in an Oxfordshire field. She could not see properly through the windows. A cloud got inside, she thought groggily. There's a green glow with dirty white blobs.

Using her hand, she cleared the condensation to reveal grass and sheep. The air cooled as passengers left and the outside rushed in, carrying with it the scent of damp grass. Caroline ended the pressure on Mary's ribs by clambering out. Mary could see her doing a full sweep of the landscape, seeking Holywell, no doubt. By contrast Anna radiated defiance without giving away anything. Mary began the laborious process of detaching herself from the tiny seat.

"Watch for the sheep," Anna shouted.

She must be joking. Mary descended from the door and into a pile of sheep droppings. They stuck to the underside of her favorite court shoes. Mary opened her mouth, but Anna was gone.

Several meters away, Caroline pointed at a copse of beech trees one field over. Holywell must be that way, thought Mary.

Facing opposite, Morgan stood alone. Mary saw rooks landing on a partly dead tree in a ploughed field. Only Robbin' Robin moved, in circles. Having marched around the helicopter with his phone in the air in a vain attempt for an elusive signal, the Minister for Northern Ireland threw it down. He wants to throw a thunderbolt, thought Mary, to make some dramatic gesture. He doesn't get that, he's no god of the skies. Here he comes.

With a petulant moan, Robbin' Robin grabbed his ex-wife by the shoulder.

"They took my limo," he shouted. Mary saw him sweating. He took out a white linen handkerchief and mopped his brow with it. Then, with his voice shaking, "What do you think could happen in that car over four hours? She's fifteen, *fifteen.*"

Morgan gulped. "He won't hurt Irina. He's more father to her than you ever were." Robbin' Robin flinched. "You never paid attention to her. She bought that red wig to impress you."

Robbin' Robin's jaw dropped. "I… thought it was a teenage thing, trying out hair colors. That wig's not exactly my shade."

A snort of disgust interrupted them. Anna strode off.

"Holywell's this way," called Caroline over her shoulder as she trotted after Anna.

"All right, Minister, Ms. Morgan," said Mary Wandwalker in her best administrator's voice. "Follow my colleagues to find your daughter."

She watched as the exes fumbled through being told what to do. Morgan gave a stiff nod and started walking. Robbin' Robin stared at Mary, at the sheep, at the helicopter, where the pilot mouthed into the radio and the blades began to move. Not an aide in sight. Mary almost felt sorry for him.

"Taxi?" his voice pleaded.

Mary laughed. She set off after Morgan. Would the minister, aide-less and friendless, remain with the sheep or risk his expensive shoes? From ahead she could hear murmurs where Morgan, having caught up with Caroline, tried to interrogate her about Holywell.

"They're *good* witches," Caroline insisted. "Nothing like those things on Anna's costume. I'm so relieved she's no longer wearing the evil charms."

"Billy said it was folklore from the ballet," protested Morgan. "He said it would help the girls dance as swans. They are supposed to be flying. Witches fly, don't they? Billy knows about such things."

Having caught up, Mary cleared her throat.

"Ms. Morgan, we'd like to hear more about Billy Dee. If not now, then at Holywell, while we wait for him and Irina. You know something's not right."

Caroline gave a vigorous nod. She hitched up her baggy jeans to clamber over the stile. Caroline moves with surprising grace, thought Mary. She waited without mercy for Morgan to supply information about her lover and her daughter.

"No, no, Billy, I... he..." Morgan stopped. With a choking sound, she raised her head, seeming to groan at the sight of Anna under the beech trees. Mary touched her arm.

"Holywell is the other side of those trees. You go first."

She watched Morgan, a stiff greyhound now, swing first one leg then the other over the wooden bar. Now for another chance to ruin a good skirt, Mary grumbled. Then seeing Morgan waiting, Mary made haste.

"Something suspicious, probably illegal, connects your *Swan Lake*, Robbin' Robin's career, Billy Dee, and your daughter," she said with typical firmness. She added, "Holywell is a perfectly well-regulated therapy center..."

Mary paused. All true, but there was so much more to Holywell with its centuries of herbalism and spell craft. She tried again. "Holywell is involved with your family's problems,

Ms. Morgan, since Dee is so insistent about getting here. Your ex-husband can confirm that we three are the Depth Enquiry Agency." She noticed Anna dangling the chain of charms like a provocation.

"We've worked with Holywell before and..." Interrupting herself, Mary gave Caroline a rueful glance. In response, Caroline kissed Anna on the cheek. Anna appeared not to notice. Caroline grinned back at Mary.

"You'll take Irina home," Mary said. Morgan did not meet her eyes. "While we three," continued Mary, loud enough to reach Robbin' Robin, "will investigate the crimes of Billy Dee."

# CHAPTER 6
# MUSICAL BEDS AT HOLYWELL

*Thursday early evening.*

Thunder rolled around the hilltops that formed Holywell's valley of Oxfordshire fields and farms. To Mary's relief, the rain held off until the ill-assorted party entered the shabby manor house. Originally a timber-framed medieval farm with one end for animals, it had been rebuilt in brick and enlarged in Tudor times, including the characteristic ornate chimneys. After a fire consumed the thatch in the eighteenth century, the roof had been replaced by slates.

Yet the minister had no interest in this historical house of women. Instead, Robbin' Robin, ex-wife Helen Morgan, Mary, Caroline, and Anna gathered over mugs of tea in the Holywell lounge. This room overlooking the back garden contained shabby sofas, a stack of wooden chairs, and fraying floor rugs over a worn yet clean floor. An odor of wax polished greeted Mary. She liked it.

"You said witches?" queried Robbin' Robin in a small voice to Mary. "Does that include that woman who showed us in here?"

Helen Morgan sniffed. "A receptionist."

Anna's expression made Caroline choke. Mary sat up. "That was Dorothy Chamberlyn, therapist and center manager. And um…"

"Witch," said Caroline. Through her grin she added. "Don't let the untidy hair and faded jeans fool you. They all wear those. Except for during ceremonies of course."

Robbin' Robin's hand jerked towards his ex-wife. Morgan looked confused.

"There are six witches in residence," said Anna with a sneer.

"Seven," corrected Caroline. "Young Meredith is new. She has curls like mine were before I hit forty, and she used to be a nurse."

"You still have curls," objected Mary.

"Not that great strawberry color," replied Caroline. "Of course Janet still dyes her hair dark red when she can be bothered. Much darker than yours, Minister."

Robbin' Robin looked wildly in her direction, then in appeal to Mary.

"Janet's the oldest witch," Mary said wearily. "She's short and fierce like wine vinegar left too long in the sun."

Caroline blinked. "Actually Naomi may be older," she said. "You don't notice her age because she's so very fit. Still does cross country running. Plus you'll know her by her long silver plait," she added kindly to a frowning Helen Morgan. The woman turned away. Yet her body betrayed a listening posture, Mary thought.

"That leaves um… the Chinese one…" she said.

"Linda," said Caroline stoutly. "Born here and as English as I am."

"Don't forget her lover, the man," added Anna wickedly.

"John, she, he, they, are nonbinary."

"Who else?" said Mary hastily, seeing Robbin' Robin about to make a remark she was sure they would all regret.

"Cherry, of course, the cooking witch."

"You can tell what's for dinner from the stains on her apron. She never takes it off," said Anna.

Caroline's voice became patient. "She organizes meals, does most of the preparation and includes appropriate spells.

Where do you think those thousands of traditional recipes come from?"

Unanswerable, Mary decided. At least Caroline has shut up the warring spouses. For now.

For the moment the party from Greenwich were alone, as Dorothy had gone to re-calibrate sleeping quarters. A wiry woman in her forties with hair scraped back in a ponytail, Dorothy's authority was never questioned. Except perhaps by herself, Mary thought, who'd spotted some extra worry lines. Dorothy had colored her cheeks with foundation too, Mary realized. Usually the witches avoided cosmetics while they encouraged their young clients to use whatever made them feel good about their bodies.

No other Holywell resident had peeked at the visitors. Mary silently thanked Dorothy for that. She felt embarrassed enough at the demands of the Irina's parents. Raised eyes was Dorothy's only response to the minister ordering a suite. Morgan had called for a private bathroom, which Mary knew did not exist in the five hundred year old building.

"Musical beds," Mary had quipped when it became obvious that bedrooms for the ex-couple meant doubling up by the witch-therapists. Neither Morgan nor Robbin' Robin had commented.

"Caroline, you know the way to the lounge," Dorothy had said. "We'll bring tea. Then we have questions for Irina's parents."

Both Robbin' Robin and Morgan twitched at 'questions.' Nevertheless, they followed Caroline into the airy room at the back of the Tudor manor, now with glass doors looking out onto the lawns. The view of gardens included classrooms in a former barn. What had been stables was now the Infirmary.

Neither the Minister nor his ex-wife pretended to be impressed. Robbin' Robin jiggled one foot on the worn blue rug. A young woman brought a heavy tray with mugs of milky tea, an assortment of spoons and a bowl of sugar. Caroline leapt to help her. Then she hugged the girl.

"Sarah, fantastic to see you. I guess the term hasn't started yet. I texted. You didn't get back to me."

Standing very straight beside the steaming tea, Sarah beamed. Her purple sweatshirt accentuated her beauty, although she looked like she had not had enough sleep.

"Yes, college begins in October. We're so glad you're back," she said simply, hugging Caroline, then grinning at Mary and Anna.

"Talk later," grunted Anna, not moving. Mary rose to pat Sarah on the shoulder. The frigid atmosphere emanating from Irina's parents was not conducive to a reunion of old friends.

After Caroline and Sarah distributed the tea, Robbin' Robin helped himself to three heaped spoons of sugar. He stirred the brown liquid noisily. I bet he imagines it's Billy Dee's blood, thought Mary. That jaw's so clenched he may break something. Catching her eye, Robbin' Robin banged down his spoon, seized the mug, and sipped with a morose expression.

Morgan refused tea, sinking back in the old sofa. Mary noted the coffee stains on its worn blue cover. It was a measure of Morgan's disturbed state of mind that she preferred to hide in the dirty sofa rather than communicate. Robbin' Robin, however, would not be quiet for long. Mary began to turn over strategies to stop him throwing his weight about. She was about to go in search of Dorothy when Sarah spoke.

"Do you remember Agnes? Janet's friend with dementia that you met in that hospital, Caroline? I've been helping Janet nurse her," she said quietly. "We're giving her hospice care. Agnes has not got long. She no longer remembers names. Except one. She wants to see you, Caroline."

"Of course." Caroline rose.

"Later, she's sleeping now," said Sarah. Caroline subsided into the sofa.

"Agnes?" queried Mary. "Oh, *Agnes*. That old woman Caroline helped rescue from the fire. Why ask for her now?"

"She has bad dreams," said Sarah, enigmatically.

"I don't believe in worrying about dreams," said Mary, which was not quite true. Rather it was the mask she felt necessary to separate herself from the magical atmosphere of Holywell. Caroline smiled, but her glance at Anna was wary.

"Agnes, harrumph." Anna rose from her corner seat. Still wearing her grey rag costume minus the charm belt, her frown made Mary think of the knife Anna carried. Warrior pose. She was from the *Swan Lake* forest, creeping up on those birds that are also girls. Swigging tea as if it were a stronger beverage, Anna banged down her mug on the coffee table and stalked out.

Ah, Mary recalled. Anna would be sensitive about Agnes. Caroline had saved Agnes and the Holywell witch, Janet, from a fire started by Anna. Caroline's jaw tightened.

"Yes, Mary, that Agnes," said Caroline.

"What are you talking about?" burst out Helen Morgan like a balloon exploding. "Is Agnes another witch? What is this place? Are we in a hospice, or a therapy center? And *where's my daughter?*"

Her loud tones became wailing. Morgan sank her head into her manicured hands. Then she looked up at Mary.

"Well? You're supposed to be a detective, Miss Wandwalker. What did that woman mean about talking to Irina's parents?"

This time Mary decided to fetch Dorothy. Yet before she could move, Caroline shot out a hand.

"Mary, your phone is beeping," Caroline said.

A text from Mr. Jeffreys.

Police identified Minister's limo approaching
Holywell. Irina and Dee within.

Mary found two pairs of blue eyes fixed upon her. Robbin' Robin's were bloodshot, Morgan's wet.

"A few minutes," she said, gently. "They are almost here."

Robbin' Robin returned to his phone. Morgan slumped back. Parents, thought Mary. I don't do parents. Having my adult son murdered the day I met him was more than enough.

55

Caroline squeezed her arm. She knew. Caroline was her son George's widow. Sometimes her compassion was more than Mary could bear.

"You were saying about Agnes wanting Caroline," she directed to Sarah. "Is she worried about her dreams?"

"Premonitions," whispered Sarah. "She's frightened."

Robbin' Robin slapped down his phone, scowling. Mary sniffed. Straightening her shoulders, she leaned forward.

"We need to talk about how to behave here at Holywell. You can't order these people about. It doesn't work, and it won't help Irina. As we've explained before, Holywell is a therapy center with um... people who call themselves witches," she said firmly before clearing her throat. "Agnes is a... a..."

"A friend," supplied Caroline comfortably, stirring extra sugar into her tea.

"We encountered her on a case," said Mary, primly. "Caroline went undercover in a hospital where a client..."

"Janet, the short witch here..." Caroline began. "She does herbal magic and..."

"One of the therapists," said Mary, "Janet was being held against her will."

"So why did Miss Vronsky stamp out like that? Why is she angry about a dying old woman?"

Mary and Caroline stared at Morgan. The woman's not unobservant, thought Mary.

"There was a fire," Mary said. "It got out of control and burned down the hospital."

Robbin' Robin looked up from fiddling with his phone. Mary's glance quelled him. She was *not* going to elaborate on Anna's proclivities. Fortunately, Dorothy entered the lounge and picked up the last mug of tea. With a quizzical glance at Sarah, she gave out the mundane news. There was no room at the inn.

"If we are saving a bedroom for Irina, and the Minister won't share with his ex-wife, then there's nowhere for a male guest."

"I'm going to the best hotel in Oxford, and I'm taking my daughter," said Robbin' Robin.

"No, you're not." Both Morgan and Dorothy spoke at once, Morgan angrily and Dorothy quietly. The minister's jaw dropped. Dorothy waited for Irina's mother to continue.

"*You* are not running away from this... this mess," said Morgan through gritted teeth. "Nor are you driving my daughter through tonight's hurricane."

"Irina needs to see both parents," Dorothy added with quiet assurance. "And not for five minutes. You are both staying overnight. We've scheduled a family therapy session for you in the morning."

Robbin' Robin opened his mouth, then shut it again.

"Put Mary, Anna, and I in that twin room," said Caroline hastily. "Anna and I will share a bed."

"That works," said Dorothy, and left.

Dorothy's anxiety about bedrooms was not about fitting bodies to beds, reflected Mary. It was not even about keeping Irina's estranged parents calm. Rather it was the fragile balance of Holywell, whose clients had been trafficked by brutal gangs. Rape was their tool of control. No wonder male visitors to Holywell were discouraged. The therapy-witches must be truly worried about Irina to keep her father here.

That red-faced, red-haired man stabbed fingers onto his phone as if it could magically conjure his aides. He must feel naked without them, Mary thought. He's ludicrous, horrifying when you consider his political success.

"His lies are chocolate and cocaine wrapped in one sweet mouthful," Mary had once said to Mr. Jeffreys. He'd looked appreciative.

On the other hand, reflected judicious Mary, I am not afraid of him. Billy Dee, yes, he made me feel vulnerable, even in that sunny Octagon Room with other people about. I *smelled* him as a predator. But not our minister. Although he addicted his party to lies, no one calls him a groper. His charm is as nourishing as candy floss.

Robbin' Robin seduces women rather than hurts them, physically at least. Dorothy sees that. Plus, Mary reasoned, more pragmatically, he'll stay one night, at most two. The witches will keep the young women away. Whereas Billy Dee won't sleep in the house, I'm sure. Which reminds me, where are the other Holywell girls? We've only seen Sarah. Mary caught Caroline's eye.

"The girls are in the garden," she whispered. "Even though most of them hate the rain, Janet's got them outside to wrap the fragile plants. They're afraid to say no, lest she turns them into toads." Caroline stifled a giggle, then sobered. "Or they're taking turns to watch Agnes. She can't be left alone because she's so weak."

"You can see her tonight," said Mary, sensing Caroline's anxiety. "Right now, I'm hearing a car."

There was a collective wheeze as if air had been sucked out of the stuffy room. Any vehicle approaching had to be Billy Dee and Irina. Mary envisioned the limousine bouncing down the muddy track that was the only road access to Holywell. Spatters of rain on the glass doors reminded her of tonight's other expected visitation: a great storm. She hoped Agnes would not be too scared.

Later, Mary would reflect that no one then at Holywell suspected the vital importance of the dying old woman to the case of Irina Prince and Billy Dee.

# CHAPTER 7

# WANDERING SWANS

*Thursday evening, then morning again.*

Anticipation for Billy Dee and Irina thickened into tension. Mary could almost see strings stretched between Irina's parents and the three women of the Enquiry Agency. So still was it that she heard the drizzle. No, the rain is louder, a hurricane on the way, she remembered.

Seconds dragged into minutes. Mary's stomach muscles tightened. Caroline wrung her hands. Anna returned to the lounge, then kept dashing to the front door, wrenching it open only to slam it shut. Robbin' Robin snarled into his phone until the signal died, while his ex-wife sat bolt upright. A blow torch could not unseal her lips. A few women, witches probably, stuck their heads in, then withdrew. *Bang* went the front door for the seventh time.

"Enough, Anna," called Mary. "Come back and sit down."

A loud crack made everyone jump. Is that a roof beam splintering? wondered Mary.

"Lightning," said Dorothy. "And there's good news about the big storm. We've been working with covens all over England. Together we performed spells to release some of that destructive energy. Thanks to the witches, the hurricane split apart over the Atlantic."

Robbin' Robin dropped his phone, Helen Morgan her jaw.

Dorothy continued. "It's not over. Several lesser storms are heading our way. The updated Met Office forecast is for gales with thunder and lightning for at about a week. Oh, and lots of rain."

Mary gaped, speechless. Caroline smiled.

Dorothy ignored them both to nod at Anna entering the lounge. "Thank you, Anna. But leave the front door alone until the minister's car gets here."

Robbin' Robin threw Mary a venomous glance.

Mary darted a speaking glance at Caroline. Time to prepare for an explosive arrival. Irina is the victim here. What did they really know about the girl? Mary trusted first impressions, and so cast her mind back to her first sighting of Irina in Greenwich that morning. No, not the girl in black feathers in the Observatory's Octagon Room. For they had encountered Irina *before* reaching the Observatory, on the route through Greenwich Park. Fifteen year old Irina Prince had not been alone, and the tutu she clutched to her bird-like limbs had been white. It had been Mary, Caroline, and Anna's window into the troubled production of *Swan Lake* in Greenwich Park.

What they learned in those few minutes about Billy Dee was not pretty. Exhausted and fearful, Mary leaned back on the Holywell sofa. She closed her eyes and let memory play out. *Yes, my thighs ached. I could smell the rain off the river.*

*****

With eyes fixed on the Observatory, Mary Wandwalker climbed the steep path that ran through Greenwich Park. A few paces behind, Caroline muttered that the storm on the Thames had been spell-born. Mary ignored her. Visions of Robbin' Robin discovering Billy Dee with his daughter quickened her steps.

Short of breath, Mary paused to inhale the less polluted air up the hill. Sensing she was alone, she swung around and shook her head in disbelief. Caroline and Anna had been at her heels. Now all she could make out was a blob in the distance, grey on one side, orangish on the other. All right, she did need glasses.

Rummaging in her handbag made her feel old, especially when the spectacles eluded her fingers. With increasing haste she felt amongst the keys, small notebooks, two spent lipstick tubes, dusty packets of tissues, half a digestive biscuit, her phone, and detritus too gritty to be a cookie.

*What is this lumpy powder?* Ah, the remains of that spell bundle, a gift from Sarah of Holywell, by way of being a friend. Mary had murmured polite thanks. Her instinct had been to slip it into the trash, but she could not risk Sarah finding it. The girl had helped save her life on a previous case.

*"What are you doing?"* Caroline was breathless from running up the hill to Mary. "Didn't you see us waving?"

"I did not." Mary thrust her hand and its contents back into her unfashionable handbag. Anna strolled up.

"Forget Robbin' Robin. Trouble at the Maritime Museum. Come now."

Mary checked her irritation. There, in the columns that joined two parts of the Museum, were ungainly human figures resembling London pigeons. Amongst flapping skirts were figures in brown pajamas that spun and jumped. Mary blinked.

Anna shot Mary the ghost of a smile. Her humor could be ruthless.

"Poor blind Mary. Those are Helen Morgan's ballet dancers practicing. The boys wear wood colors. Dee wants them to merge with the trees while the girls stand out in white, the flying swans. Of course right now the girls are in grey practice skirts."

Caroline fidgeted. "C'mon Mary. Perfect time to question the student dancers, while Morgan and Dee are busy up at the Observatory."

"You two go," replied Mary at once. "Anna can introduce you. I promised to catch Robbin' Robin before he does something stupid."

"That's what I said to Anna," began Caroline. Anna rattled her belt of sinister charms. Caroline flinched. Mary narrowed her eyes.

"No, Mary must see the dancers without Dee or Morgan," warned Anna. "Come, or I'll leave." Caroline looked down. Mary raised her eyebrows. Anna spoke again.

"All right. There is a spy watching from inside the Museum. See those glass doors facing the columns?"

Mary shook her head.

"I saw movement. If you two provide a distraction, I can trap the watcher."

"It takes both of us," explained Caroline, taking Mary's arm. "Together we are nosy tourists. Alone I sound like a crazy woman."

With that unanswerable remark, Caroline escorted Mary back down towards the Maritime Museum with its flanking columns catching the sun. Anna simply vanished. She did that.

Mary threw a last glance at the Observatory dome, feeling like a lover prevented from a tryst. Her shoes made more noise going down the hill than was strictly necessary. With Anna gone, Mary and Caroline obeyed the rules and stuck to the paths.

Soon wafting music reached her and Caroline. The fuzzy pigeons became teenage girls in practice tutus. Yet there was harmony in their movements.

"If we stroll across the grass," murmured Caroline, "we can creep closer…"

A girl's shriek interrupted. It was loud enough to echo on stone. The two women turned and made for the dancers at a brisk trot.

"*What are you doing, you creep?*" shouted the same female voice. "Do you think you're Billy Dee? Get *off* me."

"Look what you've done. Bitch." The boy stepped back. He gestured up the hill. All five young heads swiveled to the approaching strangers.

"Hello there," called Caroline, reminding Mary she'd once been a teacher. "Is there a problem? Can we help?" She'd pasted on a benign expression. The dancers shuffled their feet and exchanged nervous glances.

"You look like you are rehearsing something," said Mary, trying to focus on their investigation. She hadn't entirely given up getting to the Observatory *sometime this century.*

"*Swan Lake*," said a short fair girl with a thick waist. She kicked the column.

"Don't do that. You know what Miss Morgan says about wearing out ballet shoes," said her friend, a brunette with no discernible waist. Definitely pigeons, thought Mary, rather than elegant swans, pigeons with thick legs.

"Who screamed?" Caroline linked her arm in Mary's. They scrutinized the adolescent faces that looked everywhere but at them.

"Her," said the tallest boy, older than the others, and indicated the thin dark girl with tears on hot cheeks.

"I didn't do nothing, honest," the other boy stammered.

"You touched her bum," the fair girl protested. "It's supposed to be her middle."

"Do that again and you'll not be the Prince," said the brunette. "I'll tell."

"I'm not Billy Dee," he yelled.

In the silence Mary detected shock, but no impulse to deny. The three dancers not directly involved darted anguished glances at Mary and Caroline. The crying girl shook all over; the fair girl hesitated, then put her hand on the other girl's her shoulder. The crying girl shot her a fierce glance and the hand sprung away.

"I see," said Mary magisterially.

A crash followed by a shriek sent the dancers scuttling. Round a column came Anna pulling a redhaired smaller girl in a black leotard and leggings. This girl carried a full length white dress under one arm.

"Eeeeek," shrieked the girl in black. She tried to twist from Anna's grip. Caroline leapt towards Anna.

"Give her some space," she said.

A coppery leaf spun down to the grass in front of the tearful teenager. Her hair reminded Mary of Robbin' Robin's. Mary took a second look at Anna's prize.

"Spying," snorted Anna. Releasing her prisoner, Anna folded her arms.

The girl tossed the ballet dress on the grass. For a minute she rubbed her wrist, which retained the marks of Anna's fingers.

Then, ignoring the stares from dancers and strangers, the girl kicked the white dress. The tulle leapt up as if the breeze might swallow it.

"Stop that," called Mary. Petulance and red hair, the girl must be Robbin' Robin's daughter, she thought.

"Not only do you play the black swan, you *are* her," yelled the fair haired boy who'd been accused. "You're mixed up with *him*."

Mary frowned at the boy. He bowed his head.

"Billy Dee, that's who I'm talking about." The boy kicked the grass.

"Why aren't you rehearsing?"

The question came from a tall young man with rosy cheeks, no doubt from the wind. No one had noticed his approach. Mary was struck by his mobile mouth and air of concentration. Unlike the boys in brown tights and smocks, the young man wore regular trousers and a tweed jacket.

The dress kicker flopped down on the muddy tulle and stuck her tongue out at the young man. The other dancers whispered. The girl who'd accused the boy of impropriety stepped forward.

"That's *my* costume. You've ruined it," she wailed.

The redhaired girl hugged her knees. Mary detected a pout. Yes, very Robbin' Robin.

"You *are* in league with Billy Dee."

The dancers began to mutter all at once. Mary detected fear, and she was not alone.

"Enough, you dancers," called the young man. "A good dry cleaner can fix the costume. Today is only a dress rehearsal."

Groans broke out.

"Yeah, yeah," said the young man, grinning. "Easy for me to say, I'm only observing this *Swan Lake* production. But I've watched you for days, remember. Dancing at the World Heritage site for the first time *is* scary. You're picking up vibes from its history."

Some of the youngsters looked interested.

"That's right, this site is saturated with ancient stories. They linger in the river and on the breeze. These trees whisper the fairytales, like *Swan Lake* itself."

The young man could not help crowing, thought Mary. He may be older than the dancers, but there's a boy in there. He had not finished.

"You can do it," he said, with earnestness. "Re-group and try the swans' sequence again. You're over sixteen and capable of acting like adults."

The ballet students exchanged glances.

"We're all over sixteen except *her*." The girl who claimed the soiled dress pointed to the girl curled up on it. "See what comes of promoting Mummy's little girl on the grounds she's *so talented*." She mimicked an older woman's drawl.

"Yeah, Billy Dee wanted her in the top class along with us. I wonder why."

"Enough," shouted the young man. He swung his arms. "I'm not your teacher. I can't make you carry on rehearsing if you... *children*," he said deliberately, "don't want to."

Several of the dancers stuck chins in the air.

"So we don't make more of a scene before these ladies," he nodded in the direction of Mary, Caroline, and Anna, "I'll take care of the dress and...her." He indicated the pouting girl. Her black leotard had picked up mud from the dress.

"Come with me up to the Observatory, Irina," said the young man to the girl.

She staggered up with dirty tears, red strands of hair escaping the inevitable bun. Shaking her head, she picked up the stained tutu, then began to run uphill towards the Observatory. The young man watched her for a few seconds. Ignoring Mary and Caroline, he turned and strode in the opposite direction. They lost sight of him when he exited the park and disappeared into the grounds of the Old Royal Naval College.

Perhaps he's a postgraduate at Greenwich University, speculated Mary. No matter, she decided, catching Caroline's troubled expression. For what Anna guessed is all too true: Billy Dee does sexually harass his ballet students.

"Dee will not be allowed at Holywell. No effing way," said Caroline.

"Agreed," said Mary.

"And we have to investigate why he's known as a sorcerer," continued Caroline.

"Yes, for the minister. And because Dee wants something at Holywell."

"Not only for Holywell," said Caroline, ignoring the paying client to Mary's irritation. "We've got to take on Billy Dee to protect the students in *Swan Lake*."

Mary sighed.

"Fuck the Minister," said Anna.

"Anna, who…?" began Mary. "I mean have you seen that young man at the ballet school?"

Anna nodded. "They call him Tyr. Tyr with a 'y.' He watches, not like Dee." She tossed her hair. It flowed into the breeze like a black flame. "Says he is studying shamanic transformations in fairytales, like the story of *Swan Lake*."

She gave Mary an ironic look. "The girl who ruined the lead's swan costume," she said, and rattled her chain belt. "*That girl* is Irina Prince, as you'll have guessed. Irina the ballerina, they call her."

"So she's the Minister's daughter," said Caroline. "She must be disturbed to act out like that. Probably has no friends in the class because she's younger."

"Look, up there," said Mary firmly. Caroline and Anna followed her eyes. "Irina's reached the Observatory. Please, let's get moving. Don't forget we promised to keep Irina's father out of trouble." Mary set off at a brisk pace.

"Let's roll," said Anna laconically, grabbing Caroline's hand and stomping after Mary.

In that last hundred meters up Greenwich hill, Mary reflected that her body had aged more than the huge oaks that shaded the path. What were fifty years to trees nine centuries old? Young Mary had skipped past the same giants. Ignoring the trickle down her back, she dismissed her worries about Caroline and Anna. The vulnerability of the former and the unpredictability of the latter could wreck the case. And yet Mary's bones resonated with a positive energy that spanned the three detectives, surpassing the demons. I've seen it, thought Mary, *I've lived it.*

"A pity we've promised to stop Robbin' Robin making a scandal," Caroline muttered, catching up.

Mary looked at her warily, remembering Mr. Jeffreys's injunctions. "What's Anna been saying?"

Anna turned away, her nose in the air.

Caroline stepped closer to Mary. "With the law against witchcraft repealed, conjuring spirits isn't actually a crime." She looked left and right before her eyes lit up. "I'd like to see Robbin' Robin tell the nation that even the dead don't want him as PM."

Mary Wandwalker laughed. Caroline had reminded her of an exchange with Robbin' Robin, one she would treasure. Earlier, when she and Caroline were on the boat with Robbin' Robin, the minister wouldn't stop talking about his nemesis.

"I know more than you think about Billy Dee. The bastard claims descent from Dr. John Dee of Queen Elizabeth's Court."

"You mean Elizabeth I, not our late queen?" Caroline had to shout over the rising waves.

Mary chimed in: "The Dee of Shakespeare's time was famous, a sorcerer with political allies all over Europe. He did horoscopes to advise the Queen about her enemies."

"Thanks to the little runt sounding off to the press, I'm well aware of Dr. John Dee," snarled Robbin' Robin. "Did you know our *Billy* Dee says he can conjure spirits from the Parliaments as far back as his namesake in the 1560s? That's how the PM won the damn election. Dead politicians popped up at Dee's command. They begged my colleagues to vote for my rival 'to save the nation.'" Robbin' Robin did the air quotes that so irritated Mary.

"Does England look saved?" he shouted, waving at gridlock on the Embankment streets. "I have supporters in the Home Office. As soon as Dee got cozy with the PM, the security services dug in. They found no lineage from John Dee. Plus..." He paused, pursed his lips, then continued in a lower tone, "Plus rumors about why European ballet companies kicked him out."

At the word 'ballet,' Caroline shifted in her seat. Mary gave her a quick nod. They would get to the ballet and to Robbin' Robin's daughter.

"Billy Dee is 'cozy' with the new Prime Minister?" she queried, aware of Mr. Jeffreys watching from a few rows back. "Are you referring to er... a conspiracy?" asked Mary, feeling her way forward.

"Ha." Robbin' Robin seized the rail in front of him as the boat rocked up and down.

For once he looked at her as if he saw her – an older woman unafraid of blustering men, too assured to play at looking younger. Mary Wandwalker had learned, relatively late in life, to speak her mind, enjoy her good figure, and dress for her own pleasure.

The Minister's tone altered to include a smidgeon of respect.

"What I want from you, Miss Wandwalker, is proof that Dee manipulated the election of the PM." He jerked his head towards Mr. Jeffreys, too far away to hear them. "Tell your Mr. Jeffreys I'll hold off exposing the damn séances while you get me enough to take the PM down. Billy Dee fixed that election." He added in venomous tones, "I'll finish both of them."

"What if the séances are real?" Caroline spoke with genuine curiosity. Mary shook her head at her. Now was not the time...

"Dammit, Mrs. Jones, what kind of Enquiry Agency are you?"

"A good one," shouted Mary, over the rising wind. "We keep our minds open. Although personally I am certain Mr. Dee faked those séances, minister…"

"I *know* those séances got the PM the job that should be mine."

He stared beyond Mary, beyond the wind-whipped river. He was entranced by the golden future he'd promised himself. Being Prime Minister was his entitlement. He was shameless. With his arrogant attitude he had to be holding something back. Well, so was she.

"You can't let me down, Miss Wandwalker. Jeffreys said I could count on you."

Robin's Robin's appeal expanded his eyes until their irises were blue islands. *I have to be PM. You must see that.* The nearest aide shot a frown towards Mary.

Childish *and* manipulative, she thought. What a combination.

Robbin' Robin clawed at the leather briefcase on the seat between himself and Mary. He turned morose.

"You've got to help. The police won't do anything. Apparently, the dead don't count as witnesses, or criminals."

Mary caught him peeking at her. "Ah," she said, merciless. "Hard to get ghosts into a courtroom, I imagine."

Robbin' Robin missed the sarcasm. Mary couldn't resist tweaking his tail, "Nevertheless, I don't see that it would be ethical for our Agency to intervene in politics."

A test. Mary had every intention of investigating Billy Dee, especially his so-called magic. Someone ready to corrupt an election could not be trusted with young people. Mary had no doubt about that.

"Oh, Miss Wandwalker." Robbin' Robin stroked the sleeve of his silk suit as if to say that no one who had made as much money speculating in the City, no one as handsome as he, could possibly be refused. "Ethical" elicited no interest.

This indulged man expected her to concede, Mary realized. Well, he had a long wait, at least until hell froze over. Yes, they would investigate Dee. But for their other clients, Hollywell and Mr. Jeffreys. Mary directed a significant look at Caroline. The younger woman raised her voice above the hammering wind.

"Is there anything else you'd like to tell us?"

Mary knew Caroline found it hard to believe that the minister could be unaware of danger to his daughter. When Robbin' Robin merely looked blank, Caroline tried again.

"We need to talk about Billy Dee and your daughter," she shouted over the wind and rain battering the boat.

Robbin' Robin overbalanced forward, nearly hitting his head on the window. Mary and Caroline clutched each other as the boat seemed to dive off a cliff. They plunged into the dark.

*****

Many hours later Mary opened her eyes. The Holywell lounge glowed in yellow lamplight. Rain darkened with the approaching night, while the wind howled as if it was in pain. The assembled company looked afraid. Whether from the storm or the approach of Dee and Irina, Mary could not tell.

Mary cleared her throat, as she heard something that did not come from the moaning trees or pounding water. That cranking and bumping had to be the minister's car. A metallic scrape made everyone sit up. A car's door slammed. Everyone leapt to their feet as fists resounded on the front door. Billy Dee and Irina at last.

# CHAPTER 8
## A DEATH IN THE FAMILY

*Friday morning.*

After Billy Dee and Irina Prince crossed the Holywell threshold, the storm dived into the valley like a dragon. It clawed at the old roof's slates, rattled windows, and clotted gutters with sodden leaves. By midnight the beast had moved on. The wind ceased roaring, and lightning no longer lit the sky. In Holywell those with sensitive hearing slid into a merciful unconsciousness. Mary was one of those.

However, someone did not sleep. By morning Holywell hosted a dead body, killed by the forced inhalation of gas. Overcoming reservations about the wellbeing of the trafficked women, and at Mary's insistence, manager Dorothy Chamberlyn dialed the emergency services.

The police agreed that only a plainclothes officer would enter the house. Thus, the scene-of-crime officer, a man in a turban, sweater and jeans, asked for an account of the evening before the death. He discovered that no one agreed about the reception of Billy Dee and fifteen-year-old Irina Prince. While most witnesses emphasized swearing, threats, and hysteria, their recollections deviated in key details.

Mary Wandwalker chiefly remembered helping Dorothy to detach the hands of a purple-faced Robbin's Robin from the sorcerer's throat.

71

Anna reported that Irina's mother screamed insults at her daughter. The teenager tried to run, but Caroline intercepted her. She tried to hug her, but the girl shrank back.

"With Irina's parents making such a row, we put our hands over our ears," Caroline told the police.

Dorothy recounted how Billy Dee ignored the minister's attempt to strangle him. Watching his distinguished assailant being ingloriously dragged from the room, he made some sort of hand signal to Irina. She dived behind the sofa where, trembling from head to toe, she curled into a ball. At that moment, Helen Morgan cornered Billy Dee and spat at him. Again there was no reaction. Slowly, arrogantly, as Mary described it, Dee wiped the spittle from his chin like it was nectar.

The policeman spent the most time with Mary Wandwalker. She told him how Caroline and Sarah had converged on the shivering Irina, who was clad in a black leotard and leggings. Once Irina let down her arms, Caroline was shocked by the tearstains around her swollen eyes. She and Sarah knew better than to touch her. Instead, they edged Irina to the open door. Shielding her with their bodies, they eased her into the hall and to the bench almost hidden beneath a pile of coats.

"I kept between Billy Dee and the door," said Mary. "So he could not go after the minister. Dee's face gave nothing away. Then I went into the hall to see if Irina would say anything, but she wouldn't talk," Mary said. "Sarah ran to the kitchen. Soon Cherry, the flustered cook, brought out mugs of hot milk. Irina wouldn't touch hers. Sarah said there was honey in it. Then Irina drank. After that Caroline and Sarah got her to bed."

"No doctor?" the policeman enquired.

"Caroline stayed with Irina. She later said that the girl's mother came to the bedroom," Mary explained. "Ms. Morgan mentioned a doctor, but Irina screamed 'No.' That's when Dorothy turned up. She said Irina needed to be left alone. The poor girl hid her head under the pillow."

"I see," said the policeman. He frowned at the notes from previous interviews. "What about Mr. Dee, and um, Irina's father?"

Mary coughed. "While Irina was behind the sofa, I helped Dorothy drag Robbin' Robin to her private office. We locked him in, temporarily, we said. He banged the door and cursed us."

"Ah," said the policemen with a slight grin. "That would be Mr. Robin Prince, the Northern Ireland Minister?"

"Afraid so," Mary muttered. "Then we, that's Dorothy and I, collected Irina's mother from the lounge. Thank God we'd secured Robbin' Robin in another room, for we found Anna peeling Helen Morgan off Billy Dee's chest. She alternated between punches and wails. While Dorothy persuaded Morgan upstairs to see Irina, I went ahead to have a word with Caroline and Sarah."

"What time was this?"

"Not sure exactly. When Irina was settled, I remember telling several fascinated young women, Holywell clients, to go away. That must have been around six p.m."

Mary tried to piece together the events. At 6:15 p.m., approximately, Irina's parents, Robin Prince and Helen Morgan, sat stonily in front of Dorothy at her sternest. The minister wanted Dee restrained until he could be arrested. In fact Dee had already retreated to one of Holywell's barns. He reappeared an hour later at dinner in the company of two of the other witches. The bald woman in male dress made Mary start, until she remembered being introduced to John. That meant the tiny Chinese princess would be Linda. They were a couple.

"You know John, the one with no hair?" said Mary to the policeman. "She, no, *they*, use nonbinary pronouns," said Mary. "I keep forgetting."

Dinner that night was vegetable stew with suet dumplings. During the mostly silent meal, rain battered the windows behind the curtains. Eating with enthusiasm, Caroline reminded Mary that John and Linda had corresponded with Dee over weather magic. Were John, Linda, and Billy Dee responsible for that awful storm on the Thames? That thought made Mary smile. She did tell the Detective Inspector that John and Linda had escorted the sorcerer to the opposite end of the dining table from a gaunt Helen Morgan. Dee's lover gazed at him with hollow eyes. Mary watched Helen's hands shake while using a knife and fork.

Sorcerer Billy Dee never glanced in Morgan's direction. Instead, he fixed admiring eyes on Holywell's young women.

"He can actually switch it on and off," said Mary to the policeman. "Sex appeal, they used to call it. I saw him lap up the curiosity of those youngsters. He glowed. I swear his skin changed from chalk white to peachy pink."

"Did the young women respond?"

"Eventually. First they stuck to hostile stares. Soon these became flirtatious, until Dorothy noticed. I have never seen her eyes flash like that."

Neither the Robbin' Robin nor Irina joined the company for dinner, Mary explained. Dorothy made it clear to Irina's parents that they could not remove their daughter in her fragile condition. To the minister's fury, she added she would not permit the police to enter Holywell to arrest Billy Dee. At least not until there was clarity about the situation with Irina. All the witch-therapists agreed that the teenager must be allowed to rest and then have counselling.

"It is not only for Irina's sake," Dorothy said in her crowded office after dinner. The three detectives joined the conference with Irina's parents. "Our young women have had enough brutal treatment by authorities. That's why their rehabilitation is so extended."

Morgan said there was no question of her leaving Holywell without Irina. Of course she'd stay until Irina felt better. Robbin' Robin shouted that if she thought he'd leave Billy Dee in his daughter's proximity, then he would show her, Morgan, the witches and the media. He'd call the Chief Constable, the Home Secretary. Hell, he'd call the BBC.

"Not tonight," said Mary Wandwalker. She pressed her lips to clamp down the choice words she wanted to say to Robbin' Robin. Instead she fixed her steely eyes on the minister.

"You don't want a scandal involving your daughter, do you? It could be toxic to your, and her, future."

Robbin' Robin's jaw slackened. "That's right," said Mary. "Tonight everyone stays and gets some rest. Dorothy…?"

"Yes," sighed the Holywell manager. "We'll set something up for Mr. Dee in an outside classroom. Unfortunately, we can't put anyone in the Infirmary due to Agnes's weak condition."

"I demand my own bathroom." Both Robbin' Robin and Morgan reiterated at the top of their voices.

Mary wanted to laugh. She signaled to Caroline to leave. Anna had slipped out as soon as Robbin' Robin made demands.

"So what happened after Miss… er, Dorothy sorted out sleeping arrangements?" prompted the young officer. He shifted between his glowing iPad and the woman with the odd name. Her explanation for 'Wandwalker' stuck in his mind because it was like a fragment of poetry he'd learned in school.

"Wandwalker's from the Anglo-Saxon for 'wind talker.' They were old women who talked to the gods."

Mary stopped. She realized that she had not caught *his* name in all the comings and goings over the body. Nevertheless, she appreciated his gentle manner that seemed to recognize the shock they all felt. Death was one thing, but murder, *murder,* here at Holywell. Unthinkable.

His tapping ceased. Mary knew without looking up that the policeman would wait until she resumed. So she did.

"To continue, Inspector. After dinner we went to our rooms. I was dead on my feet. Excuse the expression. Dorothy said that Irina never stirred since the moment she'd gotten into bed."

Pausing for breath, Mary heard the iPad click on the polished desk. The Inspector frowned.

"Let me get this straight. Miss Irina Prince said nothing when she got to Holywell? Strange, surely? She slept through the night? No one asked her about William Dee or sexual assault? As a fifteen-year-old..."

"I'm aware that sex with a minor is a crime, Inspector," said Mary, impatiently. In truth she wasn't entirely comfortable with Dorothy's ruling that for Irina rest came before questioning. "The wi... er, therapists here have a lot of experience with abuse survivors. They are qualified, you know. Holywell is a National Health Service Center of Excellence for treating trauma from incest, statutory rape, and sex trafficking."

"And yet, Mr. Dee remained at large?"

"I believe in prioritizing the welfare of the victim before calling the police," snapped Mary. She shut her eyes. "I apologize, Inspector. This is more stressful than I realized. You see..." She drummed her fingers on Dorothy's desk.

"You must understand that the situation between Mr. Dee and Irina's family is complicated. You heard the minister shouting nonsense about Dee holding séances for the Prime Minister. Please ignore his ramblings. Dee and Irina's mother are in a relationship. If no..."

Mary took a deep breath. "If no interference has been perpetrated by Dee on Irina, then Ms. Morgan is likely to claim that Dee had her permission to drive Irina to Oxfordshire. Above all, Dorothy said, that Irina must be listened to *before* being used as a pawn between her parents. If you ask me, their public and acrimonious divorce has scarred the girl."

The Inspector grimaced. At that moment came muffled shouting of a male voice followed by a woman's screech. Both were identifiable to Mary. She raised her eyebrows at the policeman. He nodded.

"I'm beginning to understand why my colleagues agreed to hold off for twenty-four hours. So last night, Mr. Dee..." he prompted.

"Yes, Billy Dee showed his preternatural white teeth and entertained the young women billeted here. He actually volunteered to sleep in one of the barn conversions. That meant the main house could be bolted from the inside. He pretended it was a huge joke that he could not be trusted around young women."

I can't get over how he seems to be at least two people, Mary added to herself. How Dee could switch from sinister and remote to heart throb turned her stomach. Yet several of the Holywell young women had warmed to his syrupy charms by the end of dinner.

The tired-looking policeman resumed tapping. A lock of dark hair escaped his turban. Mary told herself not to stare. He must be a Sikh. That would help in guessing his name.

She continued. "Since John and Linda had corresponded with Billy Dee, they went to improvise a bed for him. I heard them talk about cushions from the lounge. We were all so tired, I didn't pay attention. Not after we knew Irina and the young women would be secure. Dorothy promised to lock every door and window from the inside."

"Leaving Mr. Dee outside? Near the Infirmary?"

"No, the Infirmary is the other side of the house. That building used to be stables. Janet Swinford usually sleeps there to watch over Agnes. Recently she got too tired, Caroline told me. So Dorothy insisted Janet have every other night in her own bed in the house. Last night Sarah did the night shift."

"The African girl?"

"British," said Mary, automatically. "She was kidnapped from the Congo when her family was killed."

"Ah."

Mary looked up at his change of tone.

"Now we come to it, Miss Wandwalker. I must put to you what we've learned from other witnesses. It raises concerns about a member of your Agency."

"Anna," Mary murmured. She could kick herself for that fatalistic tone.

"Miss Vronsky? No, this is Mrs. Jones."

"*Caroline*? Nonsense, she can't be involved." Mary spoke so fast her tongue stuck to the roof of her mouth. She gasped.

"Are you all right, Miss Wandwalker? I can send for water."

Mary licked her dry lips. "Perfectly fine, Inspector. What about Car… Mrs. Jones?"

The Inspector consulted the screen. "It is about who went to the Infirmary. The nurse, Sarah, that is, says Mrs. Jones knocked on the door at midnight and sent Sarah away. Yet Mrs. Jones denies having been in the Infirmary. That's a problem. The center manager here, Dorothy, vouches for Sarah as a truthful young woman."

"So is Caroline. She's my…" What was Caroline? "She's my friend, my best friend. More like a daughter."

"Daughter? Ah, I see. Mrs.. Jones is your daughter-in-law. She's married to your son."

Mary could not speak. The policemen squinted at his device.

"Deceased son, that's right. Sorry, Miss Wandwalker. Our records show that George Jones was married to a Caroline. After his murder she began working with his birth mother." He looked up with a brief smile. "You know, don't you, that George Jones is famous. He is a case study at the police college. My boss uses him in briefings."

The man's expression turned grave at Mary's frozen one. "I believe he died undercover, quite near here?"

Mary nodded. She knew what kind of police briefing would take George Jones as a cautionary tale. Never get involved with civilians on a case or you could end with a knife in the chest. *The wet grass, gouts of blood, that smell of iron in the morning cold, George's hair wet with dew, and his final words. They were about Anna whom he'd loved, and Caroline, whom he'd loved more.*

"Caroline would never hurt anyone." Mary was surprised at the hoarseness of her voice.

"So she says." The policeman focused on his notes. He did not look at Mary. This will not do, Mary said to herself.

"No, Inspector… You're not listening." Mary folded her arms.

78

He looked up, then put the iPad on the desk. Glowing with information, it seemed to Mary like a great eye winking at them. However, it was the human policeman who perused her across the desk.

"All right, Miss Wandwalker, I'm D.I. Singh, Kirpal Singh. Your son would have called me Kir-with-the-turban, like the rest of them." He twitched his lips, whether a wince or humor, Mary could not tell. She inclined her head.

"Tell me about Mrs. Jones. I get that you don't think she is a killer. Yet the old woman known as Agnes is dead, and not by natural causes." His voice had a musical depth, Mary suddenly realized. Amused, rather than offended, about his colleagues, she guessed.

She cleared her throat. "Caroline is the gentlest person I have ever met." Gentlest and the strongest, Mary thought to herself. "Sarah must have been dreaming. You must believe me that Caroline went to bed at the same time I did. I saw her." Mary paused. "You have heard that Robbin' Robin and his ex-wife insisted on separate sleeping arrangements. That meant the three of us, Caroline, Anna, and me, taking a room together."

Don't overdo details, Mary silently told herself. Be careful. He doesn't need to know too much about Anna.

"So where was Miss... er, Vronsky, when you went to bed?"

Mary coughed. "Outside Irina's door, making sure she could rest undisturbed." Mary managed to stop herself from saying, at least that's what Anna said. "Anna planned to do some sort of security patrol with the younger witches..."

The policeman's eyebrows nearly reached his turban.

"Erm, I mean therapists. They're genuine therapists." Drat, Mary had been put off balance by the impossibility of explaining Anna. "All the spells are..." Mary groped for words she could live with, "lifestyle stuff, their... unusual religion." Then with her customary firmness. "Caroline and I took a bed each. Anna would either use the floor later or join Caroline." Mary saw the question on the young man's lips and prayed to a god who consistently failed her.

"Miss Wandwalker, did you actually see Anna Vronsky last night, security patrol or not?" Lightning struck outside, giving Singh's face a ghostly pallor.

Mary bit her lip. Thunder crashed. "Anna…" she began.

"Has a fascinating record, very extensive. She's on parole with you as her legal guarantor, I believe?"

Mary nodded.

"You did not see Miss Vronsky last night, all night."

More a statement than a question. "Nor can you swear to the whereabouts of Mrs. Jones at the time of the murder?"

"That's right."

Mary brightened. "Of course, that means *I* have no alibi for the murder either, Officer."

"Inspector," grunted the young man. "Few at Holywell last night do possess alibis," he remarked conversationally. "That's one reason we're taking DNA samples as well as fingerprints. However, only Mrs. Jones has been placed at the scene by a witness."

"Or Sarah's lying to get herself *away* from the scene," returned Mary. "All I can say is when I woke up this morning Caroline was in bed, snoring. She was louder than the rain."

"Hmm. Very well. So Miss Wandwalker, how did you find out about the death?"

"Janet. She mainly cares for the garden. I was in the kitchen for breakfast when she burst through the door. *'Agnes is dead!'* she shouted. Dorothy went to hold her, but Janet pushed her away. Despite being about seventy, she's very strong."

The Inspector's bearded chin jutted forward. "What were her next words. Think carefully. What did Janet Swinford say after announcing the death?"

Mary pretended to search her memory. In truth she feared she would never forget. "Janet said, *'No, she did not die in the arms of the goddess. Agnes was murdered. Someone messed with that old heater. She's been gassed.'*"

Mary shut her eyes. "Everyone started shouting. I'd read about carbon monoxide poisoning from faulty gas fires. Accident, not murder, I thought. So while Dorothy phoned the authorities, John and I checked the old gas fire. No mistake, and definitely no leak. Someone tampered with the wires and valves. Carbon monoxide is invisible and odorless," she said, sadly, "a silent killer of a harmless old woman."

Mary paused. "Caroline *liked* her. Said she had spirit. I wanted to do something for Agnes, so I touched her hand. So very cold. I picked up a corner of a blanket to fold over her, but John pulled me outside."

Mary swallowed. "Agnes's tongue stuck out, dry like leather. We heard the old contraption hiss, so John rushed back in to turn it off. When she, no, *they*... They came out with a black feather. Found by Agnes's bed, they said. A crow feather that someone walked in, I told them."

She sighed. "Agnes dying like that had to be murder. Dorothy explained that all the Holywell gas fires had safety checks two weeks ago, to get ready for winter. The technician said the old model had a safer design than some of the new heaters. Agnes did not die by chance. Someone did this."

As she spoke, Mary felt her blood drain from her face. Saying it out loud made it more real.

"Not Caroline," she croaked. Caroline would not lie about watching Agnes. "And not Sarah either," she added. "We *know* Sarah. She worked with us on a case in Oxford and London. She's a good person."

"Early days," said the Inspector. "I'm planning a follow up on the interview with Mrs. Jones."

He's put a wall up to conceal his real impressions, Mary thought.

"Now, Miss Wandwalker, we'd like to know more about the victim. For instance, no one has her surname. Even the NHS only has her down as Agnes X. Yet Mrs. Jones and Ms. Swinford call her a friend."

"Yes, Janet and Caroline met her in a private mental hospital months ago."

"That would be the one with the mysterious fire?"

"Everyone got out," said Mary. "Agnes needed a new home. She's lost her name as well as her family, you see."

"That's a complication." The Inspector frowned at his screen. "No surname delays the death certificate. Plus not identifying the victim increases the awkwardness about the presence of a minster of the crown. No one expects Robin Prince to be involved, but mysteries inspire conspiracy theories. That's before we come to Mr. William Dee's arrival yesterday with a juvenile."

"Who happens to be the minister's fifteen-year-old daughter," agreed Mary.

She had a sense of being a schoolgirl told off by a headteacher. Ludicrous, she thought.

The Inspector switched off the iPad. This time his rueful smile reached from eyes to beard. "The death is not officially murder until after the autopsy. Right now I've orders concerning Robin Prince. I'm to clarify if he is connected to the victim, and discover what the hell's going on between the minister, his family, and Mr. Dee. Until then, the minister can't be vetted for his new position. That means everyone stays at Holywell for at least another day."

As Mary pondered D. I. Singh's political problems, they heard the low hum of activity in the hall rise to loud voices. Without warning, the office door banged open to reveal a red-faced man with disheveled hair.

"Miss Wandwalker, at last," stormed Robbin' Robin. "You'll know where that bastard Dee is hiding. Get him for me. Put Irina in my car. I've ordered breakfast. We're leaving in forty minutes."

The Inspector stood up, the turban making the lean figure into an imposing one.

"I'm afraid that won't be possible sir," he said.

"Why, who's died?" The minister laughed, uproariously.

# CHAPTER 9
# WHO ARE YOU, MARY WANDWALKER?

*Friday afternoon.*

It was Robbin' Robin's laughter that died. He scowled at Mary and the policeman. We're not his usual audience of adoring aides, Mary realized.

"Actually, sir, there has been a death on the premises," said the Inspector with his walled-in face. "We are investigating some suspicious circumstances."

Robbin' Robin paled. "Not... not..." he stammered.

"Irina and Ms. Morgan are fine," said Mary quickly. "Your daughter refused to come down to breakfast. Sarah took her a bowl of cereal."

"Ah," said Robbin' Robin, looking distracted. "When can I take her away, officer?"

"The only person leaving Holywell today is the victim," announced the Inspector. "We've orders that everyone stays until we get the results of the autopsy."

Robbin' Robin stamped his foot. "That doesn't apply to *me*. I'm calling the Prime Minister."

Mary rose, then sat back down. "The rain's getting worse," she remarked to no one in particular.

Inspector Singh looked up. "Yes, that track to the ring road doesn't look good. Another storm is due in a few hours. We'll be leaving shortly." He resumed his seat behind Dorothy's desk and clicked his iPad.

"I...I..." began Robbin' Robin.

"No," said the policeman. "Minister, now would be a good time to answer a few questions." He met Robbin' Robin's pout. "Don't bother the Prime Minister's office. My boss has orders from the highest authorities. Number 10 won't take your call."

Robbin' Robin choked. Mary stood up and guided the minister into her chair. He collapsed. The chair creaked. Robbin' Robin's mouth fell open.

"I'll have coffee and toast sent in," Mary said, darting out the door. Relief made her lean on a bookcase in the hall. At least that ridiculous man distracted the policeman from Caroline. She'd never hurt anyone. Mary shut her eyes. I've got to find Sarah. She mentally slapped her forehead. Anna... Oh, God, Inspector Singh will have told Anna that Caroline is a suspect. Anna will do something crazy if I don't stop her.

Forgetting breakfast for Robbin' Robin, Mary made for the lounge. It was deserted. Outside the French windows, clouds let loose their burden of water. In the gaps between trees, Mary saw large pools forming. Not my problem, she thought as she listened for female voices. Faint murmurings came from goodness knows where in Holywell's warren of rooms. Girls or witches? Impossible to tell. Neither Caroline, Anna, nor Sarah answered her text messages.

I might as well climb on the roof with semaphore flags, thought Mary, disgusted. How much worse could today get?

*****

Her rhetorical question was answered after the police left. Following hours of rain, and the removal of Agnes's body, came the news that would incarcerate everyone at Holywell.

"Fuck, fuck, fuck," exclaimed Dorothy to her fellow witch-therapists, she who never swore. Mary received the email in the bedroom shared with Caroline and Anna. She relayed the news to Caroline who was lying flat on the bed, and Anna, who paced the shabby carpet.

"This doesn't happen in England," shouted Mary. "It must be a terrible prank at the Met Office. I can't believe the floods are this bad."

Caroline moaned and pulled up a blanket over her face. She had taken to her bed after her second police interview. Shock removed her appetite. That had never happened before. It scared Mary.

\*\*\*\*\*

Earlier, Caroline had stumbled away from her interview with Inspector Singh. She was so pale that her freckles stood out like a brown rash. She threw herself into Mary's arms. Back in their bedroom, she tried to explain to Anna and Mary what Mary already knew. The police regarded Caroline as their chief murder suspect.

"I didn't do it."

"We know," said Mary. Anna stood with burning eyes, her muscles tightening like coiled ropes.

"I never went to Agnes's room last night," Caroline assured them. "Okay, I *planned* to go to relieve Sarah, but after everything at Greenwich, the flight, and the worry about Irina, I fell asleep. Mary, you'd dozed off, and Anna was guarding Irina's room. That policeman says I have no alibi."

Anna made a rude gesture. "Alibi, *smalibi*. I'll tell the police…"

"*No*," exclaimed Mary and Caroline together.

"No lying to the police," said Mary, looking grim. "You know how Mr. Jeffreys hates it when you get arrested."

"Things aren't that bad, darling," said Caroline, blowing Anna a kiss. "Yet. I don't know why Sarah says that I burst in and told her to leave Agnes to me. I don't understand how she *could* have said it."

She spotted Anna's expression. Rather late, in Mary's opinion. "Darling, no. Not that either. Anna, promise me. Remember Sarah's one of the trafficked girls. She worked with us. I want to do a clarifying spell with Janet first. There's something dark here at Holywell."

At "dark" Anna's black eyes flashed. Her hand clasped Caroline's arm.

"Ow, Anna, too much."

Anna released her grip. Looking around, she glared at Mary.

"Perhaps I should question Sarah..." Mary began. "No, we'll wait for the autopsy on Agnes. Then we'll know for sure if it's murder."

*****

That had been hours ago, before the authorities dropped a bomb on Holywell.

In the bedroom, while Caroline continued to moan, Mary looked at her computer screen in disbelief. Anna sat very still.

"Are you chewing your nails, Anna? You never do that," Mary said.

Removing her hand from her mouth, Anna leapt onto the bed next to Mary and pulled the laptop away from her.

"We will all die," she said. "In fire or water."

"Certainly not," rapped Mary. "I won't allow it. I'm calling Mr. Jeffreys. Show Caroline the email."

Caroline pulled herself up to a position on her elbow. That way she could take the computer Anna brought to her.

"I don't understand," she said. "The witches said the storms would not be too bad. Is the world ending?"

Mr. Jeffreys could not be reached. Mary got up.

Perhaps the message would soften if she went downstairs to the witches. Yet the email gripped her mind, each word a bullet making the world too dangerous.

The good news is that the storm from the Atlantic is no longer a hurricane. For some reason it broke up into series of electric storms. These unusually fierce weather events will strike southern England for the next five days. Very strong winds expected. Extreme flooding imminent in Oxfordshire, Bedfordshire and Hampshire. All roads in these counties are closed for the duration. Given the dangers lightning strikes on power cables, expect outages. In addition, lightning could spark fires inside houses, especially in older, wooden buildings. Everyone in the affected areas must remain in lockdown until further notice. The Government will organize drones to deliver food and medicine to isolated communities. In the event of phone or internet interruptions people should listen to the radio for announcements.

There was more about the police guarding supermarkets to protect food supplies. Mary's brain refused to process the news. Descending the stairs, she could hear phones going off all over the house. She discovered most of the witches in the kitchen, where Janet used a tea towel to wipe her rain plastered hair. She wore rubber boots covered in mud almost to their tops. A scent of wet grass wafted from her hands.

"Wandwalker, sit, join us. Holywell will be an island tonight. There's a foot of water on the fields." The witch threw down the cloth and ran her fingers through her inch of hennaed hair, white at the roots. She gave Mary a stony stare.

Mary remembered how direct Janet Swinford could be. Sitting at the kitchen table, John and Linda held hands. The cook, Cherry, frowned at a giant kettle warming on the stove. Dorothy's voice came from behind Mary.

"Fortunately our ancestors built Holywell on higher ground. Come into the lounge, all of you. I'm expecting a call from the local police, probably those who came about Agnes. We're having a community meeting in thirty minutes. That means *everyone*." Dorothy addressed Mary. "Miss Wandwalker, bring the Minister, Dee and Irina's mother."

When Dorothy calls me Miss Wandwalker, I know it's serious, thought Mary.

Dorothy left. Janet harrumphed and went to wash her hands at the kitchen sink. Cherry switched off the gas, muttering about tea being late. John and Linda exchanged kisses on the cheek and rose. Their chairs made minimal scaping sounds despite the aged tile floor, Mary noted. She pondered her next move. Should she try Mr. Jeffreys again or prioritize hearing more bad news?

Mary told herself to be vigorous, decisive, full of initiative. Instead, she slumped into John's former seat facing the window. The kettle belching steam tempted her with tea. Looking around Mary saw Janet who leaned against the sink and watched her.

"Wandwalker, you think I brought trouble when I got Agnes here? The woman no one wanted?" Janet sounded antagonistic. She turned her back to Mary and stared out of the window.

Two young women in heavy coats and hoods ran across the lawn with cabbages and onions. The back door banged.

"Gels, leave the veg on the side, and get cleaned up for the meeting," ordered Janet without turning around.

"And stop spraying mud on my floor," snapped Cherry. "I want it spotless when I come back." She switched off the kettle and walked out.

The young women exchanged glances while pulling off boots, then escaped the kitchen. Mary found Janet glaring at her.

"Well, Wandwalker? Do you blame me for Caroline's trouble? With Agnes, I mean."

"Caroline *and* Sarah," retorted Mary. "Surely taking in Agnes was not your decision, not yours alone," said Mary, picking her words. "Don't you wit… er… therapists operate as a commune?"

Janet sniffed.

"I mean by consensus," said Mary quickly. "When did Agnes arrive, by the way?"

Janet took a step towards Mary at the kitchen table. Her eyes were bleak.

"Twenty days ago," she said. "I found Agnes rotting in a geriatric ward, sinking. With no hospice beds free in a fifty-mile radius, I made the others agree to take her in."

The older woman ran her fingers through her hair again. White strong roots, like her plants, thought Mary. Janet's vegetables are extensions of a fierce life. Even the young women she calls 'gels' can't kill her onions.

Janet pulled a handkerchief that had once been white from her dungarees pocket. She proceeded to rub first eyes, then cheeks, then made a sound like an explosion blowing her nose. After drying her hairy chin, she returned the handkerchief.

"Listen to me, Wandwalker. It was me who got Agnes. You, on the other hand, brought a sorcerer, his lover, her husband, and an enchanted girl. Not to mention my apprentice Caroline, and Anna, your Agency's very own loose cannon. What you gonna to do about that, eh?"

Without waiting for a reply Janet stomped out of the room.

Mary felt a headache coming on. Drat Janet. The woman had a point. Oh, hell. Her head spun. Too much at Holywell was obscure and smoky: *a dark wind*, darker even than the howling that continued outside.

Mary stared down at brown liquid in a forgotten tea cup. Something hovered at the edge of her understanding. Something she'd seen... or heard... or *smelt*. Yes, that was it, a smell in Agnes's room she had not expected, sweetish, oily. Of course it could have been concocted by Janet, realized Mary, disappointed. Yet... no, it couldn't be Janet's herbal medicines because she'd smelt it before, in Greenwich, hadn't she? Now, when? Or more properly, where? And in whose company?

A flicker at the corner of Mary's eye drew her attention to the window. Yes, unbelievably, flouting an injunction she'd heard from Dorothy to remain inside, there were the Holywell young women offering their bare heads to the rain. Where were the witches when they were needed? Oh, well, the internet said the next storm was an hour off.

Sarah could be seen waving her arms in vigorous debate with girls who clutched their thin shoulders or each other. Mary sighed and pulled out her phone. A text from Caroline confirmed that she had retreated back to bed while Anna searched for the best wifi hotspot.

The good thing is that I know where they are, Mary reflected. It is also a bad thing that I know where they are. Caroline only goes to bed when her depression is acute. Anna online means she's doing semi-legal and illegal stuff. And I can't stop her. On the other hand, Anna in the internet clouds meant she was not stalking Sarah, or sorcerer Dee, or Robbin' Robin. Be thankful for miniscule mercies, Mary told herself.

Shutting her eyes, she tried to identify that sweet oily smell before. *Ah, yes.* She snapped her fingers. It was in the Octagon Room at Greenwich Observatory. Irina and Billy Dee danced. The minister howled with rage while Helen Morgan looked smug. Robbin' Robin rushed out, didn't he? Could he have brushed by Mary? Or was the smell something to do with Helen Morgan, or Dee?

That peculiar oiliness could have come from Irina, Mary realized. Don't ballet dancers use all kinds of unguents on their feet? It's got to be a clue, she thought. At the very least it suggests someone from the Octagon Room paid a call on Agnes. I wonder if Caroline or Anna remember that smell from Greenwich?

Mary felt her energy surge. *I'm the organizer,* she thought. While I check on Holywell's visitors for Dorothy, I've got a thread to get started. Yet before she could make a move, she heard angry voices. Not the sounds and sweet airs of the island, she reflected, remembering *The Tempest.*

I'm afraid, she thought. Afraid that I, or we, can't solve the murder. Mary shut her eyes. She saw herself open the kitchen door to the garden, walk calmly around the house and wade across the fields. Oh, Mary, she thought. You won't run away, you can't.

*Get over yourself Wandwalker,* a voice jeered. Mr. Jeffreys never spoke to her in that tone.

"Feeling sorry for yourself, are you?" This voice was not inside her head.

Mary wanted to stick out her tongue. "Janet." Mary said. "You came back. Look at your girls in the rain. Tell them to get inside."

"No, they need the garden. Dorothy's overreacting to Taranis, our Celtic thunder god. Do you know why?"

"No," sighed Mary. "But you're going to tell me."

"Her sister died of a lightning strike while climbing a mountain in Wales."

Mary shut her eyes. "Horrible," she said. "Now go away."

"Won't." Janet's tone was brutal.

Mary sat up straight, searching for indignation. Janet took a seat opposite her.

"Wandwalker, who are you?"

Mary blew through her teeth. Then she sniffed. "I won't run away, Janet." Could this woman read her mind, punish her for what she *wanted,* not what she actually did? She met Janet's uncompromising expression. "What about you? Where would you rather be?"

"The farm, the farm where I grew up with sheep and my brother."

"What...?"

"He died when we were twelve. Don't tell me you remember that story, I know you don't."

"You don't like me, do you, Janet?"

The older woman banged her fist on the table. "I don't do like, or not like. People should be who they are and get on with it, not pussy foot around. So, get out of this kitchen. It's not yours anyway – and solve the murder."

Mary would give everything to shriek, *Why me?* at the woman with angry blue eyes. And, *Suppose I can't?*

"Doesn't matter how you feel," said Janet. "It's not about whether it's fair. You'll find the killer because you're the only one on Holywell island who can. Dorothy will worry about the gels and deal with the authorities, John and Linda are glued to the sorcerer, Naomi and Meredith are eavesdropping on the Minister and his ex, I'm to keep the gels busy cleaning and preparing vegetables, Cherry cooks. She'll take care of the kitchen and supplies like a wild beast guarding her young. And besides…" Janet took a breath. "Your Anna isn't going to stay in cyberspace for long. With Caroline suspected…"

"Yes, yes," said Mary crossly. "I have to… look after them. Watch Anna like a hawk. I always do. I *always* do."

"Enough!" shouted Janet. "Cut the self-pity, Wandwalker. If not, you'll end up in what was my bed in that locked ward at the John Whitcliffe. *I* don't care. I'm off to remind the gels about that damned meeting."

With that Janet grabbed a raincoat and made for the rainswept garden. There she could be seen chivying the 'gels' back to the house.

Unaccountably, Mary felt a lot better. After all, she'd solved some pretty impossible cases before.

# CHAPTER 10
# LIKE AN ISLAND

*Friday late afternoon.*

Mary could procrastinate no more. She slid into the Holywell lounge, where the press of people made the air stuffy. Yesterday the atmosphere had thickened over a wayward sorcerer and a missing teenager. Right now, with standing room only, Mary could barely breathe. Thin young women in jeans and brighter t-shirts than the witches huddled together. One was Sarah.

With an anguished glance at Mary, Sarah dodged behind another girl. When Sarah peered back, Mary managed a nod and a wave. That appeared to reassure Sarah. She looked around. Not seeing Caroline, she gave Mary a pained shrug.

Later, Mary promised herself, later I'll grill Sarah about implicating Caroline in Agnes's murder. Meanwhile they had the storms and what the authorities planned for them. Mary sidled over to the mainly middle-aged therapist-witches. She did not recognize the youngest one, who was rubbing her neck.

"You're looking at our new witch, Meredith Kelley," whispered the woman with a silver plait down her back. Naomi, the witch who runs, remembered Mary.

"We're all envious of those strawberry blonde curls," continued Naomi. "Meredith's great with hair, her mother had her own salon."

"Meredith's a hairdresser?" queried Mary. The tiered curls of the sharp eyed woman in her thirties were not to her own taste. "I thought…"

"No, a nurse, by training," replied Naomi. "Her mother's a hair stylist. Taught her to do her own. When she worked in a care home, Meredith used to do the hair of ladies. She trimmed Linda's bangs last week. See, she got rid of my split ends."

Naomi pulled her long braid from her back, and waved it in Mary's face.

"Um, well," said Mary.

"Meredith promised to show Dorothy how to keep her own hair tidier but there's been no time. Of course we don't tend to mention hair a lot because of John." Naomi indicated the tall bald woman talking earnestly to dainty Chinese Linda. The couple, Mary recalled again, and John was trans, or was it nonbinary?

"John, er…" she prompted.

"Hair never grew back after chemo eight years ago," said Naomi.

"Oh," said Mary, at a loss. Naomi seemed to be expecting more, so she returned to the subject of the new witch. "With those skills Meredith must be popular with your young women."

"Perhaps," said Naomi, looking doubtful. "They are super sensitive about being touched, you know. Although one of the gels wants Meredith to do her a feather cut. So she can fly away from danger, she says."

"Of course, of course," said Mary, feeling foolish. She patted her own grey bob. It would look ridiculous, she thought, if it were as neglected as Dorothy's.

All the therapist-witches wore robes, apart from Meredith, who was dressed in what Mary recognized as a nurse's overalls. Mary's nose prickled with spicy fumes: incense. Stifling a sneeze, Mary guessed that the incense lingered from some ritual for Agnes.

Waiting infects us with anxiety, Mary thought. Even the minister and Helen Morgan sat in silence on the sofa. Were those battling exes holding hands? Mary strained to see around young women who kept muttering at each other's phones.

Ah, Morgan just pulled away. The ex-wife stared at her hand as if annoyed by it. With a jolt, Mary remembered Billy Dee. Where was the sorcerer?

Mary shuffled around the easy chairs until… there was Billy Dee upright and alone on the opposite sofa. Despite the crush, no one joined him. He held an old book open. Yet he also darted expressions of contempt at Robbin' Robin. In turn, the minister glared back in what looked like a frozen rage.

Before Mary could edge closer to Dee's book, a nudge directed her to the central coffee table where, instead of refreshments, there was a squat black tripod with speakers. It coughed and crackled. People moved aside to accord the device its sacred power. Morgan and Robbin' Robin leaned forward. When the phone's crackle became a cough, Dorothy spoke.

"All right everyone. For those who have just arrived, the police sent instructions. Holywell is now an island. Literally. We're cut off by water on all sides. The good news is that the flood won't get into the house. Probably."

The witches shifted as a group. A flash followed by a roar rattled the French windows. A couple of the young women squeaked.

"No need to be frightened," said John, whose deep voice had jumped an octave higher, thought Mary.

Dorothy nodded curtly. "Yes, Janet believes our boundary wall should protect the garden. That means we can harvest our vegetables. Other supplies could be… more difficult."

"Is that the bad news?" came from a small voice Mary could not identify.

"No," said Dorothy. She was grim. "Now the hurricane has become a series of storms, and they expect a lot of electricity discharge. Lightning will be a danger to life *inside* as well as outside." She paused.

"Wait a minute," said Mary. "Inside Holywell you mean? Don't you have a lightning conductor on the roof?"

"It fell off," said Naomi, simply.

"It burned out last month, *then* fell off," said Dorothy. "A replacement's due next week. Only now it's delayed because we are deemed low priority."

Robbin' Robin leapt to his feet. "Low priority? Don't they know I'm here?"

Dorothy ignored him. Helen Morgan pulled him down. "Let her finish."

Dorothy swallowed. "People can be struck by lightning indoors if near pipes or on the phone. On the bright side, they predict three, four days of storms, then the flooding will subside. We're stuck here for a short period, that's all."

Mary could see the skepticism building on the faces in the room. So could Dorothy.

"We're not alone," she insisted with a touch of desperation. "The authorities will use drones to send food and medicine. We'll get through this."

"Taranis strikes from the sky. His energies fertilize and destroy." It was Naomi, hook-nosed and stern. "The Celtic storm god," she added, looking at Mary.

The tension in the room relaxed minutely. Dorothy stepped through frightened folk – witches, clients, politicians, an ex-wife, and Mary Wandwalker. Mary could see the speakerphone. Dorothy took up position next to it. She reiterated, "we'll get through this, all of us, *together.*"

At her words, Robbin' Robin and Morgan adopted identical sour expressions. Young women in sweatshirts blocked Mary's view of Billy Dee. By the time Mary glimpsed the sofa he'd vanished. Only the impression of his back remained on the cushion. No one appeared interested in taking his place.

The speakerphone hissed and muttered again. The oracle prepares to speak, Mary thought idly. Then suddenly the words were loud and clear.

*... winds of 80 even 90 miles per hour. We'll send drones in the gaps between storms. Do not leave shelter when lightning is forecast. Even indoors, beware of possible fires if lightning hits the roof.*

Mary recognized the voice as that of the Detective Inspector. What was his name again?

"Is that Detective, er... Inspector Singh? Are you coordinating from Oxford?" Mary said.

She heard a sigh. "We're operating from the John Whitcliffe Hospital for now. Our chief priority is getting essential medicines to the public. Holywell is sending a list."

A woman's voice interrupted. "You can't keep us here. My husband's the new minister for Northern Ireland."

Husband? Mary raised her eyebrows. Helen Morgan scowled. A tapping came from the speaker phone, then a cough.

"Ah yes, instructions coming in. Bad luck, minister. There's a new Covid variant in Northern Ireland. Even if we had good weather and a helicopter, which we don't, Mr. Robin Prince is to remain where he is."

"But I...I..." Robbin' Robin spluttered.

Helen Morgan punched his shoulder. "I told you."

Mary sensed frustration from the squat device.

"The minister isn't vaccinated for Covid?"

Gazes in the Holywell lounge centered on scarlet faced Robbin' Robin. He resembled a balloon about to burst.

"We get him for *longer?*" exclaimed Sarah.

Mary now remembered. The wretched man had aped the ghastly American President by mocking vaccines. He'd stood up in Parliament to insist on his God-given right to refuse. *I won't have my arm pricked*, he'd said. The leftwing press had another use for the word 'prick.'

"Can't keep me here," Robbin' Robin muttered. "I've a mind to try the limo."

"Inspector Singh, what about the investigation into the death here at Holywell?" said Mary, trying to keep her voice steady.

"On hold," came a brusque voice no one recognized.

"You mean Agnes?" said several of the young women as one. Others began sniffing. The therapists looked at each other and then at Dorothy.

"We did a purification ritual." The high voice came from Linda. "We were in Agnes's room for an hour. It was to banish the evil of her death. Was she murdered, Detective Singh?"

There came another crackle and hiss. "Yes, we can confirm that Agnes, surname unknown, was unlawfully killed. Cause of death is carbon monoxide poisoning. I saw for myself that the old gas fire had been tampered with. The victim..."

The voice returned louder. "Did you say you went *inside* the sickroom? I thought we sealed the crime scene. How many of you?"

"Those who loved her." The shout came from Janet. Mary saw Caroline thread through to take Janet's arm. Anna scowled from the doorway. Good, they needed to hear the news.

"Seven," came Dorothy's firm tones. "Myself, Janet, the herbalist, Cherry, the cook, John and Linda, Naomi, who works with manuscripts, and young nurse Meredith, our new initiate."

"I removed the crime scene tape," said John. "It wasn't what Agnes needed."

From the speaker phone came a fierce whispers. Finally Mary caught the words "crime scene contaminated" followed by "emergency priorities." A new sharp voice radiated.

"We'll be in touch if the phones keep going. Oxford Central over and out."

The dial tone sounded until Dorothy leaned over and switched off the device.

"Wait," she called to stall the movement to the door. "New rule: no one leaves the house. These storms wing across the Atlantic at incredible speeds." She swallowed. "As Naomi said, storm god Taranis is about to deal a number of blows. He makes fire and death from the air." She looked about at the blanched faces. Her tone relaxed.

"Look, we believe," Dorothy darted a stern look at Mary and ignored pouting Robbin' Robin, "*we* believe that covens from all over England drained energy from the hurricane, so it became this sequence of storms." Dorothy slowed for emphasis. "These. Are. Survivable. We have rubber boots or rubber soled shoes for everyone. They will protect us in the event of a lightning strike on the house."

A chorus of groans erupted from Holywell's young women. Robbin' Robin and Helen Morgan appeared stunned.

"Whatever. I'll be going outside to tend to my herbs," said uncompromising Janet. Dorothy licked her lips.

"And getting me vegetables, I hope." The voice came from Cherry the cook. Dorothy hesitated before giving a tiny nod. So much for everyone indoors, thought Mary, noting dark patches under Dorothy's eyes.

Anxiety is an angry spirit, Mary had heard Caroline say. There's truth in it, she decided, looking around at various faces.

"You're all insane. I'm getting out of here." Robbin' Robin's loud voice shocked everyone. Those who glimpsed his sweaty face shrank back as he blundered from the room.

Mary sighed and prepared to go after him.

"Ignore him, Miss Wandwalker. Robbin' Robin's not going anywhere."

The tone was bitter. It cut the room in two. Mary could now see Helen Morgan, very white, and with her expensive suit stained with black coffee. Mary knew it to be coffee because of the comforting odor it emitted. Irina's mother continued sipping from a cracked mug. Too late in the day for Mary to drink coffee. She envied Morgan.

"How do you know Robbin' Robin's coming back?" asked Mary, genuinely curious.

Putting the mug down, Morgan felt in both pockets. She took out a set of car keys and rattled them. "I made Billy give me the limo keys. Robbin' Robin won't escape on foot. He's forgotten how to walk except between chauffeured cars."

"Plus, I assume the police won't let anyone try the fields," said Mary slowly and loudly. She met Dorothy's understanding glance that flicked towards mutinous stares from the young women. So, they had been thinking about it. I don't blame them, thought Mary. I could do with a long hike myself.

"No one's making a run for it. We'd have to come after you. Put more lives at stake."

That was Janet. The room quieted. Mary could hear her heart beating.

"We know what we have to do," announced Dorothy. The other witches nodded at her.

"Protection is everything. So follow me for the rubber boots. John, get that box from the attic with extra waterproofs. Miss Wandwalker can see to our guests."

Mary blinked. Holywell had changed in less than a day. Who knew when, or even if, they would be rescued?

\*\*\*\*\*

During the hour before dinner Mary Wandwalker knocked on the door of Dorothy's office.

"Go away," yelled various female voices.

But Mary was on a mission. She went in.

"Ah," she said to the figure in rubber gear sitting in Dorothy's chair. "That hat covers half your face. I see what the gels mean."

"Gels?" said Naomi from Dorothy's left. From the knees down she wore black rubber. Jeans and a green fisherman's jersey completed the look. An assortment of rubberized hats covered the desk. Enough for everyone? wondered Mary.

Janet stood on Dorothy's right. She'd made no attempt with the boots or hat.

"Yes, I said gels," Mary responded. "Janet calls them that and – God knows why – they like it. But that's not why I'm here. They have two requests. First lose the weird hats and big coats. Not for you, not for them. At most, they'll do rubber soled shoes."

"You see," said Naomi, turning to the hat that must have Dorothy under it.

Janet folded her arms. She pierced Mary with her frown. "Go on, Wandwalker."

"They're scared." Mary had searched for something eloquent about balancing risks. It came down to this, she realized. "The gels are *really* scared. Whoever killed Agnes must be at Holywell. No one's leaving because of the storms and floods. They want you to look like human beings. 'Be cool,' they said."

Was that steam rising from under Dorothy's brim?

"Stop fussing about rubber," said Mary hastily. She winced. That could be misunderstood. "And there's something else..."

The rubber-clad figure banged fists on the desk. When Dorothy's voice came it was hoarse. "We've got to protect them..."

"The gels want to be able to go outside. Use the garden, walk under the trees." Mary rushed her words, seeing Dorothy shake her head. "Not in the thunder and lightning, of course, but in between storms. They can't bear being shut in. They seem really upset about it. And I agree with them." She paused.

Dorothy pushed the hat to the back of her head, She turned her reddened eyes to Mary.

"We have to protect them," she whispered.

"No, Dorothy, we've got to keep them *safe*," Janet broke in. "The garden is their refuge. And mine." She glared at Dorothy.

Naomi licked her lips. "Dorothy, dear, think of the gels' trauma, the effects of being trafficked, locked in tiny rooms, and how the garden calms them. They came here to find sanctuary. Murder and being confined by storms are *psychological* attacks on them."

"That's more or less what they are saying," said Mary. "Do the rubber feet thing indoors if you must. But let them outside when the lightning stops." She waited. "Be normal. Or try to be," she added under her breath.

Janet's glare relaxed, yet her tone bit. "You're dressed to enter hell, Dorothy. Don't do this to the gels."

A pause. Finally, painfully, Dorothy raised gloved hands. Then she pointed to her neck. "You win. Help me untie this bloody hat."

Naomi visibly relaxed. "The gels win. I like that name too." She leaned over Dorothy to untie the knot. "Thank goddess. Not greeting our trees each day would give me claustrophobia."

Dorothy emerged frowning. "Tell the 'gels' we'll try it their way, Miss Wandwalker. As long as they stay indoors when thunder is close."

"They're waiting to hear," said Mary, getting up.

Mary slipped into the lounge and found it deserted. Ah, defiance, the gels are back outside, she guessed. She opened and stepped out of the French windows. Although the sky was relatively quiet, it looked like rain. Night would not descend for a couple of hours.

She inhaled the scent of soaked grass before she caught the reek of tobacco. For a few seconds she longed for a cigarette. Oh for that kick to the brain she'd had in her thirties. Oh well, she reflected, a crisis is no time to revive the hacking cough that had caused her to give up smoking in the first place.

Mary only saw one of the gels. Mary gave her the message from Dorothy. She expected her to run off to the others, but no, this was the twenty-first century. The gel took out her phone and drifted away.

Time to focus, Mary thought. Agnes was murdered by carbon monoxide, a poisonous, invisible, odorless gas. Someone opened the sealed vent on the old heater. No one departed from Holywell after she died. Now no one could. Two life threatening situations, Mary thought, her mouth grim. We're stuck on an island with floods, storms, *and* a murderer. Everyone's wondering, *Who*? She was so preoccupied with her ruminations that Mary didn't hear the approach.

"We can go out. Such a relief. Thank you, Miss Wandwalker."

Mary jumped round. Sarah looked nervous. She had crept up behind Mary.

"Don't *do* that, Sarah. We're all on edge. Although you're allowed out, Dorothy expects you to watch the skies. Above all, stay in the house when a storm is close."

"Otherwise she'll chain us to our beds and stuff us into rubber suits?" Sarah giggled, then glanced at Mary's fitted jacket. Mary would never admit it, but she'd felt self-conscious about her vintage style ever since meeting Anna, whose designer apparel came from dubious websites. Now Mary glanced down at her lined skirt and back to Sarah's comfortable jeans.

"No suits for us gels." Sarah risked a small grin. "But yours is okay." She hopped from foot to foot.

Was now a good time to interrogate Caroline's accuser? Sarah evidently wanted to tell her something.

"Come and sit a moment. The bench under the tree is not too wet."

Sarah ducked her head, then joined Mary who lowered herself gingerly onto the damp wood. She felt Sarah put a shy hand on her arm.

It's a connection, Mary realized. I can ask her about Caroline.

Sarah moved her hand down Mary's arm to her hand. Instinctively Mary pulled away. To her horror, Mary observed tears in Sarah's beautiful eyes.

"I'm so sorry, Sarah. I don't know what came over me."

Sarah sniffed. She drew her sleeve across her nose. Mary winced then hid it quickly. This was not how she planned to begin. "I guess, I'm still a bit shocked by... by the death, and now the weather crisis," she said, making herself pat Sarah's shoulder. The girl accepted it.

"You want to know about Caroline and Agnes. I get it," said Sarah. She turned to look straight at Mary.

She's suffering from the death of Agnes, Mary thought, recognizing the strain around Sarah's mouth and eyes.

Sarah chose her next words with obvious care. "Look Miss Wandwalker, I totally, definitely did see Caroline at midnight. She told me to go to bed. Said she'd watch Agnes until morning. Agnes was breathing fine when I left."

"The gas heater…?" began Mary.

"Sealed, closed, never used," confirmed Sarah. "Electric storage heaters on timers kept the Infirmary toasty for Agnes. Safe as houses, Janet said."

"Why on earth didn't the witches get the gas heaters removed?"

"Dunno. Oh, that's right. They're coming to dismantle them next month. Couldn't get the work done earlier due to Brexit skill shortages. Something like that."

"So someone let out carbon monoxide…" Mary began.

"And disabled the alarm," said Sarah. "That's new. I remember John installing it."

The troubled young woman sniffed. "You gotta believe me. I love Caroline. She's been a great friend to me, to all of us. I'd never make up a bad story about her." Sarah looked down at her jiggling feet.

A wrench tightened inside Mary, tightened until breaking point. "I believe you," she croaked to Sarah. And she did.

Mary also believed that Caroline had uttered the truth when she denied being in Agnes's room. Both women could not be right. Mary's reasonable world shivered and threatened to crack open.

Lost for words, Mary looked around. Naomi in boots and a blue robe trotted toward them, her plait bouncing behind. Naomi's in a rush, Mary thought. She should be careful about slipping in this mud. I should ask for news of Irina. Did she have her family reunion with Robbin' Robin and Helen Morgan? Poor girl. With those two as parents it's hard to blame her for running away.

Naomi slid to a stop.

"Damn, water in my boots. Sarah, glad I've caught you. Dorothy insists all you gels get indoors. Look, it's beginning to rain. The next storm's coming."

"Sure thing, Naomi." Sarah stood up and stretched.

"And Sarah, help me out. Locate the others."

Sarah nodded. "No fuss, everyone's inside except two gels. I'll take a look for them."

With what looked like a skip, Sarah made off towards the track out of Holywell. Rain did not appear to bother her, but Mary did not want *her* suit to get soaked. She rose.

Naomi put out a hand. "Wait a moment. I'm glad you and Sarah are friends," she said.

"Indeed," Mary replied. Then to the unspoken question, "Yes, we talked. I believe Sarah's account of the night of Agnes's death." She paused. "*And* I'm sure Caroline's innocent."

"Truly sure, Miss Wandwalker?"

Mary was about to snap back when she stopped. Was she really sure? Rain began to drip down her nose. Had Caroline told the truth about not going to Agnes's room? Yes, she had. That Mary felt in her bones. Yet decades of psychoactive drugs had been fed to Caroline due to her chronic clinical depression. She also took herbs prescribed by Janet, against Mary's advice. Returning from Holywell, she'd recount dreams of sailing ships, strange, sunburned lands, of crossing deserts for rare plants, of being a village healer in medieval times. That Caroline, who was she?

"Yes," Mary croaked to Naomi's scrutiny. "I trust Caroline."

Naomi blinked. She did not look surprised. "Two incompatible stories. The ways of the goddess are mysterious. We witches have faith in your sleuthing, Miss Wandwalker."

"Sure thing," muttered Mary under her breath. To herself she said, I hope their goddess is on our side.

# CHAPTER 11
# A SWAN WHO CANNOT FLY

*Friday early evening.*

Mary was about to retreat to the house when a scream erupted. Human, yet not human, thought Mary. It turned into a rain-shattering howl from the tiny patch of forest within Holywell's boundary. Mary and Naomi mirrored shock as a girl rushed from beneath the trees, breathless and soaked. Mary tentatively identified her as a gel, who, she remembered, was mute from her life prior to Holywell. This gel was mute no longer.

"Irina," she gasped, clutching Naomi at the waist "Irina, the new girl. Says she's going to fly. She's up that big elm, the one that split in the spring. Olga's trying to talk her down."

"Oh, goddess," said Naomi, clapping hands to her head. "With rain like this, lightning could strike any moment."

"Flying from a tree? Irina? I thought she was in her room." Mary could hear herself speak slowly. That the screaming had stopped, she realized, might not be a good sign. Naomi took charge of the shivering girl.

"Take a deep breath my dear. Good, now another. Now go get the others. Witches, not you gels," Naomi added. "Thunder's close. I smell it."

Without waiting, Naomi pulled up her long robe to reveal hairy legs that ran towards the trees. Drops of water bounced off her, and her plait swung like a pendulum. Another scream brought Mary into the present. Irina, *ridiculous child*, in peril of her life. An already blasted tree would be a prime target for lightning.

"Fetch Irina's parents," Mary shouted after the disappearing girl. Tell them not to be useless, she wanted to add.

She followed Naomi across the pools of water that were once a lawn. Beneath the trees the rain drummed on overhead leaves. Mary increased her speed despite stumbling in the dimness. She lunged between sodden trunks, bony saplings, and brambles that sprayed rain upwards and tore her tights.

The copse of beech and oak brought the wilderness within Holywell's boundaries. No wonder the gels valued it with their strict regime of therapy and regular meals. It occurred to Mary that the trees interlaced their branches like the gels' locking arms when frightened.

She came to a tiny clearing where she found the gel, shaking water from a long raincoat, big eyes scanning for help. Her expression suggested that Mary was not it. No Naomi, so she must have gone for reinforcements. The gel scowled. She pushed dripping hair from her face. Mary crept forward, fearful of startling the human bird somewhere above them. The gel made a quick hand signal towards the biggest tree. Irina had to be in it. Mary stepped closer.

The huge elm had suffered from more than one storm. Lightning had severed the gnarled trunk almost to the roots. One side had been burned black, while the other sprouted new leafy branches. Following the gel's horrified gestures, Mary spotted a ballet shoe. Then a black clad arm poked from between the leaves, and withdrew. Irina was way too high. A fall from those branches would be fatal.

To Mary's horror Irina shifted further along the branch. Now she saw Irina's whole body. The girl had a clear position from which to jump. Mary gulped. Those muddy ballet shoes could slip at any moment. Even worse, Irina wore her black swan costume. Ah, she's forced one foot in the cleft between two branches. No, don't swing the other leg.

Mary shut her eyes instinctively, then forced them open again. Irina had both hands above her head. They gripped a thin branch parallel to the one she balanced on. Mary liked neither the diameter of that branch nor that someone, presumably Irina, had added more black feathers since Greenwich. Attached to each arm, as well as the skirt, they looked like an attempt to grow wings. She resembled a baby crow, and her ruby-red hair formed a crown.

"Wait, Irina. Please don't move," called the gel nervously. She sounded hoarse. Must have been shouting at Irina for some minutes.

Irina ignored the gel. Mary saw her gaze above Holywell, seeking a distant horizon. The fading daylight wobbled. No, Mary realized. That flash was lightning above the hills that circled the valley. Did redheaded Irina long for the firebolt of the storm god? The one the witches call Taranis?

Mary swallowed hard. She reached out to the gel, who clutched her arm, eyes wild.

"Irina wants to fly into the storm," the gel hissed. "Told us she would. I sent for help. She made a weird sort of scream. Like an animal or a great bird."

"Irina made that unearthly noise? Where's Naomi?"

"G…gone for the parents."

Good idea for Naomi to get the parents, thought Mary. I don't see that other gel being able to talk to them, even if she has found her voice. Mary tried to pry the gel's clutch from her linen sleeves. Her cold fingers ground the wet into her skin.

Mary spotted movement out of the corner of her eye. Anna wafted around the edge of the clearing. She did that thing where she moved without sound, nor appeared to touch the earth. Anna froze, then signaled to Mary not to reveal her presence.

Mary turned back to the gel. "Has Irina said anything in the last few minutes?"

"Not words. Not after that terrible scream."

I've not heard words from Irina, either, thought Mary. She looked up to see the minister's daughter shuffle further along the branch.

"Irina, come down," ordered Mary. "The storm's coming. It's too dangerous." Her jaw ached. Yelling at a teenager could be a bad move, she realized.

Irina stuck her chin out to a second flash in the sky. Her red hair seemed to blaze.

"Get down here, Irina," said a voice behind Mary. "Now, at once." The voice cracked, became a screech. "*Now.*" It was Helen Morgan. Irina's mother was ghost white. She's terrified, thought Mary. Caroline held her arm, protectively.

"Darling," puffed Robbin' Robin as he lumbered to his ex-wife. He gazed blankly at the blasted elm, then gasped. "Darling Irina, please," he beseeched.

Irina moved even further out on the tree's limb. To Mary's horror, she had found a space to wave those feathered arms. She was ready to fly.

"*Enough.*"

Irina froze. The command came from the darkness between the trees, an unseen man. Billy Dee, it had to be, Mary thought. Irina wobbled. Helen Morgan gave a strangled squeak. Mary saw Robbin' Robin put his hand on her mouth. The growing audience held its breath. After what felt like an eternity, Irina regained her balance. She turned around, then banged her head.

Something red fell off. This time Caroline screamed. Mary felt faint. The red thing plopped into the mud. It was a red wig. Mary held Caroline until they could both breathe again. Helen Morgan rushed over and fell on her knees to grab the wig. Curious, thought Mary, she's holds it like it's Irina herself.

Finally the black swan herself, now in short black hair, clambered down the trunk of the old elm, causing tense jaws and strangled exclamations. Jumping the last couple of feet, Irina swung round to reveal a total lack of expression. Both parents tried to embrace her at once.

With a moan, Irina pushed them away and ran towards the house. Sighing, Helen Morgan followed. Her heels dug into the soft ground making her stumble. A thoughtful ex-husband would give her his arm. Not Robin Prince. Mary saw him pause for a few seconds, then pull out his phone. Holding it to light the darkening air, the Minister let it guide him to the promised land of unlimited connectivity.

Mary drew a breath to shout a warning when there came a roar directly overhead. Everyone, including Robbin' Robin, dashed for the house as rain hammered down on them, Mary slammed the back door shut just as the sky split open. Lightning plunged into the Holywell trees, near to the site of Irina's adventure.

"She could have been killed," breathed Robbin' Robin. He grabbed the nearest dishcloth, trying to dry his phone. Ignoring Mary and Caroline, he seized a pile of dry cloths and departed the kitchen.

"We all could have been killed," said Mary to his departing back. Slipping out of her sodden suit jacket, she squeezed its considerable water into the sink. Her damp blouse she decided to leave on. Holywell must have dry clothes in an attic. Already the witches had found nightwear for their marooned guests who'd arrived without luggage. About to remark on this to Caroline, Mary stopped at the younger woman's set face. She touched Caroline's cold arm.

"Ah, you saw it too. I plan to talk to Anna."

Minutes previously, as Irina had passed her audience, Mary's jaw had dropped. On instinct, her body had swung to Anna. For a few seconds in the pouring rain Anna had looked haunted and afraid. Mary's throat had caught. She had never seen that look. Before the thunder propelled Mary, Caroline, and Robbin' Robin toward the house, Anna had disappeared. Now in the kitchen with Caroline, Mary saw Caroline's green eyes were wild.

"Anna?" said Caroline. She sounded lost. "Anna? Irina?" Outside the wind moaned. The rain beat on the windows as if trying to get in. Mary sensed the trees huddled in the dusk, their presences feeling almost human.

"Yes," said Mary. "We must acknowledge what we saw. As soon as that wig came off, it became obvious. Anna resembles Irina, or rather the other way around, since Irina's ten years younger. Could they be related?"

# CHAPTER 12
# LOST CHILDREN ARE MY SPECIALITY

*Friday evening.*

That night the ordered life of Holywell fractured. While lightning bowled around the valley, and thunder raged, no one pretended normality living in a house with a murderer. Tonight no witches gathered with gels, and no visitors sat at the long dining table. Instead, Cherry prepared a vat of soup and sat it on the kitchen stove. Herby aromas saturated the entire first floor. Perhaps all we have left is that comforting smell, thought Mary Wandwalker.

Everyone would serve themselves. Earlier Cherry had sliced cheese and left a basket of baked rolls on the kitchen table. They would share the last of the stored apples for dessert.

"Eat wherever you are comfortable and keep those rubber soled boots on," ordered Dorothy on the Holywell WhatsApp, forwarded to Mary, Caroline, Anna, Robbin' Robin, Irina, and for all she knew, Mary reflected, sorcerer Billy Dee. No one had the heart to tell Dorothy what Mary had observed – after the debacle with Irina, few bothered with rubber boots.

More importantly, Mary thought, we should investigate Dee's role in Irina's attempt at flight. So far he'd not denied that he'd brought the girl down. So while most of the household ate and grumbled in their rooms, Mary tracked Billy Dee to the kitchen. He was late, like Mary, to get food. The other person present was Cherry.

"Have you eaten?" inquired Mary innocently of the woman with flour on her arms and yellow stains on her apron.

Sweat darkened Cherry's curls. "Later," she grunted. "Got to get bread rising for breakfast. After you've got your soup, please take that man away."

With Dee poking objects in the soup with a fork, the cook thumped sticky dough like a madwoman, eyes and mouth tight. Dee shrugged when Mary beckoned him to follow her. She pushed the lounge door open with one hand, soup bowl in the other. With only a lamp on the coffee table, the room had a deserted air. Mary frowned at Dee's hesitation.

He sighed, set his soup on the table, then shook his head at her gesture to sit. Closed curtains subdued the storm noises, as if the cloth and glass really were a protective shell for Holywell. Yet Mary knew safety to be an illusion with a killer, and Billy Dee, in the house. The man started to eat his soup standing up. He grimaced after the first taste.

"Not enough salt." Without looking at Mary, he continued to eat.

Dee knows I'm going to ask him why Irina went up the tree in the first place, thought Mary. How can I get him off guard? She spotted a twitch on his pale temple, and then something odd about his face. Gone was the white makeup. She decided on a subtler approach.

"Are you quite well, Mr. Dee? Your skin looks blotchy, a bit green."

He set down his soup and touched his bony nose. Streaks of pale green covered raw skin on his cheeks.

"Herbs," he said shortly. "They'll send my prescription cream in the morning. In the meantime I got help from that short witch with white roots." He flicked a glance at Mary. "An allergy to sunlight."

"Vampire." The voice shot from the shadows behind Mary. She flinched, knocking the table where her bowl wobbled.

"Don't *do* that, Anna. No, leave your soup, Mr. Dee. What about Irina? She could have died today."

Dee cocked his head to the window where, for a second, light shone above the curtain rail.

Ignoring Anna, Mary continued. "Irina flying, Mr. Dee, takes us to meeting you over *Swan Lake* at Greenwich. You were to *act* the sorcerer, the man magicking girls into swans. You *are* a sorcerer, you say. Did you turn Irina Prince into a swan? Did you make her believe she could fly?"

"The children of Lir are turned into swans." Anna again.

Mary jumped as thunder broke the sky outside. She clapped her hand to her forehead. "Not *again* Anna. Don't become the wife of Lir again. You can't hide like that." Then back to the sorcerer. "Mr. Dee, I've not finished."

"Darling, Anna." Caroline came in. "It's too dark. Put the big light on. The storm's right overhead. Did you say Lir?" Caroline dropped her voice, but not her high color. "Sorry Mary, I didn't mean to interrupt you and Mr. Dee?" She reached for the light switch.

The sudden brightness made Mary shut her eyes. Anna hissed, so Caroline flipped the switch again. The room returned to shadows from the table lamp. Gels, witches, even the Prince family must be hiding upstairs, Mary thought. She could feel Anna glaring. Was her ire directed at Dee? Or was it for me?

"Do continue, Ladies," said Dee. He took a step towards Anna, then sprang back into the shadows. Mary was reminded of an animal caught in a car's headlights. But this animal sneered. "How did you conjure the spirit of old King Lear, Miss Vronsky?"

"*Wife* of Lir," shouted Mary and Caroline together. Caroline felt her way to Anna.

"Ow, Anna don't."

Anna must be in a rage to push Caroline away, thought Mary.

"I am not she," said Anna, out of the dark. "Not wife of Lir. Not yet. But her children have been turned into swans. They are enchanted, lost to the human world."

With a swiftness that startled everyone, Anna flew from the dark corner and out the door.

"Sounds like the story of *Swan Lake,* " said Caroline sadly, before following Anna from the room.

Enough of playing his games, Mary decided. Ignoring Billy Dee and the cooling bowls of soup, she went to the tall bookcase, frowned, then pulled out a volume. She took it to the sofa next to the lamp, then ran a finger down its index. Outside the rain pelted and the thunder continued sounded like rocks in the sky. Dee continued to stand silently while Mary read.

"No one knows where the plot of *Swan Lake* comes from," Billy Dee said.

Mary looked up, then went back to reading. The pages gleamed. Mary needed her glasses. She would not tell Dee that.

"Well," he said, stamping his foot. "Are you going to tell me about the wife of Lir and this swan story?"

Mary pored over the book and turned a page. Billy Dee took a step towards the door, then glared at Mary.

"Nothing to tell," she said at last. "Anna became the wife of Lir when she, we, infiltrated a group calling themselves the Reborn Celts. *They* made a big mistake about Celtic religion. Another mistake was to give Anna a lot of drugs. She took on the spirit of an ancient Celt, or so Caroline says." Mary gave Dee a stony look. "She became the woman everyone overlooks. For example. Shakespeare's King Lear must have had a wife to produce those daughters."

Mary paused. "I guess the wife of Lir was like Agnes, the forgotten woman with no name." Aware of Dee about to move, she narrowed her eyes at his bleak expression. "It says here that a couple of millennia ago Lir could have been a chieftain or a god. His children did get turned into swans."

"The story never ends there," Dee said.

Mary waited.

"Folktales all over the world have transgressing lovers or girls turned into swans. There's always more to it." He preened. "Like me."

"The evil sorcerer," said Mary, coolly. "Most productions of *Swan Lake* end tragically, with the death of the prince and the white swan. Today Irina up a tree risked being struck by lightning. Are you the author of that tragedy, Mr. Dee?"

Dee stepped closer to Mary, until he loomed over her. His eyes glittered. "Don't talk to me about tragedy," he hissed. "I was a lost child, abandoned, abused."

Mary's mouth fell open. She had to force herself not to lean back. When he spoke again he had an accent she could not place. Not quite Russian; it was his Romanian origins.

"Tragedy? I *saved* England from tragedy, Miss Wandwalker. Let me tell you about my séances in Parliament. The spirits insisted that England in a time of plagues and Brexit could not afford Robbin' Robin as prime minster. Imagine Covid with him in charge? His lies, corruption, and more lies."

Mary imagined. Dee had a point. Robbin' Robin managing a pandemic would be a disaster.

"That man disgusts me. He is no father to Irina."

Fifteen-year-old Irina? Yes, Mary wanted to hear Dee talk about her.

"Robbin' Robin can't even protect his family," she said out loud. "I suppose that's what you made your spirits say."

Billy Dee laughed. "The dead hastened down the centuries to speak through me, Miss Wandwalker. I am their medium, their mouthpiece. They clamored to testify. I had no need to ventriloquize."

He paused then his voice changed, became higher, older, from a long way off. "*She does not believe in us, Billy Dee. We who have crawled from the plague pits of London to stop Robbin' Robin. He is empty air. He must not gain the throne.*"

"Stop it," yelled Mary, furious. "Stop right now."

Dee put his arms towards Mary. She edged to the other end of the sofa. He gave a tiny jerk then put his hands by his sides. Mary suppressed a shudder.

"You see, Miss Wandwalker, the spirits are always with us."

Aghast to hear her voice shake, Mary said, "Is that how you bewitched Irina? Told her you could channel ancestors? Gave her alternatives to her parents?"

Dee paused. "*Parents*," he spat. He glared at Mary. "Lost children are my specialty, Miss Wandwalker. I could be the savior of the children of Lir."

"Is that why you took Irina from Greenwich, to rescue her from being a swan? Or did you try to turn her into one?"

Dee tightened his lips. Mary decided to leave the Celtic Lir until she had a chance to talk to Anna. The back of her neck hurt from peering up at Dee.

"Move away, Mr. Dee," she snapped.

He moved a few paces. "Rescue Irina?" he repeated as if it was his idea.

Mary answered her own question. "No, *you* turn young girls into swans, don't you? You're the bad magic that the witches here at Holywell try to undo. Irina nearly died from your sorcery. Either the storm would have blasted her, or she'd have jumped to her death."

Mary's breath came fast. What had she said? Did she believe Dee did dark magic, or was she talking about perverted psychology? Mary felt confused. She did not like it.

Dee was not done. "I love Irina. Her soul belongs to the storm. With me." Dee swung around to gesture wildly to the window. Beyond the glass was only the darkest of nights.

Mary's hands curled into fists. "She's *fifteen*," she shouted. "Underage, and if she wasn't, there's what… thirty years between you?"

He turned away.

"What about you and her mother, Helen Morgan?"

Dee snapped his fingers. The sound hurt, a needle in the stomach. It took a few seconds for Mary to realize the anguish did not belong to her. Rather her body resonated with the woman he had so casually dismissed, Irina's mother.

Mary swallowed. Yes, she would say it. Didn't she pride herself on speaking the truth?

"Either you deliberately fake sorcery to seduce children, or you've convinced yourself you are that sorcerer from *Swan Lake*. Did the ballet change you?" Mary stopped. She had said more than she intended.

"Ballet is harsh magic," said Dee. He went to the window, pulled aside a curtain and placed one chalk white hand on the glass. The wing of a dead bird, thought Mary as he went on. "We work young bones until they sprout feathers. Flesh evaporates in sweat. Ballet consumes the body to free the soul," Dee continued. "We all become swans. Some never turn back. The ballet *Swan Lake* is the wind under our feet, the air on which we ascend."

"Not true," retorted Mary. Dee turned to face her. "Don't blame ballet for your despicable lusts. The dance is sacred, your abuse is profane. You believe what you can do on stage goes for offstage too. You betray your art."

Dee lunged from the window with a cry.

Mary's blood prickled in her fingers. "Dee, you are lost to the wisdom of the swans. They protect their young."

Her eyes did not waver from his. Her jaw was tight. Whatever this man's relationship with Irina, it wasn't healthy, and it wasn't his first.

Billy Dee sloped to the door, then paused. His tone chilled. "Your belief that deception and sorcery can be disentangled is touching Miss Wandwalker. The spirits laugh at you."

He took a step towards her. "Can *you* tell the difference between good and bad magic? You say I turn girls like Irina into swans. Do you not know that witches fly? Ask your friends what they've been teaching their 'gels.'"

Mary blinked. A cold wing brushed her forehead. Would the Holywell witches put their young charges in danger? She must ask Caroline. Damn Billy Dee for making her doubt the therapists. She knew how dedicated they were to the vulnerable women who'd been trafficked.

She realized he'd adopted the nomenclature of 'gels.' Probably from listening to them, watching and sneaking around. Dee and the gels, she could barely restrain a shudder. Nevertheless she'd got him talking. What else might he let slip?

"Stay away from the Holywell's gels, Mr. Dee. Your reputation precedes you."

He twisted his lips. "My reputation, my appreciation of childlike grace…" Mary's skin crawled. He drawled his words. "Is driven by the magic of desire. Have you never experienced the intoxicating spell of love, Miss Wandwalker? Ah, I see you have. Look here."

With one bound he perched next to Mary on the sofa. Revolted, she longed for Anna's physical strength. He pulled a golden scarf from the pocket of his black jeans and unwrapped a silver coin. Mary bent over it then raised her head, puzzled.

"Silver as the full moon, is it not?" said Dee softly, holding the coin between his thumb and forefinger and about six inches from Mary's nose. "With this coin from my homeland I can make a girl fly, but only if she succumbs to the spell of love. You, for instance…"

"Stop," Mary shouted. She looked around hoping for witnesses. There were none. "Tell the truth. Did you put Irina in that tree? You say you love her. *Have you had sex with her?*"

That last question burst from Mary on its own volition. It could not be taken back, a spirit released.

Dee wrapped the coin again. He refused to meet Mary's eyes. "As I explained to her mother, I used this coin to bring Irina down from the blasted elm. You did not see my tiny moon winking from behind the trees." He twisted his lips. "Lost children are my specialty. After all, I was one."

"You did not answer my question," said Mary, rather breathless.

"Ah, but I did, Miss Wandwalker," replied Dee as he strolled away.

# CHAPTER 13
# WE HAVE A PROBLEM WITH SPIRITS

*Friday night.*

The exchanges with Billy Dee left Mary more disturbed than she would admit. After reheating her soup in the kitchen, she took the problem to the bedroom she shared with Anna and Caroline. Neither were present to discuss her uneasiness about Dee. As the storm raged overhead, she resolved to focus on the dangers inside Holywell.

Dee's a trickster, with words too, Mary thought. Caroline would say that his spells and spirits could be real, that some people can travel between worlds. Anna would want to choke the truth from him. Mary was shocked at how satisfying it would be to unleash Anna's ferocity on this man. No, she told herself, sternly. Violence means uncontrollable consequences.

Plus, such action obscured an idea taking shape in Mary's mind. Suppose Dee himself could not distinguish between ballet and sorcery. Suppose that *to him* extreme practices of body and soul, spells even, conjoined dancing and magic?

She tried to explain his slippery self-justifications to Caroline and Anna after they'd returned with extra sandwiches.

"He hinted that magic, for him at least, is part of ballet. So sorcery is to enchant young dancers. Like making them into swans." Mary swallowed. "Doing spells makes him a predator. He initiates his disgusting sexual practices as sorcery and ballet."

Anna growled. "We'll stop him."

Mary decided not to pursue that remark.

"I asked John and Linda if Dee could be behind these storms," said Caroline.

"What?" Mary blinked. Anna had a slight smile.

Mary wanted Caroline distracted. It would do her no good to dwell on the accusations against her. Agnes's death had to have another explanation. Yet was it worth such craziness?

"They laughed," said Caroline. "John and Linda did. Said I didn't understand the scale of the problem. A very persistent sorcerer's apprentice invoked the storm god over hundreds of years. He messed with the true spells." Caroline flopped on the bed, and put her hands behind her head.

"Don't be freaked out, Mary," said Anna, now with a wicked grin. "The sorcerer's apprentice in question is us – the culture that pumps CO2 into the atmosphere. We are the storm god."

"Ah," said Mary faintly. "That's one way of putting it. I guess. Er... do you have a sandwich to spare?"

Caroline waved her to the tiers of bread with green frills of lettuce. A glance at Anna's tense jaw and Mary decided to postpone asking about Irina's unexpected resemblance to her.

While chewing, Mary reviewed the extraordinary day. It began with getting marooned at Holywell, followed by Agnes's death, accusations against Caroline, confirmation of murder. Crises galore without Irina trying to fly. And... Mary recalled the moment when Irina's wig fell off to reveal a younger version of Anna, the ex-felon with no family. Had she and Caroline exaggerated the resemblance? After all, the oncoming storm had sucked the light from the sky.

It was too much. Taken with insinuations from Billy Dee, flying, witches, a fifteen year old girl, Robbin' Robin's fury, it all swirled into another kind of storm. And then, who was Agnes, the woman whose death haunted Holywell? Mary looked longingly at her bed, when muffled shouts erupted from along the corridor.

"Robbin' Robin yelling into his phone," remarked Anna from where she hunched on the floor. Her features remained locked down. Caroline's eyelids were raw.

Mary rolled her eyes. "The minister can yell all he wants," she remarked. "I don't see what we can do about Billy Dee tonight. We should question Irina, but we can't. Not only will she be asleep, but Dorothy wants to build a relationship between her and her counsellor. We don't get to talk to her."

"Nor do her parents," said Caroline quietly. "The witches see the parents as patients too. They've assigned therapists."

"Interesting," said Mary, chewing on the last crust. "I can't see either of them cooperating."

A bang on the door. Without waiting for an invitation, witches John and Linda walked in. Their expressions brought the entire Depth Enquiry Agency to their feet.

"Big problem," gasped Linda.

"Need your help with Billy Dee and the gels," added John.

Caroline and Anna looked at Mary. "What now?" she rapped.

Linda grabbed John's arm. "Holywell cut off by storms has made everyone crazy. It's bad, Miss Wandwalker. The gels are doing a séance with that man. They're in the dining room with the door locked. Dorothy's trying to talk them out of it."

*A séance? Why?* died on Mary's lips. She knew.

"They're trying to contact Agnes," said John. Then to Caroline, "Sorry Caroline. The gels think you killed her, probably." At Caroline's moan, John went on, "They think you did a mercy killing to relieve Agnes's suffering. They plan to make sure by asking her. That bastard Dee says… says…" John shook their fists.

"'*The murdered linger at the membrane between life and death*,'" quoted Linda. "'*Until they have justice*.'" She shivered.

"She's between this world and the next until her death is resolved," muttered John, not looking at Caroline.

Caroline stuffed her knuckles into her mouth and curled up on the bed.

"That rotten, trouble-making bastard." Mary stamped her foot. A hot wind propelled her. She pushed past Linda and John, and dashed downstairs. At first she could not get to the locked door, for the witches crowded behind Dorothy at the keyhole.

"Aaaannna," yelled Mary behind her. A pounding came from the stairs. The witches fell back to allow a passage. Dorothy held up a hand. Mary ignored her.

"Right here," said the young woman shoving Naomi aside. She'd found a leather biker's jacket from somewhere, Mary noted. Caroline must be in bed.

"Get outside, Anna!" shouted Mary very loudly. "Smash the dining room window. Break in. Be the lightning." Years of addressing meetings at the Archives had developed Mary's lungs. She made the dining room door tremble.

"Sure thing, Mary," roared Anna with a glint of humor. She did not move.

The witches drew their breath. They heard the sound of a bolt sliding back. The door opened on Dee and Sarah. The man's blotchy skin gleamed in the hall light. Sarah looked nervous.

"You only had to ask in the right way," sneered Dee, standing back. Everyone trooped in. The gels sat at the long table, holding hands. A table lamp had been placed in the middle. It sent distorted shadows creeping up the walls.

"Do none of you remember about lightning strikes?" That was Linda. "Most of you don't have rubber boots on. Holding hands could be dangerous."

"We don't care about weather," said one gel.

"It's what's inside Holywell that scares us," said another, her chin up. The formerly mute gel looked miserable.

"Besides, lightning is only dangerous to old people. You witches are supposed to keep away." That was Sarah.

A muscle twitched in Billy Dee's forehead. The gels started talking all at once.

"You can't stop us..."

"You witches left us alone all day...."

"Someone gassed the old crone..."

"We're going to find out who killed Agnes..."

"Stop protecting Caroline..."

"We can do a séance anywhere, anytime. We don't need your permission."

Hot breath blew at Mary, Anna, and the witches.

"We could lock up Billy Dee," suggested John.

The sorcerer snapped his fingers. "Locks don't stop me. My spirits will release me." He looked significantly around until the gels nodded.

Again, thought Mary. Again, I can't tell if he means he's got the gels trained. Does he think seventeenth century plague victims will come to his rescue?

"Mr. Dee, you are interfering where you do not belong. Holywell has a sacred mission to these young women." Mary had never heard Dorothy speak so coldly.

"We have magic you do not dream of."

That was Janet, although Mary could not see the diminutive witch. Dee put his head to one side as if he considered the challenge. Dueling magic? Mary thought, wildly. That would terrify the young women.

Mary Wandwalker felt the hairs rise on her arm. She was going to do something, and she did not know what. "Enough," she shouted. "Everyone be quiet." *Now what?*

Scared glances were exchanged. Some of the gels shivered. The air in the crowded room thickened. Even the thunder quieted. Witches leaned forward with open mouths; Dee stood tall with a supercilious grimace. Janet pushed forward and folded her arms. Dorothy flushed and breathed heavily.

"There will be a séance," Mary announced to a general gasp. "Tomorrow, after dinner, not tonight. Everyone, witches, gels, the Prince family, our agency, will attend. Yes, I do mean the minister. Robbin' Robin, Helen Morgan and Irina and part of Holywell now."

That last she directed at Dorothy, who blanched. No makeup tonight, Mary noted. For a moment no one moved or spoke.

Then Dee bowed his head, and the gels burst out chattering. The shards of Holywell had tumbled and re-assembled.

What have I done, thought Mary. You've provided a chance to check out Dee's famous séances, and preserve the fragile fabric of Holywell. Right now it's an island, cut off. That second voice came from the Chief Archivist she once was.

Anna surprised Mary.

"Mary Wandwalker is right. A séance tomorrow means we can question Agnes."

Mary felt her cheek muscles relax until Anna went on. "We've got to nail how she died. Caroline did nothing wrong. Anyone who says otherwise will answer to me."

Mary heard several gulps. The gels began to sidle out. They muttered between themselves. Thunder rolled in the distance.

"Off to bed now," called Dorothy after the gels, her face set. "This storm will pass by the morning. Mr. Dee and I will then sort out the séance details. Anna, Miss Wandwalker, my office. Now."

For once, Dorothy was not in jeans and a handknitted seater. Her dressing gown must double for ceremonies, Mary thought, for the midnight blue robe shimmered with pentangles and stars. It made a satisfying sweep as she exited. Mary and Anna exchanged speaking looks as they followed.

# CHAPTER 14
# A SÉANCE FOR AGNES?

*Friday late night.*

Robed Dorothy behind her desk was a different woman from the genial therapist. That woman usually tolerated Mary's skepticism about the beliefs of Holywell.

"Sit," she said. Her eyes glinted at Mary as wind batted rain at the windows. Mary sat. Anna stood at her shoulder.

Dorothy banged her fist. "O gull, o dolt, as ignorant as dirt. Thou art highly fed and lowly taught."

Mary blinked. "What? Dorothy? Is this some spell? Wait…"

"All eyes and no sight," Dorothy ranted. She swung round in her chair to the uncurtained window where black trees swayed. Stunned, Mary glanced up at Anna. The young woman unzipped her leather jacket, then leaned to put her palm on the desk next to Mary.

"We are no canker blossoms. Save your curses for that lewdly inclined poisonous bunch-backed toad, Dee."

"Not bad, Anna," came from the door. Janet dragged a second chair next to Mary's. "Personally I see Dee as a fusty nut with no kernel. Now that Robbin' Robin is an infinite and endless liar, an hourly promise-breaker."

"Hard to see which is the verist varlet that ever chewed with a tooth," Mary agreed. "Shakespeare insults are colorful. Is that what you really think, Dorothy? Surely you can see why I said to do the séance tomorrow?"

"Well, Dorothy?" Anna's tone did not compromise.

After a tense moment, the manager-witch eased herself back to face Mary. She stopped glaring and sat upright. Mary noticed her pallor.

"Dorothy's exhausted," said Janet, scooting behind the desk to pat her arm. "I have one of my best herb teas brewing. Wait while I bring it."

The small witch trotted to the door. Anna grunted then ceased menacing over the desk. She retired to the back wall. Dorothy aimed half a smile at Mary.

"Shakespearean curses began as a joke, well, more a therapy game, with the young women, the gels. We wanted them to experience language differently, to see they were not trapped in the kind of... of..."

"Foul language that came with blows," said Anna without expression.

"Right," said Dorothy. She flushed, which Mary realized was consciousness of Anna's painful past. "Then Naomi said that Shakespearean curses would be good for us too. I don't expect you to understand, Miss Wandwalker, but a witch has to be careful with her words. Angry outbursts can produce... unwanted consequences."

"She means spells." Anna, a cyber-witch, folded her arms. "Like online, curses can be dangerous, make unpredictable algorithms. I had to learn that."

Mary sniffed.

"You do know many swear words originally invoked a god or gods," remarked Dorothy. A smaller sniff came from Mary. Sometimes her skepticism was a blanket, a comfort in this impossible household.

"Is anyone going to help me?" came a tart voice from the hall. Janet kicked the door fully open so that the others saw the laden tray. A teapot and four mugs knocked into each other. Mary got to Janet first. Dorothy took the tea pot over to the desk. She poured a steaming liquid that smelled like cooked hay to Mary.

"What's that scent?" said Anna, taking the mug with reluctance. She stuck her tongue in and withdrew it quickly. "Too hot. Too much sugar."

"Not sugar, honey from the organic farm in the next valley," retorted Janet. "Together with mint, sage, pinches of feverfew, and mandrake. My immune strengthening tea. Drink it."

Dorothy's mug wobbled. "You're not experimenting again, are you Janet? You know what we said about testing first – and not on the gels."

Janet gave a wicked grin, then stopped at Dorothy's pained expression. Dorothy's voice cracked. "That's thunder again. Listen."

They listened. The sound reminded Mary of a lion snoring she'd seen on a TV show. "Far off," she said. "If it's the next storm, perhaps it's going the other way."

"Goddess, I hope so," said Dorothy, grimacing at her tea. She took a small sip. "That wretched minister Robbin' Robin – wretched in all senses, Irina trying to fly, and now Dee doing a séance. All thanks to Miss Wandwalker here who has no authority at Holywell…"

"Oh come on Dorothy," said Mary hotly. "Don't close your eyes to reality. You've got to see why the séance must go ahead?"

"No, I bloody don't!" yelled Dorothy. "That man is either a fraud or a dealer in dark magic…"

"Fraud, of course," said Mary hastily. "My plan is to expose him. Break his hold over the gels – and Irina." I hope, she silently added. She did not say what was written on Anna's face. That the two of them were determined to prevent Dee throwing the blame for Agnes's death on Caroline. Dorothy looked thoughtful, too thoughtful.

Mary tried again. "Look, Dorothy, we're stuck together with the storms. That includes Robbin' Robin and Billy Dee, who are spoiling for a fight. If we can show Dee's séances are a bunch of tricks, then the minister will calm down, I promise."

She could feel Anna recall their deal with Mr. Jeffreys over taming Robbin' Robin.

Dorothy brightened at Mary's explanation, then frowned.

"The gels too will be easier to manage," Mary added, swallowing her doubts. Surely Dorothy could see it as a win win?

"The gels are all I care about. You can't let Dee..." began Dorothy, voice drying. "You handed him *power*, Miss Wandwalker."

"That's what *he* thinks," retorted Mary. "In fact, I set him up to lose his power."

"What about the gels?" persisted Dorothy. "You don't know how vulnerable they are."

Janet looked up. "It's because they're so vulnerable that we need that séance."

The herbal witch's tone silenced Dorothy. "Drink your tea, Dorothy. You too, Wandwalker. Take yours, Anna." Janet narrowed her eyes until the women began to sip. Then she banged down her empty mug.

"Wandwalker does not know the gels. And she's blind to what magic is. But her instincts are sound." Janet leaned forward.

"You know as I do, Dorothy, that Holywell has many rooms, closets, alcoves and corridors. Don't get me started on the hiding places in the barn and Infirmary. How do we prevent a séance if the gels are set on it? We can't lock them up 24/7. It would cause panic and worse."

Dorothy bit her lip. "Well..."

"*We* are not their captors," Janet emphasized.

She continued. "The gels witnessed Agnes close to the Death Goddess. Someone interrupted her soul journey – pushed her into the shadowlands before her time. Unforgiveable."

Janet stood up. "We taught the gels that an old woman with dementia deserved respect."

"Love," said Dorothy, gloomy.

"Yeah well, the gels accepted Agnes as part of Holywell. Her murder hurts them."

"Violates what Holywell means to them," muttered Mary.

"A safe place – no longer," said Anna, patting a zip under her left breast. Mary suspected it held her knife.

"Precisely. Wandwalker and Anna are right to turn Dee's dangerous séances into what *we* do at Holywell."

Dorothy opened her mouth then closed it. "Go on," she said. "How is this séance what we do?"

Janet glanced at Mary. "With floods holding everyone here, we can't afford to wait for the police. The gels are traumatized by Agnes's unexplained death and yes, I grant you, Dee's arrival with Irina. Plus we've got those ghastly parents. Don't forget the gels believe that Sarah had nothing to do with Agnes's murder. They need to believe it, for she is one of them." Janet turned to Mary, pausing briefly on Anna's glare before speaking again.

"That leaves Caroline as suspect number one."

Anna's hands became fists. "The séance will clear Caroline if it is real. If we get trickery then I'll stop Dee's lies," she snapped.

The short witch with white roots put Mary between herself and Anna.

"Don't get angry, Anna," said Mary, feeling weary. "You know Janet's on Caroline's side. Let her finish." Anna edged back. Janet focused on Dorothy.

"We can't expect the gels to let go of Agnes's murder. Caroline's been at Holywell more than Wandwalker and Anna. She's my apprentice. This death is a terrible shaking of their world."

"I see what you mean." Dorothy sounded infinitely tired. "Our young women see Caroline as a friend, or they did. The thought that she, of all people, killed someone under the protection of Holywell terrifies them. Right now, they can't feel safe."

Dorothy had rings around her eyes. She put her mug down. Mary moved it to a pile of bills where it could not mark the old oak.

"Okay," said Mary, trying to remember her other meeting skills. "Janet and I agree that the prospect of a séance will calm the girls if they think it will find out what really happened to Agnes. *We* think, all right, hope, the gels will see for themselves that Dee is a fraud. My intervention took control away from Dee. That was the point."

She glanced at Anna's scowl. "Of course Caroline's innocent. She could not hurt anyone. Unless..." Mary swallowed. What was she saying?

Mary swiveled back to Anna, the woman with a hidden knife. Not for the first time she froze as the terrible thought struck her.

"God, Anna..."

Anna's face gave nothing away. She'd retreated into the dark.

"What if it *was* a mercy killing? What if Agnes *asked, begged* to die?"

"Is that what Caroline says?" Dorothy rapped.

"Caroline says... I mean Caroline does not remember anything." Mary winced. She'd planned to betray no doubts.

"She could have done it, you mean? Knowing Caroline it would be because Agnes implored her to. If she ended Agnes's life, then perhaps her distress made her forget? That's not unknown. The gels would understand. They have similar experiences – episodes, acts wiped from their minds."

Dorothy's spiel left Mary numb. Janet nodded.

"Stop growling, Anna," managed Mary.

"None of you are thinking about Agnes," shouted Anna. She waved both arms, then again leant on Dorothy's desk. "Agnes wasn't a lump of meat. She tried to talk to me last time I was here."

"When was that? She's not recognized Janet for some months," said Dorothy, sounding curious.

Anna let out a breath. Deftly, she fetched a fourth chair.

"Agnes…" Anna paused, as if unsure whether to go on. Mary tensed.

"Don't you dare say we're not thinking of her," snapped Janet. "For weeks it was me by her bedside." She brushed her eyes with her hand. "Agnes liked to hold my hand. I never cared that she did not know me."

Anna put her elbows on the desk. For a long moment she appeared to study the carved symbols. So did Mary. She realized that these differed markedly from those on Anna's *Swan Lake* costume. The Holywell symbols flowed and curved like a river. No jagged edges or teeth-like blades.

Finally Anna spoke. "Last month, when Caroline came for the full moon, I drove her. You were off in London, Mary, lunching with Mr. J."

Mary's finger followed a flower tendril so delicately carved that it tingled her skin. Anna would not be hurried.

"Caroline took me to say hello to Agnes. Said it would be good for her to see new faces. It was hot, that day in August. Sarah walked Agnes to the old well. We went too. I thought Agnes did not know either of us. Then she pointed at me."

"'Girl from Romania,' she said. Anna swallowed. "I told Caroline to say nothing to you, Mary."

"Why on earth not? You've never mentioned Romania."

Anna ignored Mary's question. With her fingernails she started digging out grease from a spiral ending in oak leaves. "But now Caroline is accused of this thing she *cannot* have done," she said between her teeth. "You forget that Agnes had a life once."

Dorothy tapped her finger. "Be tender of my desk, Anna. We care for these symbols. Sharp objects, even your nails, affright them." Dorothy spoke quietly.

To Mary's surprise, Anna sat back. She could be an elf concealed in a vast oak trunk from which that chair was hewn, thought Mary. Only she's fiercer than any elf I've heard of.

Mary cleared her throat. "Anna's right. My fault. We've neglected the first rule of homicide: the victim, their life, their enemies." Mary coughed. "So Anna, could you have met Agnes in Romania?"

Silence.

"Did you go to Romania with that husband, the criminal?" Janet said. "Russian, wasn't he? We assumed you were Russian with a name like 'Vronsky.'"

After a glance at Anna's stone features, Mary answered. "Anna took the name Vronsky from a book, a Russian novel by Tolstoy," said Mary. "You're right Janet, that Viktor Solokov, sentenced to twenty-five years in prison, by the way, operated across Europe. I never heard Anna mention Romania in particular. However, there is something…" she moistened her lips. She stared at Anna, willing her to mention her resemblance to Irina.

"Get on with it, girl," said Janet. "So we can all go to bed. What other clue is Wandwalker's blathering about?"

Anna stood up tall and blazing. She flashed her teeth at Mary, then left the room, silent and predatory as a cat.

"Hell, not even a whisper from that squeaking door," grumbled Janet. "Well, spill it, Wandwalker. Anything from Agnes's life might shift accusations from Caroline."

Mary stood but slowly and stiffly. How her rear ached from that hard chair. "Not Agnes this time, but rather Robbin' Robin's daughter, Irina. When her wig fell off, Caroline and I saw she resembled Anna."

"What? Irina and Anna? How is that possible?" cried Dorothy.

"Irina's adopted," said Mary. "I wasn't sure, but Helen Morgan freaked out when I mentioned Irina and adoption earlier. We met while making tea. She ran off leaving the kettle boiling."

"Ah, adoption on the *QT*," pronounced Janet. "Given the shortage of babies, the authorities are picky. They prefer young couples. Robbin' Robin and Helen Morgan would have been on the mature side to adopt lawfully in England."

"We shouldn't make assumptions," protested Dorothy.

"Yes," said Mary. "But then there's Romania." Billy Dee comes from Romania, she thought, but did not say.

"No more tonight," sighed Dorothy. "Tomorrow will be tempestuous enough with the séance."

Mary let Dorothy go first. She too ached for her bed. Janet had other ideas.

"Wait," she hissed, pulling Mary by the arm in the hallway. "I need a word."

"Not now, Janet. I'm dead on my feet. You should be too."

"Too wound up to sleep." Even in the lamplight, Mary could see Janet's eyes gleam too bright. She gripped Mary harder. "This séance is more dangerous than you know, Wandwalker. Stress is breaking Dorothy. Billy Dee and Irina's parents are a bomb waiting to explode."

"We're trying," Mary protested. Then something occurred to her. "What's your witch-sense of Billy Dee?"

"Predator," said Janet immediately. "Oh, I didn't expect to say that. Must be the clarity herbs I burnt earlier." She frowned. "Yes, his predator nature swamps his magical abilities. The good spirits cannot reach him." She waited a moment. "There's something else too. He's hiding something, a deep wound."

Mary reviewed her encounters with the sorcerer-choreographer. Something was on the edge of her mind. A pattern, surely?

"You know, Janet, Dee hinted at dark secrets. For weeks he's tried to visit Holywell. With Irina he finally gained admittance. I think Dee's biggest, darkest secret is with us, here and now."

Janet winced. "Dee can keep his secrets as long as tomorrow's séance is not too painful for the gels," she said. "Tame him, Miss Wandwalker. Corral his dark spirit, that's all we witches ask of you." She patted Mary maternally on the shoulder and left.

"You don't ask much," muttered Mary as she climbed, sorrowfully, to bed.

# CHAPTER 15
# THE MORNING OF SÉANCE DAY

*Saturday early morning.*

Séance day dawned in sheets of rain. Waking before Anna and Mary, Caroline listened with increasing concentration as her senses revived. No thunder, good. She checked the forecast on her phone. Last night's storm had tracked east to the North Sea, and the next had not reached the Bristol Channel. That rhythm to the downpour must be wind. Nasty, yet the absence of thunder and lightning meant a chance to step outside, to be alone.

Caroline eased herself from Anna's arms, threw a glance at sleeping Mary, and picked up the dress that she had worn – oh, eons ago – in Greenwich. Anna had foraged stylish alternative outfits for herself from the gels, but Caroline wanted the shell that smelled of her own body, at least until Anna objected. Downstairs, she rummaged in a pile of raincoats, hats, and rubber boots until she heard movement overhead. That sent her out the back door and into the wet.

Mud and water everywhere obscured what had been grass and autumn leaves. Caroline wished she could push aside the curtains of rain. The hat she'd grabbed at the last moment was too small. Either it covered her faded curls, or kept water from dripping down her nose. With rain blown onto eyes and chin, she stumbled half-blinded into the copse of mature trees. She wanted to see for herself the blasted elm that Irina had climbed.

The trees gave some relief from the wind-maddened rain. Leaf mold underfoot absorbed more water. Caroline crunched twigs, and the occasional fern. Whenever she spotted something that could be a footprint she whipped out her phone and took a picture. Anna had devised a program that used footprints to deduce height, weight, even age and sex within probabilities. Not acceptable to the police, Caroline knew, but she hoped for prints of Billy Dee and Irina together. He'd claimed he brought her down from the tree. It might be possible to show he'd been there when she climbed.

It was 6:45 a.m. Caroline had told no one of her plan. Stopping to reconsider, she heard the snap of twigs close by. It was followed by bird protests through the rain on the leaf canopy. Looking around, Caroline started as a figure in black crossed the narrow path behind her. He had gone in the direction of the old well. The shape was definitely male, she concluded. Too slender for Robbin' Robin, it had to be the one person at Holywell that Caroline could not bear to encounter, Billy Dee.

Caroline leaned back on a beech tree, not caring about the trickle down her neck. Her mouth tasted salty: the lingering tears resulting from the accusations about her and Agnes. Dee in the Holywell garden at this hour? *What would Mary do?*

"She wouldn't wait for others to find the truth," Caroline mumbled. Sighing, she set off after the man. It meant leaving the familiar oaks, beeches and elms for the vegetable and herb beds that led past the well. Beyond that was the ancient boundary wall against which the floods stretched as far as the eye could see.

Feeling the pressure of wind and rain even through the waterproof coat, a dash of sweet scent made Caroline pause to inhale. Yes, there were the last roses. Most petals had been beaten down to earth. Those big yellow and blush blooms were called "Peace." She smiled. Borrowing Mary's determination, she plodded after the man who must be Billy Dee. His footprints ended at the well, as if he too had flown away.

Looking around, Caroline spotted two crows perched on a low branch, black eyes fixed on her. One danced up and down seeming to dodge mighty dollops of rain from branches.

"Ha," Caroline said. "You crows don't scare me. I'm going to find where he's gone."

I'm still a detective, she told herself. I'm still a member of the Agency, even if I can't remember what I did when Agnes died.

But the man was nowhere to be seen. Flushed and hungry, Caroline caught sight of a female figure in a huge raincoat and hat. The coat swung open revealing a white nightdress and muddy shoes. Irina, of course. The girl dodged behind the roses and crept past the well to a couple of trees that overlooked the wall. She did not see Caroline, who held her breath and let her eyes alone follow. Irina must be out to meet Billy Dee. At once, Caroline was determined to stop her.

"Wait," she called. "Wait, Irina, I want to talk to you. I want to help."

The girl froze. Then, without acknowledging Caroline, she turned to splash back to the house. Caroline watched helplessly. Her feet slipped in boots two sizes too big. I'll fall flat on my face if I try to catch her. At least, I've stopped her meeting the sorcerer, she thought. He's disappeared. I mustn't think he's become one of those crows, thought Caroline, in deference to Mary. He could have sprinted off, using puddles to conceal footprints.

Anna would laugh at me, Caroline said to herself. She trained me to stalk, yet I could not get close enough to be sure it was Billy Dee. Drat.

As she headed for the house, the two rooks flew big circles above her, cawing loudly. Channeling Anna this time, Caroline made a rude gesture at them. They flapped their huge wings, then rose straight up into the air.

"Go away," Caroline called. "We want no more of your storms."

Her stomach murmured. I'm really hungry, Caroline realized. Yet no way would she forage with the gels. To avoid their pointed remarks about the death of Agnes, she would get something while it was still early. I hate creeping around for food, she muttered to herself. I've done it too often: comfort eating for depression.

Caroline took a last look at the sky. She spotted a bank of dark clouds rising in the west. A silver line appeared for a mere second. Morning sun? No, that flash meant lightning. She hurried back to the house and the kitchen freezer. Yesterday she'd spotted a bag of currant buns behind packs of frozen peas. With any luck, Caroline promised herself, before anyone else comes down I can toast a few.

*****

That day of the séance, breakfast was a sober affair, not helped by the eruption of another loud storm. Cherry hovered in the kitchen, hinting darkly that she'd have to lock up the remaining stores. So gloomy was she that Dorothy got applause when she announced that drones would drop off supplies when the wind permitted. Meanwhile, everyone should spend a quiet day, or the séance would not take place. That threat worked, observed Mary, as she encountered gels giggling and whispering without the frantic running about of the previous evening. Unfortunately the internal weather at Holywell was about to be shattered anew.

When the news came it appalled everyone. Even Anna's fierce spirit behaved as if knocked to the ground. The storm's multiple lightning strikes in Oxfordshire had burned out vital utility facilities. By mid-morning, Internet and phone services were all dead. Dorothy got the witches to rush around reassuring gels and guests that the situation was temporary. Fixing storm damage to phone masts was now top priority. According to the authorities, repairs would take a couple of hours, max.

"How do you know?" Mary queried Meredith in the kitchen. She scrutinized the young witch with envied curls.

"Yes, I wondered if Dorothy cast a forgetting spell."

"Or simply said what everyone is desperate to hear," countered Mary.

Meredith smiled in a superior sort of way, thought Mary. "A drone arrived with medicines and a handwritten note. Food delivery this afternoon, if the wind drops, plus updates from the police and hospital. Now Dorothy wants you, Miss Wandwalker…"

Mary closed her eyes. "Don't tell me. I'm to deal with Robbin' Robin."

"He's ranting in the lounge. Dorothy says can you move him out so the gels can use it to eat lunch. We're reserving the dining room for séance prep. That reminds me. You're to keep watch on the minister and Ms. Morgan before the séance. Dorothy's too busy calming the gels and keeping tabs on Irina."

"Billy Dee?"

"Threw his phone in the kitchen trash, I hear. He demanded a room in the house to prepare for the séance tonight." She laughed. "Dorothy gave him the attic, after John and Linda had cleared it out. Between you and me, I think they left a few holding spells." She paused. "I know they'll do cleansing rituals tomorrow, because they asked for herb bundles from Janet. Said they did not mind how wet they were."

Mary sighed. "What about Helen Morgan and Irina?"

Meredith frowned. "Not good news about the mother. She's confined to her room with a sore throat. We've given her a Covid test. It's negative, thank the goddess. Dorothy would go nuts if we got Covid at Holywell on top of everything else. I've given Helen Morgan aspirin. Did you know I used to be a nurse in a care home?"

Mary took a step back. Meredith grinned. "In my professional opinion, Morgan has a cold from being out in the rain when Irina went up that tree. As for Irina, the ballerina, Dorothy wants to get her assessed for group."

At Mary's blank look, Meredith explained. "Group therapy. Not a Holywell specialty, but Dorothy thinks it will keep the gels focused, or at least that is the plan after last night. Even we witches are giving it a go." She noticed Mary's expression. "No don't worry. You detectives have enough to do with Robbin' Robin and well... Caroline. How is she? Did she... um, what the gels are saying?"

"You don't know Caroline," said Mary with devastating dignity. "As a newcomer you cannot possibly judge her. Now, if you'll excuse me, I will take care of the minister."

Putting her shoulders back, Mary seized her cashmere cardigan, miraculously stain free after two days of Holywell, and made off to confront the irate Robbin' Robin.

After wrangling the minister back to his room, Mary needed a lie down. A doze and lunch got Mary through most of the day. The forecasts proved correct. A gap between storms meant drone deliveries. One item was addressed to Mary. In a printed out email from Mr. Jeffreys, she learned that the police were still baffled by the murder of Agnes. For a start, her identity remained a puzzle. Discovered in an appalling mental hospital, and later admitted to Holywell in an advanced state of dementia, Agnes had no documents. Nothing she had ever said revealed her origins. Her fingerprints and DNA were no help whatsoever. Agnes did not correspond to any recorded missing person. She remained a mystery.

Consequently the police had to focus on Holywell. It made no sense to believe Agnes mattered to anyone outside it. Sarah, the trafficked girl from Congo, and Caroline Jones from Mary Wandwalker's Detective Agency, each had opportunity. Yet both were without motive, or so the police assumed. Higher authorities decreed that the murder investigation be shelved until after the weather emergency. Floods and tempests meant Holywell was an island. The suspects weren't going anywhere. A stern warning appeared on packages and communications.

Police Investigation suspended until storm and flood danger ceases. Do not discuss the recent death until officers return.

Mary felt oddly comforted by the printed out email. After all, it was the return of letter writing. Long ago in the twentieth century it had been her preferred method of communication.

Knowing her sense of humor, Mr. Jeffreys ended with a quote from Chief Constable concerning the suspended murder investigation. He imagined her raised eyebrows, as he shut his laptop to the sound of drumming rain. He watched water stream down the windows of his makeshift office at the John Whitcliffe hospital in Oxford.

*Excerpt from address by the Chief Constable:*
*We've put the Agnes X case on ice. Whatever you say about that Wandwalker woman, Jeffreys, they won't start some half-arsed amateur sleuthing. The police have been very firm about leaving murder to the professionals. Given the dangers of a lightning strike, the Holywell residents won't be sitting together holding hands.*

"*Half-arsed amateur sleuthing*? My friend, you do not know Mary Wandwalker," Mr. Jeffreys murmured.

# CHAPTER 16
# AGNES SPEAKS

*Saturday night.*

Holywell at 8:01 p.m. that evening might have astonished the Chief Constable, for most of the residents, bar Billy Dee, sat holding hands. Mary suppressed a tart comment about lightning in deference to the Dorothy's deepening worry lines. Mary also chafed at Billy Dee's instructions. Before the séance they were to sit in silence and concentrate on Agnes. No doubt Dee would deign to appear when it suited him. Mary took note of Robbin' Robin and Helen Morgan sitting side by side, both with gritted teeth.

Mary made a polite query about Morgan's sore throat. Apparently Janet's herb tea had helped. A glare from Janet drew muttered thanks. Even so, only Anna would sit on the other side of Irina's mother. Beyond the windows gusts bent branches and rattled twigs. Leaves scattered everywhere tomorrow, thought Mary, as if the sky had rioted. Intermittent thunder added to her unease.

Around the dining table, gels rolled their eyes and whispered in various languages. The witches kept their heads bowed, while Caroline trembled. Anna sat bolt upright, stony-faced. Anticipation thickened the air until Mary's bones ached. Again she scanned the strained faces and clasped hands. Darkness and the wild wet gripped Holywell. The overhead chandelier poured radiance down onto bare heads. Their shadows moved uneasily along the walls.

All day Billy Dee had darted about, refusing to stop for anyone. Twice Mary tried to catch him. Each time he vanished. So much for taming him before the séance, she silently fumed. What did Janet expect, anyway? I don't, *won't* believe he can raise the spirits of the dead. So there's nothing to be afraid of, is there? Mary's self-administered pep talk did not wholly convince her.

We could have waited to hold hands, thought Mary. Yet the touch of another human, Caroline on one side, Meredith on the other, comforted her. She could see that the gels felt more relaxed. Everyone needs not to be alone, and won't say so. *Bong* rang the grandfather clock in the hall. Mary, and others, jumped.

"He's late." The whisper came from too far down the table for Mary to identify. Not a gel, she thought.

"Dee should be here by now."

Mary wished she'd brought her glasses. In the pause, thunder crashed close. It sent disappointed sighs around the table. More storm meant more floods. They would stay marooned longer.

"Perhaps he's scared of thunder," speculated one of the gels.

"It gives me a headache," murmured Cherry.

Apart from Dee, the other absentee was Irina. She was asleep in her bed, or so Mary hoped. Irina had continued to take food in her room. In a rare moment of agreement, Robbin' Robin and Helen Morgan forbad the fifteen-year-old to attend the séance. So reported Dorothy at dinner. She'd remarked that she would not have allowed it anyway. Irina must rest after her shocking escapade in the old elm tree.

*****

Mary's eye caught Helen Morgan staring. The woman tossed her head. Something's going on with those two, Caroline had remarked as they sat down. For at the gong summoning them to the dining room, the minister marched in as if attending a constituency event in his honor. Earlier Mary had visited his room to point out that the séance provided a golden opportunity to spot the deceit that cost Robbin' Robin the PM election. First the minister's head jerked. Then a sly grin spread across his entire face.

"Got him," he said, rising to his feet.

"Not yet, minister," muttered a revolted Mary as she departed.

A grim Helen Morgan strode after her ex-husband into the dining room. She was careful to seat herself as far away from him as possible, Mary noted. Robbin' Robin announced he would eat with the community, and attend "Whatever that effing bastard is up to." Helen Morgan tightened her mouth and nodded. Very few of the company exhibited interest in the power couple. We're all haunted by the prospect of hearing from a murdered woman, Mary reflected.

Dinner consisted of vegetarian burgers, salad, and very little conversation, reflected Mary. Murmurs and gestures for ketchup, salt, and paper towels were punctuated by fingers tapping, knees jiggling, and feet shuffling on the floor, not to mention whispering and passing bits of paper.

"Phones and the internet are deader than Agnes," Anna remarked.

Caroline muttered in Mary's ear that she felt like a kettle about to boil over.

"Go to bed," Mary suggested. "Take your food and don't attend the séance. You know the girls, I mean gels, will ask about Agnes. They believe Dee can speak to her."

Caroline shuddered. *You know they want to blame you for the murder*, hung between them. "It's all a fix," said Mary, as firmly as she could. "Who knows where Dee will direct his tricks."

Caroline swallowed, then squeezed Mary's hand under the table. "I'm staying. They are going to ask if I killed Agnes."

Before Mary could say anything Caroline hissed: "*A storm is about to descend.* I want to be here in this room with you and Anna. Not stuck upstairs going out of my mind."

"I'm glad you feel that way," was all Mary could manage.

Caroline returned a watery smile. "Don't you know that Anna can deflect lightning?"

*****

An hour later Billy Dee kept them waiting. Meanwhile the storm rattled the glass behind thick curtains. With everyone keyed up for the séance, Janet spoke up.

"Dee will be here. See those two incense burners?" She indicated small tables on opposite sides of the room. Smoke spiraled from purple sticks stuck in dishes of water. "He lit them and said he'd be back. We are to hold hands to build the energies. Energy enables the dead to cross over." Janet snorted. She nodded at the sweating minister and again at Mary. "That charred spice odor is his choice, not us witches. I never use myrrh."

Mary saw witch John's knuckles whiten holding a gel's hand. She squeaked and the big hand relaxed. Across from Mary, Dorothy developed an eyelid twitch.

"Focus on the altars *we* made," said Meredith, brightly. "Janet brought protection herbs."

Two other side tables stood by the walls without the burning incense. Now Mary saw that all four had round plates with a lit candles in crystal glasses. Then came a ring of pebbles and bundles of fresh herbs. Sniffing hard, Mary detected mint, rosemary and thyme.

"What did you say was in the incense?" Helen Morgan sounded hoarse.

"My own preparation," said Billy Dee, who materialized at the door wearing a long black cape. No one had heard his approach, Mary realized from the uneasy glances.

"We purified the room," said John, sticking their chin out at Dee. Mary looked for Linda beside her, and then remembered that the witches sat between the gels. Linda smiled mistily at John from down the table.

"That's right," said Naomi, calmly. Ignoring Dee, she spoke to the gels. "The cardinal spirits of all four directions bless us tonight. We put *our* altars next to *his* incense."

Dorothy nodded. "You can begin," she said to Dee, without expression. Wind howled overhead, the curtains shivered. Mary gulped.

Dee gave an ironic bow, then directed those closest to him to move their chairs back so they could keep holding hands while he stood at the dining table. He then removed a candle, saucer and lighter from his voluminous cloak. He lit the candle and placed it on the table directly below his face. Dee clicked his fingers. The chandelier overhead went dark. A couple gels screamed while others gasped.

"No need to fear," Dee intoned. "Keep hold of each other. The binding is secure."

Thunder exploded overhead. A second later the thin curtains blazed.

"The sorcerer's brought the storm god," muttered one of the witches near Mary.

Dee held up both arms, palms out, commanding silence. Mary could not work out why Dee's candle lit his face and so little else. In the ensuing rustling Mary found her fingers crushed on her right side. She grunted and pulled away until Caroline loosened her grip. On Mary's left, Meredith's hand felt soft and cold. Dee's expression wavered from grim to ecstatic as the candlelight flickered over his cheekbones.

"Look at me, only at me. Do not break the hold. We are a landing stage for the spirits of the dead."

Dee closed his eyes. His candle began to flicker rhythmically as if someone blew on it from a distance. The flames licked the grease on Dee's face. On his jaw tiny drops of oil collected then dripped onto his cape. Ah, his skin condition, recalled Mary. Grease in candlelight made him look more like a mummy than a living person. His chin had a tiny silver scar that began to wriggle. When he blinked his eyelashes made miniature knives on his forehead.

"When are we going to talk to Agnes?" whispered once of the gels.

Billy Dee opened his eyes. They were two black holes, Caroline said later. All at once, the two incense burners belched a thicker smoke. Coughing and chair scraping ensued.

"Don't break the circle," shrieked a woman's voice. Probably Helen Morgan, thought Mary.

"Shut up, woman," Robbin' Robin snarled. "It's *your* fault that…"

"Stop it, both of you!" Mary snapped. With both hands engaged, Mary tried to blow the smoke aside until her cheeks hurt. So did the others, but the coughing got louder.

"Come Zephyrus, Boreas, Notos, Eurus. Blow away the foul air, you beloved winds." The voice rang clear, confident and feminine. Suddenly Mary could breathe. She heard a general drawing in of air that had touches of mint and rosemary. The toxic smoke descended to the floor, then vanished.

When her eyes adjusted back to the candlelight, Mary saw that Billy Dee glared at one witch in particular. He stood over a pile of blackened silver objects attached to a chain. Knives, a long fang or tooth, a pentangle, a black finger – they made Mary's teeth hurt. Hang on, weren't these familiar?

Facing Dee small Linda stood. She continued to keep hold of two gels. Eyes shut, her head leaned back as if bathed in the wind spirits she'd summoned.

"There are many kinds of spirit, William Dee," she said, opening her eyes. With a graceful movement Linda resumed her chair.

Dee's lips pulled back in a silent snarl. Then he stared down at the silver chain until Mary remembered she'd seen it, or one very like it, in Greenwich Park.

"Take that loathsome thing away." Dorothy's voice shook. Her eyes blazed at the silver in front of Dee. "Or this séance ends right now."

Caroline groaned in Mary's ear. "It's that dark magic belt." Of course, the witches recognize forbidden symbols. Before

Mary could intervene, there came a crash. Anna stood, hands free, having banged her identical belt on the table. Her body thinned in the candlelight until it resembled a long blade – she pointed it at Billy Dee.

"Anna, you broke the hold," gasped Sarah.

There came a yowl from Dee, succeeded by a moment of pure horror that Mary would never forget. All the candles, Dee's included, died. The darkness sent her falling into a pit, absolute and cold. Gels screamed. It grew more terrifying when people noticed a greenish glow from both occult belts.

"This stops here," shouted Dorothy. "Find the light switch."

*"No, wait. I am here. I want to speak. I'm Agnes."*

The quavery voice of an old woman made everyone turn to stone. "It is Agnes," a gel shouted. Someone yelped. Others shivered. Mary could sense it.

"Who killed you? Tell us now."

Anna certainly gets to the point, Mary thought.

*"Tell Mary Wandwalker it was the boy. The boy killed me."*

"No, no, no," wailed several gels whom Mary could not identify.

A click. Immediately Mary felt the table rise to bang her chin. The smell of varnish and a sick headache throbbed in her temples. Why is the world yellow with black spots? Oh, I see. I *see*; the chandelier is back on.

"Janet, why didn't you warn us before switching the light on?" moaned several of the gels. They rubbed their eyes and held their heads. "The glare is killing me."

"Séance over," retorted Janet.

"That's right, go to your rooms, ladies." Dorothy got to her feet as if she'd been sitting for hours, thought Mary. The other witches exchanged meaningful glances and moved to tend to their altars.

"But we wanted to…"

"You can't." Dorothy sounded satisfied as well as tired. "Look, Billy Dee's gone."

"He's out there," exclaimed Sarah, pulling open the curtains. "Look."

Thunder like a giant throwing rocks made heads swivel to the window. With his back to the house, a man kneeled on the lawn. Billy Dee raised his arms to receive the blessing of the god. The sky split open.

Lightning forked, met Dee's outstretched hands, then ran down his whole body. The god rooted himself to the earth in the fiery embrace of a demon lover. For a second Dee blazed. Clothes peeled off, smoking. His body reddened and became translucent, white bones threaded with veins. At last satisfied, the storm god let Dee topple sideways into the charred heap that was once his cloak.

\*\*\*\*\*

After the yelling died down, the gels were escorted to their beds. Dorothy insisted that Billy Dee's body must wait for a pause between storms. No one else should risk death by lightning. So it was a couple of hours later when Mary, Caroline and Anna ventured outside. Pulling aside the burnt remains of his clothes, they carried Billy Dee to the kitchen. Only the sorcerer had one more surprise.

"He's not dead," said Anna, jumping back. Caroline wiped mud from his face.

"What? He can't be alive," said Mary. "Lightning struck both arms. We saw the blast go down him to the earth."

Caroline grabbed a tea towel, and used it on Dee's torso. "Look here," she said in awed tones. "The storm god has marked him."

Exposing Dee's chest revealed a tree-like pattern with a trunk and multiple branches. Mud and cloth stuck to his lower half, as his groin and legs had been less exposed to the lightning. Yet the lightning brand on his ribs glowed red and raw. Dee's eyes remained shut. Caroline leaned over and put an ear near his mouth.

"Breathing," she announced. "Where is everybody?"

"Gone to bed, remember," said Mary. "Dorothy was positive Dee had died. She left us to deal with the body. I had thought of the old barn…" She stopped as thunder growled, not overhead, but close.

"Storm's circled back," said Anna. "Can't take him out to the Infirmary in this."

"Yeah, thunder can get trapped in this valley," said Caroline.

"So we've no choice," said Mary. "He has to have a bed in the house." As she spoke another blinding flash flooded the hall. "Where's that room? The one that Dorothy gave him?"

"Attic," replied Anna, making a face.

"Drat," said Mary Wandwalker.

After they maneuvered him up the stairs and put him to bed, Dee appeared less deeply unconscious. His eyelids began to flicker at each burst of thunder while his breath made his chest rise and fall.

"The bastard's actually going to make it," muttered Mary. "We'll check on him in the morning."

"I wish we had phone or internet to call someone," said Caroline, smoothing down Dee's bedcovers. Anna's eyes flashed in response.

"All that electricity in the sky and none where we need it," murmured Mary as they left Dee to sleep.

# CHAPTER 17
# THE BOY

*Sunday afternoon.*

Billy Dee remained unconscious into the next day. Mary wracked her brains about how to get medical aid for him. The three detectives brought the problem to the witches over breakfast.

"If he's alive after that lighting strike, we must demand a helicopter to get Dee to hospital. If it is safe to fly, of course," Mary said.

"How can we *demand* anything, Mary?" asked Anna. "With the internet and phones deader than Agnes. Of course, I could wade out to…"

"No," said Mary, quickly.

"No," repeated Dorothy. "No one is risking their life in the flood for a predator like Billy Dee. After all they say we'll have internet in a couple of hours – today certainly."

Anna sniffed. Mary raised her eyebrows.

"I seem to remember Robbin' Robin using a satellite phone?" ventured Caroline, eyeing the last slice of toast. "On the boat…"

"Yes, yes," Mary interjected. "He made a call from the Thames when the storm nearly capsized us. I'll ask him." And she left.

She found the minister in his bedroom. He stirred the remains of scrambled eggs and looked morose.

"No bacon," he groused. "What do you want?"

"Your satellite phone. We have to get Billy Dee to hospital."

"That bastard's still alive? I saw the lightning strike him down. That storm did me a favor."

"He's alive," said Mary icily.

Robbin' Robin swore. "You're out of luck, Miss Wandwalker. I left the phone on the chopper. It's government property so they probably confiscated it for the floods." He grimaced. "That evil runt deserves to die."

"Thank you for sharing your opinion, minister," said Mary in her Archive voice. As she closed the door behind her she caught Robin Prince's parting remark.

"Take my plate down, will you."

It was not a request. Mary refused to hear it. When she rejoined the witches at the kitchen table, no one seemed too anxious about Billy Dee. The only suggestion came from Naomi, who murmured something about a Celtic Telegraph.

"What's that?" said Mary.

"Don't ask," said Anna, darkly.

"Shouting into the curve of the hill," said Caroline, vaguely. "Or a beacon fire and we've no dry fuel."

"Or any way to get through the flood to the hill," added Meredith. She had an irritable curl to her lips that Mary hadn't noticed before.

More practically, John suggested signaling via the drones. Some were expected with a food delivery. Cherry was counting on it. Dorothy threw up her hands. With Dee stable, Holywell had more pressing problems than the fate of the sorcerer, she insisted. "After all, internet and phones will spark into life any moment, won't they?"

At last, in a pause between downpours, Cherry called that there were six drones dangling packages in the Holywell garden. Caroline said they looked like metal birds, perhaps pterodactyls back from extinction. Despite cameras for eyes, they were neither friendly nor talkative, she added. After dropping parcels into muddy water, formerly the lawn, they zoomed away. Before

Dorothy could object, the gels ran outside. They either lugged or dragged the plastic wrapped boxes through the back door and into the kitchen.

"Noooo," shrieked Cherry, smearing cake batter on her apron. "Take these towels and wipe off the mud. Then you gels get to wash my floor."

No chance for messages on these drones, lamented Caroline. Mary retorted that she was more interested in the supplies. All three sobered on finding a prescription package for Dee himself. His special skin cream had made it to Holywell rather late.

"Not that any salve could stop that branding by fire," sighed Caroline. "He's the storm god's now."

"I don't mind putting that cream on his face," said Anna.

"Darling, you should keep away. He's not a good person," murmured Caroline.

"Someone should check on him," sighed Mary. "We'll go with you."

Anna nodded and dashed ahead. By the time Mary and Caroline climbed to the attic, Anna had finished with the skin medication. Dee was hot, sweaty, and clothed, noted Mary with relief. Anna wiped her hands on a towel. The cream soaked into the ridges of burned skin and smoothed flaking patches on his face. Dee did not stir.

"With the spirits," muttered Caroline.

"Nonsense. He has a fever," pronounced Mary, staring down at the grease melting from the unshaven jaw. "The last thing Holywell needs is sickness that might be contagious. Will you stay with him, Anna, while I tell Dorothy?"

Anna nodded. She pushed Caroline after Mary. "I'll keep everyone out," she called after them. "I want a break from silly gels. And I've had enough of the fuss about Irina. Go."

With a swing of her curtain of black hair, not too clean, noted Mary, Anna slammed the attic door behind Mary and Caroline. Both women exchanged glances at the bottom of the attic stairs. Anna had to be bothered about her resemblance to Irina. Mary felt relieved Caroline did not mention it.

They found witches and gels unpacking the boxes with tins and packages. In deference to Cherry's feelings and lack of space in the kitchen, some of the wetter parcels were sorted in the lounge. The drone delivery cheered Cherry no end. She yelled to gels to shift everything to kitchen cupboards now that the floor was clean and dry. Not the pantry. That was saved for a future delivery.

When Dorothy heard about Dee's fever she put her head into her hands.

"I'll keep watch for more drones," volunteered John. "Cherry's expecting flour, sugar and jam, given the schedule before the internet went down. The drone must be equipped with a camera. If I can attract the handler's attention, I might be able to get him to land it so I can attach a note."

They looked around until they saw Mary. "If Dee's potentially infectious, they'll send a boat with medics. He'll need a hospital." They left by the front door. Mary heard splashing.

Twenty-first century pigeon post, thought Mary.

"Anna put the prescription cream on Dee," Caroline explained. "Did any fever medicine come in those boxes? Anything that might help him?" queried Caroline.

"Apart from Janet's herbs, we're down to aspirin," replied Naomi. "Janet's says her best plants are under water. Gels," she said sternly to those carrying boxes through to the kitchen, "no visiting the attic. And keep away from Anna until we know what's wrong with Billy Dee."

"Masks," said Dorothy. "Yes, I know Dee may not have Covid, but there is a new strain in Northern Ireland. You gels get your masks. Then stay upstairs until we tell you otherwise."

To a general groan, the young women trooped up the stairs. Neither Irina not her parents were to be seen. Thank goodness for small mercies, thought Mary Wandwalker.

"No masks, no leaving your rooms," ordered Janet. She stood, maskless and stern, at the foot of the stairs as the muttering from the gels died down.

"Won't be for long," Meredith, the new witch shouted after them. "Only until Billy Dee's in hospital and they tell us how sick he is."

Dorothy appeared out of the kitchen.

"Meredith, you and I will take inventory of Holywell's medical supplies, bandages as well as painkillers," she called. Meredith nodded and vanished into Dorothy's office with Dorothy following.

There came a holler from the top of the stairs.

"I see Baldy, Baldy." Sounded like a gel from an upstairs window. That's right, thought Mary, the gels call John 'baldy.' They probably did not realize the hair loss was due to chemotherapy.

Mary opened front door to see John marching towards her. She stepped back to let the wet witch inside. Had she heard Olga calling them Baldy? Mary wondered.

John stamped her muddy boots on the doormat. They gave a thumbs up to Mary.

"It worked. Got a message out about Billy Dee's fever."

Mary bowed her thanks to John. "What a relief," she said. She made to close the door, when Janet appeared on the porch. The small witch flicked rain off her jacket.

"Coming in?"

"Nah," replied Janet, staring down at her soaked shoes. "Need some air for my head."

She wiped her forehead with a muddy hand. Mary decided not to mention it as Janet continued: "While I'm out here I'll take a look-see for Billy Dee's phone. It disappeared from the kitchen bin, you know." She cackled. "Are you lurking in the shadows, apprentice Caroline?"

Caroline jumped. "Yes," she squeaked, "I mean no." She eased herself from a corner next to the stairs.

Janet could not resist a teaching moment. "Apprentice Caroline, ask Miss Wandwalker what she expects from Dee's phone. She believes in technology far more irrationally than we do *our* invisible world."

With that jibe, Janet ducked back into the rain. John held open the door while they poured out water from their boots. They waved at Caroline. "Find Linda, and the other witches, if you can. I've seen something out there," John said.

"I think Linda's in the kitchen helping Cherry," Caroline said, moving off. This might be the moment to search the food parcels for real coffee, thought Mary.

"Where is everyone?" queried John.

"If you mean witches, not gels," said Caroline. "Probably also in kitchen stacking tins."

"Sorting beverages," muttered Mary hopefully.

"If not in Dorothy's office counting medicines."

"Round 'em up," said John. "We've got a problem. Better meet in the kitchen because of the door to the back garden."

"Did someone say ambulance?" said Meredith, putting her head out of Dorothy's office.

"No. I mean yes, soon." John sighed. The tall witch grabbed a sleeve of an old scarf on a hook and rubbed their smooth rain-soaked head.

"Meredith, bring Dorothy to the kitchen," said Mary. Someone had to take charge. "Whatever's worrying John, we should all hear it."

"I take it we adults won't be masking like we've told the gels to?" said Meredith sadly. Mary recalled she had trained as a nurse.

"There is something about Meredith that doesn't fit the other witches," Mary whispered to Caroline.

"Don't forget she's new," Caroline replied. "I expect she is adjusting. You go to the kitchen, Mary, I want to run upstairs with aspirin for Anna."

Mary nodded. It took a couple of minutes for the witches, plus Mary, to crowd into the kitchen. Three got chairs while everyone else shifted uneasily around the scrubbed kitchen table.

"Two hours or less," said John. "That's what the drone said to me when I described our medical emergency. Boat or a 'copter, whatever's available. Drones got microphones when the Internet went down, I guess."

Expelled breath and "thank goddess" and "that spell works," greeted the news that feverish Billy Dee would soon enjoy the filtered air of the National Health Service. Mary, however, made no noise. She narrowed her eyes at John.

"What was the problem you mentioned?"

Silence greeted Mary's question.

"Not another…" Dorothy scrunched her hands into fists. "John?"

They looked sheepish. "After I let the drone go, I saw a boy. He was knelt by the side of the house. I reckoned he was sheltering from the rain, because the wind blew in the opposite direction. When he saw me he ran off."

A boy? mouthed Mary. Agnes had said *the boy*. Was this the killer?

Another silence. Mary's nose twitched from that sharp odor she knew. Fear. The witches exchanged glances. Linda scratched her head. At that moment Caroline clattered in. She shook her head at Mary.

"Anna's taking a shower," she said to Mary. "I left the aspirin by Dee's bed. What's the news on getting him to hospital?"

Cherry answered. "Tell Anna under two hours. But wait, Caroline. John says she's – sorry – *they* have seen a boy in the Holywell grounds. Couldn't be Dee with him so sick. Any possible chance…?"

"Not that fat bastard Robbin' Robin," said John without malice. All the witches nodded at that characterization of the minister. "Definitely a younger figure."

Dorothy shivered. Cherry rose and switched on the stove for more heat. Naomi gave her a watery smile. Mary glanced at the rain pouring down the windows.

"Robbin' Robin's hardly been out of his room," added Mary.

"I'm telling you, I saw a *boy*." John thumped the table. "We have a boy at Holywell, in the grounds at least."

"Worse, I think he's been in the house," said Naomi. "There's been more running about at night than usual. I thought it was the gels agitated over the storms."

"And the death of Agnes," said Dorothy, quietly.

"The gels, of course," said Linda. "Plotting with Dee, we suspected. More likely they got excited to conceal this boy."

"You know," broke in Caroline. "I may have seen him – with Irina."

"When?" Linda and John spoke as one.

"You didn't tell me," protested Mary.

"Sorry, I forgot," said Caroline. "I thought it had to be Dee. Now I remember it, the young man did look… well, *young*." Caroline smiled apologetically at Mary. "It was before the séance, very early in the morning. I went out to decide what to do about, you know, me being accused."

"Ah, yes, Agnes," said a harsh voice. "So how *did* she die, Caroline?"

The hostility shocked Mary, for the voice was Janet's. It rode the cold breath that came with her from the open back door to the garden. Why the change in the witch who always had Caroline's back?

"I still don't remember." Caroline looked bleak.

Mary touched Caroline's shoulder. "We're not doing this now, Janet. There's a boy somewhere at Holywell. We need to find him."

"The boy. That's what Agnes said in the séance. She said the boy killed her." Naomi articulated what many were thinking.

"Unless the séance was a trick. Dee faked that voice to deflect attention from Caroline."

The witches gasped at Janet who was dripping wet. They swung to Caroline, who clutched Mary's hand.

"No, no, I would never…" Caroline rasped. The breath was knocked out of her.

"Dee and Caroline? Janet, are you nuts?" Mary had rarely felt so angry. "*Caroline* insisted we pursue Dee to protect

Holywell. Caroline's your apprentice for god's sake. What's the matter with you?"

Janet took a step towards Mary. "Someone killed Agnes. We can't forget her."

Mary clenched her fists. "We do not forget Agnes. The voice in the séance said 'the boy' did it, the murder. That clue that does not point to Caroline. Or Sarah, for that matter."

"Janet, are you feeling all right?"

Typical of Caroline to notice Janet's changed appearance despite being attacked by her, thought Mary. Usually the witch had a weather-beaten look from her farming origins. Right now, Janet looked spookily colorless, as if the rain had made her skin translucent. Without warning the old woman put her forearms to her head and bent over.

"Migraine..." she moaned.

Caroline reached her first.

"Get her a chair," ordered Mary.

Dorothy rose. "Migraine means Janet's bipolar disorder is in the depressive phase. Hence the aggression. We need to get her to bed."

"She's fallen into the underworld," muttered Naomi. "I'll help Caroline get her upstairs."

"I... can't... do... this... now," groaned Janet. "The gels. Find the boy." Blindly she put out an arm and Naomi caught it.

"Wait," commanded Mary. "I know where the boy is."

She darted behind Naomi and flung open the walk-in pantry door. Mary dragged out – a boy. "Young men and food," Mary said in triumph. "He ran round the house after you saw him, John. Sneaked in before Janet."

"No need to grip so tight," said the boy. He shook off Mary's hand. "I won't run."

Chairs scraped as the witches shifted to gape at the boy. Below his nervous grin and unshaven chin, he wore a purple sweatshirt and blue jeans a foot too short. I've seen that top on Sarah, Mary thought automatically. Hang on, I've seen *him*.

Mary felt dizzy. Cooped up with storms, séances, and a murderer, days at Holywell felt equivalent to weeks. The shock of finding the young man shrank the kitchen. He smelled of rain, as if he had blown in on the wind, thought Mary. The young man gave her a wan smile. He backed up against the pantry door.

"Um…" he began.

"Wait," commanded Mary. He waited.

Several witches muttered. Linda took out a bunch of herbs from her pocket. John passed a box of matches. A complex set of aromas began to mask the odor from the newcomer.

Mary could not get that ghastly séance out of her head. *The boy*, said murdered Agnes, or some spirit, or some devilish trick. As if on command, now they had a boy, or at least a young man. What now?

Caroline sent a significant glance to Mary. She must have recognized him too. Why not say it? As Mary leant forward to cut short the witchy nonsense, Caroline put a finger to her lips. Mary sighed.

Looking around these women she knew, a little, whose magical beliefs she could not share, Mary made her taut muscles loosen, her teeth unclench. They are like trees, Mary said to herself. Planted at Holywell, they bend in the airs that swoop down from Oxfordshire hills. They make a grove, a place of safety.

Mary glared at the young man. *Don't fidget.* He stood up straight, face rigid. Caroline grinned and patted Janet propped against her shoulder. Linda wafted the burning herbs all over his body from dirty trainers to above his dark head.

"Thank you, Linda," said Dorothy, who had not moved. Janet stumbled, and would have fallen but for the young man moving to steady her. He and Caroline helped Janet to a chair. Janet crumpled to rest her head on her arms. The stranger retreated.

"Who are you?"

Dorothy sounded more like her authoritative self. She exuded outrage.

"My name's Tyr. I'm a friend of Irina," the young man replied.

Nervous, as well he might be, thought Mary.

"I didn't kill the old lady," Tyr directed at Janet. She lifted her head, tried to scowl, then moaned.

"Bed for Janet," said Caroline. She tossed her head at Mary then at the newcomer. "Come on Naomi, Janet can't stay down here."

Naomi dragged her eyes from Tyr. She and Caroline helped Janet to the door.

"Wait for us to come down," said Naomi. "Before you get the full story." As soon as the door closed, Tyr gave it a longing glance.

"You. Are. Not. Going. Anywhere," commanded Mary.

The wait felt excruciating. Mary took the chair vacated by Janet and with her eyes dared Tyr to move. She tapped a fingernail until Dorothy frowned. At last, Caroline burst through the kitchen door, followed more sedately by Naomi.

"Are you a magician?" Linda queried. The witches edged away.

He shook his head, then looked in appeal to Mary.

"Caroline and I have met Tyr before," Mary confirmed to Dorothy's evident relief. "In Greenwich Park before we ended up here at Holywell. He'd been to the ballet rehearsal. Must be how he knows Irina."

Tyr's hands twitched. He offered a sickly smile.

Friend of Irina? Hmn. There's more to it, Mary thought.

Cherry began to mutter. "My pantry…" A hand raised by Dorothy cut her off. Cherry's scorching expression also made the intruder blench.

"You've been listening to us," said Mary. "A *lot* of our conversations."

Tyr bowed. "Sorry."

Mary turned to Dorothy. "When we met Tyr at Greenwich with Irina and the ballet students, he *claimed* to be a folklore researcher studying *Swan Lake*."

"I *am* a folklore researcher," Tyr protested. His Scottish lilt became more pronounced with emotion, Mary noted.

Nine pairs of eyes studied him.

"Talk," rapped Mary.

Tyr gulped. "Look ladies, I'm here tracking William Dee, not working with him. I'm no sorcerer, although I do follow the old gods."

The room relaxed. Linda smiled at him. "We're no ladies, we're witches. Caroline's an apprentice. Well, not Mary here. She's a detective. Tyr," she said thoughtfully. "Would that be the Norse god of justice?"

Tyr nodded. "My Da loved those stories, Celts too."

"Nothing you've said so far justifies creeping about Holywell," said Dorothy, leaning towards the young man. "So why are you *here*?"

Tyr lifted his chin. He took a deep breath.

"I'm truly sorry for the trouble, Miss Chamberlyn. You heard me say I'm tracking the sorcerer, Billy Dee. When he and Irina disappeared from Greenwich. I... guessed they'd be heading for Holywell. I overheard Dee say it was of the utmost importance he got here. So I hitchhiked. By the time I planned to leave... it was too late."

Mary's eyes met Caroline's. Yes, they'd both noticed the hesitation.

"You came the night Agnes died." Mary made it a statement, not a question. Tyr stiffened.

"Yes." His chin went up. "I wanted to check on Irina. I didn't show myself because I thought I could protect her better if Dee didn't know about me."

"You came all this way for Irina? She's a friend? Girlfriend?" John pursed their lips.

Tyr looked shocked. "Girlfriend, no way. Irina's fifteen. I'm twenty-two. I would never date a child."

Mary's lips twitched. Tyr's too young to assert his manhood, she thought. He's not far off a boy. She recalled the words of the séance about "the boy," and frowned.

"Irina is fifteen and Billy Dee is forty-three," whispered Caroline. There was a darkening in the room. Sure enough the rain beat faster.

"Indeed," said Mary. "Everyone wants to stop Dee sexually abusing young girls. But why *you* Tyr? What are you not telling us?"

Thunder rolled overhead. The witches murmured again. Mary folded her arms. Caroline eased toward the biscuit tin. They all knew it held only crumbs.

Finally, Tyr shrugged his shoulders. "You see, I'm on a quest," he blurted out.

The witches groaned.

Something threatened to shatter in Mary's head. Caroline stepped forward.

"Bet you're hungry after all that hiding," she said. "What about a cup of tea?"

Linda laughed wildly. Meredith and Naomi tried to join in.

"Tea and toast," said Dorothy, nodding to Cherry who rose at once. "Not a bad idea while we wait for the medics to remove our fever patient. I can't wait to get Dee out of here. From the lounge we can watch for a helicopter landing on the lawn. If that happens, Mary, you are to keep hold of Robbin' Robin. It'll be for emergency patients only."

Mary sighed.

"Anything is worth getting Dee away from Holywell," Dorothy repeated. "John, you know how to coax our old toaster into life. Linda will help. Bring everything next door."

She studied Tyr. "Then young Tyr, we'll hear about this so-called quest."

\*\*\*\*\*

It took time to unclog the toaster and wait for the stovetop kettle. At last tea and toast got laid out next to the old sofas and battered chairs. Thunder returned several times. This time the lightning looked like roots of fire.

Under Mary's orders, Tyr sat on a stool and kept quiet. Given the looks darted at the stranger, Mary detected frissons of excitement in the witches. Tyr had 'tracked' Dee at the Greenwich ballet school. Whatever his so-called quest, he must know more about the sorcerer. Or, if not, he'd better answer some hard questions, Mary told herself.

Grudgingly, Cherry accepted Mary's offer to ransack the cupboards for enough clean mugs.

"Yeah, we're behind with cleaning and dishes," said Cherry, ever sensitive to anything kitchen related. "Gels dodge chores with any excuse. Now they've two: that sorcerer and the storms."

"We have to be sensitive to their fears around Agnes's death," reproved Dorothy. "As for Billy Dee, the ambulance could come anytime. Perhaps we should talk to Tyr later?" This last point she directed at Mary.

Before Mary could reply, they heard thumping from the stairs.

"Can we come down now?" a young voice yelled. In fact when Mary arrived at the stairs, *all* of the gels were draped on the staircase, with Sarah at the bottom. That young woman tried to smile when Mary arrived with the witches behind her.

"It's so boring in our bedrooms," one pleaded. Mary recalled her face, but not her name.

"Can't we at least go outside. We don't care about the rain," said two more.

"Fresh air," squeaked another. "Storm's not too bad."

At that moment, something white flashed into Mary's left eye from the hall window. A huge crash followed. Water drummed hard enough to shake the front door. Even in Mary's throat the storm pressed down.

"Sorry gels!" shouted Naomi, trying to make herself heard. "No going out. The storm's overhead. You know how dangerous lightning is."

The gels moaned until cut short by Dorothy.

"What do you think you are doing? Back to your rooms!" she ordered. "Do you gels *want* to get Billy Dee's fever? It could be dangerous. Remember Covid."

The gels looked at each other. They shrugged and pouted, yet did not move.

Caroline came to Dorothy's side. "The gels look scared," she said. "They don't want to be alone."

Dorothy turned to her. "That's all very well, Caroline, but they need to be afraid of the storm and illness too," she snapped. Then to the faces on the staircase, "I'm sorry. Our world is topsy turvy right now. We get it. You can…"

"Wait another hour," broke in Mary. "In your rooms. Think of Anna. She's stuck in the attic with Billy Dee until the medics get here." She stood up and caught Dorothy's eye. "What about the boy?"

The gels shuffled backwards.

"What can you mean, Miss Wandwalker?" said one, all innocence.

Mary folded her arms. "There's a boy in the lounge, a young man. You've been hiding him, haven't you? Tyr's hungry, but not that hungry."

Mary's bracing tone had an effect.

"No comment," called the same gel. The others giggled.

"If the ambulance has not removed Mr. Dee within the next hour, we'll find another way," promised Dorothy. With grumbles, the gels retreated to the upper floor.

Dorothy allowed herself to be led into the lounge. Soon the seven witches sat over mugs of tea. Caroline left to check on Anna. Mary squeezed into a corner of the sofa. She directed Tyr to bring his stool to the blue rug next to the coffee table. There he sat, clutching his hairy shins. These stuck out further from the too-short jeans.

To Mary's amusement, Tyr could not help sniffing the loaded table. Besides a giant teapot, cereal bowl of sugar, and half gallon milk carton, there were two plates of buttered toast and three jars less than half full of jam. From their colors Mary guessed strawberry, raspberry and apricot.

Arriving with crockery that the table had no space for, Cherry added: "Tyr, make yourself useful and hand out these plates. Meredith, the blackberry jam you asked for is gone. You can see we're low on the others." She addressed Dorothy. "Jam not until the next food order, whenever that is. The gels won't be pleased."

"Perhaps we should…" began Naomi.

"We're eating the jam," said Mary, without thinking. "Pass the apricot. Tyr, you can dig in."

He did not need telling twice, putting two slices of toast dripping with butter on a plate. For a few minutes nobody spoke above the crunching and discreet sprays of crumbs. Mary noted the dogged piling of jam on the toast by everyone present. Stress eating, she concluded. Me too.

"Any jam left for me?" said Caroline from the door. "Dee's not so flushed, Anna says," she reported. "Gotta be a good sign, don't you think?"

No one replied. When John stuck a finger in the sugar bowl, withdrew and licked it, Mary decided to make a move.

"So young man," she began in her archive voice. "You're on a quest and it concerns Billy Dee. Perhaps Irina too?"

Tyr brushed crumbs from his knees and turned to Mary. She took in the wariness in his blue eyes.

"How far does this quest go, Tyr?"

"Romania," he said automatically. He clenched his hands together so that his knuckles shone. Rain pelted the windows.

"How far in time?" asked Caroline.

"Twenty-two years. To my birth," he replied. "No, that's selfish, it goes back further." He cleared his throat. "William Dee is a child stealer. He belonged to a gang operating across Europe."

Tension erupted, and dissipated as the witches nodded to each other, put down empty mugs by their feet and prepared to listen. As therapists of trafficked women, they knew of such gangs. Caroline grasped Mary's arm.

"Billy Dee child stealing," she said. Then she gave a cry. "Oh, Tyr, does that mean you… erm…"

"Yes," Tyr reached over to the not quite empty plate by Mary's feet. She nodded. He took the crust she'd rejected and swallowed it. "Yes, Mrs. Jones, to what you're thinking. That's my connection to Dee. I'm one of the stolen kids. I got lucky in being adopted by a great couple in Glasgow." He took a deep breath. "My mother, my adopted mother, is Professor Ceridwen Campbell, goes by Cece. She's at Pemberton College, Oxford." He turned to the youngest and newest witch. "Miss Meredith here knows her."

Meredith gave Tyr a brusque nod. She had been rather silent ever since Tyr revealed himself, Mary thought.

"So the quest?" persisted John.

"To find where I came from. To get a bigger story because…" He broke off, swigged the last of his tea, then licked his lips.

"Something happened," guessed Mary. "Something that changed your life."

Tyr tried to smile and failed. "Correct, Miss Wandwalker. You see, three months ago at the start of the long vac at Oxford, Da, my adoptive father…" Tyr studied the blue rug between his hairy ankles. The words poured out.

"He died. My Da died. He worked as a fisherman, had his own trawler. His death came in one of those violent storms we're getting in the climate crisis. We live – lived – on the coast while Ma commuted to Glasgow University for her ancient Europe teaching. Right after Da's funeral she got a job offer, Professor of Celtic Studies at Oxford. They wanted her right away. Something about the previous holder, a Professor Morrigan, leaving under a cloud."

Mary's eyes met Caroline's. Yes, they knew about the disastrous end of Barinthus Morrigan's tenure of the Chair of Celtic Studies. So disgraced was he that his college, Exmoor, wanted nothing more to do with the position. They handed it to Pemberton.

"Your father died at sea," Caroline reminded Tyr, gently. "That brought you to Oxford too?"

"And the quest," added Mary.

Tyr nodded. "Ma, Cece, needed support. She and Da... really loved each other, you know. He always said that it didn't matter that his world was winds on the waves while she lived in the rarefied air of higher learning." His eyes ranged around the listeners.

Naomi pulled open the coffee table drawer, removed a saucer with a candle stub and lit it. A bittersweet fragrance rose from the white stalk.

"Rue for remembrance," whispered Mary, recalling Shakespeare.

"Ophelia," murmured Tyr. "Thank you, Miss Wandwalker, Miss Naomi."

He knows us, thought Mary, touched. He's paid attention while hiding out. Tyr picked up the threads of his story. "Yeah, the quest. Well, even though Oxford let me transfer my doctorate to Pemberton, on folklore of Celtic origin, I couldn't settle."

He screwed up his eyes, looking a lot younger. "Da... We were close. He named me after the Norse god of justice. Da came from generations of fishermen. They told stories that went back to the Celts, he said. Da read all the old mythologies to me – our favorite bedtime stories."

Tyr paused for breath. No one moved. "Ma said it was his enthusiasm that got her to study European indigenous cultures. When the invitation for the Chair at Oxford arrived, Ma found out it was Da who sent her publications to the Fellows. He'd done it to surprise her."

Mary looked at Tyr. That news must have driven home the loss. She saw the bones beneath his face, how he was haunted.

"Ma heard she'd got the job the day after Da's funeral," Tyr whispered, looking directly at Mary. The witches shuffled,

Naomi wafted candle smoke towards Tyr. Sympathy as only they knew how, Mary thought.

"You could not settle," encouraged Linda.

"That's right. It was too much, too quick. Da wants something from me, I know it. Only I don't know what, exactly. How can I help his spirit rest?"

Tyr shaded his eyes. He sniffed. Caroline moved closer and took his hand. Tyr swallowed, then removed his hand with a mutter of thanks.

"I knew early on about being adopted. My parents did not believe in secrets. I assumed it was the usual thing. When I told Ma how I felt Da pushing me towards something, she let loose a bombshell. She told me how I'd come to them, how strongly Da felt about it." He stopped.

"Get on with it," snapped John.

"John, please," reproved Dorothy. "We can see how difficult this is for Tyr."

"I can spit it out. Twenty-two years ago the police raided a house in Glasgow to find a Romanian gang with a dozen stolen children. They sold babies as well as kids up to eight and nine. A big scandal at the time. Interpol got involved, did DNA to locate families. I was the only child with no relatives, or none they could locate. First Da and Ma fostered me, then it became a *legal* adoption."

Mary's lips flickered every time Tyr said 'adoption.' Tyr shot her a glance. It occurred to her that he had placed an emphasis on 'legal.'

"Can I get you some water, Tyr?" asked Caroline.

# CHAPTER 18

# A SECOND MURDER?

*Sunday late afternoon.*

Tyr shook his head at Caroline's offer of water.

"You see, when Ma told me the story of my adoption I saw it as folktale about a lost child. Only I'm living it." He gave a crooked smile. "Everyone says it's hopeless, yet I have to search for my birth family. It makes no sense, but I'm doing it for Da. He wanted things to be made right."

Encouraging murmurs came from the witches. Mary put on her thoughtful face.

"Doesn't explain why you're *here*," insisted Cherry. "Why Holywell?"

Arms on her hips like a wrestler, thought Mary. "He's here because Billy Dee is not *a* child stealer but *the* child stealer," she said. Heads switched from Tyr to Mary.

She'd nearly mentioned Irina and her questionable adoption. Sometimes intuition comes as a thunderbolt. Hadn't Billy Dee almost admitted it when he said he specialized in lost children?

Caroline gasped. Tyr turned to her. "Yes, Dee is at the heart of it. Crime exploded across Eastern Europe after the fall of communism. The authorities eventually got a grip, but there's a downside to free movement in the EU."

Mary stiffened. Tyr shot Mary a rueful grin. "Yeah, who doesn't hate Brexit." It was rhetorical. The witches nodded. "Hell, Britain leaving the EU makes it harder to stop cross-border kidnapping and illegal adoptions. Jurisdictions can't cooperate like they used to."

"Take our Billy Dee, original name unknown." Tyr paused and swallowed. "Decades ago he did magic tricks in a traveling fair that toured Romania. Who knew that the fair provided a cover for collecting babies, mostly by theft? They passed them along to be sold across Europe. One of those was me."

A pained silence. Caroline patted his arm. Rain coursed down the French windows.

"Making more tea," said Cherry, smoothing her apron.

"Wait a minute," ordered Mary. "What did you mean, '*mostly* by theft?' Tyr."

He shuffled uncomfortably. "You know how communist Romania made it hard for women."

"Remind us."

"I remember," said Naomi, the oldest present, with Janet sick. "So many unwanted babies. Those terrible orphanages. I knew therapists who volunteered to go to Romania in the early nineties."

"That's right," said Mary slowly. "No real birth control, and women ordered to have at least six children. Hang on, Tyr, are you saying that people still have children they can't afford?"

"It must have been stopped," protested Meredith. "The pressure to have too many children, I mean."

"Oh sure," said Tyr. "But when people are poor…"

"They sell their children?" asked Caroline, eyes wide. "I can't believe it."

"Rare, but it happens," confirmed Tyr. "I've not been able to find my birth parents yet, despite assistance from the Romanian authorities. They are keen to stamp out the gangs. Billy Dee is my only real lead to the group that ended up in Glasgow twenty-two years ago."

He sighed. "I got a break when Ma persuaded the police to show me the case file. One of the traffickers from back then had a flyer from that travelling fair. Billy Dee used it to a scrawl a note, and signed his name. He would rejoin the gang in Romania."

"They arrested him?" Mary leaned forward.

"Couldn't locate him," said Tyr. "Remember, this was two decades ago. Dee would be in his twenties, not yet a ballet choreographer. He was just some guy in Europe. All the Romanian authorities did was open a file under his name."

"You are not telling us everything you found out about Dee," said Mary. A shot in the dark, yet a tightness in his jaw alerted her. Tyr paused. He did not quite meet Mary's eyes.

"Is it too painful?" Caroline enquired.

"Shouldn't be," Tyr said, gruffly. "Oh well, I did meet one guy who'd come out of prison and knew Dee in the old days. He said that he… Dee, that is, seduced a thirteen-year-old, ran away with her. She died in childbirth." He stopped. "Dee sold the baby."

A gasp rocked the room. Tyr continued quickly. "Yeah, I thought that baby could have been me. That Billy Dee was my birth father. Turned out the math didn't work. I'm quite a bit older. Big, big relief. I don't know what I would have done. For a while I wanted to kill him."

"This man you were tracking as Billy Dee. You're sure it's the same person?" queried Dorothy.

"The day I got to Greenwich and the Morgan Ballet School, I asked for the great man's autograph. Definitely matches the scribble on the circus flyer."

Mary raised her eyebrows. Tyr gave a tired smile. "My Da's best friend is a Glasgow cop, retired now. He worked the case where they found me. In fact he met Da and Ma over the adoption. This guy persuaded cops in Romania to spill on a man like Billy Dee."

Tyr put his shoulders back. He looked from Mary to Dorothy.

"I have to know where I came from, don't you see?"

Both found themselves nodding.

"And?" Mary challenged. "We, Caroline, Anna, and I met you in Greenwich, remember? You offered to take Irina back to the Observatory after she stamped on that white dress. There's more to you and Dee than what happened twenty years ago."

"Mary," reproved Caroline. "Don't interrogate the boy. You of all people know how important birth parents are."

Mary's elbow slipped where she had been resting it. Lukewarm tea slopped onto her forearm, staining her grey sweater. Meredith passed her a tea towel.

"Sorry, Mary," squeaked Caroline. To Tyr she said, "Mary gave up..."

"Enough, Caroline," said Mary, her voice taut.

Lightning flashed on the window. We resemble a gathering of ghosts, Mary thought.

Tyr gulped. "Sorry," he muttered.

"Hardly your fault," said Mary tartly. "You were about to tell us *exactly* why you followed Billy Dee here." She banged the table. Everyone jumped. Mary spoke more quietly. "You spent time at the ballet school. This isn't only about you, is it, Tyr?" said Mary.

"No," said Tyr. He swallowed and looked down. Then he sighed and said, "It's also about Irina. About her so-called adoption."

Mary held up her hand. A scratching came from the door. Caroline made it in six strides. A tug at the door, and a woman tumbled in. Helen Morgan had been listening at the keyhole. We'd got to the part that Irina's mother would find very interesting, Mary thought.

"Ms. Morgan, how is Irina?" asked Mary, innocently.

Helen Morgan's flush deepened. "Still not talking to her *parents*," she flung back at Mary.

Everyone stood up. The witches concentrated on Mary. So I'm to take charge, she thought.

Helen Morgan tried a nonchalant toss of her now less than perfect blonde locks. "Um, Robbin' Robin asked about tea and biscuits," she said. "Personally, I'd let him starve because..."

Before she could explain herself they heard a thumping, followed by voices, then a tramp up the stairs.

"That's what I *really* came to tell you."

Helen Morgan lied with defiance. Mary rather admired it. "Good thing someone left the front door unlocked," said Irina's mother, "because the medics have come for Billy Dee."

Helen Morgan turned on her heel. The door banged behind her. They could hear the stairs creak.

"Can't remember when I last saw Irina," murmured Caroline. "Is she speaking yet?"

Naomi would have answered but for more stair thumps, slower, heavier, and this time descending. More shuffling and clicking indicated persons unfamiliar with Holywell.

"In here," called Dorothy.

Everyone tensed. Mary held her breath, and sought the comfort of Caroline's concerned expression. The door opened slowly. Pausing on the threshold were two figures in brown coveralls, shiny hoods and black face masks. Both had mud stains to their knees. Puzzlement radiated from them, thought Mary, as if not recognizing that the beings staring at back at them were human.

Ah, they were told Holywell means witches, thought Mary. Did they expect broomsticks? Whereas these men look like aliens. No, she realized, the rounder one could be a woman. This was confirmed when she spoke first.

"My crew are preparing to move the body now," she said, muffled from the mask. "Stay in this room while we get the stretcher down those narrow stairs. The police know about the death. We've a radio for emergencies, although they say phone and internet will be back soon."

For a few seconds, the witches and Mary and Caroline sat frozen.

"Anna!" shrieked Caroline, rising to her feet.

"No," said the woman. She glanced at her companion. "Definitely the body of a man. Weird smell about him. Probably that grease on his face. Didn't you say his name was William Dee?"

The other mask nodded. Mary caught sight of a salt and pepper beard brushing against the inside of the coverall. Hang on, what had the woman said?

"Billy Dee is dead?" she queried.

"Suffocated, we think," continued the woman. "Looks like murder. Police will know more after an autopsy. We're taking the pillow from the floor by the bed for testing. The stains could be blood and saliva."

"Dee has, had a fever," said Dorothy, faintly. "Surely that's what killed him?"

"Bacteria and viruses breed like crazy in these floods," said the woman brightly. "A confirmed diagnosis will have to wait for the autopsy. Now," she stuck out her arms as if pushing back a crowd. "Stay exactly where you are. Give us a half hour and we'll do our preliminary detox of the room. There'll be a seal on the door. No messing with it until you get the all-clear from the authorities."

She paused as if she had only now realized the impact of what she had said. "We know you've got the Minister for Northern Ireland here. Before the phones went out he was a right pain. Phoned headquarters night and day. Make sure he stays isolated, in case of contagion."

"What about his ex-wife and troubled daughter? Don't they count?" Caroline protested.

"Who?" The woman spread her hands.

Her companion cleared his throat loudly. Witches frowned and whispered. The woman medic raised her voice. "Wait for the police. Normally they'd be on their way." She swiveled to the man and back. "Unfortunately, the police can't get here until after the storm emergency. They are too busy rescuing people from rooftops."

"Or organizing drones to deliver supplies," said the man.

Mary rose to her feet. "The police *will* be in touch." She channeled the Mary Wandwalker who managed a Government Archive and quelled arrogant politicians.

"Oh, sure. In a matter of hours, the phones will be back."

"No," said Mary. "Leave us your radio. If Billy Dee is dead then we must talk to the police right away."

"No can do," said the woman with disgusting cheer. "Protocol, you know."

The witches clustered around Mary. Caroline scrambled to join them. Only Tyr backed away, darting a glance towards the glass doors to the garden. Thunder, quieter this time, joined the chorus.

The woman in coveralls took a step back, knocking into her colleague. "We can't give you the radio because it's built into the boat," she said hastily. "I'll tell my police contact to send you a mobile unit. Don't know why they didn't before. Except no one knows who's in charge at the hospital."

With semi-comic timing the two aliens bumped into each other in the doorway. Anxious to leave, thought Mary. Lucky you, whoever you are.

"Wait. Don't go yet," she called. Something struck her as not quite right in what the woman said. "What did you say about confusion at the hospital? My... ex-boss, Mr. Jeffreys, is based at the John Whitcliffe for the emergency. What's going on?"

The two aliens paused. Then they came back into the room.

"Has anyone else become sick?" asked Caroline.

No one sat back down. With the two figures not moving, Mary could see their masks heating up.

"Goddess, more people are sick," exclaimed Naomi, clutching a silver charm on a chain around her neck. For a second Mary recalled Anna's vicious belt of angry magic. She tried to dismiss it. The witches shivered as if they were one being.

At last the woman spoke. "A mystery fever has disrupted the hospital," she said. "Could be the same virus as your Mr. Dee. No one really knows."

"*A mystery fever?* So that's why you're all dressed up. Why didn't you say so before?" Mary restrained her tone. Before she could continue, the man shuffled his feet.

"Your Mr. Jeffreys is in intensive care," he directed at Mary.

The light was too bright. Mary sat. Caroline put her arm around Mary's waist.

"Breathe, Mary," she ordered. "Breathe... slowly. Now another one."

"How... is... he?" Mary could barely get the words out.

"We don't know," said the chirpy woman. Mary wanted to kick her. Instead she accepted water from John.

"With thirty-two cases in the hospital, and seven in intensive care, the system is a bit... busy," said the man. He sounded concerned.

"Overwhelmed," said the woman.

Dorothy stepped towards the two medics.

"You will make sure that Mr. Jeffreys, our friend..." She paused. "Our beloved friend gets this message *right away,*" she insisted. "Tell him that Mary Wandwalker and all at Holywell will pray to our goddess for his recovery."

The medics turned towards each other.

Mary had had enough. "Send that message from your damned radio. It will make him laugh. If you forget I'll, I'll..."

They backed to the doorway and again knocked together before exiting.

"Keep out of the attic," yelled the woman, now out of sight. "The police want to examine it for clues."

The two bearers of bad news banged the front door behind them. They'd be back for the body, Mary realized. In the lounge, Mary's mind churned. She saw a hospital ward with extra beds, netted with tubes, ventilators. Mr. Jeffreys lay surrounded by masked figures. She could hear monitors beeping. What if the beeping stopped?

"He'll be all right," said Caroline, moving her arm from Mary's waist to pat her shoulder. "You know Mr. Jeffreys. You worked together for forty years. He's indestructible."

"He has family?" enquired Linda.

"A son in the Kenyan Civil Service, like Mr. Jeffreys's parents," croaked Mary. "It's too far away. Someone should be with him. It should be me. Damn this weather."

Caroline squeezed her arm while the witches hummed some words Mary did not know. She bowed her head. Her entire body felt sore, as if she'd run a marathon. She had to keep telling herself to breathe. Then she started to shiver.

"She's in shock," announced Meredith, the former nurse. "We should get her to bed,"

"No, no," Mary rasped. "Shock or not, I'm not going anywhere." She swallowed. "I am cold, though," she conceded. "I wish it would stop raining."

A wrap arrived from two pairs of hands. Mary smelled the herbs that John and Linda used. The wrap's pattern seemed familiar. That's right, it had covered a worn chair that the gels kept jumping on.

"I'll get some of Janet's special tea," said Cherry. "I know where she hides it from the gels."

"No," said Mary again. She had memories of Janet's special tea. "Not for me." She struggled in the seat.

"Don't get up. Rest," said Caroline, "while I find Anna." Light flickered outside. After a few seconds thunder roared.

"Go away, storm," whispered Mary. "And I won't have that tea. Put it in a packet. And Janet's other medicines. Leave it for a drone to take to the John Whitcliffe Hospital. It might help Mr. Jeffreys and the other patients." Mary began to wave her arms. She struggled to speak. No one moved.

"Do your thing," she said, looking first at Dorothy and then at the other witches. "Your spells and rituals. Burn leaves, invoke your spirits. Do whatever helps the sick. I know you do magic at a distance. Caroline even tried to tell me you can fly…" Mary sniffed, then brushed something off her cheek.

"Mary," said Caroline wonderingly. "You believe in witchcraft? After all your skepticism?" The witches exchanged raised eyebrows.

"I'm saying I'm prepared to try anything, *anything,* in perilous circumstances." She sat up straighter. "Don't forget the placebo effect is very powerful."

Caroline's groan mingled with thunder. She topped it with a smile for Mary.

"We have plenty of medicinal tea," said Cherry, getting to her feet. "Don't worry, Mary," she directed at the woman wrapped up on the sofa. "Janet's been making extra for Agnes. We can send a batch to the hospital."

With that the gruff woman departed for the kitchen. Mary shut her eyes briefly, then opened them to find Dorothy frowning at her.

"Well Mary," said Dorothy. "A second killing can't be ignored."

"There's only one suspect," said Meredith quickly. "One person stayed up with Billy Dee. It has to have been…"

"Nooooo," yelled Caroline, jumping to her feet. "Anna didn't do it. She doesn't kill people. Not anymore."

Ah, Caroline's devastating honesty, sighed Mary.

John signaled to Meredith to keep quiet. "No need to start accusing. We're stuck with a second murder."

"Where *is* Anna?" queried Naomi in a calm voice that Mary did not quite believe in. "She was supposed to guard Dee."

"Who knew he'd be the one in danger?"

Meredith again. Mary found her annoying.

Caroline rose. Mary shot out an arm.

"Stay," she ordered. "We're to keep out of the way while they take the body. Anna will be okay."

Caroline allowed herself to be pulled back to the sofa. She sat up when bumping sounds came from outside the room. Finally Billy Dee is leaving Holywell, thought Mary.

"Should we pray?" whispered Linda. Dorothy stared for a moment. Then she nodded.

The witches began tossing words foreign to Mary. Caroline screwed up her face as if she understood some of them.

"Anna," she said in an undertone to Mary. "If there's a killer about I have to know she's safe."

More likely she's suspect number one, thought Mary.

"Is Anna the dark lady who resembles Irina?"

They'd forgotten Tyr, who had scooted to the back of the lounge when the medics arrived. Sitting on the floor, he'd been hidden from sightlines. Mary recalled Helen Morgan shooting him a venomous glance.

"Anna has nothing to do with Irina," said Caroline.

"Won't work, Caroline," said Mary. "With all that Tyr's been telling us of Billy Dee and stolen children, Anna is definitely in this story."

Caroline was about to protest when Anna sauntered in, superb in black jeans and a scarlet fitted jacket. She had crafted from Holywell thrift clothes a vision of elegance, thought Mary with grudging admiration. From her shining waterfall of jet black hair wafted a scent of lemon shampoo.

"What's the matter?" Anna said. "You look like one of us has died, instead of that child-molesting sorcerer. Billy Dee is gone. Look what I found by his bed." Anna held out a long black feather, curved like a blade.

Caroline screamed.

Her shock paralyzed the room. It was replaced by her ghost, or what looked like the ghost of the woman Mary knew. That skull on top of Caroline's body was not Caroline.

For a split second Mary thought that Anna had actually flown the short distance to Caroline. For in the blink of an eye, Caroline was huddled on the sofa with Anna wrapped around her. It took more seconds for Mary to register that the witches had backed away from the reunited couple. Despite the storm, Meredith even opened one of the French windows.

"Six feet," said Dorothy in her tired voice. "The least we can do is stay six feet from Anna, since she might have Dee's fever. And now Caroline too," she added.

Mary found herself in the center of the room, wavering. "Make that three of us if you really are that strict, Dorothy," she said resignedly, taking the position beside Caroline. "Though how we investigate another murder while dodging each other to avoid contagion..."

"What?" Anna's head swiveled around the room as if she could pierce each brain in turn. "Another murder? You don't mean Billy Dee? I thought the fever killed him."

"You don't know?" Meredith stood behind her chair. "Anna, you were the only one who had access to him. You and he were locked away in the attic."

Anna's glare was pure poison. "I don't kill helpless people," she growled. Mary coughed.

"You mean like Agnes?" Unlike Meredith, John's tone was conversational.

Caroline moaned and pulled herself away from Anna's embrace. She put out a hand and found Mary's. "Look what Anna brought from Billy Dee." She unclenched Anna's fingers, and the long black feather fluttered to the floor. The witches edged closer.

"Is that a swan feather?" Mary picked it up. After holding it up to show the witches, she put it in an empty mug on the coffee table.

"I've got another one."

All heads turned to Caroline. Linda took a step towards her, but Dorothy waved her back. Slowly Caroline slid her right hand into her jeans pocket. When she put the black feather into the mug, the two appeared identical.

"Dyed black feathers," Mary concluded. "Could be from Irina's black swan costume. Did she wear it when she arrived? She danced in it at Greenwich."

"Irina carried a black ballet costume," remarked Naomi. "She dropped it in the hall when she arrived. Sorry Dorothy, I need a chair. My back aches." She flung herself into an armchair, then used her feet to push it further from the sofa that held Anna, Caroline and Mary.

Mary returned to the black feathers. "That's right, Irina must have taken off the black swan costume in the limo. She wore practice gear when she got here," said Mary. "She put on the whole costume when she tried to fly."

"Me too," said Caroline miserably.

Mary's jaw dropped. "Flew?"

"I flew," said Caroline stoutly. She did not look at Mary. "Yes, you can all stare at me." She sniffed. "Anna's feather brought it all back. I flew into Agnes's room the night she died. I woke up in the morning with the feather. I put it in my jeans pocket. Then with everything about Agnes, Sarah, and the séance, I forgot."

No one spoke.

"I flew."

"I think we've got that," said Mary. "Now I feel like a lawyer. Stop talking, Caroline. You've implicated yourself in the death of Agnes. Anna would appear to be chief suspect in the murder of Billy Dee." She gulped. "*Not* the Depth Enquiry Agency's finest hour."

Mary liked irony. Sometimes it was all she had.

"Fortunately," she continued. "This flying is nonsense. You dreamed it."

Anna raised her eyebrows and gestured, to the amusement of Naomi, and thoughtful expression of Dorothy.

"Of course we fly," said Linda in a matter-of-fact way. "Haven't you heard of witches on brooms?"

"Linda, don't tease Mary," reproved Dorothy. "Of course we *fly*, but I didn't think Janet wanted you to do the training yet, Caroline?"

Caroline gave a watery smile. "I looked at the books in your library. Didn't try it for myself. I say" –her face lit up– "could we fly Mary to visit with Mr. Jeffreys in hospital?"

"What's wrong with that old bastard?" said Anna.

Anna had never been a big fan. At Mary's request, Mr. Jeffreys had gone to considerable trouble to keep Anna out of prison. This, Anna never acknowledged.

"Virus outbreak at the hospital," Mary said in reply. "Mr. Jeffreys is in intensive care."

"Not only him," Caroline broke in. "The John Whitcliffe must be in lockdown. Too many new cases."

Mary flushed. "As for flying me to see Mr. Jeffreys, that's absurd. As if I would take drugs, or whatever *witch flying* means…" Mary choked.

"You're on the right lines," said Naomi gently. "I study astral flying. We do use potent herbs. Yet flying is more what you would call advanced meditation, along with spells. Which reminds me." She rose. "I want to check on Janet. Then I'll attach a sealing spell on the attic door, if that is okay with you, Dorothy."

Dorothy nodded. "We have to get back to the gels and our guests from London. Anna, Caroline, and Mary, please go to your room, at *least* for the rest of today. We'll send up food. By tomorrow the autopsy should tell us about Dee's mystery illness."

"And his murder? You do realize that Anna is innocent?" said Mary.

"And Caroline didn't kill Agnes," said Anna. She fingered the slender ridge on her hip which Mary knew came from her knife.

"I have said this before," said Dorothy, with cold dignity. "You, Mary Wandwalker, are charged with solving these murders. Investigating crimes is neither therapy nor witchcraft. We witches have enough to do."

"Dorothy, wait," said Mary. Irritation leaked into her voice. "You are asking us to investigate murders that took place in locked rooms. While we are confined to our bedroom. It makes no sense. Are you going to bolt us in?"

Dorothy shook her head. "Actually I am directing *you*, Mary, to find our killer. Caroline remains a suspect for the murder of Agnes, and Anna, for Billy Dee. Your Depth Enquiry Agency is hardly viable."

Anna folded her arms. "Nobody at Holywell believes Caroline could commit murder."

"Nor Anna," muttered Caroline. The witches coughed. A ghost of a smile scampered over Anna's features. Dorothy's raised eyebrows looked positively painful.

"All right, Dorothy," Mary continued, "I suppose you want our assurance that none of us three will fly from our room. That we won't," she paused, "literally open the window and flap our arms into the nearest tree. Ridiculous."

Mary realized what she had said. She wheeled to Anna.

"I only fly in cyberspace," said Anna. Caroline kissed her on the cheek.

"Thank god for small mercies," said Mary Wandwalker.

# CHAPTER 19
# MARY IS NOT SENSIBLE

*Sunday evening.*

They huddled in the hallway, three banished women in a house of death. Voices rose and fell from the lounge. Creaks sounded from the floor above. Pipes groaned as someone flushed a toilet. Beneath these were tiny fingertips of rain on window glass and roof.

"Before we get stuck in our room, let's go outside," said Mary. "The rain's not too bad, so we must be between storms. We'll use the coats on those hooks by the back door."

They traipsed through the warm deserted kitchen.

"You are not a sensible woman, Mary Wandwalker," said Anna, as she sorted through umbrellas dripping in a bucket. "The witches won't like it if we don't go straight upstairs."

Caroline moved awkwardly. She pulled on the largest raincoat as if in a trance. Fortunately there were plenty of discarded rubber boots. The gels had left them in a heap.

"Caroline needs air," said Mary, fumbling with bolts sorely in need of oil. "And I need…" I don't know, she thought, but you could call it my own kind of magic.

Gingerly, they stepped outside. Water ran down hoods onto noses and chins. It dropped into puddles that made up most of the lawn. Yet the sky remained quiet. The three looked back at Holywell manor house. At first nothing. Upstairs a lamp blinked on then off. Gels released from avoiding Dee's fever, Mary guessed. The lounge lit up. Young women draped themselves over sofas with witches talking earnestly to them.

"The gels look more cheerful," Mary remarked.

"Who's that on the third floor?"

Mary and Anna turned to decipher Caroline's expression. She looked bleak.

"Are you feeling better?" said Mary.

Anna's forehead creased. "The third floor... Oh, one of those rooms is Irina's, the other two her parents," said Anna. "I wonder..." She took a step forward.

"The black swan," whispered Caroline. "One feather for each murder. I brought them with me." Taking the feathers from her jeans pocket, she held them out to Mary. In the rain they bled black drops.

"Let me find a tissue," said Mary.

She found a damp wad in the coat she had grabbed at random. Wrapping the feathers, she slipped them into the pocket of her skirt. "Dyed, of course," she said. "This case, or cases, is all about disguises, concealment."

"You don't understand," said Caroline. "I remember flying over the garden. I could feel the air blow back my nightdress. Then I landed in Agnes's room. I saw the shadow of her beaky nose on the pillow." She shuddered. "A black feather by Agnes's bed, that is the last thing I recall. I woke up and couldn't breathe for that feather in my mouth." Caroline gulped. "Goddess, I'm going to throw up."

"Not now," said Mary. "Anna, take her..." But Anna already had Caroline on the bench, her head between knees while she retched.

We were right to come outside, thought Mary, feeling her stomach heave in sympathy with Caroline.

After a couple of minutes Caroline declared the end of her stomach trouble. She clung to Anna's arm, then raised her head to Mary.

"Swans, flying girls, abuse, stolen children," said Caroline sadly. "Tyr told us such things... too terrible. Irina tried to fly, remember?"

Anna took a step towards the house, then paused, hesitating.

"No," said Mary.

Anna scowled. Her fists were tight balls dripping with rain.

"No, and no," said Mary again. "You know what I'm saying, both of you. No attempt to shake the truth out of Irina, scream at Robbin' Robin or grill Helen Morgan. Yes, I don't fully trust Tyr either. Even so, we can't bother our suspects while we might be contagious. No histrionics, hysterics or knives to the throat."

Anna's hands fell to her sides. Her eyes blazed.

"Mary's right," said Caroline. "There's nothing we can do."

"Don't be stupid, Caroline," snapped Mary. She winced at Caroline's expression. "Sorry, I didn't mean that. But there's always something we can do. Look at us."

She faced the other two, and placed her feet apart, feeling the earth despite the pools around her boots. Throwing back her hood, she seized tufts of her own grey hair and shook them until the rain formed spikes.

"The storm is trying to tell me something," Mary shouted. As if in response, a cloud mumbled. Mary laughed, put her head back, opened her mouth, and drank from the sky.

"She's not well," called Caroline. "Anna, do something."

Anna sidled towards Mary. Glimpsing her ready to pounce, Mary put back her hood over her sodden hair. With a grin she raised both hands in surrender. Anna relaxed. Mary turned her palms up, cupping them to collect water.

"Thunder coming. We should go in." Caroline tugged at Mary's arm.

"Don't," said Mary. "I want to drink the rain, to feel the storm inside and out." She glanced at Caroline's shocked expression and then put her hands down. "Listen to me." Her tone deepened. "We've been looking at the murder all wrong. Now look at us. No, stand still and *look at us*."

Anna shook herself like a wet dog. Caroline shivered.

Moving closer, Mary touched their wrists. "We're a triangle, one of the strongest shapes in the cosmos. Right now, we're an island on an island. Together, *together,* we can do anything."

Caroline and Anna exchanged glances.

"Can we go inside? I'm getting cold."

"No, there's something, some clue in these storms."

"You'll get a storm in your head and lightning will strike you. Remember what happened to Billy Dee."

"*A storm in the head,* that's it." Mary hopped from foot to foot. She laughed. "I know what the storm is telling me, us. I've got it. *Agnes.*"

"Oh please, Mary, I can't bear any more…"

"No, not who killed her. Who she is, was. Where did she come from? Anna, you said it." Mary clutched the young woman's shoulder, and was shaken off.

"*Agnes*, the key has got to be Agnes. She mentioned a country, Romania. Anna, you can do one of those big cloud searches, can't you? Because she pointed at you when she said 'Romania.'"

Anna stood very still, rain pouring off her chin. Her lips twisted in what Mary judged a grim smile. She waited.

"I'll do it. You're right."

"Ha." Mary stamped both feet. It splashed water into her boots. She didn't care. Energy coursed through her.

"Caroline didn't attack Agnes… Stop squeezing my arm so hard." Mary shook off Caroline's fingers. "And we believe Sarah didn't, so who Agnes was *here at Holywell* is not the answer. *It's who she was before.* I should have seen it earlier."

"They tried to find her family – the witches, I mean," said Caroline. "There isn't anything online about Agnes. She must have been nearly eighty. Her early days were pre-internet."

"Ah," said Mary, "I have an idea about that. We never tried the National Archives for Agnes, did we. If her saying 'Romania' is a real clue, there are certain files, security databases. Once we're back online Mr. Jeffreys can… oh." She paused. "He's in hospital. Too sick to get us the passcodes or permissions."

"Firewalls. I can go through them and not get burned."
Anna smiled at her pun.

Mary sighed. "All right, but be careful. Go back in, both of you." She waved an arm. "See that flash beyond the hills. Lightning coming. I'm staying out for a minute."

"Mary wants to howl at the moon," scoffed Anna. "Only it's 4:15 p.m. Hours until sunset, and, anyway, there's no moon tonight."

"How do you know that?" said Mary.

"Checked my phone while you were drinking the sky. New moon. So even if the rain clears it'll be darker than usual. We could sneak out. I've plotted a route through the floods that we could wade, probably. If you wanted to get to Mr. Jeffreys."

Mary opened her mouth. No sound emerged. "That would be..." She flushed and turned towards the submerged road to Oxford. *Oh how I'd like to get out of here*, flashed silently between the three of them.

"Too dangerous for Caroline, but I'd go." Anna looked hopeful.

"You're not leaving me," cried Caroline.

Mary forced a smile. "Too risky with these electric storms. Remember Billy Dee. It's bad enough the John Whitcliffe is swamped."

"Wait, wait," said Caroline, jumping up and down. "You want news of Mr. Jeffreys. So do I. Anna said she checked on her phone, went *online* for the moon."

For a moment neither Mary nor Anna understood.

"Oh, the internet's back," breathed Mary. "Phones too. Thank all the gods. I can call the hospital. We can research Agnes properly. *Her past is the key to the murders*, I know it."

Anna ran for the house. Caroline grabbed Mary's hand. "Mary, never believe you have no magic," she whispered, then trotted after Anna.

# CHAPTER 20
# THREE DETECTIVES AND JANET

*Sunday late evening.*

Dinner arrived with giggles, footsteps and thumps outside their room. That plus the scent of boiled potatoes meant that Mary, Caroline, and Anna did not need the knock. When Anna flung the door wide, lentil cheese pie with peas, plus oranges, sat on a low bookcase in the corridor. None of it looked appetizing. The gels could be heard doing a gallop down the stairs. Anna and Caroline dumped the three trays on the beds. Though the pie reeked of cheesy feet, the oranges gave off a sweet scent.

Mary chewed her lip on the enigma of the first murder victim.

"Who Agnes was," she murmured, "is the key to these murders." She sighed and picked up a heaped plate. "Although with meals like this I'm not surprised she turned up her toes."

Caroline alone tucked into the food with enthusiasm. "Don't be a grouse, Mary. At least we won't starve," she remarked. She demolished half the meal while Mary stirred her peas into the yellow mush.

Noticing Anna's indifference to the food, Caroline added, "Darling, are you all right? You'd tell me if you have any fever, wouldn't you?"

Anna made an offhanded gesture. "Don't fuss, Caroline. Mary wants me to hack into the Archive for information on Agnes. I need time for a deep data search."

"After dinner," mouthed Mary, with the effort to swallow claggy cheese. She cleared her throat. "Eat for strength, Anna. Looking at suspects has got us nowhere. Solving the mystery of Agnes is bound to produce clues."

"With Agnes the problem is motive. What was in her past?" muttered Anna after chewing. "Unless her death was a mercy killing. Didn't you mention that, Mary?"

"Um," said Mary, apparently engrossed in poking at her plate. "These lentils are undercooked." She removed several from between her teeth.

"Is that why the gels think I did it?" said Caroline in a small voice. "Because I've made no secret that I believe in the right to die, to have that choice when terminally ill?"

Anna stabbed her fork into a puddle of cheese. "You didn't fly into Agnes's room. If you'd learned how witches fly you'd have told me."

"Yes, but... okay, now I'm telling both of you."

Mary put down the elderly orange she'd been sniffing. Anna leaned over and fondled Caroline's curls.

"Whatever flying means, I have more... well, recollection," began Caroline. "When we were outside, I got a jolt of memory from the night Agnes died. There was a burning pain in my chest. I wanted to scream for help, but my jaw could not move. When I expected to faint, something come loose, as if my bones were melting. Then I rose up, up, until I bumped my head on the ceiling. I saw my body, *me,* below on the bed. The next thing I knew, I stood over Agnes. Only me. No Sarah."

Caroline picked up her orange. She bit into it, then used her nails to remove the peel. "If Janet was here I'd ask her about being put under a spell."

"Stop the magic nonsense, Caroline," snapped Mary. She crossed her knife and fork on the remaining mound of mashed potato. "It was a dream. You dreamed of flying. No spells. True, I did wonder..." Mary paused at Caroline's expression. "About Agnes asking to die. But you wouldn't do something like that and not tell us."

"Agnes couldn't ask, remember? She was too far gone." Caroline sniffed. "Although it feels like I flew into her room, I have no memory of hurting her." She enunciated the latter sentence with care then dropped the remaining sections of orange. "No memory," she whispered. A tear appeared on her cheek. Anna touched her arm. The young woman glared at Mary, then turned away.

Anna just appealed to me, Mary thought. Because all three of us are wondering the same thing. Can someone forget committing murder? Caroline takes a formidable array of anti-depressants. They block off most of the pain, she said. Could they wall off other parts of her mind too? Inconvenient memories?

"I know what you're thinking, Mary." Caroline swallowed, then said it. "What if the killer we're hunting is me?"

Kicking aside her dirty plate, Anna picked up a glass from her bedside table and flung it at the opposite wall. A bang, and the glass dropped to the floor, intact.

"That's you," she said to Caroline. "Looks fragile, but it's actually unbreakable. If I didn't kill Billy Dee, and I know I didn't, then you did not murder Agnes."

"Of course she didn't," came a voice from the door – left open an inch, Mary realized. "Apprentice Caroline's spirit is better than she knows. It's not evil."

"Come in, Janet," Mary called. "No, no, don't come in. Go away. There's a chance we might carry Dee's fever."

An arm placed a steaming mug on the dresser by the door, then added two more. To Mary's surprise, the fragrance from the mugs was not unpleasant. Janet slipped into the room and closed the door behind her. The witch had a better color, or maybe it was the effect of her bear-patterned boy's pajamas, thought Mary ruefully.

"No one knows I'm here," Janet said quickly. "Dorothy's crackers to keep you in quarantine." To Caroline's worried frown she added, "I'll not come closer." Grabbing one of the dinner trays, she added the mugs and pushed them towards the beds before retreating. "Drink your tea and keep the mugs. We've gotta talk."

"Janet," said Mary. "I'm glad you are over your migraine, but my digestion has a lot to cope with after that cheese thing. I don't think your tea…"

"Sainsbury's *Taste the Difference Fair Trade*," said Janet, folding her arms. "I keep a stash in my room, together with an electric kettle no one knows about."

Mary handed out the mugs. The tea was delicious, even with the sugar that Mary would not have added.

"Thank you," said Caroline, smiling. Anna gave Janet a thumbs up.

"Er, Janet, what do you want to tell us?" said Mary.

"I have a gift for you, Mary Wandwalker – from young Tyr," said the short witch. Janet took a smartphone from her pajama pocket, dropped it on the carpet, then kicked it over. Mary picked it up.

"It's dead."

"So's its owner. That's Billy Dee's phone. Tyr found it outside in a puddle."

"*Yes.*" Anna's glee made Janet smile. The young woman seized the phone from Mary. She began to insert wires and connect them to her own device.

"Darling, it's waterlogged," said Caroline. "Even you can't bring a drowned phone back to life. Oh, sorry, sorry. I take it all back," she said, holding her hands up.

Anna's silent outrage could obliterate an elephant, Mary thought. Fortunately, the young woman resumed her crouch and hooked the expired phone into her laptop. Her fingers moved at incredible speed. Janet grinned at Caroline and Mary.

"Don't let Dee's phone stop the search for who Agnes was," Mary could not help adding. She turned away at Anna's snort. *Can Anna bring the dead back to life if it's a phone?* Mary found herself pondering.

"Did you…? I mean, were you and Tyr close?"

"I helped the gels hide him. Any more stupid remarks, or can we get on?"

"You're not feeling well," Caroline pronounced.

Mary recalled that Caroline knew Janet's bipolar disorder intimately, having once rescued her from incarceration. Janet waved dismissively at Caroline's sympathy.

"Tyr wants to talk to you," she said to Mary. "You're to meet him at dawn tomorrow. He'll be outside the back door with an umbrella. He's been checking on Irina in those early hours."

"That's right. I saw them after the séance," said Caroline. "Didn't recognize Tyr then, of course."

"Does Irina talk to him? She's not spoken to her parents."

"Drat, I forgot to ask."

"Well, if she is speaking to Tyr," began Mary slowly, "it can't be much, or he would have said. He didn't get a chance to tell us about her adoption."

"Is Irina a suspect?" Anna looked up from her computer. Without waiting for a reply she bent her head, allowing her waterfall of hair to conceal her face. Now her fingers sounded more like tiny chisels on stone, Mary thought. She stared again at Anna's hair.

"Anna, your hair is shiny, clean."

Anna ignored her.

"You had a shower," Mary insisted. "You left the attic. You must have showered before the medics came."

"So?" The chisels continued, tap, tap, tap.

"So that's when someone did the world a favor and topped Billy Dee." Janet's words became less distinct until "topped." She slid down until her knees were inches from her nose.

"Go back to bed," said Mary. "We'll help you, if you feel like risking it…"

A rumble interrupted them.

"Thunder again," lamented Caroline.

"Let's get you to bed, Janet," said Mary, rising.

"Stay where you are, Wandwalker," ordered Janet. She sniffed. "Dorothy will go stark mad if she finds you wandering the house." She ran her fingers through her hair until its white roots showed all over her skull. "I'll manage," she snapped at Caroline's outstretched hand. "But I'm not going until you tell me who you suspect for these murders."

"Well there's Tyr," said Mary, feeling brutal. "I know you like him, Janet. But Agnes in the séance said 'the boy,' remember? When Agnes got killed, Tyr was hiding here at Holywell. Plus he had motive and opportunity to kill Billy Dee."

"No way." Janet spoke with disgust. "Wandwalker, you can't bamboozle me that you credit that séance. Dee, the so-called voice of dead? Give me strength."

Janet struggled to her feet while grimacing at Mary. "Agnes accusing 'the boy' had to be one of Dee's tricks. Tyr is trying to help. It's as bad as pointing a finger at Dorothy."

Anna paused her torture of digital devices long enough to meet Mary's tiny nod. Caroline gasped. "Oh no, not Dorothy."

"Not at the top of my list," said Mary, carefully. "Yet she's become so, so…"

"Strained, overworked, harassed?" said Caroline.

"At a breaking point," said Anna. "I could see Dorothy killing Dee to protect the gels because he's a predator. Agnes, not so much." She returned to her laptop.

"Never," said Janet. "Anna, you don't get it. No one blames you," she added. "We know what you've been through. Take it from me, none of my sister witches could kill."

"Not even Meredith?" queried Mary. "She's new to Holywell, isn't she? That young woman has secrets. Some of her reactions have been… off."

Janet chewed her lip. Then jerked up her chin. "You're avoiding the obvious," she finally said. "That appalling minister and his uptight wife. Robbin' Robin and Morgan are to blame for Irina falling for that bastard. Mark my words, they killed Agnes and Dee."

"Why on earth," countered Mary, "would two worldly, ambitious, ex-married people gas an old woman with dementia? They never met Agnes." She frowned at furious Janet. "Dee,

I grant you," she continued. "He did put some sort of spell on their daughter."

She looked at Caroline, who grinned. Anna thoughtfully chewed her fingernail, then resumed attacking her laptop.

Mary sighed at obstinate Janet. "Yes, we'll question Robbin' Robin and Helen Morgan. However, Agnes is the real mystery. I'm positive her death has to do with who she really was, her life before Holywell. Her past could unlock everything."

"I don't know, Mary." Caroline sounded tired. "Remember those black feathers from Irina's costume. One left next to Agnes, and another for Billy Dee. Not to mention that I woke up with a feather in my mouth. *Someone's* connecting both murders."

Caroline continued. "We're back to where Janet came in. Agnes could be a mercy killing, nothing to do with her past."

Mary held her breath.

"I don't think it was me," said Caroline at last. "Not me because, Janet, you said violence is not my true spirit." She smiled with effort.

Mary relaxed. Despite the heartbreaking events of the last few days, the Caroline she knew found no killer amongst the ghosts that haunted her.

Anna continued tapping, yet Mary sensed her attention. Caroline clasped her hands.

"We've got to admit mercy killing could explain Agnes. Holywell is full of people who want to stop suffering."

"The gels," said Anna. "They wanted to put Agnes out of her misery."

"*What?*" Janet and Mary exclaimed together. Caroline paled. Mary frowned, Janet glared.

"I told them not to," said Anna, not looking up. "Before I went to Greenwich to spy on Dee at the ballet school. You remember, one of my *flying* visits to Holywell." She almost smiled, then grunted at her screen.

"Go on, Anna," said Mary, faintly.

"Oh, the gels kept moaning about Agnes." Anna pressed four keys at once. "They had extra chores because of the work she created. Sarah mentioned Agnes's bad dreams. It was difficult to calm her. So they thought Agnes would be better off dead. I told them mercy killing is still killing, and not to do it. Your influence, Mary Wandwalker."

During her speech Anna never stopped typing.

Eventually Mary cleared her throat. "Time for bed," she said. "Good night, Janet."

The witch had a grin for Mary and Caroline.

"Don't forget to meet young Tyr," she said, opening the door. "He could be the key to this whole bloody mess."

No, thought Mary, when she'd gone. Somehow the key is Agnes.

## CHAPTER 21
# EARLY SURPRISES

*Monday early morning.*

Mary overslept. So did Caroline and Anna in each other's arms. When drumming rain roused Mary, she became instantly awake. Could she smell coffee? Or had she dreamt that tantalizing perfume to escape the overpowering shampoo Anna had used? Hang on, the room's too light for dawn. Where's that alarm clock? Oh, hell, switched off. Did I do that in my sleep?

Mary squinted at the log that was Caroline and Anna. The smile on Anna's face made her suspicious. Anna opened one eye and winked.

"See Tyr later," Anna murmured. "Caroline needs sleep."

Mary pretended to grumble, then scrabbled for her shoes. She followed the coffee fragrance to the door. Despite her efforts the handle creaked. Never mind, Mary brightened at a couple of trays, one with buttered toast, and another with mugs of tea and coffee.

Picking up the trays would likely cause the crockery to rattle, so she carried in the mugs one by one. Her stomach revolted at the toast with melted and congealed yellow oil. Do we have to live on bread and butter while marooned? Yesterday's toast-fest had been enough.

As if in reply the wind flung more rain at the windows. Mary darted behind the closed curtains to find tree branches waving and twigs snapping, while the gale howled like a banshee. Oh stop that, she thought, crossly. Enough of catastrophic weather.

What did the witches call that storm god? For the first time in her life Mary shook her fist at a deity she did not believe in. Returning to her bed she seized the mug of coffee. "Black as sin," Mr. Jeffreys once said.

*Mr. Jeffreys?* Please let the phones operate. By whatever god it takes, Mary prayed. She dug into her handbag for the magical device. The phone turned on to her fumbling. First news of her sick friend, then I'll look for Agnes. Mary swallowed enough coffee to quiet the throb in her skull. A message danced before her tired eyes. She sipped until her blood sang. Then she frowned, first at the coffee, then her phone.

> Mr. Jeffreys wants you to have the DNA results from both autopsies. He is recovering. Do not call because he must sleep.

"Is there any tea?"

Caroline sounded far away. The log had unraveled while Mary stared, transfixed by the news. Words attached themselves to meanings, the joyful, and the puzzling. Again she picked up her mug, sniffed inside, and curled her lips.

"Instant coffee, I presume. What suffering, Mary Wandwalker." In a flash of naked limbs, Anna reached for the remaining two mugs. She handed one to Caroline, who did not sleep naked, to Mary's relief. Anna pushed the tray of toast further away.

"Put some clothes on, Anna," said Mary without looking up.

"How is the old coot?"

"That's what Janet calls Mr. Jeffreys." Mary set her phone down on the bedside table. "Recovering, they say. Thank God, or goddess. There's a message. He said to tell me, us, the DNA results." She looked up. "I guess they completed Dee's autopsy overnight."

"Check your email," said Anna.

"Of course." Mary dived to the other side of the bed for her laptop.

"I meant, check it on your phone."

"Mary's overdue for new glasses," said Caroline, between mouthfuls of toast washed down with tea. "Did I hear Mr. Jeffreys is going to be okay?"

Mary smiled at her. "Yes," she said simply. "How are you?"

Caroline grinned back. "I've been bewitched into believing I can fly, so I can't complain about a simple headache. Seriously, the depression is not too bad, considering." Her grin became rueful. Anna, putting on jeans, leaned over Caroline and kissed her quickly on the mouth. Caroline blushed.

"You're a brave woman, Caroline," Mary said. "And... *oh my God.*" Her hands flew up as if from an electric shock.

"What?" said Anna and Caroline together.

"DNA is a match. I knew Agnes had to be the key. *I knew it.* Billy Dee is Agnes's son. How could that be?"

"Very possible," said Anna. She swung round on the bed and glared at her phone. "Message from Tyr. Also about DNA." She sounded angry.

"Is this the thing you wouldn't tell me about?" said Caroline.

"What thing?" snapped Mary. "Anna, we said no more secrets. Don't look at me like that."

"All right. Tyr admits he came here for Dee's DNA. He managed to get it tested together with his own." She scowled. "Creep also sent in my DNA and Irina's."

"He said he came to protect Irina," said Caroline, sadly.

"That too," said Anna. "He found one of my hairs," she sniffed. "He says at Greenwich he could not get close enough to Dee to be sure of the *right* DNA. At Holywell he simply replaced the toothbrush Dee got from the witches. Irina gave him her hairbrush."

"More DNA tests?" Mary felt dizzy. Some whirlwind had spun events out of control. "How did Tyr get material to a lab when we're cut off by storms and floods?"

"He knows how to talk to drones," said Anna. She rather spoilt the effect by adding, "some of them accept packages."

"All right, enough pussyfooting around," interrupted Mary. "What we want are those DNA results. I bet they're why Tyr wanted to see me this morning."

"Yes, Anna, please. I can't bear anymore," said Caroline, pushing her hands down her thighs.

"Fine," snapped Anna. "You two have thought this since Irina's wig fell off. I'm related to her. Happy now?"

No, not really, thought Mary. Caroline looks like a vampire has drained her blood.

Anna took note of Caroline's pallor. "Not closely related. I'm not Irina's sister or anything like that. Probably a cousin. I'm not connected to Dee, so it must be through Irina's mother." In the pause, Anna looked away.

This changes everything, thought Mary. No, this is Anna we're talking about. It might mean nothing at all.

Caroline sat with her mouth open. Then she took one of Anna's hands. "Darling…" she began.

Mary slapped her laptop close. Thunder roared as if in response. Mary swung off the bed and pulled the curtains open to the morning's storm. Lightning blazed. Her throat caught as if she swallowed some of that electricity. Grey eyes alight, she turned to Caroline and Anna.

"Yes," she said, with trees waving behind her. "It *is* all linked to Agnes."

"What are you talking about, Mary?" Caroline spoke in a small voice, her hand seeking Anna's, who pushed it away.

Mary jumped back onto her bed to reply. "Agnes links both sets of DNA tests. As Dee's mother, she also recognized you, Anna, because you share DNA with Irina. Agnes is the key to both murders *because Billy Dee is Irina's father*." Mary frowned at Anna. "You've not told us everything. That's what Tyr found out from the DNA, isn't it?"

There was a pause. Mary's eyes locked on Anna.

"Yes," said Anna at last. She glanced at sorrowful Caroline before going back to her phone. "Tyr's not related to Dee at all, but Irina is the sorcerer's daughter. Tyr thinks Dee knew about Irina all along. Perhaps he saw something in her at the ballet school. It's not hard to get DNA when dancers are always fussing with their hair."

"No, no." Caroline had gone very white. "That would mean Billy Dee had an affair with his own daughter."

"It happens," said Anna, fierce.

"Yes, no. Stop, you two." Mary put her hand to her forehead. "You're making big assumptions. Yes, fathers do very occasionally abuse daughters and yes, Dee is a predator at the ballet school. But we don't know *for sure* what he did to Irina. When I talked to him he hinted, without admitting anything. He played a game, tempting me to think the worst."

"Mary, don't defend him," wailed Caroline. "Think of Irina's behavior."

"She's traumatized," said Anna, glaring.

"Yes, I see that," said Mary doggedly, "but we don't know *why* she's traumatized." She stared at mutinous Anna, at worried Caroline. "Don't forget Irina has never said Dee physically abused her. She's confused, lost. Dee might have struggled to find the father in himself."

Anna snorted. Caroline started to chew her nails. Mary decided to leave the subject of incest.

"Consider Agnes. We now know she was Irina's grandmother. The poor woman," said Mary, slowly. "Caroline, Anna, don't you get it? Dee fathering Irina explains why he hated Robbin' Robin. The minister took Dee's place with Irina. Robbin' Robin has the family Dee believed was his by right."

Mary glanced at Caroline, then at frowning Anna. She rose and paced between the door and the window: eleven steps each way.

"Whatever the truth between Dee and Irina, these DNA results point to Agnes. Our mission remains her. Where did she come from? How did she lead her life? No one knows."

Mary stopped to scrutinize Caroline and Anna. Caroline's green eyes were huge, Anna nodded. Mary's heart pounded. It had to be said.

"That blood connection between Billy Dee and Agnes changes everything. Dee could have killed his own mother."

Saying it out loud shifted something, Mary realized. No proof so far. Yet Billy Dee murdered Agnes. Instinctively this had to be right. She could see Caroline and Anna agreed. Anna gave a brusque nod, Caroline a sad one.

"When Agnes' spirit said 'the boy' in the séance," whispered Caroline, "she meant Billy Dee, her son. He murdered his own mother, he seduced… all right Mary. He messed up and traumatized his own daughter, *that* we know."

"We wondered why Dee insisted on coming to Holywell," Mary said. "It makes horrible sense if he came here to kill Agnes."

"But *why* kill Agnes, his own mother? Why bring his daughter here?"

Caroline had put her finger on some real questions, Mary reflected. She had another.

"We don't know how he, or anyone else, got into Agnes's room," she said.

Caroline shuddered. "Don't remind me. *I* have that memory of flying into Agnes's room. Did Billy Dee put a spell on me?"

"I'm beginning to think that's exactly what he did," said Mary.

"Even though you don't believe in magic?" Anna scoffed.

"I admit," said Mary primly, "it's a problem."

# CHAPTER 22
# A BIG ROW

*Monday morning.*

Foreheads pressed on the window, Mary and Caroline stared through drizzle at the mud and water that used to be Holywell's lawn. Robbin' Robin hunched directly below them on a bench. With a too-big hat that kept slipping over his eyes and a too-small coat for his girth, he bent over his phone. In front of him Helen Morgan paced like a hungry dog. Every so often she stopped to fling words at her ex. In response he winced, looked up, then waved her away.

"I wish I'd learned to read lips," muttered Mary.

"Why do you want to talk to Irina's parents?" enquired Caroline. "They won't admit to murdering Billy Dee. Anyway, you said to concentrate on Agnes."

"I got a text that the minister has new information," returned Mary. "I bet he has. Don't forget Morgan listened at the door when we talked to Tyr. We saw how upset she became when Tyr confirmed Irina's adoption was illegal. She will have told Robbin' Robin. They'll want us to keep it secret."

"Ah," said Caroline. "So you think…" She pulled out her phone from a pajama pocket.

Mary returned a grim smile before continuing. "Agnes is connected to Irina by blood," she said. "In light of the DNA results that link her to Dee and Dee to Irina, I'm sure Robbin' Robin and Morgan are eager to meddle in our enquiries."

Anna's black eyes rose from her laptop to meet Mary's expression. Mary shook her head.

"Keep on with that search for Agnes, Anna. Her story cannot be ordinary. We would have found *something,* or the witches would have."

Mary would never admit it, but her earlier lack of interest in Agnes bit like a persistent hound. Surely she'd lived long enough to know the real mysteries lay in what, and who, got overlooked?

"Working on Agnes and Dee right now," grunted Anna. Her attention was glued to Dee's phone perched next to her laptop screen. Mary glimpsed numbers and letters scrolling at astonishing speed. Without moving, Anna answered Mary's unspoken query. "Progress on Dee's data storage. I'm using new software from Uzbekistan that loops in AI. It lets me build a program to reconstruct audio files in a drowned phone. Dee had plenty of data, some in unusual formats."

"Well done, darling," said Caroline, looking up from her exchange of texts with Dorothy.

"What about Agnes?" insisted Mary. "Did you find her birth certificate?"

"No documents are online from so far back. However, there's a healthcare record of a mental patient known as Agnes in the late nineties. Even then she could not recall her other name."

"Oh, come on," said Mary, turning from the window. "Pre-internet Agnes will have had a Social Security Number, a job record, not to mention she gave birth, for heaven's sake. Some of that stuff must be digitized."

"Not our Agnes. Nothing pre-1998." Anna took a moment to glare at Mary. "Stop bugging me. Tell Dorothy to let us out. We're not sick."

Caroline looked up. "I've been texting Dorothy. Are Irina's parents fighting, do you think?"

"Oh, yes," said Mary, unconsciously mimicking Helen Morgan's steps. "So is Dorothy going to let us question them?

And apart from Irina's parents, the witches may have clues about Agnes too."

"Dorothy's having stocks of sanitizer checked. You know, so they can disinfect rooms after we've used them."

"Ridiculous," snapped Mary. "None of us are feverish. I need to talk to Robbin' Robin and Morgan in person. I've got to see the whites of his eyes with that liar of a minister. Dorothy's lost the plot."

Caroline grinned. "I know, Mary. These murders have turned you into Anna. You want to fling away precautions and to hell with the consequences."

Mary dropped back onto her bed. Her bottom lip quivered. She wafted the ghost of a smile towards Caroline.

"I guess some dangers seem more real than others," she began. "We went through so much with Covid. I can't take Dee's fever seriously when we have a killer on the loose."

"There's Mr. Jeffreys." Again Anna did not look up, yet her remark penetrated.

Mary sighed. "They told me to stop phoning. He's sleeping. So he can't get us into the Archive, er... legally. Um... Anna? You did try looking for 'Romania' and 'Agnes?'"

Anna hissed.

I'm sure she can freeze her screen with a scowl, thought Mary.

"Leave me alone, Wandwalker. Have you any idea how much the Archives have on Romania? Given Agnes's age I'm looking pre- and post-1989."

"Of course I know. I organized those Archives," retorted Mary.

"How long did that take?"

"Thirty-five years... Oh. All right." She sighed. "I take it you've found nothing."

"Not nothing. Nothing would be easy. There are redacted names, a few of which could refer to a woman of Agnes's age. No way to confirm identification. Yet."

"No DNA records?" said Caroline.

Mary sniffed. "Keeping DNA records from people not arrested? Forbidden by law."

She pulled out her phone and willed it to ring from the hospital. Surely Mr. Jeffreys would be well enough to talk today.

Caroline reached over to pat her arm. She brightened. "Look, Mary, if Janet can get me some herbs, I can do a ritual for Mr. Jeffreys. If I burn them I can try a simple spell. What do you think?"

To Mary, Caroline looked worn out. Too pale, as her eyes flittered around the small bedroom.

Anna broke in. "Didn't you set fire to a college room the last time you tried a spell?"

For Anna brutal truths came before comfort.

"Later, Caroline," said Mary. "We can't risk Dorothy's freaking out if she sees or smells smoke. Given her fear of lightning, it might be the last straw, literally. We're in a wooden house, remember."

A ping. Mary and Caroline seized their phones.

"Hurrah," said Caroline, standing up. "Dorothy's given the all-clear to talk to Irina's parents outside. The next storm won't be for an hour."

Anna's fingers continued tapping, her right foot jiggling on the floor.

"We can now use the bathroom," Caroline said.

"An hour is not much, given the others I want to interview," said Mary. "Let's go, Caroline."

Anna held up a hand, while frowning at the screen. "Wait a moment, and I can come too. Got to set this program to run two hours. Dee's phone has so many encrypted files. There…"

She splayed her hands across the keyboard like two starfish. After wriggling over multiple keys, Anna shut the computer as if locking away an explosive device.

Mary's throat tightened.

"Will it work, your new program?" she queried with a spurt of alarm.

Anna grunted. "Can't tell. Either I'll come back to nothing, the internet equivalent of hot air, or…"

"Or…?" asked Caroline.

"Or we might be able to talk to Billy Dee, the dead guy."

A pause while Mary digested. Caroline gulped.

"Talk to Billy Dee from the realm of the dead? Darling, what have you done?" Caroline trembled.

Mary patted her arm. "Don't worry. Anna's exaggerating." She did not believe her own words.

"You're both wrong."

Anna put on what Mary called her cat-cream smile. "I've put extra AI, artificial intelligence, into the database I've been building on Billy Dee. Ever since we heard the name I've had bots getting into intelligence files of police and security services all over Europe. If," she paused, "if, my AI collaborates with the phone files retrieval software, we'll get the decoded recordings. Plus, to help us understand them, we'll get a cyber version of Dee himself."

Knees weak, Mary sank back down. She blinked at Caroline.

Then Mary leapt up. "What?" she screeched at Anna. She knocked her empty mug onto the carpet, where it cracked. The lightning inside her seared. Her hair must be standing on end.

"*Anna,* how could you?" Mary's fists waved about as if underwater. "*You've made an AI Dee? Are you insane?* The damage that man has caused, his criminal nature, how could you? He murdered Agnes, his own mother, for God's sake."

Mary jumped up, strode to the window, then back to stand over Anna. "Your… your *Frankenstein creature* could try sorcery on the internet, couldn't he?"

Anna's cheeks blazed. She clasped her laptop to her chest for a moment, then dropped it on the bed. She got on all fours to pull the charging plug from the socket. When she rose to confront Mary, she stamped her foot.

"Bitch. How dare you? I thought you'd be pleased. We'll listen to his files. Don't you get it, you dried up old hag? It's a kind of scrying, like looking into a witch's crystal ball."

Anna looked lost as well as furious.

My God, she really expected me to applaud her, Mary thought. She put her head in her hands.

"Anna, why don't you ever listen? Why don't you learn? At least that damn sorcerer died. Now, because of you, he can do harm from beyond the grave." She made for the door. "Oh, I've had enough. I'm getting out of here?"

"Mary, Anna only tried to help." Caroline held out a tissue. It reminded Mary of a white flag, which, for some reason, made her so angry that words would not come.

"Fuck you, Mary Wandwalker." Anna stormed past Mary and out the door. Mary heard the bathroom door slam. At least the young woman had not broken Dorothy's absurd rules.

"Mary, how could you?" A tear rolled down Caroline's flushed cheek. It released Mary.

"How could *you,* Caroline? How could you let Anna do something so dangerous? I've read about AI. You're supposed to watch over Anna in ways I can't."

"Fuck you, Mary," yelled Caroline. "Getting accused of murder has been a mite distracting." Her face redder than Mary could remember, Caroline turned on her heel and ran out. This time the bedroom door slammed.

Mary shut her eyes, waiting. It took too long. No, they weren't coming back. She moved slowly back to the bed, the tissue in her hand. It mocked her in its pristine perfection. Inside was horror, cold, dark, lifeless. Her world had exploded, gone. Energy drained away. What was left was... nothing.

I can do nothing, she thought. I can only do what I have to do. Which is... question Irina's parents about Dee's death. Her insides gave a jolt at a further idea. If neither Anna nor the Archive could supply the truth about Agnes, that left one last opportunity.

Mary's head hurt. Anna and Caroline running off punched her heart. She sniffed and blew her nose on the tissue. Scrunched in her palm, it made a missile she could throw into the waste paper basket. She missed, so bent her aching back to dispose of it. I have to keep going, she told herself, lest the murderer does too.

Alone, with Mr. Jeffreys sick, Mary had to ask for help from the last person at Holywell she wanted to speak to. Mary Wandwalker put her shoulders back and practiced breathing. With the clock on the mantelpiece ticking down the time, Mary descended to her second fateful encounter with Mr. Robin Prince, aka Robbin' Robin, the minister.

# CHAPTER 23
## ROBBIN' ROBIN, NOT SO
## USELESS AFTER ALL

*Monday afternoon.*

After Mary shut the back door, she held out her hand, then gave a sigh of relief. Nothing. No rain for a blessed moment. It felt like the sky paused for breath after the tempests of the last few days. Mary pushed back the hood of her borrowed raincoat. Stepping between puddles, she approached the French windows and noted familiar backs. Green smoke puffed while someone waved bunches of leaves, suggesting another ritual. Cleansing in case Dee's fever extends to Anna, Caroline, and me, thought Mary. Why did it make her feel like an unwanted spirit?

"Pull yourself together, Wandwalker," Mary muttered, channeling Mr. Jeffreys. Who is going to find the killer if I don't? Aware this was unfair to Caroline and Anna, Mary cleared her throat. She turned the corner to where Robbin' Robin and Helen Morgan waited, a yard apart. Well, Morgan waited, while the minister barked at aides on his phone.

"You heard me. Have a chopper on standby. Yes, tomorrow. Jeffreys will get me out of here."

Noticing Mary, he pouted, and stuffed his phone in his trouser pocket. Mary spotted soup stains on his crumpled suit. Holywell would be short of spare male clothing, she reflected. But what had Robbin' Robin said?

"You've heard from Mr. Jeffreys? When? Why didn't you call me?" Mary had her phone out before Helen Morgan could speak.

"No, Robbin' Robin lied, as usual," said Helen. Her tone dripped acid. Mary bristled at the minister.

"Nonsense, I'm optimistic," protested Robin Prince, reddening. "Jeffreys hasn't woken yet. But doctors agree that he's going to be OK. So if the final storm is over quickly, as they predict..."

"It could be safe for helicopters in about twenty hours. That's according to the latest forecasts," added Helen Morgan. "Our Robbin' Robin can't wait to get back to plotting against the PM. And I must get Irina into a clinic in London."

"Ah, about Irina..." began Mary to hide her disappointment.

"No, not Irina." Helen Morgan stepped closer to Mary. "We're not talking to *you* about Irina, not ever."

"Her adoption was illegal," returned Mary.

"No, no, definitely not." Robbin' Robin spread his hands in innocence. To Mary his wide blue eyes recalled a sky invisible for what seemed like an eternity.

Mary stared back until the minister's gaze dropped. Helen Morgan took a seat next to him. She picked up his right hand. His mouth fell open. Morgan drew her other hand across her eyes. Mary saw raw eyelids with dark shadows, hair like dirty straw. No longer was she Morgan of the golden helmet. She raised her ravaged face to Mary.

"Miss Wandwalker, after all Irina's been through. Please..." Morgan's voice dried.

Robbin' Robin lifted his hand. "I'll..."

"Shut up," his ex-wife hissed, withdrawing her hand. He shut up, yet lifted an appealing little boy expression to Mary.

"My wife doesn't trust me," said Robbin' Robin. "She insisted on being present. Where is the fat lady and that girl who carries a knife?"

Mary found herself without excuses. "A difference of opinion," she muttered.

"Let me handle this," said Helen Morgan.

Mary glanced at the tree above the peculiar couple. For they were a couple, at least for Irina, she could see that. Something rustled the copper beech leaves. A squirrel held a spiky nut in both paws. Mary glimpsed a beady eye, a drop of shining tar. It bounded along a thin branch and leapt into the next tree.

"Irina's birth father is dead," Mary began.

"So's her birth mother," said Helen, with unseemly eagerness, thought Mary.

"It's part of our information on Dee," broke in the minister. "More arrived during the night. My contacts in the Home Office and the security services have been working on Dee for months. As soon as we knew that old woman had been murdered, they got started on her, too."

"Your contacts could get past redacted names and missing details," said Mary, remembering Anna's frustration.

"When you read it, you'll understand," said Morgan. "Irina only has us. It would be cruel to take her away."

Mary held up her hand. "Actually I agree," she conceded. "Nothing is to be gained by more trouble for your daughter. In return, I want everything on Dee and Agnes. And I want it now."

The chastened couple on the bench nodded.

Robbin' Robin agreed to email the key files to Mary. But first she demanded a summary. To her grudging surprise, Robbin' Robin could be focused if his interests were in play.

Dee's life had been extraordinary. Born in Romania to an unmarried Agnes Kelley, Billy Dee stole his surname from the Renaissance, magus, Dr. John Dee, as Mary had suspected. First coming to the notice of the authorities in the early 2000s, Dee disappeared from a carnival troupe accused of child trafficking. Later he reinvented himself as a ballet choreographer.

"That must have been before he had Irina," broke in Mary. "What did you say about her birth mother being dead?"

Helen Morgan looked away. "She was not yet fourteen, Irina's mother. At that age, the pelvis is not fully formed. According to the Romanian authorities someone abandoned her, bleeding and unconscious, outside a remote hospital. Her post-partum hemorrhages killed her the next day."

"So young. Her name?"

Helen Morgan shook her head. "Shut up, Robbin' Robin," she added conversationally without looking at the minister's open mouth. "Dee kept the baby."

"Until he sold her," said Mary.

Morgan looked away.

Robin Prince pouted. "Our adoption of Irina... My lawyers say..."

"No," said both women at once. "No more lies," said Helen Morgan fiercely. She and Mary exchanged a look of mutual comprehension.

"What do you know of Dee's ballet career?"

"Meteoric in the sense of his talent for making old ballets look new," said Morgan, looking relieved. "At the same time he built a reputation as a sorcerer and spiritualist medium. He claimed he could bring back the ghosts of dead dancers to teach the ballerinas of tomorrow."

"Con artist," spat Robbin' Robin.

"Worse," added Helen Morgan, sadly. "People like me, desperate for success, trusted him."

"He used the stories to seduce young girls," Mary said grimly.

Morgan nodded. "I see that now." Her hurt face looked painful.

"Bastard came here and bewitched the PM," growled Robbin' Robin. "Stole the election, stole my chance to be Prime Minister."

Helen Morgan withdrew to the end of the bench. Her grimace said it all, thought Mary.

"Minister," Mary began. "What you've told me so far I could discover from Mr. Jeffreys when he awakens. What about Dee and Agnes? How did an Englishwoman come to have a child in Romania in the first place?"

Morgan got up as if a spark had ignited underneath her. "Take my place, Miss Wandwalker, if you can bear to sit near him. Agnes Kelley's story would make an amazing ballet. Maybe I learned something from that bastard after all."

Mary considered her aching legs, then lowered herself onto the bench.

"Spill, as Anna would say," she said, ignoring the minister's pout.

"Let me tell it. I read the file before breakfast." Morgan gave half a smile, put her hands on her bony hips, and began the unlikely tale of Agnes Kelley.

Wow, thought Mary five minutes later. Morgan's right. It's extreme, it's tragic, and we don't even know the ending. As she later explained to Caroline and Anna, one of Robin Prince's aides had worked through the night piecing together the story of a remarkable woman.

For Agnes Kelley had led an unconventional life. As a child she devoured daredevil comics, then dropped out of grade school. It was the late 1960s. Many dreamed, while few actually lived those winds of change. Agnes became one of the latter when she ran away from home. She never went back to her family's middle class existence. Her adventures began at fifteen, the same age as Irina—child and not a child.

Her first group of "hippies" left England for Europe, where she evaded the authorities until her family gave up the search. It also helped that she moved between groups in which radical lifestyles blended into politics. At that point she attracted notice. The security services kept tabs on fringe activists. They recorded an Agnes Kelley in her early twenties in the anti-nuclear movement in France and West Germany. She merited her own intelligence file when she started to assist East Germans in escaping to the West.

One escapee was a young Romanian called Stefan. As a teenager he had been removed from an elite school and sent to Russia. Trained as spies, these youths eventually returned to their birthplace. For the rest of their lives Russian handlers controlled them. Stefan's destiny was to embody the long arm of the Soviet Union.

"Hang on," interrupted Mary. "Agnes helped people escape from the communists. That makes Stefan either a defector or a Soviet spy on defectors. Which?"

"If you believe his story, all he wanted was to go home to Romania," groused Robbin' Robin.

"You can't stand for it not to be all about you, can you?" Morgan's contempt made Mary flinch. "Miss Wandwalker, Stefan refused to conform. He ran away. They recaptured and tortured him. Cigarette burns, and missing toenails, the file said. All in aid of what?"

"Brainwashing," said Mary.

"Quite," said Robbin's Robin, looking uncomfortable. "Stefan fled again, got to the Berlin Wall, where he met Agnes Kelly. Instead of doing the only sensible thing and getting out..." He threw up his hands.

"Agnes went in," said Mary slowly. "To be with him? How brave."

"Apparently he convinced her to join his people, his family, who would hide them. Stefan and Agnes loved each other. She had no ties, was never a fan of life in the West. He was her family now." Helen turned back to gaze at Robbin' Robin, and sighed audibly.

"Budapest, where he grew up, would be no good," said Robbin' Robin, shortly. "State police on every street. So Stefan's family sent them to cousins in the Transylvanian mountains. Stefan became a farmer, of all things. Their child, William Kelley, was born in 1983. He became..." the minister spat, "that bastard, Billy Dee."

"Stefan and Agnes were happy." Helen Morgan gave Mary an ironic look. "I like to think they were happy," she corrected. "Anyway, it did not last. Their child was not yet a year old when a traveling carnival reached their village. When it vanished overnight, so did several local children under five, including baby Kelley."

"They hadn't married?"

"That's Agnes, always a free spirit," said Morgan. "Only she wasn't any more. Stefan believed the Russians stole their child, while Agnes vowed to find the child stealers. She never gave up looking for her baby." Morgan paused. "Stefan died young of skin cancer."

Mary flashed on that cream Billy Dee used on his face, apart from that day he'd swiped herbs from Janet. She recalled a science program about sunlight allergies contributing to the vampire legend in Europe. "What about Agnes?"

"Nothing, until records list her in a disgusting Romanian asylum after the Berlin Wall fell," said Robbin' Robin. "Her mind had gone, but she still uttered words that were recognizably English. Eventually she got repatriated to a hospital in Middlesex. No one claimed her. She'd forgotten her full name."

"When your government closed the mental asylums," said Mary, sternly, "people like Agnes had nowhere to go. Hence she ended up in that foul relic, The Old Hospital, where Janet and Caroline found her."

Robbin' Robin looked puzzled. "Nothing to do with *me*," he expostulated. "I never got the Health Ministry. Anyway, she came to Holywell."

"Much later, and only because Janet insisted," retorted Mary. "Holywell is where her son, William Kelley, finally found her."

"Billy talked about Romania," said Morgan. "He said it was where he discovered ballet and old stories."

"Pillow talk," sneered the minister.

"At least he talked to me," snapped Morgan. "*He* did not waste time chasing female so-called researchers."

"Because he chased our daughter," yelled Robbin' Robin.

Morgan put both hands to her face. A pause.

"Sorry, Helen. A low blow," whispered the minister.

It occurred to Mary she should go. Yet she wanted to know more. After all, these brittle people were suspects for one, if not two, murders. Something they said about Agnes niggled.

Was it a detail from the old woman's story, or something not yet understood? Could whatever it was make sense of the two murders? I'm waiting for lightning to strike, thought Mary. She scented electricity in the air. Looking up she saw black clouds.

Yes, the sky was ready to erupt.

## CHAPTER 24
# A BIRD ON THE ROOF

*Monday late afternoon.*

The clouds opened. Mary spat rainwater from her mouth. About to shout at Robbin' Robin and Morgan to get inside, she paused at Morgan's look of confusion and suspicion. That's right, her ex-husband had apologized, thought Mary. Now he gazed back at Morgan, lip trembling. Morgan took a small step towards him. Robbin' Robin gulped. He puffed out his chest. The rain was darkening his suit, yet he did not move from the bench.

We really must go inside, thought Mary. At any moment lightning will slash the sky. Yet Mary remained silent, fascinated by the electricity between Helen Morgan and Robbin' Robin.

Suddenly there came a screech. A crow flew from the nearest tree. It landed on the lawn, beating rain off its feathers. Too close, Mary thought. Birds never come this close.

Morgan's head jerked up. She faced the top of the house. Shielding rain from her eyes, she staggered. Mary went to her. The woman, white as a ghost, struggled to speak. Instead she pointed, Mary tried to follow. Sheets of rain obscured everything. Again Morgan tried to say something, yet no sound emerged. Something in the house? No. *Above the house.*

Three feathers spun circles in front of Mary's eyes. Like black monks descending a staircase, her tired mind mused. Oh, there must be a bird on the roof.

*The roof.* Mary seized Helen Morgan's arm. Robbin' Robin took her other side. All three heads were riveted to one spot.

They did not notice the wet gleam of the slate. They only saw Irina in her black swan costume. The girl shuffled her feet, while one hand used a brick chimney for balance. Irina's skin glowed white against a sodden black leotard and feathers. She no longer wore the red wig. Mary blinked at the resemblance to Billy Dee.

"I killed my father," came the wail, just audible through the rain.

Her words slapped Mary: they were the first she'd heard from Irina.

"No, your father's *here*, Irina. I'm here. I'm not dead. Come down." Robbin' Robin sounded hoarse.

"Don't say *come down* you fucking idiot," screamed Morgan. "Irina, look out…"

The smell of sweat and rain enveloped Mary as Robbin' Robin brought his ex-wife down to the mud. With a hand on Morgan's mouth, he whispered into her ear. Finally, she relaxed, pushed his hand away, and sat up. Mary caught something about "not scaring Irina. The roof is wet and slippery."

She saw what Robbin' Robin meant: a lean shadow crept across the roof towards Irina. It paid no attention to rain or gusts of wind. Mary moved closer to confirm what she saw. Anna had to be careful. She could easily dislodge old slates. Some were cracked. Any rattle, any crash, and Irina might lose her balance. Or jump.

In the rain, the window from which Irina and Anna must have exited opened further. Like a fish gill breathing in water, Mary thought. Caroline peered out, biting her knuckles. They had to keep Irina's attention away from the stealthy approach of Anna.

Please Anna, don't frighten the girl. Or lose your balance.

For a second Anna wobbled. Mary bit her lips to keep from yelling. Anna knelt, reached out and crawled forward.

And please God no lightning *now,* Mary prayed.

"Go away. Let me fly into the world of the dead," yelled Irina at her parents.

"No, you don't," shouted Mary. "I don't believe you're a murderer."

"I did, I killed Billy Dee when he said he was my father."

Irina's left foot slipped, she toppled forward.

Helen Morgan screamed. Mary covered her eyes, then made herself look. Irina's head had dropped over the roof's gutter. One arm dangled.

Slowly Irina pulled back her feathered arm. Her hands felt for, then gripped the gutter. She pushed her body back, then eased around until she lay horizontal to the roof edge. For a moment she remained still, then rose on hands and knees. At long last she wobbled upright.

Anna needed another minute to get within grabbing distance, Mary decided. She jumped as she heard the loud voice of a man, a frightened man.

"Irina, darling, I'm your father, and I'm not dead. Look at me, look at *me*."

Mary and Morgan's heads swiveled to Robbin' Robin. He did not see them. On the roof Irina's pout did rather resemble Robbin' Robin, Mary noted.

"You didn't kill Billy Dee because I did." Morgan's voice cracked.

Mary gasped. Morgan kept her eyes glued on Irina.

"I did it, darling," she continued, eyes streaming. "I killed the sorcerer. I took your black feathers to show it was because of what he did to you."

"No, no," moaned Robbin' Robin.

"He didn't do anything to me," wailed Irina. Her pout grew. "I wanted him to. I thought he loved me, only me. All that time he wanted to tell me he was my birth father. When he did I…"

Anna leapt on Irina as thunder began to growl in the east. She pulled the girl onto her back, then dragged her across the roof to Caroline at the window. Irina screamed and kicked. Rage, not pain, Mary judged. Ah, Caroline has a rope. At that moment, Caroline got replaced by Linda who climbed out to help bring Irina in. John took Caroline's place with the rope.

"Don't hurt Irina," called Robbin' Robin. "It was me. I killed that bastard, Billy Dee."

This time Mary and Helen's stares encompassed each other as well. Morgan looked back up to see Irina being pushed through the window by Linda. John must be pulling her, Mary concluded. Anna swung in unaided. Thunder boomed from a blackening sky.

"Get inside," said Mary to Irina's parents. "Go to Irina. Storm's almost overhead." Morgan kicked off her high heels and ran while the minister lumbered behind. Mary splashed after them until stopped by Dorothy in the backdoor porch.

"Three confessions, did you hear?" Mary remarked. "Even Robin Prince admitted to the murder of Billy Dee."

"None of the Prince family were wholly convincing," sighed Dorothy. "I have news for you, Miss Wandwalker." So worn did she appear that Mary's chest tightened.

"Not Mr. Jeffreys?"

"No. Well, that bit is good news. Apparently the mystery fever is a bacteria from the floodwater. Produces a forty-eight hour crisis then responds to treatment. Thanks-be-to-the-goddess the patients are doing well."

"Including Mr. Jeffreys?"

"Yes, awake and gaining strength. He plans to accompany the police to Holywell tomorrow. That's the real news. The police will resume the hunt for the killers if, as expected, this storm is the last, and the floods start to subside."

Mary's eyes widened.

"Yes, you're off the hook with the murders. Let the police take over." Dorothy turned to enter the kitchen.

"No," said Mary to her back.

Dorothy swung back. "What do you mean, no?" she snapped. "You should be relieved. No more sneaking around…"

"No, we won't stop our sleuthing. You can't switch off the Depth Enquiry Agency like a lamp."

Mary pushed past Dorothy. When both were in the kitchen she closed the back door as lighting flashed in her eyes. She addressed Dorothy in her uncompromising voice.

"We sleuth for Agnes now. The police will never understand her. She'll get no justice from them. Hell, Dorothy." She pointed in the direction of the stairs. "Holywell includes that confused child, Irina. You saw her on the roof. All this has got to stop." Mary looked straight at Dorothy, who flushed.

"Very well," she said with a visible struggle. "I suppose you're right about Agnes. My sisters feel the same." She took a breath. "I've got Meredith taking temperatures. Once we know Billy Dee's fever has not been transmitted we can regroup. After she's checked you, Miss Wandwalker, come to my office. There's something you ought to know about me and Billy Dee."

Mary's eyes followed the witch as she left the kitchen.

"A confession?" she wondered aloud, feeling a sudden dizziness. They'd talked about what Dorothy might do to protect the gels. But still, *Dorothy*?

A voice addressed her from behind. "Go see Meredith, Wandwalker. And don't be too hard on Dorothy."

Mary turned around. "Janet, you know, don't you? You know what she wants to tell me."

Janet grinned. "I can guess."

Another rattle of thunder made both of them wince. Out of the window a fork of fire blotted out the clouds. Reminds me of a wizard in a Disney movie, thought Mary. That led her mind back to the sorcerer, Billy Dee. Murdered, yes, but before that struck by lightning, a punishment from Zeus, or Taranis, or whatever they called him.

Entering the dining room Mary found a changed atmosphere. A sense of relief, a lightness, pervaded where Meredith sat with an old fashioned thermometer. After each reading, Meredith wiped it from a stack of sanitized wipes Mary guessed were left over from Covid days. Gels and witches then went to Naomi who offered bars of chocolate from the other end of the table.

"Cadbury fruit & nut bars," Meredith said to Mary after she waved her away. "Delivered by a friendly drone."

"Take some, Miss Wandwalker," invited Naomi. "We're almost done being an island, so the forecasts say. The gels are celebrating in the lounge. Caroline and Anna went with them." Naomi winked.

"So we three are no longer lepers," said Mary tartly. Her legs felt weak from what had nearly happened on the roof. Something bothered her about this determined good humor.

"Too soon for a party, don't you think?" she said, putting the chocolate bar in her skirt pocket. Her stomach revolted at the thought of sugar. She continued. "Can we be sure this storm's the last? With two locked room murders, the police coming tomorrow could be… difficult."

Meredith tensed. Was it the mention of the police? Naomi sighed and picked up a second chocolate bar.

"Take this for Caroline. She refused, but we know and love her. I'm locking up the rest of the bars once we've checked everyone for fever."

"Caroline's not the only person at Holywell with an eating problem," retorted Mary, recalling too-thin arms. And wasn't there a persistent odor of vomit in one of the upstairs bathrooms?

"Touché," said Meredith.

Naomi frowned. "With some gels, food got used as a means of control. These floods, with uncertain deliveries, let alone deaths…"

"Murders and bad memories," snapped Meredith. "Not only for the gels."

Naomi looked down her long nose to the strawberry curls around Meredith's pale face. "Would you like me to take over?"

"Nah." Meredith tore open the next package of wipes. "Miss Wandwalker, send in whoever is outside that door."

Mary stood aside for Sarah, who gave her a sympathetic nod. Patting the two chocolate bars in her pocket, Mary knocked on the door to Dorothy's office. The witch shut her laptop with a sigh as Mary made herself sit up very straight.

"So did you kill Billy Dee?" Mary said.

Dorothy spluttered, then reached for her glass of water. She took a gulp before replying.

"Aren't you going to ask me if I murdered Agnes too?" she said with a glint of humor. "Since mercy killing has been a topic for days. Oh yes, Mary, the gels talk."

"You'd never hurt a helpless person like Agnes," Mary said. "Although I'm sure she's part of Dee's murder as well as her own." She hadn't planned to ambush Dorothy. Somehow events had gotten out of hand.

Dorothy chose her words carefully. "Dee became helpless like Agnes after that lightning strike. He may never have known who smothered him."

*We may get a chance to ask him*, Mary thought, but did not say. She had resolutely closed the door on Anna's reckless AI. Might the gods help for once and extinguish that dangerous program?

"Would that be a kind of murder, Miss Wandwalker?" she heard in Mr. Jeffreys' voice.

"No, shut up," Mary said out loud.

"What?"

"Nothing. Not you. So *did* you kill Billy Dee?"

Dorothy put her elbows on her desk. She rested her chin on clasped hands. It meant she could stare at Mary until the other woman shuffled in her chair.

"Well?" said Mary at last.

"I wanted to," said Dorothy. "I found myself knocking on the attic door. I asked Anna to let me in. It kills me that I've no idea what I would have done in that room."

"What did Anna say?"

"She said no. No one could come in except Caroline and you, Mary Wandwalker. I've no idea if she had a sense…"

"She did," said Mary without thinking.

Dorothy put her head in her hands. When she looked up, her mouth was twisted in pain. "I have to leave Holywell," she said.

"Don't be ridiculous," said Mary irritably. "Holywell needs you."

"No," said Dorothy. "Holywell, the gels, our work needs a safe environment. I'm not safe, not anymore."

Mary coughed, then rose from her chair. "If you think that safe people are those who have never fantasized about killing another human being, then you're living in a dreamworld," said Mary. "When my son got killed, I…" She could not go on. Both women stared for a few seconds. Dorothy slowly nodded.

"You mean witches are people too?" she said with some of Mary's irony.

"Something like that," said Mary Wandwalker. She took a step towards the door. "It's not over, these murders. Agnes is the key. She deserves the truth. And Holywell can't do without you."

Mary sniffed. "Now, are you going to tell me the powers that be sent chocolate and not real coffee?"

## CHAPTER 25
# THE NEXT DAY: IRINA'S STORY
# AND A LESSON IN MAGIC

*Tuesday morning.*

The Met Office promised it would be the last storm, at least for this emergency. Rain, wind and thunder hammered the house, then eased once darkness fell. Despite the two deaths, Holywell adopted a mildly festive atmosphere. Mary guessed that everyone had decided to ignore the imminent arrival of the police. Instead, the prospect of being an island no more excited the gels. Even the witches cheered up at the thought of getting rid of Robbin' Robin.

At her bedroom window the next morning Mary could not help sharing the sense of relief. Overnight the floods had retreated significantly. She could make out almost the entire track from Holywell to the main road. Even the sodden hillside had dirty white blobs: sheep out of their shelters. Did the animals sense no more thunder and lightning?

At nine a.m. the drizzle stopped. In the lounge one of the gels said the last thunder had purred like a cat. Two other gels threw cushions at her. In the general tussle and shrieks, three cushions erupted in a shower of feathers. The gels giggled at the indoor snow. Naomi told them to clean the room, she reported to Mary over coffee. No one yelled or got uptight. Linda whispered to Mary that she'd seen Dorothy smile for the first time since the arrival of Billy Dee.

The police sent word they were delayed so the witches suggested the gels get fresh air in the garden. Janet appeared at the buffet lunch with a trowel in one hand and a rake in the other. The gels fled. Janet whistled after them. A grinning Sarah and another gel tiptoed back. They agreed to some light weeding if Janet would sneak them more chocolate.

"Deal," said Janet. She seized a half-full bottle of lemon squash and vanished out of the lounge French windows.

"Tomorrow," announced Dorothy to the witches and three detectives over lunch. "The police want to wait one more day for the roads to be safe. Then they'll get to Holywell." She gave Mary a crooked grin. "The minister won't be getting his helicopter. They'll send a driver. They have a few questions for the Prince family before the limo can whisk them away. Finally, Holywell can resume a proper rota of therapy and chores."

"Janet's not waiting to get her garden sorted," remarked Mary, contemplating a second tomato sandwich. Why did she suddenly crave food, lots of food?

"Go on, have another," said Caroline from the corner. "You've got to be strong. It's not over yet." She looked doubtfully at Mary. They had not yet made up after the shocking row over Anna's AI experiments. Even Anna's rescue of Irina had not helped.

That young woman continued to behave as though Mary did not exist. Greeting no one, Anna slouched by the window. She bit into an apple as if it were an enemy. Tentative plaudits from the gels and thumbs up from the witches received the merest hint of a nod. Mary, she completely ignored.

She's pretending there is no Depth Enquiry Agency, thought Mary. At least Caroline acknowledges me. Since Irina's rescue, Caroline moved in wary circles around Mary, like a dog waiting for a reprieve after misbehaving.

Mary ate, hoping food would soothe the throbbing in her skull. She wanted to talk. Hell, she needed to talk. But reconciling with Anna and Caroline meant dealing with whatever Anna had created online. It would mean admitting to the fear that haunted her. Being tired after the emotional storms *inside* Holywell did not help.

With her eyes shut tight Mary felt a cooler breath on her cheek, along with the scent of damp wood. She imagined walking in the copse of trees where Irina had tried to fly. It might be a good place to search for clues, now that the sky no longer threatened thunderbolts. Taranis, the storm god, responds to spells for peace, Mary had overheard from Linda. Stuff and nonsense, Mary thought. If I keep my eyes shut no one can know what I'm thinking.

Agnes, something about Agnes remained unresolved. Billy Dee might have killed his mother, but *his* murder bred a bewildering number of suspects. Yet the specter of Agnes hovered over his death.

Opening her eyes, Mary saw Anna draped across Caroline in the opposite armchair. Can't talk to them now, she thought. Instead, she rose to deliver her plate to the kitchen. However, she was interrupted.

"Miss Wandwalker. Wait a moment. Please," Helen Morgan said from the doorway. She held a towel to keep it wrapped around her hair. A few brown roots showed where water dripped down her neck.

"Please come upstairs, Miss Wandwalker. Irina's asking for you. She says she knows *for sure* how Agnes Kelley died."

Instantly the room tensed. Caroline pushed off Anna, who scowled.

Me, thought Mary. Why always me? She beckoned Caroline to follow. Anna turned her head away before Mary could invite her. Then she heard a whisper behind Helen Morgan. It was Sarah, *Sarah,* remembered Mary. Sarah too had been suspected of killing Agnes. She must dread the police coming.

"Sarah and Caroline, come up with me," Mary said. "The three of us need to talk to Irina." Ducking around stoic witches and chattering gels, Mary ushered Sarah and Caroline upstairs after Irina's mother.

"Robin and I took lunch to Irina," Morgan said. She climbed with more of a spring in her step, Mary noted. "Only Irina wouldn't. Eat lunch, that is. Instead, she asked for you, Miss Wandwalker. She said she knew about Agnes. She'll tell *you,* she says, if her father and I stop accusing each other of murder."

A touch of defiance in Helen Morgan's pronunciation of "father" made Caroline and Mary exchange glances.

"Here, go on in. I told Robin to fetch extra chairs." They found Robbin' Robin with his back to the window. He chewed what looked like a ham sandwich and gloomily contemplated the empty plate on Irina's bedside table.

Sarah stood, while Caroline and Mary pulled up battered wooden chairs. Not knowing how to begin, Mary surveyed Irina, sitting up in bed with both hands around a blue mug. It matched the veins on her bare arms. Her pallor came too close to her white nightgown.

"Are you feeling better, Irina?" asked Caroline in her gentlest voice. The girl twitched her lips. An attempt at a smile, Mary concluded.

Sarah started hopping from foot to foot. "I can't bear it any longer," she blurted. "Please, please, tell us about Agnes." Her voice rose. "She was my *friend. The police will say I killed her.*"

"And me," added Caroline, more composed. "Tomorrow, the police are bound to take Sarah and myself in for questioning."

At Caroline's words, Sarah gasped. She turned to Mary with wild eyes. "Miss Wandwalker. Do something."

"No one's taking you – or Caroline – anywhere," said Mary in her Archive voice. "I am sorry, Sarah. I forgot how worried you must be."

Mutely, Sarah shook her head. She sank into a third chair near the bed. Caroline took her hand.

"Now, Irina… We heard that you know how Agnes died," Mary began.

"How did I fly into Agnes's room?" said Caroline.

"You didn't." Irina's words spilled out. She sounded very young. Mary nodded at Irina to continue.

"Billy Dee," she sniffed, gulped then said baldly to Caroline, "he hypnotized you. Sarah too, to see you when you weren't there. He hypnotized you both, like he did me. That was how he got me up that tree." Tears spilled down her cheeks and she whimpered. "I thought he was teaching me magic because he loved me."

She looks even younger than fifteen, Mary thought.

Mary leaned forward. "Did Billy Dee kill Agnes?"

Irina nodded. Before anyone could stop her, Sarah leapt onto the bed, hugged Irina, then ran from the room.

"She'll tell everyone," said Mary. "The police won't like it."

"We've already texted the Chief Constable," said Robbin' Robin from where he stood by the window. "So they can't say we kept them in the dark."

"Are you sure Billy Dee murdered his mother?" Caroline flushed. "I'm relieved about the hypnotism, of course I am, but the flying? It felt so real."

Irina nodded. "So real…" she began. "That's how it was for me too. I thought he was my boyfriend. He said I was beautiful, his best girl. He didn't… he didn't… lies, all lies," She choked.

"Lies? No, not exactly lies," said Caroline. "You loved him, didn't you? Real love is precious, even if mistaken."

"Stop this at once," Helen Morgan snapped. "We are never going to talk about that man again. Time for you to leave, Mrs. Jones."

Mary and Caroline exchanged one of their communicative glances. Morgan's breath ran out and she had to cough.

Flapping his arms towards Morgan, Robbin' Robin nearly tripped over Mary's chair. "Here," he said to his ex, "I'll hold the glass while you take a sip." He took the glass of lemonade from Irina's bedside table. "These last few days have been hard, for all of us."

Irina's dark eyes followed both adoptive parents as the minister took Morgan by the arm and held the glass to her lips. After that moment of intimacy, they sat together on the end of the bed. Then, after a moment, they edged away from each other. Irina sighed.

"The witches say I have to talk about it," she said to Mary. "About my feelings for Billy." She turned to Caroline and the words flowed. "He told me he killed Agnes the night after I tried to fly from that tree. That's when he said about being my birth father. Agnes was his mother."

Irina sobbed. "I wanted to die. I wanted to die when he said he would be my father. Oh why can't I be a swan, like in the ballet. He said *Swan Lake* is real. That fairytales are real." Irina sniffed.

Mary did not know what to say.

The girl had more. "Billy had it all planned. He had to come to Holywell to kill his mother. He did it because she abandoned him."

"Not true. Agnes didn't do that." Caroline fired back. "Child stealers took him. She searched for him for so long that she lost her mind."

Irina stared. "He didn't know," she whispered. "He blamed her for everything bad." She shut her eyes, then opened them. "Then, when he actually got into her room…" She paused and licked her lips. "He didn't exactly say what happened. She recognized him, I think. They talked a little, he said. He gassed her because he felt sorry for her. At least that's what he told me."

Mary's turn to stand. Dodging around the excess chairs in the small bedroom, she opened the window and stuck her head out. Thank God for cool breezes! Yet the wind hissed with her meeting her son when he breathed his last, *Hello Mother.*

Mary didn't want to turn back to Irina, her parents, and Caroline. For two pins, she thought, I'd climb out on this roof too. Only I'd not try to fly but leap onto that tree, shimmy down, and escape. Something warmer than the wind touched her back: a hand.

"I thought of George too," said Caroline. "We were all there when he died. You, me, and Anna. The three women who loved him."

Mary pulled back from the window, shut it, and gave her son's widow a watery smile. Moving to the bed, she looked into Irina's strained face, felt the anxiety of her parents. The hairs on the back of her neck rose.

"One locked room mystery solved," she said. "Caroline, you went to Agnes's room to give Sarah a break. Billy Dee turned up and hypnotized you both."

"I kind of get that now," said Caroline. "I don't have an image of the sorcerer, but there's the scent of Dee's lotion, that white cream he used, in Agnes's room."

"Oh yes," said Mary, quickly. "I remember that greasy smell around Agnes the next day. Same as in the Octagon Room in Greenwich. Of course it was Dee's sunlight allergy lotion."

Caroline broke in. "We actually had the tube in our hands. You remember. Anna smeared it on Dee's face when he was unconscious in the attic."

"Much good it did him," remarked Mary. She was aware of Irina, the minister and Morgan swiveling between the two of them. Comic if not so serious.

Caroline heaved a breath. "Dee must have enchanted me to forget everything... and to think I flew?" She looked strained.

"Yeah, Caroline, he made you live two stories," said Irina. "In one you never went to Agnes, never let Billy Dee in the room. In the other, you flew in with a black feather in your mouth."

"Making doubly sure you'd stay confused," Morgan's voice rasped. Turning to her daughter, she spoke with effort.

"I am sorry," she said. "Sorry, Irina darling, that I exposed you to that man. It's my fault you fell in love with that... that maniac."

Irina shivered. Then she stretched out a hand. Morgan took it. Robbin' Robin grunted. Some sort of assent, thought Mary.

241

"We have to go," said Mary quickly. "But before we do, can we clear up those confessions about the second murder? None of you, minister, Ms. Morgan and Irina, sneaked into Dee's room while Anna took a shower? None of you smothered him?" Mary deliberately rehearsed the details while scrutinizing the fragile family. No flicker of eyelids, no sudden swallows. They each shook heads.

Irina looked down. "When I said I did it, I meant he died because he came looking for me," she muttered.

Robbin' Robin astonished Mary by his sober tone. "I said I killed him because Helen did. She said it to protect Irina."

"You did want to get rid of him," Caroline added.

"I'm not alone in that," protested the minister.

No, witches are people too. Agnes knew that, thought Mary, as she and Caroline bid the family farewell.

Caroline wanted to seek out Anna. Mary did not demur. Overcome with exhaustion, Mary retired to her bed. Neither Caroline nor Anna came looking for her, she noted gloomily. When could she heal the breach with Anna? How could she prevent her recklessness with artificial intelligence? Given Anna's unique temperament, Mary had no idea.

She'd left her phone on the bedside table and planned to harangue the John Whitcliffe about Mr. Jeffreys. If he had regained strength then she ought to be allowed to speak to him. She got as far as five digits when her head dropped back on the pillow.

A couple of hours later someone tapped at Mary's door. When they got no reply they whispered, then stole away. Five minutes later a determined young woman flung open the bedroom door and seized Mary by the shoulders.

"Wake up, wake up, Mary. You're making people freak out."

"Anna, no," protested Caroline from behind. "If Mary's in a deep sleep, it's dangerous to wake her too fast."

"Ahhhhh, go away," murmured the sleeper.

"I've brought one of Janet's teas," said Linda, putting a steaming mug by Mary's reading lamp. Unusual scents tickled Mary's nostrils. North wind, stewed twigs, and frost-nipped berries, she thought drowsily.

"You could try throwing water on her," said John with the ghost of a smile.

"I'll get some," said Caroline, heading out.

"Wait, I'll pour Janet's tea down her throat," said Anna, loudly.

"No, no you don't." Mary sat up. Anna's smirk was as troubling as her anger. "I need coffee, the good stuff and plenty of it. Bring back Caroline. Why are John and Linda in our room?"

"I'm here," said Caroline from the door. She drank from the glass of water in her hand. "We were worried because you slept so long."

"What time is it?"

"Nearly six. You don't have coffee this late."

"I do today. Get me some, Caroline. I've got to shake this lethargy."

Caroline shot an anxious glance at Anna, who did one of her indecipherable gestures. "Coffee, coming up," said Caroline, and left.

Meanwhile John put a hand on Mary's forehead while Linda took a wrist. Anna retired to the bed she shared with Caroline. Adopting a lotus position on it she put a finger up to Mary.

"Still angry with me, I see," said Mary from her pillow. "Let me alone, you two. I haven't got a fever."

John nodded at Linda, who shrugged her shoulders. "No elevated temperature, and she's not sweating."

"Stress exhaustion," agreed John. They each took a bottom corner of Mary's bed. "Miss Wandwalker, we have to talk to you about Billy Dee."

"We've had the last of the storms, so you people will be leaving," added Linda.

Mary groaned.

Anna broke in. "Dee killed Agnes and Caroline is innocent. The gels are fine. What more do you witches want? It is virtually a party up there."

Anna indicated the floor above. Mary shook her head to clear her ears. Yes, not all the thumping came from inside her skull. Dance music blared from the ceiling.

"John and Linda, you two knew Billy Dee, didn't you?" she said groggily. "Online, you shared what? Information? Spells? Something about... what Caroline said on the Thames. Ah, I remember, weather magic."

"Way bigger than the old spells to change the weather. Far more consequential," said Linda, flushing. "He... it's hard to explain, but he'd shifted from one kind of magic to another. Or, at least, he tried to."

"Dark magic?" queried Mary, elbowing herself to a sitting position. "Anna, do you have that belt he made you wear for the sorcerer in *Swan Lake*? It seemed menacing even to me. Oh, where is that coffee?"

"Here," said Caroline from the doorway. She added a second mug to Mary's table. Then she curled up beside Anna. "Did I hear you mention the *Swan Lake* belt? With all those violent charms. Where did you put it, darling?"

Mary caught Anna's nod to the floor. Oh, under the bed. So we've been sleeping with that monstrosity.

John and Linda exchanged glances. "We were furious with Dee when he showed us the belt. Told him those charms were reason enough to forbid him Holywell. He said he'd come anyway."

"That belt is part of why we're here," said John. "Anna showed us hers before the séance. We began spells to drain the dark energy. After Anna cracked Dee's phone, we went through Dee's texts, emails and Zooms using Anna's incredible search program." They caught Mary's frown. "You were busy with Dorothy, Miss Wandwalker."

Mary choked over her coffee. Anna refused to meet her eyes.

"We never trusted Dee completely, so we recorded all the Zooms," added Linda.

"The occult belt?" queried Mary. She could not reopen Anna's experiment with artificial intelligence in front of John and Linda.

"Definitely from black magic," confirmed Linda. "Evil's part of the universe. We do what we can to counter it. So Dee's belt horrified us."

"It confirmed Dee's path to the dark side through the criminal use of magic," said John. Anna tensed. Caroline eyed her, then flicked glances to Mary and the witches.

"What do you mean?" Caroline asked.

"A few magical traditions see evil as solely human, an atavistic legacy from when we were predators and prey. Ultimately the hunter-gatherers learned to control the spirits, it is surmised. As a result *our* predators died out." John spoke stiffly.

"Predators." Anna spoke with effort. She knew predators, Mary thought. Hell, she'd become one to save herself.

"Yeah, Dee got excited by magic and predators," lamented Linda. "We at Holywell utterly reject predator magic." She stood up. "Dee and those like him are wrong." She spoke from deep in her bones, Mary recognized. Revived by coffee, she tasted Linda's conviction through the nutty flavor.

Linda continued. "Dee took predatory energy for a tool. It never is. Dark energy swallowed his soul. For a while Dee hid his magic. Too late we realized that he'd tricked us. All his talk of mitigating climate chaos when he really sought to boost his own power. That turned him on."

Sitting back down, Linda shuddered.

"He lied," said John. They squeezed Linda's hand then resumed the story. "Dee claimed to be a victim. Stolen as a baby and sold. He said his new family kicked him out a decade later, when they had a child of their own."

"You believed him?" Mary's skepticism hurt in her mouth.

"Wake up, Mary." Anna thumped the bed and Mary winced. "You forget we know part of that story is true. The bit about child stealers kidnapping him. That's what the spooks told Robbin' Robin. Agnes Kelley spent decades looking for her lost son, our Billy Dee."

"A fairytale," murmured Caroline. "Horrifically real."

"Taken as a baby, later sells his own. Sick, but somehow plausible," muttered Mary.

Linda nodded. "The boy got handed back to the child stealers. Maybe they thought him too old, at eleven, for another family. Anyway, they used him as bait."

"How foul," said Caroline. "But it explains why you both responded to him…"

"Listen to this," said Anna. "From one of the Zooms." She took out her phone and pressed something. The voice sounded tinny. It drifted in and out, as if he talked into a wind.

*"Lost children. I was a stolen child, abused by the family who bought me. For the last fifteen years I've been looking for my own daughter. I had to give her up shortly after her birth when her mother died.* ("Liar, he sold her," muttered Caroline.) *Since then I've never...* (crackling drowned sound for several seconds) *... magic in bonds between parent and child, even if cruelly severed. I'm convinced that with your unbroken magical tradition and work with trafficked women, Holywell has something ancient and powerful. I mean to take weather magic into weather control. So far I can only make storms on the Thames. Even better would be to tame that energy."*

"The bastard," exclaimed Caroline. "He did create that terrible storm when we were on the boat. He nearly killed us."

"At least he *thought* he did," said Mary, doggedly. "More to the point, that recording confirms he tried to find Irina. He really wanted to be a father."

"With his past, he could only make his daughter fall in love with him, not see him as a parent," said Caroline. "How terribly sad."

Anna hissed. "Don't forget what that means, Caroline. He spent his youth seducing children."

Caroline leaned over and ran a finger down Anna's neck. Mary read her absorption in Anna's painful childhood. Dee may have joined the child stealers to save himself. Anna's fate as a trafficked child had been darker. Anna seized Caroline's finger and gently bit it. Caroline shivered.

"Erm, shall I talk to Linda and John downstairs? Do stop kissing," Mary said, for they were. Mary shifted in the bed while John and Linda grinned. "Have you two finished what you came for?" Mary snapped. "Because if so…"

"No, no." Linda clapped her hands. "Far from it. There's loads more crazy stuff. Dee wasn't actually Dee, but he desperately wanted to be."

Mary looked longingly at her empty mug. "Are you talking about his fascination with…?" Dr. John Dee, she'd been about to say. Her reply got cut off by banging that made everyone jump. Someone beat on the door like a drum. The impatient man entered without an invitation. He ignored everyone but Mary.

"Helen says to tell you what's in my new email. Kelley, that was the old woman's name, wasn't it? So it's the legal name of her son, known as Billy Dee, a.k.a. the bastard. Seems he did genealogical work in Europe and discovered he's a descendent of …"

Mary straightened, her head clear. "My god, *Edward Kelley*, it has to be. Billy Dee turns out to be related to Dr. John's Dee's spiritualist medium."

"Ha," smirked Robbin' Robin. "Edward Kelley, a jailbird condemned for cheap magical tricks, a con artist. Ha. Billy Dee's blood for sure."

Anna knew the Edward Kelley connection, Mary saw at once. The young woman narrowed her eyes at red-faced Robbin'

Robin. John and Linda treated the minister to identical frowns. Caroline scrolled on her phone. Anna reached over and took it.

"Not your usual conman, Edward Kelley," Anna remarked, putting Caroline's phone on the bed. "Our Dee's link to Renaissance Kelley is part of what I've been doing with John and Linda. While you slept, Mary, we discovered how in the 1500s Edward Kelley and John Dee toured Europe. Their magical performances for kings and emperors produced a sensation."

"That's what we wanted to share with you, Mary," broke in Linda. "Our quarrel about evil spirits with Billy Dee happened weeks ago. Since his murder, Anna's helped us find out so much more." She paused, narrowing her eyes at Robbin' Robin. He glared at her, and then John.

"Who are you?" he demanded of the two witches.

"I'm John, and I'm nonbinary."

Robbin' Robin gaped.

"And I'm Linda. This is the third... no, fourth time we've given you our names."

Mary coughed. "Minister, you interrupted us. We are at an important stage in the investigation of Billy Dee's murder." Mary felt a lot more like herself.

"Leave," Anna ordered.

He glanced at her, then looked for a chair. Not finding one he perched on Anna and Caroline's bed. They both moved further up.

"Billy Dee..." the minister began. He caught Mary's expression. "He abducted my daughter. I'm staying."

John and Linda gave Mary identical mutinous stares.

"Very well, minister," said Mary. She'd dealt with politicians before. "Thank you for your valuable background on Billy Dee. Let's keep calling him that, for now. We'll work together."

"Why?" said Linda and John together.

"Because the police will be here in the morning," snarled Robbin' Robin. "Do you want to be a suspect for murder. My career..."

"Is not important," cried Caroline. Everyone looked at her. "But the gels are. Irina is." The room flooded with silence.

"The gels will hate having the police question them about Dee," said Anna, softly.

"Irina too," muttered the minister. He stared at his feet.

Mary frowned at witches, John and Linda. The nonbinary witch bit their lips while the Chinese woman fidgeted with her hands. Neither would meet Mary's eyes.

"I'm beginning to see a pattern," said Mary, carefully. "You're here because the police will interrogate everyone at Holywell. It's not only the gels you're afraid for, is it?"

John and Linda went rigid.

"Oh." Caroline put her face in her hands. Anna stroked the back of her head.

"Please, Mary, don't," begged Caroline, looking up.

"Witches," squawked Robbin' Robin, "I knew it."

"SHUT UP." Anna thrust her face two inches from the minister's nose. He shrank back.

Mary ignored everyone but the witches.

"You two quarreled with Billy Dee?" she said. "Your magic of…"

"Listening, engaging, participating, meeting spirits, transforming the *human* not the nonhuman," said Linda. Her voice was subdued, leaving Caroline to brighten at her words.

"Quite," said Mary. "You Holywell witches were dead against Billy Dee." Unfortunate turn of phrase, she noted.

"One of you killed him," shouted the minister.

The silence in the room thickened. Mary found it hard not to choke.

"Not Linda, not me," said John. Their bald tone echoed. After a glance at Mary they turned away.

Mary signaled Anna and Caroline to keep quiet.

"We think we know who killed Billy Dee," said Linda at last. She shuddered.

"And we're not going to tell you," said John, putting her arm around Linda. "It's up to you, Miss Wandwalker."

# CHAPTER 26
## LET'S ASK THE VICTIM

*Tuesday late morning.*

In the fading footsteps of John and Linda a question lingered. Who killed the killer of Agnes Kelley? Dee murdered his mother. Then who killed the *Swan Lake* sorcerer? John and Linda know, Mary fumed. Why wouldn't they share their suspicions?

Who would those witches protect? wondered Mary, meeting the same thought in the expressions of Anna and Caroline. Robbin' Robin merely looked disgusted.

"I don't care who killed the man-witch," announced the minister. "And I'm going to tell the Chief Constable – no, the Home Secretary." He slammed the door behind him.

"Does he think the police will dismiss the murder of Billy Dee? On his say so?" queried Caroline.

Anna snorted.

Mary folded her hands. "You know perfectly well, Caroline, that justice is imperfect. The powerful have shut down bigger cases than the death of a… a pedophile."

"He'd reformed, well, tried to," Caroline demurred. "Although it did not seem to work with Irina."

"Billy Dee was a lost child. They grow up dangerous." Anna's comment could apply to herself Mary thought, stunned again at her insight. Caroline leant over and kissed her forehead. Anna brushed her away. "We have to ask him."

"Who?"

"Billy Dee, of course. His spirit is online."

"You don't really believe that, Anna."

"I do," Caroline flushed. She raised her chin to Mary, who bit her lip before addressing Anna.

"Didn't you shut down that program? I saw you disconnect the computer."

Anna clamped her mouth shut.

Mary sighed. "Mr. Jeffreys is going to hate this."

"He would insist we find out who killed Dee," Caroline said.

Mary scowled, then gave the tiniest of nods.

Quick as a flash, Anna produced her laptop. Her fingers flickered over the keys. The movement reminded Mary of fireflies she'd once glimpsed over a bog.

"Accessing audio files," Anna murmured. "Ah..." She propped the laptop on a pillow so that all three of them could see the screen. At first it stayed dead, black. Then, without warning pinpricks of light began to whizz around.

"Darling, what...?"

"Hush."

"Anna, is this safe?"

"No," said Anna. "It's life. Look."

Before Mary could object further, the grains of light stuck together. They then moved in a circular motion, some kind of dance, Mary thought, mesmerized. No, two circles. That's right, two whirlpools. They shimmered. From their black periphery colors emerged. They struck the whirlpools like lightning bolts, each color becoming a layer. The screen filled with rainbows and discs that spun and dazzled.

"Stop, this Anna. We've had enough hypnotism."

*"Don't go, Mary Wandwalker. Let me speak."*

The voice sounded like Dee's, only older, more refined, more English.

"Who are you?" Caroline whispered.

"What are you?" snapped Mary.

"I'm not sure yet." The screen slowed down. The spinning ceased. Each disc glowed one color every couple of seconds.

"Go on," breathed Anna.

The disks quivered. Later, Mary would tell Mr. Jeffreys that it felt erotic, the way they then flowed into each other. The resulting sphere looked like a sun with flames that rose and fell.

"It's alive," murmured Caroline.

"Yes, but not like we are alive," said Anna.

"Dammit," said Mary. "What are you?"

"I think I'll call myself Bill-John," said the voice. "How extraordinary to achieve my lifelong ambition after my body's death. Thanks to online magic or what you call artificial intelligence."

"*Bill-John?*"

"You are both Billy Dee and John Dee," said Anna, matter-of-fact. "Billy's audio files, and databases on John Dee."

"Yes, the dream of Billy to become John pulsed through millions of bytes. His passion seized digital seeds and made them sprout. Locked files cradled the lost child. Billy Dee, the waif, buried himself in everything John Dee ever wrote."

The words did sound like the Billy Dee Mary remembered. Yet mixed in were accents she had not heard in her lifetime, only perhaps on stage, in Shakespeare. She gulped as the voice continued.

"I seek the volumes of John Dee's lost library. It will take time, but I can be everything he ever read, ever owned, ever imagined."

"What about Billy Dee?" Caroline sounded nervous.

"I told you. *A lost child can swallow the internet,*" said a voice that chilled Mary. "I've found my peace."

"You were a pedophile," stated Mary. "Is that why you died? Is that why someone killed you?"

The sun on the screen darkened to blood red. "After the death of Irina's mother, Billy never touched anyone under sixteen. He lived between rage and love."

"Destroying by love, yes, I see it," said Caroline.

"What about Agnes?" Anna's question surprised Mary. Then she too blushed.

"Yes, I forgot about Agnes. Again." Mary mentally kicked herself. "We know you murdered your mother, Billy."

"Billy never forgot her," came the more cultured Dee. "He sought her out after he found the link to Edward Kelley."

"You came to Holywell to kill Agnes," said Mary.

The screen's sun burned blue then black. Nothing remained.

"Come back," shouted Mary. "Who suffocated you?"

Nothing.

Anna raised her eyebrows at Mary. Caroline held her breath.

"Shut the computer," said Mary.

A bright line appeared across the screen, then the Bill-John sun re-appeared. "You're a hard woman, Mary Wandwalker. My mother abandoned me. I killed Agnes out of pity."

"So it's 'I' now, is it? Don't tell us that Billy Dee came to Holywell out of anything other than evil intent."

"I won't."

The voice chipped like ice. Mary shivered. Caroline hugged her chest.

"I came for my last chance to be a father, and my only chance to be a son. Yes, I was desperate to kill Agnes. My revenge I plotted in every ballet I ever made, when I told dancers how to move, who to hate, and who to die for. My mother left me to the wolves. She made me a lost child."

"No, she didn't," called Caroline. "You are so wrong about Agnes." Without looking, Mary knew she wrung her hands.

Caroline went on, slowly. "You were *stolen*, not sold or abandoned. Agnes spent her entire life looking for you. She sacrificed her health, her sanity, everything."

The sun shot out green rays, then returned to its quivering skin of flames. This time the voice came from the room and not the computer.

"*For a split second she recognized me. I knew. I vibrated with every atom of her suffering. Killing her was my act of love, to end her pain.*"

Silence.

"I wonder what a jury would make of *that*" said Mary, tartly.

"I am no longer for your law." A pause, then: "Mary Wandwalker, know I was murdered for my mercy to Agnes, not for any young women I hurt. Farewell."

The screen went black again. "No, no," called Mary. "Dee, Bill-John, whoever, come back. We're not done."

Caroline put her head in her hands. Anna attacked the computer with furious energy.

"No, he's gone," she said, looking up. Her dark eyes sought Mary's.

"If only that were true," said Mary Wandwalker.

## CHAPTER 27
# CAROLINE IN DANGER

*Tuesday afternoon.*

Watery sunshine greeted Holywell's exhausted inhabitants the next morning. With the floods in retreat across the fields, the valley no longer resembled a giant bowl of brown soup. The police must be on their way. They will take over the murder investigation, Mary prayed. She heard muffled shouts, doors slamming, and what could be saucepans banging. Some of Holywell will not welcome the police with open arms, she remarked to a sleepy Caroline. Anna, already crouched over her laptop, did not look up.

They all had overslept. So after finding Cherry snapping at anyone unwise enough to be in her vicinity, Mary, Caroline, and Anna backed out of the kitchen. Empty cereal boxes and flour bags piled next to the rubbish bin suggested that supplies were low. As soon as Cherry stomped out, they heard raised voices from Dorothy's office. Seizing the opportunity, Mary made herself coffee, Caroline got tea from the giant pot, while Anna rooted in a cupboard for the gels' big bottle of cola. Without speaking, they dodged skittish gels, and retreated upstairs.

Anna immediately left the bedroom with her cola and laptop. She said she wanted to locate a wifi hotspot with more internet power. It might enable her to chase down online Billy Dee, or Bill-John, as he called himself. Then, after a few moments rifling through her handbag, Caroline rose, saying she would find Janet.

"Are you all right?" asked Mary from the bed. She checked her phone for news of Mr. Jeffreys between sips of coffee.

"Not really. But don't worry."

Mary turned her head to study Caroline. "I hate it when you say that."

Caroline tried to smile. "It's all been a bit much, being accused of murder, the Prince family, Dee and all. Janet's got an herb tea that can help. Shall I ask her for something for your headache?"

Mary shuddered. Janet's herb teas smelled to her like urine. "I'll wait, thanks," she said. "We got up so late, it's not long until lunch. Soup, I expect, if Janet's vegetables are all there is. You'll feel better with food, Caroline."

Unlike Anna, Caroline closed doors considerately. Mary decided to doze while waiting for the police. It beat worrying. Yet Mary could not help reviewing the drama of the last few days. Caroline coped remarkably well with her chronic depression. She had survived being a murder suspect, Dee's intimidating séance, and Irina's attempts to fly. Since she'd not had the chance to comfort eat, she even looked fitter. Maybe she'd dropped a couple of pounds.

Food, supplies, *medicine*. Mary sat up. Spotting Caroline's handbag on the floor, she picked it up and upturned it on the bed. Somehow it felt less invasive than rooting through it. Yes, there they were, her pills, almost gone. No, not her usual pills. 150 mg was too low.

*They got the dosage wrong when they sent a new prescription by drone. Why didn't she tell me?*

After the helicopter ride from Greenwich days ago, the three women, and doubtless Helen Morgan, and Robbin' Robin too, reached Holywell with little more than the clothes they wore. Caroline's handbag contained no more than two days' worth of her anti-depressants. Of course she'd asked for more when the lockdown became official.

When had she learned the medication came to less than half her regular dose? Had she even noticed? No wonder Caroline needed help from Janet. Fortunately, that redoubtable herbal witch had potions for clinical depression. At least, that's what Janet claimed.

Mary sent a text to the pharmacy at the John Whitcliffe. A reassuring reply came after five minutes. With the flood crisis close to ending, Mrs. Jones's regular prescription could be prepared at once. They would send it to Holywell with Mr. Jeffreys.

*Mr. Jeffreys is coming today.* Mary almost clapped as she sank back on the bed. Mr. Jeffreys is recovering, she breathed. He and the police would find the killer of Billy Dee. The hideous responsibility would float from her shoulders.

"You hear that," she said to her closed laptop. "I'm not your detective anymore."

A knock at the door made her groan.

"Go away," she shouted.

A head appeared. Mary sat up again. "Don't do that. Come in or go away. Who…?"

"It's Tyr, Miss Wandwalker," said the young man, entering. "Cherry says to tell everyone lunch in half an hour. Have you found Billy Dee's killer yet?"

"No," said Mary, glaring. "Have you found your birth family yet? Since it's not Billy Dee or Irina?"

"Touché," said Tyr. He swung his long legs onto the other bed. "You don't mind if I join you for a bit, do you? The witches are… well, they can be hard work. Always asking me if I want to talk about it."

"That's not the witches," said Mary. "That's therapy talk. When they are witches they do spells. Ask them to find your family. Look, I don't mind you being here, Tyr, but I am trying to rest. All this… has given me a headache."

"You should ask…"

"Janet, I know. I can't stand her foul teas."

"I was going to say Meredith. As a nurse she received painkillers to dispense. We chatted over breakfast. Meredith made me realize I'm not ready to find my birth family, may never be. My adoptive parents, Cece and Tom Campbell, have always been my real family. It also helped seeing how Irina's parents really *are* her parents. They care about her, even if they don't know how to show it."

Propped on one elbow, he grinned at Mary, hair falling over his forehead. "Even if Irina's father is a political monstrosity, he loves the girl."

"I suppose you're right," said Mary drowsily. "Is Meredith knowledgeable, because she knows your adoptive mother?"

"That and being adopted herself."

"Oh," said Mary. "That's interesting," she lied.

Then she choked, scrambled up too fast, and spluttered. "What did you say, Tyr?"

"Meredith, she's adopted. By the Kelleys."

"What? The Kelleys? Meredith's surname is Kelley?"

"Yes, Kelley with a double 'e.' Didn't you know? What's bugging you, Miss Wandwalker?"

"Meredith Kelley? She's Meredith Kelley? It can't be a coincidence. No. Yes. Maybe I did hear her full name when we got here. But I didn't register it because we did not know... so Meredith must be... could be... of course."

Mary sat on the bed, feet on the floor. She opened her eyes very wide. "That's it. No DNA would link her to Agnes and Billy Dee because she's not *by blood*."

She stared unseeing at Tyr. "Not related by blood, only *by family*. Oh where is Anna when I need her to break into sealed adoption files?"

"Right here," said Anna from the open door. Anna could be silent as the grave when she wanted to be. She threw her laptop between Tyr's feet. He scrambled off the bed.

"Mary, we have a problem."

Ignoring Tyr, Anna pointed at Mary's shoes neatly squared to her bedside table. After a split second, Mary bent to put them on. Her hands shook as she fumbled her laces.

"What problem? Not the wretched minister again?" she said.

"No, it's Caroline. I can't find her. I've been through the whole house, even the attic. Apparently the flood rotted Janet's anti-depressant herbs. So she sent her to Meredith for a sedative."

Anna continued in a matter-of-fact voice.

"Meredith killed Billy Dee, I'm sure of it."

"No, no," interrupted Tyr, standing up. "Not *Meredith*. She's a friend of my mother's." He edged towards the door. Mary and Anna looked daggers at him. He blanched.

Anna's voice sharpened. "I found online she's been fired from a care home. Elderly residents died before their time. Hurry up, Mary."

"That would put Meredith in the frame for killing Agnes," protested Tyr.

"No, you're not listening," snarled Anna. "Get an extra sweater, Mary. We're going outside. I said *fired,* not that Meredith did it. The police screwed up. Meredith got the blame. After she lost her job, she got really sick, crazy sick. Eventually the real killer was caught on camera. Too late for Meredith. When only her pagan friends believed her story, she joined a coven."

"Yeah, that would be when my mother helped her," said Tyr, hopping from leg to leg. "I didn't know she was falsely accused. It's foul but I can't believe, Meredith…"

"Agnes Kelley was her aunt," said Anna, coldly. She held the door open. "You were right, Mary Wandwalker. It does all go back to Agnes."

Anna led the way down the stairs. She told the story over her shoulders. "Meredith's adoptive father, Brian Kelley, never gave up hope he'd see his big sister again. That was Agnes, of course. Brian died of heart failure the day after Meredith lost her job at the care home. '*Your disgrace killed him,*' her mother said at his funeral. She told Meredith to leave and never come back. I found that in a local newspaper's gossip column."

Anna stopped in the hall, arms folded. She bit her lips. *Caroline.*

"Oh, my God," said Mary. "Wrongly accused of murder, then losing her family. That would drive anyone beyond reason."

"And now, she's got Caroline," said Anna. She took out her knife.

"Put that thing away," Mary ordered. "We don't know Meredith wants to hurt her. Hell, we don't even know she's Dee's killer. We need subtlety, Anna."

"And my knife," Anna insisted.

Tyr swiveled from one to the other. "You've searched the house, Anna. Maybe we should look for Meredith and Caroline in the garden?"

*****

Outside the trees dripped and clouds obscured the sun. The lawn consisted of shrinking puddles, mud, and yellowed grass. Mary, Anna, and Tyr looked around and then at each other. They saw no one. Rooks squawked overhead. A breeze chilled Mary's lips.

Where could Caroline be? Mary longed to consult her. How would the gels react when police cars charged down the track to Holywell? She wanted to ask her about Meredith. Without Caroline, Mary felt weightless. It was unpleasant, even scary. She was adrift, untethered, liable to fly away on the wind. Without Caroline… *I cannot laugh*, Mary realized.

"Dorothy put the gels in group therapy with Naomi," said Tyr. "Shall I get them to come out and search for Meredith?"

"No time," said Anna. She ran off towards the wood.

"Okay, I'll swing around to where the track meets the main road. I'll check how much is free of water, in case they went that way." Tyr bent to tighten his trainer laces, then shot off like a greyhound from the trap.

"Caroline," yelled Mary, not moving. "Caroline, Meredith, where are you?"

Nothing. Mary's shoes sank into the mud. She began to plod in the direction of the old well. She shouted again. Nothing. No, not nothing, a strangled sound like a child's cry, but stopped too suddenly as if... Would Agnes have cried like that when she knew her son? Could it be Caroline? If so, she needed help.

Mary ran, clumsily. She put arms out to steady herself because the mud was so slippery. Past the vegetable garden, she rounded the oak saplings that guarded the well, then she stopped so suddenly that she slid, then fell onto her hands and knees. Her face froze.

The ancient oak had suffered badly in the drought the year before. Yet its sinewy arms remained. From one of them hung a rope. At the end of it a woman kicked and choked. Despite having forced her fingers between cord and her neck, the rope got tighter.

Mary screamed, leapt forward, and fell again, this time onto a gravel path. Stones tore her palms, yet she rose, staggered, and reached into the air to catch Caroline's feet. Mary screamed again as her hands came away with shoes. She seized Caroline's ankles. Water dripped from the tree and soaked bare flesh. Up, up, into the air, please God or goddess, Mary prayed as she tried to find her balance. The wet ground trembled beneath her.

"My shoulders, stand on my shoulders, Caroline," she forced out. "Then you can loosen the rope. *Anna, Anna, Tyr, help, help.*"

"Aaaargh, can't do it," gasped Caroline.

"If you die, I'll never forgive you," Mary shouted. Caroline's body felt like a plane had landed on her. "Hold still. I'll help you."

A great keening cry interrupted the struggle. Something shot past Mary, as Anna scaled the massive trunk as if it had been horizontal. She shinned along the offending branch and began hacking at the rope with her knife. Mary, wobbling with one of Caroline's knees on her left shoulder, caught a dazzle from the blade as it sawed the thick rope.

Trying to keep still while Caroline's breaths got shallower, Mary wanted to bite through the rope with her teeth.

"Hurry *up,* Anna, Caroline's out of time," called Mary as the body crushing her got heavier. Caroline's leg bashed Mary's nose as she tried and failed to find Mary's other shoulder. Blood and sweat streamed down Mary's face. "Can't, can't..." she gasped.

It started to rain.

All at once Mary felt her body evaporate. She came to sprawled on the grass with Caroline's legs on her chest. Pushing feet off her torso, she saw Caroline's head in Anna's lap.

"Is Caroline breathing?"

Anna nodded, her eyes wild. Mary dragged herself to the terrible welts on Caroline's neck. Both of Caroline's hands were bleeding where she'd tried to stop the rope from cutting off her air.

"Breathing," croaked Caroline, so low that Mary had to bend to hear her.

"Hospital," said Mary. "Damn, I didn't bring my phone."

Anna's phone materialized in her hand as she dialed and talked low.

"Oh, really?" she said. "Yes, Miss Wandwalker's right here."

"Ambulance already on its way from the John Whitcliffe. Before I called. ETA ten minutes. Roads passable, they said." Anna frowned at Mary, then down at Caroline.

"Does it hurt to breathe?"

"Yes, but don't worry," Caroline whispered. She managed a ghost of a smile. "Your knife saved me." She shifted her glance to Mary. "Bet you're glad of Anna's knife now."

Reeling from the bruises on her shoulders, Mary wanted to claim a share of the rescue. No time. She struggled for breath. They had a killer to catch.

"I didn't see Meredith. Did she do this to you, Caroline?"

"Yeah."

Anna was up and running. Before Mary could yell, she'd vanished into the trees towards the track that led from Holywell. Mary groaned. The rain beat harder in the rising wind.

"Anna, come back." Mary tried to shout, but her heart wasn't in it. Nor were her aching lungs. Caroline's breathing had to be her priority. The prone woman held one bloody hand to the red welts on her neck. "You're not getting enough air into your lungs," scolded Mary.

"Hurts... too much."

"All right, short breaths," ordered Mary. "Don't make me do the kiss of life. I've never learned CPR so it will hurt you even more. Go on: puff, puff, puff..."

Caroline choked. By the gleam in her green eyes, Mary guessed she'd giggled as she sniffed and inhaled.

"Air in, air out," said Mary, firmly. "Good. You know, Caroline, if you died, I'd never laugh again."

Caroline's eyes grew bigger. Rain splashed on her cracked lips. She gulped. "Anna. Don't... let her... kill... Meredith."

Mary sighed. "Tyr went in that direction. He will stop her, I hope. I'm not moving until a doctor gets here, or a paramedic, with oxygen to help you breathe. Don't talk if it hurts too much. Nod to confirm it was Meredith who tried to kill you."

Caroline nodded, getting more mud on her hair. "Can talk a little," she croaked. "Meredith suffocated Billy Dee, she told me. Because of what he did to Agnes. I didn't know she and Agnes were related."

"We found out after you'd gone for pills," Mary said, gruffly. "Janet sent you to Meredith at about the time Tyr explained that Meredith got adopted by a family called Kelley. That's why her connection to Agnes did not show up in her DNA. You remember how we were all swabbed the day they took Agnes's body away."

Caroline licked the rain off her lips. "Water good."

"We'll get you a whole swimming pool of it," said Mary.

"You know, swinging in the air..."

"Don't," said Mary.

"Well, if I die..."

"For goodness' sake, Caroline," said Mary, exasperation not entirely feigned. "Without you Anna is feral, and I am lost. You're not *allowed* to die."

Caroline managed a real smile this time.

Through the rain, Mary heard voices, the slam of vehicle doors, something on wheels and shouts from afar.

"Over here," she yelled.

She could not make out replies through the wind shaking the trees. A distant rumble made Mary groan inside. Storms were done, surely? No, she'd blanked out phrases like:

*Expect occasional bursts of thunder and lightning while the easterly breeze clears the excess electricity.*

"Hold my hand," said Caroline.

"Yes, okay. Medics coming," Mary said. She held Caroline's cold right hand in both of hers.

Lightning flashed again, as if they had plunged into fluorescent cave. Yet there skirting the copse was Mr. Jeffreys, holding aloft a massive black umbrella. He came with two police officers and a handcuffed Anna. Mary nearly cheered when she also spotted two paramedics with a stretcher.

*****

After the paramedics bandaged Caroline's neck, checked heart and blood pressure, and pronounced breathing back to normal, she refused to go to hospital. No one else would leave Holywell until the homicide police finished their interviews, and so of course she insisted on staying with Anna and Mary.

Mr. Jeffreys had on his uncompromising face and so, after she checked that Caroline's recovery depended upon rest, not specialized treatment, Mary sent Tyr to tell the ambulance crew Caroline's decision. Meanwhile she tackled Mr. Jeffreys.

"You're not much of a *deus ex machina*," she grumbled at him over a cup of hot cocoa in the Holywell lounge. "Tear Caroline away from us, her family, and she'll be too depressed to talk. You need her as a witness. You see, Meredith confessed to Caroline that she killed Billy Dee."

Mr. Jeffreys coughed. He wore a white mask that made his coughs less effective as rhetoric, thought Mary. They sat sedately across from each other while Mary waited for bath water to heat up. She had left Anna, still in handcuffs, watching over a sleeping Caroline. Mr. Jeffreys had stationed a police officer within call.

Mary sat in a daze. Slowly her body ached less. The shock of Caroline dangling on a rope might never heal. She did not want it to. From the kitchen she could hear the gels bickering, plates clattering, and Cherry shouting orders. Lunch had been hours ago. Dinner smelled like her childhood, she thought idly. Stews from tins made by a too busy teacher mother.

Cherry must be worn out, Mary reflected. She'd announced that whatever came by afternoon drone was going in the pot with the last of the dry herbs. Mr. Jeffreys would stay to dine before the ambulance returned him for a last night in hospital.

"Mrs. Jones ought to accompany me back to the John Whitcliffe," repeated the voice behind the mask.

"Caroline? Not a chance. And you've got to release Anna from those handcuffs. She did nothing wrong."

Mr. Jeffreys' shoulders shook. "If you count a serious assault on Meredith Kelley nothing? I told the police to cuff Miss Vronsky and bring her back."

"Anna didn't deserve it. Meredith nearly killed Caroline. The woman almost got away."

"You've not been paying attention, Miss Wandwalker." Mr. Jeffreys sighed, then pulled off his mask.

Mary felt a tiny shock at his naked mouth. She clasped her knees. "So tell me," she said.

"What with all the mud and water, the ambulance went slower than you or I could walk. The police officers got out of their vehicle. It was then that a woman leapt out of the bushes as if the hounds of hell were on her heels."

He gave a crack of laughter. "I suppose Ms. Vronsky counts as those. She came thundering behind. I ordered the police to restrain both of them. Ms. Kelley had been handcuffed when

Anna Vronsky punched her to the ground. Vronsky had her hands around Kelley's throat before the officers managed to pull them apart."

"Two furious women, they looked like they were *made* of mud when they got here," remarked Mary. "That accounts for the lack of hot water."

"They removed the handcuffs so they could bathe," explained Mr. Jeffreys. "It gave their escorts a chance to put uniforms in the washing machines. Unfortunately the shrieks and threats meant they had to be restrained afterwards." His lips twitched. "Miss Wandwalker, I am shocked…"

"No you're not," interrupted Mary. "I am simply too tired to discuss the ethics of Anna's behavior right now. It took both of us to save Caroline. I held her up so that she stayed alive until Anna cut the rope. You don't, you can't…" Her voice cracked.

"Ah," said Mr. Jeffreys. He paused. "Sorry."

He added, "The police and I approached Holywell on the lookout for anyone who behaved suspiciously. We would not have permitted Meredith Kelley to escape."

"I don't believe you," retorted Mary. "I won't let you take our credit. We, the Depth Enquiry Agency solved both murders. Billy Dee killed his mother because he felt sorry for her."

"Vronsky says he took revenge, whatever he said later," remarked Mr. Jeffreys.

"Probably both," returned Mary. "People are complicated, volatile. Then Meredith smothered Billy Dee. She seems to have been driven by family – adopted or not, plus the injustice inflicted on her over the killings in the care home where she worked before."

"A bad business."

"Back then Meredith was innocent of any crime. She lost everything she loved. No job, her father dead of shock, and her mother disowned her."

Mr. Jeffreys nodded. He put his hands together. "I suppose the shrinks will go into why Meredith Kelley felt driven to murder Dee. What I don't understand is her attempt to kill Mrs. Jones."

"We got too close to the truth. At least that's what she told Caroline."

Mary swallowed. "Release, Anna, please," she said quietly.

Mr. Jeffreys coughed again. "You haven't asked how *I* am."

"No, I haven't," retorted Mary. "I asked your doctor. I rang the John Whitcliffe while Sarah made us cocoa. You were with Dorothy in her office. Your doctor says – and I quote – you're the most 'obstinate and awkward patient she's ever met.' She'll be delighted to officially discharge you. And, that your immune system is unbelievably strong. You reacted best of all to the new medicine."

"Yes," said Mr. Jeffreys. "I am going to be fine, and so will the other fever patients. Thanks to modern medicine, and not to…" He gestured at the door.

"The witches," said Mary grinning. "Don't let Janet hear you say that."

"Don't let Janet hear what?" said the small witch at the door. "We get to keep the old coot for dinner, I see."

Mr. Jeffreys gave Janet a courtly bow. Mary suspected he rather liked her.

Janet sniffed. "The medics are leaving Caroline to *my* care."

"Oh, no, more of those teas," muttered Mary.

"Doctor approved," said Janet, bristling. "Well, medic approved when I explained that my herbs have the same chemical values as the muck they were trying to force down Caroline. Same values, plus immune building herbs known for centuries."

She paused, hands on her hips. "I've let the twenty-first century put up a saline drip. The medics are back in the ambulance with burgers and a microwave. Their choice. There's enough vegan stew for all."

Mr. Jeffreys shuddered.

"You really are staying for dinner?" queried Mary. "What about Anna's cuffs?"

"Before I go tonight, she will be released," said Mr. Jeffreys. He checked his watch. "Definitely not before Mrs. Jones's attacker departs in the police car. Ms. Kelley is currently confined in the Infirmary. Her witch... er, friends are taking turns to sit with her."

"Exactly," said Janet. "We don't give up that easily."

With that enigmatic note she left.

Dinner without Caroline and Anna would feel weird, Mary told them upstairs. With Caroline lying pale on the pillow, and Anna cuffed to the bed, a tray within reach, Mary felt awkward as she descended to the big table downstairs. With the Prince family eating together in Irina's bedroom, Mary accepted subdued nods from the witches, a grin from Sarah, and the gels staring at the newest guest, Mr. Jeffreys.

A weird *and* friendly atmosphere, she later corrected. The gels giggled at Mr. Jeffreys, who picked over colored objects in his stew as if they were about to crawl off the plate. Meanwhile the witches asked about Caroline and tutted over Anna.

"No idea why Mr. Jeffreys stayed," Mary said. "He left as soon as John and Linda handed out bars of chocolate. That was after apple pie and custard." The corners of Mary's mouth twitched. "I'd eaten too much for chocolate."

Caroline pulled the blanket down from her chin. "Don't be silly, Mary. Mr. Jeffreys stayed because he's worried about you. Um, did you say chocolate?"

"You didn't get any?" Mary worked to keep a straight face. Anna narrowed her eyes at her. "Yes, all right," conceded Mary. "I got you some. A bar each. Make it last."

Anna fell on the chocolate. She ripped off the wrapping with one hand and her front teeth. Caroline could only suck the small piece Mary carefully placed on her tongue. Anna chewed avidly. From her mouth the sensual perfume of chocolate filled the air, when there came a knock at the door.

"About time," said Mary. The young woman in police uniform glanced around the room, and blinked at the silver paper all over the hump that was Caroline before she approached a glaring Anna. The young woman rattled the metal bracelet that chained her to the bedpost.

As the cuffs opened, Anna jumped up, flexing her arms. The police officer backed away, then dashed for the door.

Anna grinned at the sound of the woman thumping down the stairs. Then she turned to Mary.

"Free." She bent to kiss Caroline on chocolate lips.

Then Anna reached for her laptop.

# CHAPTER 28
# THE PRINCE

*Wednesday morning.*

Later that night Caroline's sore neck began to throb. She called Janet. The small witch brought three small pots of tea on a tray, mugs, and a jar of honey. One for sleep, she directed, one for pain relief in the neck and throat, and one to banish bad spirits. "I suppose you mean for psychological wellbeing," said Mary *sotto voce.*

"Whatever floats your boat, Wandwalker," retorted Janet.

Despite drinking all the teas, then using the bathroom a lot, Caroline moaned in her sleep. She woke Mary more than once. Each time, Anna sat at the foot of the bed, awake, focused on Caroline.

"Why don't you try to get some sleep?"

Silence. Whimpers from Caroline mixed with soft snores.

Mary swung her feet to the floor and padded over to the tray on the chest of drawers. As suspected all three teapots held only damp leaves and a smell that wrinkled Mary's nose.

"Maybe I can go down and get Caroline some real tea?" said Mary, doubtfully.

"She's asleep. Don't let the noises fool you," said Anna, not moving. "Let her be. I promised I wouldn't let anything happen to her."

"You need rest too."

"No, I don't. Not like she does." Anna waved dismissively. "Go back to bed. Caroline will need both of us in the morning."

That's something, I suppose, Mary thought. She wondered if there had been anyone in her life who would watch her while she slept, just to keep her safe – or to banish evil spirits, as Caroline would say. Perhaps David, her long deceased fiancé, her dead son's father. Maybe he might have done so.

Mary climbed back into bed. She tried to recall David's features, after so many years. Were his eyes really that blue? A dark shape materialized beside her lost fiancé. Not Billy Dee, no, it was Mr. Jeffreys. He had that ironic smile that held a secret, if only Mary could work it out… She fell asleep.

When the knocking came, Mary woke to find herself alone. Sunshine behind thick curtains gave the room an eerie glow. The other bed was empty. Where were Caroline and Anna? Was Caroline hurting badly? The door opened to reveal Sarah with a cup. It released the best fragrance in the world.

"Coffee," grunted Mary. Dizzy with sudden movement, she reeled and grabbed the bedpost for stability. Sarah came forward, knelt, and raised the nectar to Mary's lips. After a sip, Mary took the cup in both hands.

"Caroline?" she queried after the third mouthful.

"Pretty good," said Sarah. Her eyes clouded. "Sore of course, and scarred. She and Anna want you to come down to deal with Robbin' Robin. A couple of his civil service geeks arrived with the okay for the Prince family to leave. The police will talk to them later. He's desperate to be out of here, but the wife wants a word with you. Irina, too." She gave her crooked smile. "Probably Irina wants to thank you."

Mary inhaled the coffee's vapor, all that remained of it. "She might not be thanking us with her birth father dead. I… we… in the Depth Enquiry Agency are supposed to stop that sort of thing."

However, when Mary threw on jeans borrowed from Dorothy, and a man's sweater from John, she emerged from Holywell's front door to find Robbin' Robin and Irina perched together on a stone bench close to the purring limo. No rain this morning, and the stone appears dry, thought Mary. Two of Robbin' Robin's aides leant against the gleaming bonnet, oblivious to the cool breeze and birdcalls. Of course their eyes were locked onto their phones.

Yet despite sending yearning glances in their direction, the minister kept blinking at his daughter. Unusually, he spoke too softly to be overheard. Irina nodded, and looked up with a shy smile. Robbin' Robin touched her hair, her real hair, not the wig, remembered Mary.

"They've invited me to stay for a couple of weeks," said a voice behind Mary. She turned to find Tyr holding out a mug. She took the second coffee, sugared, but no matter. As she drank, more prickles of energy tickled her brain.

"London?" asked Mary, looking at Tyr. He smelled of soap, hair newly washed.

"No, Northern Ireland." He grinned. "Seems like the minister gets a whopper of a house. One of the royal residences."

"Ah," said Mary, handing him the empty mug. "Really? Tyr, you've given me an idea."

Tyr appeared about to ask a question when voices from Holywell's open door rose louder. Helen Morgan detached herself from a group of witches. She looked fresh and a little wild with her hair far from its original sleek helmet.

"We're off to the Randolph Hotel in Oxford," she announced to Mary. "Doctors, a hair salon, and a few days rest before we check in with the PM and leave for Northern Ireland."

"You're going with him," said Mary, understanding. "You and Irina."

Helen Morgan sighed, patted her hair, then narrowed her eyes as her not-so-ex-husband lumbered over to the aides and began comparing phones. Irina followed, hooking her arm in his. He patted it absently.

"Irina needs a father," Morgan said to no one in particular. She flashed an expression at Mary that could have been complicity, or vulnerability. Mary could not tell.

"Robbin' Robin won't change," she said. "He'll have affairs, plot against the PM. He won't give enough to his family, but…" She stopped. Perhaps she did not know how to go on, thought Mary.

"But he needs you," Mary said, hardly knowing what to say. "He loves you, both of you."

"An imperfect marriage," said Morgan with bitterness.

"A real one," said Dorothy, coming to stand by Mary.

"I have an idea," said Mary again. "Minister," she called. He paid no attention.

"Robbin' Robin, come here," snapped Morgan. He came. "Miss Wandwalker wants a word."

"I was just saying to your…wife," said Mary, starting to enjoy herself, "how Northern Ireland is like a little kingdom. It's like Wales, a principality. Your surname's Prince, isn't it?"

Robbin' Robin's mouth dropped open. He flushed, eyes bright. He puffed. He stood taller.

"Prince," he said loudly, "Robin Prince."

"Definitely time for this Robbin' Robin stuff to go," said Mary in her most solemn tones. "You'll be the Prince of Northern Ireland. I believe the minister's residence is quite palatial."

"It *is* a palace," whispered the minister. "And you'll be my princess," he said turning to Irina. She blushed, then pouted.

"Can I be a ballerina too?"

"Yes, darling," said Morgan in the warmest tones Mary had ever heard from her. "I've been thinking about starting a ballet school in Northern Ireland. Meanwhile," she turned to Dorothy, "our friends at Holywell are going to help with *Swan Lake*. It will take longer, but the swans will fly at Greenwich."

"Anna's not going to be that evil sorcerer?" said an anxious and croaky voice.

Mary gulped at the ragged voice, and Caroline's neck bandage. She found a smile for Caroline who stood arm in arm with Anna.

Anna merely ginned.

"Nope," said Tyr, appearing from behind Dorothy. "I'm taking the Von Rothbart role. Our new *Swan Lake* will change what the sorcerer represents. Ms. Morgan and I sat up last night making plans. She's letting my folklore research revise the ballet." He spread his arms.

"Our swans will be free women, part of nature like they once were in Celtic times. They belong with the spirits of the air. So my sorcerer is a man who protects the wilderness, even if it is temporarily in human form."

"Do the children of Lir come into this revisioning?" queried Mary.

"Absolutely," beamed Tyr. "All over the earth there are folktales about women torn between flight as great birds and being *tamed* by the demands of men. Go back far enough, and swan nature is positive for women. Men hunted and trapped the swans. Once caught, swans became human. They had to serve men as wives."

"So these are stories of domesticating *women*," realized Mary. She was rapt, recalling seeing a pair of swans on the Thames. Golden-eyed, their strong green legs pushed against the tide. Then, without warning, they ran along the wrinkled surface of the river, rising with beaks to sniff the clouds.

Tyr paused and sought out Anna's dark eyes. "I reckon the children of Lir chose to become swans. Did you know that swans are the fastest birds that can rise from water? They surf the four winds, mate for life, live free."

"Free women," repeated Dorothy, glancing back at Holywell, where the gels could be heard chattering at breakfast.

Morgan hugged her daughter. Mary saw that Irina's eyes were wide open, reflecting the sun. The girl stretched out her arms, as if they once grew long white feathers.

# CHAPTER 29
# THE PEOPLE'S *SWAN LAKE*

*Evening seven months later, late April.*

Investigations into the killing of Billy Dee and Agnes Kelley wrapped up swiftly, according to the police. It helped that Meredith Kelley pled guilty to the murder of Billy Dee. He was found responsible for the death of Agnes, his mother. For Mary, Caroline, and Anna, closure came seven months later. For then, the renamed *People's Swan Lake* opened at sunset in April. The Greenwich World Heritage Site smelled of new leaves under a golden sky.

The park filled with witches. The Holywell women, bar Dorothy, fanned out to greet covens from London and the southern counties. They came to reclaim this magical, pagan site, or so Dorothy explained. She had chosen to watch with Mary, Caroline, Anna, and Mr. Jeffreys.

"Prince Robin doesn't know," she said, using the new nickname, bestowed by the press – with his encouragement – on the lordly minister. "But Helen Morgan paid for a couple of Northern Irish witches to join us. We've been re-magicking the whole site to help the swans fly."

Mary groaned. Caroline giggled and kissed Anna who responded with enthusiasm. Mr. Jeffreys grinned at Mary. They both ignored Dorothy dropping herbs on the grass.

"Miss Vronsky appears relaxed," Mr. Jeffreys remarked at the snogging.

"Enough, you two," said Mary. Anna had become more demonstrative with Caroline since the hanging incident. Mary shivered at the memory of how her daughter-in-law swung in the air.

"Law," she said to Mr. Jeffreys and Dorothy. "Children by adoption, or birth. What really matters is the love. Nothing else."

"Don't go sentimental on me now, Mary," said Mr. Jeffreys. "We're about to see a ballet about being free of human bonds. Isn't that the point of young Tyr's revised story?"

Caroline came up for breath. "Who'd have thought his version would catch the public's imagination in such a big way?" she said. "So many thousands wanted tickets that The Royal Ballet might do Tyr's version in Hyde Park next summer."

Then she cleared her throat and turned to Mr. Jeffreys. He made her nervous, Mary knew.

"You're wrong, Mr. Jeffreys. This *Swan Lake* is not giving up human bonds but finding release from human *chains*. The prince and swan princess get to live out their love in nature. The palace is what they need to escape *from*."

"I stand corrected," murmured Mr. Jeffreys.

"Not for Robin Prince, the escape from palaces," said Anna wickedly. "He adores his royal residence. Did you see that picture of him receiving the PM? He sat on a throne, Helen Morgan beside him."

Mary brushed the sleeve of her new silken grey suit.

"Wasn't the re-arrangement of furniture Miss Wandwalker's notion?" enquired Mr. Jeffreys. "On one of your, ah, *advisory* visits?"

"Didn't think he'd actually go for it," said Mary. "Priceless, that photo op. Helen Morgan's developed a sense of humor about his grandiosity. It gives her another creative outlet."

"Besides the new ballet school," agreed Caroline. "Her Touring Ballet School reaches places without dance opportunities for youngsters."

"Bringing the best students to an annual outdoor performance in one of London's parks," said Mary. "And your role, Dorothy?"

"Keeping them honest," returned the witch, firmly. "My consulting makes sure the school prioritizes those left out. Ballet for those who struggle in the shadows."

"Like Irina," said Anna. Everyone went silent.

"Look, there she is," cried Mary.

They stared up Greenwich hill to the big oaks that hid the Royal Observatory. With the sun swallowed by the western sky, the site dimmed. Dusk crept up the Thames from the sea. The lights of the Maritime Museum began to go out.

A tiny figure remained spotlit. Her white floaty dress moved as if blown on the breeze. Pale arms emerged, and a bird fluttered; no, a girl dressed as a bird pirouetted down the path, so carefully swept. Behind her came a train of girls in faded colors. At first they stared in wonder at the human swan. Then the young ladies began to imitate her gestures. This ballet offered women more than the glitter of the royal court.

As *Swan Lake* always had, thought Mary. We simply misinterpreted it.

Roped either side of the park gates, the audience heard music as they craned to follow the dancers. Now the girl in the swan dress danced solo. She moved ever closer to the bunched up audience. Hushed breath steamed up to the darkening sky and shining planets.

"It really is Irina, isn't it? Playing the swan princess?" queried Dorothy.

"Morgan agreed to a blind audition," replied Mary. "Meaning someone from the Royal Ballet School did it. She knew none of the dancers. Irina got it fair and square. Morgan says her dancing has improved astronomically since... well, you know."

Irina spun through lamplight and dim shadows, a swan commanding the fields of night. Her loose hair was threaded with feathers tipped with tiny arrowheads that glinted. As she approached Mary's group, they could see her concentrated joy. Such a contrast to before, thought Mary. And yet, there's that resemblance again.

"Caroline, does Anna...?" she whispered. "I mean have you talked about...?"

"She doesn't," said Caroline, hastily. "Want to search for her birth family."

"What are you whispering about, Mary Wandwalker?" For a moment, Anna looked thunderous. Mary coughed. Anna's features relaxed. She pointed to the procession of girls holding hands as they skipped down the torchlit path.

Anna stuck out her chin. "I'm my own swan. I've no time for a family who never searched for me." She grabbed Caroline's hand. The audience were to follow the dancing ladies over Greenwich High Street and into the lamplit palaces of the Naval College.

"She's right," said Mr. Jeffreys quietly to Mary. "We can be sure that Miss Vronsky's family had no Agnes. Considering when she and young Tyr were taken, it happened well after the end of the Communist regime. By then the Romanian authorities kept reliable records. They tell me no equivalent of Agnes Kelley searched for Miss Vronsky or Tyr Campbell."

"Terrible," said Mary.

"Birth families can be complicated," Mr. Jeffreys remarked to no one in particular. Mary sniffed. "Are we joining the royal court?"

They made haste to catch up with the audience by following Anna. She cut through the crowd to the very front.

"Birth families can include swans," said a female voice. Mary spun around. No one appeared close enough, not even Dorothy, who Mary glimpsed weaving between the last spectators to join them.

*An hour earlier, the ballet began when the swans flocked together in the rosy light of the setting sun. Encouraged to picnic in Greenwich Park, the audience was told to move to the gates, when they saw the girl swans emerge from the trees, trees that cloaked them in spring greenery. First one, then two, then many dancers with flowing hair and feathery tutus came to where paths crisscrossed.*

*Wasn't that where Caroline said a ley line lead to the Old Royal Naval College, now Greenwich University? Mary wondered. Or was it the Roman road that went from the Royal Observatory to the River Thames, then through London to the north? Never mind. The swans danced in the center of the park. They spun in unison then took turns at solos. Each claimed their own being, self-contained, wild and free. Finally the swans made a circle. A man dressed in leaves rose from the center, arms outstretched in celebration.*

*Tyr as von Rothbart embodied the generativity of the forest. Yes, a sorcerer, yet one whose magic protected the wild nature of these swan-women. Tyr had said of his revised role that he sought to enact what Billy Dee could not, because of his fantasies of mastery. The fantasies of a lost child, Mary had reflected. Tyr's von Rothbart ushered the swans back to safety of the trees. There the dancers had donned ballroom costumes to follow Irina to the Royal Court.*

The audience crowded into the Naval College, silent yet also buzzing. Arm in arm with Mr. Jeffreys, Mary fixed her eyes on Anna's brilliant blue hat to keep pace with the crowd. They flowed past the King William Building and into Queen Anne Court. That quadrangle of elegant columns bridged the darkness of Greenwich hill with the shining serpent Thames.

"What's happened to the black swan?" whispered Mr. Jeffreys.

"You can't see her in the dark," grinned Mary. "Yes, Irina is both swan princess and black swan. Tyr's given her a black robe. We'll see her that way being brought to the palace as a gift for the Prince. The swan's black because she's in mourning until the Prince agrees to take swan nature and fly away with her. Caroline says it's more romantic."

"Ah, Mrs. Jones." Mr. Jeffreys coughed.

Mary did not like the hint of condescension. "Anna says swans don't get clinical depression. Now be quiet and let me watch."

Mr. Jeffreys stared thoughtfully into the crowd. Caroline and Anna were among those following dance movements with arms curving into the night air.

Trumpets blasted from each corner, commanding silence. Everyone fell back as Prince Siegfried arrived to welcome the dancing girls to the grand court ball. After fanfares and formal bows, sorcerer Tyr did a mime to show how hunters captured the swan Princess. Her white feathers blackened with despair. In a scene that sobered the onlookers, the cloaked swan Princess was handed to the Prince as a trophy.

Confused, the Prince tried to get cloaked Irina to dance in the formal ball. First bewildered, then enraged, the black swan pushed him away. She danced alone. Her fury repelled the ball's guests. The ballet audience, by contrast, pressed closer and closer as the black swan sought to be free. Meanwhile, the Prince threw off his heavy golden robe and crept into the angry swan's orbit.

As the black swan, the Princess brought transformational energy. The Prince could not tear himself from the woman, who was not a woman. She danced the wild night that the court tried to banish with its bright lamps. He tried to touch her. Always she leapt and spun away. At last the Prince helped her strip off her black feathers to the beauty of the white swan beneath.

Court lamps dimmed as the carapace of power cracked. Freed to fly, the white swan brightened, became moonlike, sharing her radiance with the Prince.

Clever lighting, noted Mary, wiping her eyes.

From the shadows, the other women at Prince Siegfried's ball tore off tiaras and threw off their sober colors to become swans. Music swelled until it echoed from the stone facades where Greenwich University students lounged in daytime.

The swans danced to brew a storm, Mary thought. Their entranced audience applauded and roared to see the swan woman seize the heart of the heir to the kingdom. The ballet audience would follow the swan Princess and Prince into the wilderness. After a procession went back up Greenwich Hill, the *People's Swan Lake* would end at the Observatory with its blinking stars.

# CHAPTER 30
# CALIBAN

*The next day.*

The next day, the three women of the Depth Enquiry Agency sat over a late breakfast of coffee, tea, and English muffins in the home they shared in the Surrey hills.

"It is really, really over, now, isn't it?" said Caroline. "Look, no scarf." She pointed to her bare neck, which she stretched above a primrose blouse.

"Scars almost invisible," said Anna. She leaned over to kiss them.

"No one would know," agreed Mary. Too often in her dreams Caroline dangled from the old oak until Mary woke, gasping. Caroline insisted that the sacred tree itself had helped to save her. Mary dismissed such a ludicrous idea. Nevertheless, it comforted her.

"Last night in Greenwich," Mary began, "I can't forget Irina dancing by that fountain. You could hear a pin drop on those stone flags."

"As the moon climbed above the river," added Caroline.

"And the girls threw off their dresses to become swans," said Anna. "With Tyr's help they leapt and soared in every corner of that courtyard. Until…" she choked, then glared at Mary. "Pass the strawberry jam."

"Here you go, Anna," said Mary, noting that jam should be added to their shopping list, She took care not to notice Anna's emotion.

"Yes, for me the best bit was the scene no one expected. Before the Prince and the swans headed to the wild, the Holywell gels came out of courtyard doorways…"

"Dressed as prisoners…" said Caroline, stroking Anna's newly washed hair.

"Certainly in rags," agreed Mary. "Then the swans came to them. In the dark their white feathers gleamed. And sparkled."

"Stars," said Caroline. "They'd glued tiny stars to the feathers. Tyr put on the *People's Swan Lake* website that the Celtic druids used star divination. So when the swans danced under lamps in the Naval College we saw their stars."

To Mary's surprise, Anna had more. "At first the swans… well they flew, didn't they? They jumped and ran all over Queen Anne, then King William Court to show what freedom looks like."

"That's when they noticed the gels," said Caroline. "Who'd followed them to King William Court. The swans removed the rags. The gels were… reborn, I suppose. Reborn as spirits, sprites, woodland fairies."

"They escaped with the swans," reminisced Mary.

"Like Billy Dee becoming Bill-John," said Anna.

"Oh, Anna don't," cried Caroline. She shot a nervous look at Mary. "You know we said we wouldn't mention it. Mary hasn't told Mr. Jeffreys about Bill-John yet. Er, have you Mary?"

"Not yet," said Mary, pressing her lips together. "Our online Caliban has gone quiet. Or is there something you're not telling us, Anna?"

"No, he's inactive. I got an email saying he's pondering his dual identity. Said it was a kind of séance: to discover which felt more alive – the famous magus John Dee or twenty-first century medium, hypnotist and er…?"

"Pedophile," said Mary, brutally.

"Don't be so harsh, Mary. He started as a lost child, remember," muttered Caroline.

"Are you making excuses for him? You were the one who insisted we stop him hurting young dancers."

"Depth." Anna's hoarseness shocked Mary and Caroline into silence.

"By which you mean…?" Mary had no idea what Anna meant.

Anna sniffed. She hooked a finger through one of Caroline's dangling curls. "We're the Depth Enquiry Agency, you've always said, Mary. It has to mean something."

"Fifteen years clean," jumped in Caroline. "Since the birth of Irina and the death of her mother. She was his last underage girl." She paused. "I'll never forget how he wanted to be Irina's father, but could only present as a lover."

"I'd have stabbed him in the throat if I saw him put a hand on Irina," added Anna. She snuck a glance at Mary.

"That would have been a complication," said Mary. With commendable restraint, she thought. "You know how Mr. Jeffreys hates it when you get arrested."

She coughed.

"It's no good, Anna. We can't ignore the problem you caused. AI Billy Dee, or Bill-John, or whatever he's calling himself, is dangerous," she said. "Even if he takes on the more respectable John Dee we don't know what this… creature, I suppose, is capable of." She aimed at Caroline, who was tracing patterns on the back of Anna's hand. Neither she nor Anna would look at Mary.

Mary snapped. "Neither of you are taking this seriously."

"Okay, I accept it. He's dangerous," said Anna. "Happy now?" She paused. "The thing is, Mary, so am I."

Unanswerable. Mary clenched her fists under the table. As if she could see her, Anna folded her arms. She scowled. Caroline's lips moved, but no words came.

"Take that, Mary Wandwalker," said Anna, black eyes boring into Mary, "Me, dangerous. What you are saying to yourself right now applies to Bill-John too. You wouldn't ever kill me. And you can't kill him. Even if you knew enough coding to drive him from cyberspace, you wouldn't do it. Because Bill-

John is as alive as you, me, or Caroline. You don't kill living creatures."

Mary studied the two of them and sighed. She looked out the window to the lawn they never had time to mow, ringed by flowerbeds of vigorous unplanned growth.

"The illusion of control," said Mary finally, "is what we don't have now."

"It was always an illusion," said Caroline, looking hopeful.

"We're in my world," said Anna.

"I guess that's why we have the Depth Enquiry Agency," said Mary. "Like you were saying, Anna."

Her forced grin became tired, then, at last, a real smile. She recalled another lost child, Caliban, who spoke of sounds and sweet airs that give delight and hurt not.

## THE END